Nirali's New Series

CONCISE STUDY SERIES

(50 Marks)

DIGITAL ELECTRONICS

Sem - I

S.E ELECTRONICS / ELECTRONICS AND TELECOMMUNICATION

As per New Revised Syllabus of University of Pune

(Pattern 2012)

S. S. Kulkarni

M. E. (E & TC)
Associate Professor
Sinhgad Academy of Engineering
Kondhawa, Pune.

NIRALI ®
PRAKASHAN
ADVANCEMENT OF KNOWLEDGE

N 2805

DIGITAL ELECTRONICS (SE E & TC)

First Edition : June 2014

© :

Published By :
NIRALI PRAKASHAN
Abhyudaya Pragati, 1312, Shivaji Nagar,
Off J.M. Road, PUNE – 411005
Tel - (020) 25512336/37/39, Fax - (020) 25511379
Email : niralipune@pragationline.com

DISTRIBUTION CENTRES
PUNE

Nirali Prakashan
119, Budhwar Peth, Jogeshwari Mandir Lane
Pune 411002, Maharashtra
Tel : (020) 2445 2044, 66022708, Fax : (020) 2445 1538
Email : bookorder@pragationline.com

Nirali Prakashan
S. No. 28/25, Dhyari,
Near Pari Company, Pune 411041
Tel : (022) 24690204 Fax : (020) 24690316
Email : dhyari@pragationline.com
bookorder@pragationline.com

MUMBAI
Nirali Prakashan
385, S.V.P. Road, Rasdhara Co-op. Hsg. Society Ltd.,
Girgaum, Mumbai 400004, Maharashtra
Tel : (022) 2385 6339 / 2386 9976, Fax : (022) 2386 9976
Email : niralimumbai@pragationline.com

DISTRIBUTION BRANCHES

NAGPUR
Pratibha Book Distributors
Above Maratha Mandir, Shop No. 3, First Floor,
Rani Jhanshi Square, Sitabuldi, Nagpur 440012,
Maharashtra, Tel : (0712) 254 7129

JALGAON
Nirali Prakashan
34, V. V. Golani Market, Navi Peth, Jalgaon 425001,
Maharashtra, Tel : (0257) 222 0395
Mob : 94234 91860

BENGALURU
Pragati Book House
House No. 1, Sanjeevappa Lane, Avenue Road Cross,
Opp. Rice Church, Bengaluru – 560002.
Tel : (080) 64513344, 64513355,
Mob : 9880582331, 9845021552
Email:bharatsavla@yahoo.com

KOLHAPUR
Nirali Prakashan
New Mahadvar Road,
Kedar Plaza, 1st Floor Opp. IDBI Bank
Kolhapur 416 012, Maharashtra. Mob : 9855046155

CHENNAI
Pragati Books
9/1, Montieth Road, Behind Taas Mahal, Egmore,
Chennai 600008 Tamil Nadu, Tel : (044) 6518 3535,
Mob : 94440 01782 / 98450 21552 / 98805 82331, Email : bharatsavla@yahoo.com

RETAIL OUTLETS
PUNE

Pragati Book Centre
157, Budhwar Peth, Opp. Ratan Talkies,
Pune 411002, Maharashtra
Tel : (020) 2445 8887 / 6602 2707, Fax : (020) 2445 8887

Pragati Book Centre
Amber Chamber, 28/A, Budhwar Peth,
Appa Balwant Chowk, Pune : 411002, Maharashtra,
Tel : (020) 20240335 / 66281669
Email : pbcpune@pragationline.com

Pragati Book Centre
676/B, Budhwar Peth, Opp. Jogeshwari Mandir,
Pune 411002, Maharashtra
Tel : (020) 6601 7784 / 6602 0855

PBC Book Sellers & Stationers
152, Budhwar Peth, Pune 411002, Maharashtra
Tel : (020) 2445 2254 / 6609 2463

MUMBAI
Pragati Book Corner
Indira Niwas, 111 - A, Bhavani Shankar Road, Dadar (W), Mumbai 400028, Maharashtra
Tel : (022) 2422 3526 / 6662 5254, Email : pbcmumbai@pragationline.com

www.pragationline.com   info@pragationline.com

Dear Students,

It gives us great pleasure to introduce a New Series "**C**oncise **S**tudy **S**eries" for Second Year Engineering students. These "**CSS**" books are written by Experienced and Eminent Professors of respective subjects.

The specialty of this new Series "**CSS**" is that it:

➤ Covers full syllabus of University of Pune.

➤ Contains Matter written in Simple and Lucid language.

➤ Includes "To the Point" Topics and well arranged articles.

➤ Includes Most Likely Questions.

➤ Includes Previous Years University Question Papers.

➤ Available in all leading stores at Affordable Price.

Happy Studying and Best of Luck!!!

Nirali Prakashan

SYLLABUS

Unit I : Digital Logic Families

Classification of logic families, Characteristics of digital ICs-Speed of operation, power dissipation, figure of merit, fan in, fan out, current and voltage parameters, noise immunity, operating temperatures and power supply requirements.TTL logic. Operation of TTL NAND gate, active pull up, wired AND, open collector output, unconnected inputs. Tri-State logic. CMOS logic – CMOS inverter, NAND, NOR gates, unconnected inputs, wired logic , open drain output. Interfacing CMOS and TTL. Comparison table of Characteristics of TTL, CMOS, ECL, RTL, I2L, DCTL.

Unit II : Combinational Logic Design

Standard representations for logic functions, k map representation of logic functions (SOP m POS forms), minimization of logical functions for min-terms and max-terms (upto 4 variables), don't care conditions, Design Examples: Arithmetic Circuits, BCD - to – 7 segment decoder, Code converters. Adders and their use as subtractions, look ahead carry, ALU, Digital Comparator, Parity generators/checkers, Multiplexers and their use in combinational logic designs, multiplexer trees, Demultiplexers and their use in combinational logic designs, Decoders, demultiplexer trees. Introduction to Quine McCluskey method.

Unit III : Sequential Logic Design

1 Bit Memory Cell, Clocked SR, JK, MS J-K flip flop, D and T flip-flops. Use of preset and clear terminals, Excitation Table for flip flops. Conversion of flip flops. Application of Flip flops: Registers, Shift registers, Counters (ring counters, twisted ring counters), Sequence Generators, ripple counters, up/down counters, synchronous counters, lock out, Clock Skew, Clock jitter. Effect on synchronous designs.

Unit IV : State Machines

Basic design steps- State diagram, State table, State reduction, State assignment, Mealy and Moore machines representation, Implementation, finite state machine implementation, Sequence detector.

Unit V : Programmable Logic Devices and Semiconductor Memories-

Programmable logic devices: Detail architecture, Study of PROM, PAL, PLA, Designing combinational circuits using PLDs. General Architecture of FPGA and CPLD Semiconductor memories: memory organization and operation, expanding memory size, Classification and characteristics of memories, RAM, ROM, EPROM, EEPROM, NVRAM, SRAM,DRAM.

Unit VI : Introduction to HDLs

Library, Entity, Architecture, Modeling styles, Data objects, Concurrent and sequential statements, Design examples, using VHDL for basic combinational and sequential circuits, Attributes (required for practical) (Test benches and FSM included)

CONTENTS

DIGITAL LOGIC FAMILIES

1.1   IC LOGIC FAMILIES AND CHARACTERISTICS

1.1.1   Introduction

> **Q.** What are ICs? How are they categorized?
>
> **Q.** What is the basic difference between unipolar IC and bipolar IC?

- ICs are miniature, low – cost electronic circuits whose components are fabricated on a single, continuous piece of semiconductor material to perform a high – level function.
- Usually referred to as a monolithic IC.
- First introduced in 1958
- Categorized as digital or linear ICs or according to the level of complexity of the IC.

Category		Number of Gates
Small scale integration	SSI	< 12
Medium scale integration	MSI	12 to 99
Large scale integration	LSI	100 to 9999
Very Large Scale Integration	VLSI	10,000 or more

- Digital IC can be categorized into bipolar or unipolar IC. Bipolar ICs are devices whose active components are current controlled while unipolar ICs are devices whose active components are voltage controlled.

1.1.2 Packaging

> **Q.** Why good packaging of an IC is necessary?

- Protects the chip from mechanical damage and chemical contamination.
- Provides a complete unit large enough to handle.
- It is made large enough so that electrical connections can be made.
- Material is molded plastic, epoxy, resin or Silicon. Ceramic is used if higher thermal dissipation capabilities are required. Metal/glass is used in special cases.

Three most common packages for ICs are

(a) Dual–in–line ((DIPs) most common)

(b) Flat pack

(c) Axial lead (TO5)

1.1.3 Classification of Logic Families

IC Logic Families

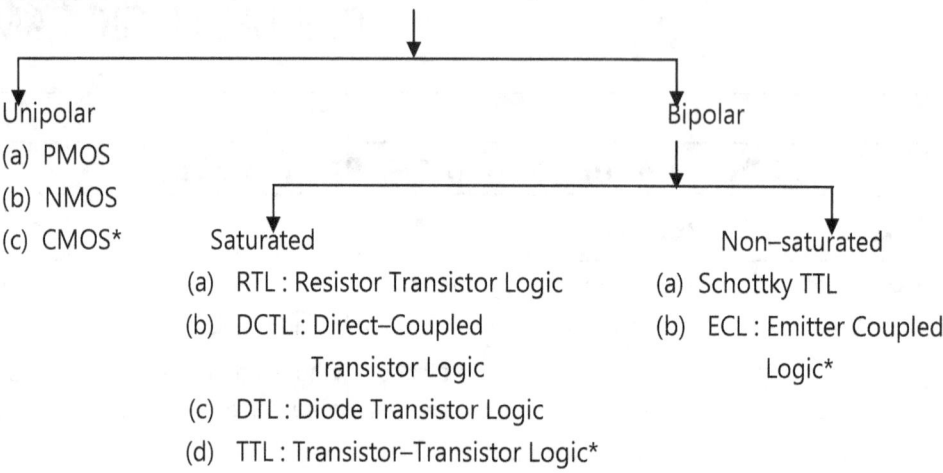

Unipolar	Bipolar
(a) PMOS	
(b) NMOS	
(c) CMOS*	

Saturated

(a) RTL : Resistor Transistor Logic

(b) DCTL : Direct–Coupled
   Transistor Logic

(c) DTL : Diode Transistor Logic

(d) TTL : Transistor–Transistor Logic*

(e) HTL : High Threshold Logic

(f) IIL : Integrated Injected Logic*

Non–saturated

(a) Schottky TTL

(b) ECL : Emitter Coupled
   Logic*

* These logic families are currently being used and others are obsolete.

• Complementary MOS or CMOS is very popular as it consumes less power.

CMOS and IIL logic families are suitable for Very Large Scale Integration (VLSI) technology.

1.2   CHARACTERISTICS OF DIGITAL ICS

Q. Define the following parameters of digital 1C families fan–in and fan–out.	
	[Dec. 06, 10, 11, 2 M]
Q. Define and explain fan out.	**[May 07, Dec. 08, 12, 2 M]**

1.2.1   Fan–in

• Fan – in (input load factor) is the number of input signals that can be connected to a gate without causing it to operate outside its intended operating range.

• Expressed in terms of standard inputs or units loads (ULs)

Example : A fan–in of 8 means that 8 unit loads can be safely connected to the gate inputs.

1.2.2   Fan–out

Fan – out (output load factor) is the maximum number of inputs that can be driven by a logic gate. A fan–out of 10 means that 10 unit loads can be driven by the gate while still maintaining the output voltage within specifications for logic levels 0 and 1.

1.2.3   Propagation Delays

> **Q.** Define the following parameters of digital IC families : propagation delay
>   **[Dec. 06, 10, 2 M]**
> **Q.** Define and explain : propagation delay.   **[Dec. 08, 12, 2 M]**

The delay before a change in the input is reflected at the output is known as propagation delay.

t_{PHL} : delay time in going from logic 1 to logic 0 (turn – off delay)

t_{PLH} : delay time in going from logic 0 to logic 1 (turn – on delay)

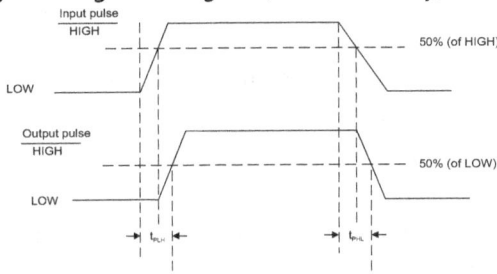

Fig. 1.1

$$\text{Total delay} = \frac{t_{PLH} + t_{PHL}}{2}$$

1.2.4   Voltage and Current Parameters

- Theoretically, the input voltage levels are 0V and +5V(TTL) for logic 0 and logic 1 respectively.

- Practically, it is impossible to maintain these perfect voltage levels. Hence, there is a need to define the worst case input and output voltage levels to consider whether the input or output should be considered as logic 0 or logic 1.

Voltage Parameters (Refer to Fig. 1.2)

1. **$V_{IL(max)}$:** Maximum low level input voltage. It is the maximum input voltage which is considered as a logic 1. If the input voltage is higher than $V_{IL(max)}$, then it is not considered as logic 0 level.

2. **$V_{IH(min)}$:** Minimum high level input voltage. It is the minimum input voltage which is considered as logic 1 level . If the input voltage is lower than $V_{IH(min)}$, then it is not considered as logic 1 level.

3. **$V_{OH(min)}$:** Minimum high level output voltage. It is the minimum output voltage which is considered as logic 1 level.

4. **$V_{OL(max)}$:** Maximum low level output voltage. It is the maximum output voltage which is considered as logic 0 level. If the input voltage is higher than $V_{OL(max)}$, then it is not considered as logic 0 level.

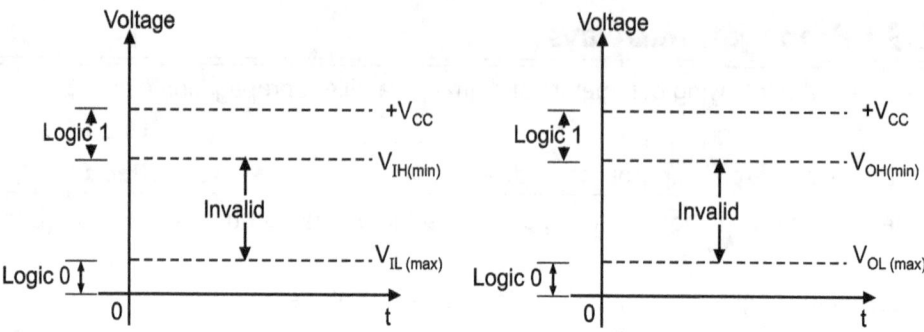

Fig. 1.2 : Voltage parameter

Current Parameters :

1. I_{IL} : Low level input current – It is the current flowing in an input terminal when the input voltage corresponds to logic 0.

2. I_{IH} : High level input current – It is the current flowing in an input terminal when the input voltage corresponds to logic 1.

3. I_{OH} : High level output current – It is the current flowing from the output when the output voltage corresponds to logic 1.

4. I_{OL} : Low level output current – It is the current flowing from an output when the output voltage corresponds to logic 0.

1.2.5 Current Sourcing and Current Sinking

- **Current Sourcing :** A device output is said to source current when current flows from the power supply, out of the device output and through the load to ground. Refer Fig. 1.3 (a)

- **Current Sinking :** Current sinking is when current flows from the power supply, to the load and through the device output to ground. Refer Fig. 1.3 (b).

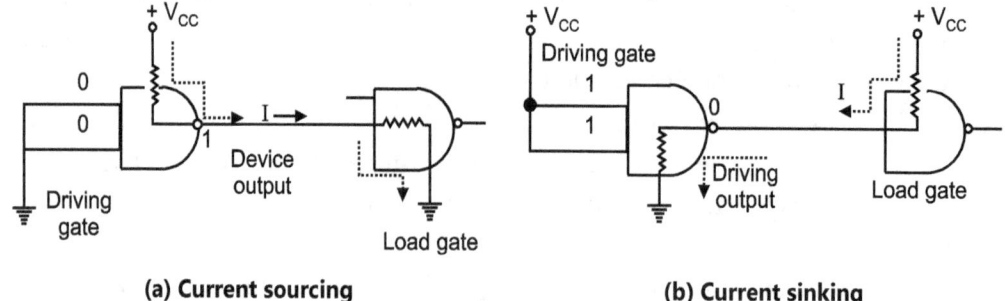

      (a) Current sourcing   **(b) Current sinking**

Fig. 1.3

1.2.6 Noise Margin/Immunity

Q. Define the following parameters of digital 1C families : Noise margin.

                                              [Dec. 06, 10, 11, May 07 2 M]

Q. Explain the following characteristics of CMOS logic family : Noise margin.

                                                   [May 12, 2 M]

- Any unwanted electrical signal which can induce some voltage in the wires used in between the gates or load is known as Noise.
- The ability of a device or a circuit to tolerate noise such that there is no unwanted change in the output.
- A quantitative measure of noise immunity is called as Noise Margin.
- The voltage levels $V_{OH(min)}$ and $V_{IH(Min)}$ are adjusted to different levels with some difference between them so that the effect of noise voltage are minimized.

$$\therefore \quad V_{NH} = V_{OH(min)} - V_{IH(min)}$$
$$V_{NL} = V_{IL(max)} - V_{OL(max)}$$

Where V_{NH} – is the high level noise margin and V_{NL} – is the low level noise margin

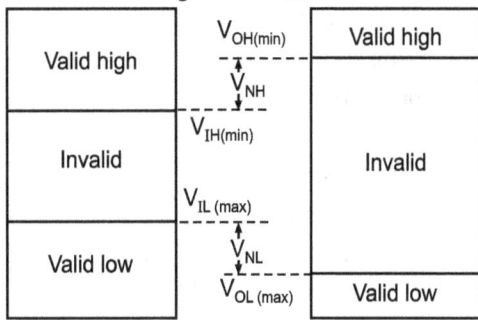

Fig. 1.4 : Noise margins

1.2.7 Power Dissipation

Q. Define and explain power dissipation.   **[Dec. 08, 2 M]**

- The amount of energy (in milliWatts) that the IC dissipates in the form of heat is known as power dissipation.
- Due to excessive temperature, the IC can get damaged. So, care should be taken so that power dissipation is not much and loading on power supplies is reduced.

Operating Temperature

- For consumer and industrial applications , the acceptable temperature range is 0° to 70° and for military applications it is –55°C to 125°C.

1.2.8 Figure of Merit

- Also known as Speed Power Product (SPP).
- It is defined as the product of power dissipation and propagation delay where speed is in seconds and power is specified in Watts.
- Mathematically,
  Figure of merit = Propagation delay × Power dissipation
- Figure of merit is constant. So, if power dissipation is decreased, propagation delay increases and vice versa.
- Practically, the value of figure of merit should be as low as possible.

1.2.9 Slew Rate

> **Q.** Define Slew rate.

- Slew Rate is defined as the ratio of output voltage swing to propagation delay. Its unit is V/ns. The slew rate determines the overall delay in the digital circuit. The larger the slew rate better is the speed of the digital IC. Smaller slew rate may cause the set–up and hold time violations leading to malfunctioning of the digital IC function.

1.3   IC LOGIC FAMILIES

So far, we have specified the logic level as either 0 or 1, or HIGH or LOW. In circuit implementation, we will have to specify the actual voltage/current levels that constitute a HIGH or a LOW. These standardized voltage/current levels are grouped in families of digital ICs so that ICs belonging to the same family will have the same characteristics.

Common families are

RTL	:	Resistor – Transistor Logic
DTL	:	Diode – Transistor Logic
TTL	:	Transistor – Transistor Logic
ECL	:	Emitter Coupled Logic
IIL	:	Integrated Injection Logic.

CMOS ICs   : Complementary metal – oxide – semiconductor ICs

1.4 TRANSISTOR – TRANSISTOR LOGIC (TTL)

- Transistor –Transistor Logic, or TTL refers to the technology for designing and fabricating digital integrated circuits that employ logic gates consisting primarily of bipolar transistors. It overcomes the main problem associated with DTL, i.e., lack of speed.

Most popular and widely used IC logic family.

- Introduced by Texas Instruments in 1964.
- Operates from a + 5V power supply.
- Standardized labeling system starting with 54 or 74. For example 7400, 7401, 74121 etc.
- A HIGH is normally + 5V while a LOW is normally 0V or GROUND.

To provide greater flexibility with regard to speed and power dissipation considerations, the following sub–families have been developed :

7400 Standard series.

74L00 low–power series

74H00 high–speed series

74S00 Schottky series

74LS00 low–power Schottky series.

1.4.1 TTL NAND gate

Q. Draw and explain the working of 2–input TTL NAND gate.　　**[Dec. 05, 06, 08, 6 M]**

Q. Draw and explain working of TTL NAND gate.

Q. Explain with neat diagrams and compare different types of output configurations in case of family.　　　　　　　　　　　　　　　　　　　　　　　**[Dec. 04, 12 M]**

Concept of Multi– emitter transistor :

Consider a transistor with not one emitter but three emitters, one base and one collector as shown in Fig. 1.5 (a) below.

- Its equivalent circuit can be drawn with two diodes as shown in the Fig. 1.5 (b).

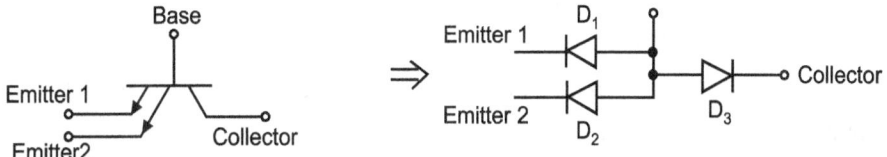

(a) Multi emitter transistor　　　　　　　**(b) Equivalent circuit**

Fig. 1.5 : Multi emitter transistor

1.4.2　2 – input TTL NAND Gate (Totem pole output)

- Let A and B be the input terminals. Therefore, for 2 inputs , four combinations are possible as shown in the truth table.

- The inputs or outputs are ideally 0V or +5V for logic 0 and 1 respectively.

Table 1.1 : Truth table

Input		Output
A	B	Y
0	0	1
0	1	1
1	0	1
1	1	0

Fig. 1.6 (a) shows a two – input TTL NAND gate

Fig. 1.6 (b) shows the equivalent circuit of transistor T_1.

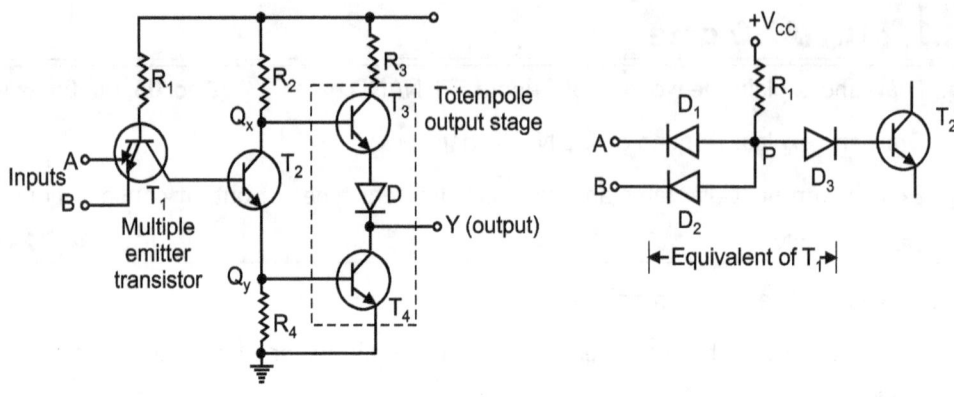

(a) Two input TTL NAND gate   **(b) Equivalent circuit of transistor T₁**

Fig. 1.6 : 2-Input TTL NAND gate

Case 1 : When A = 0 B = 0

- When both the inputs are low , then both the diodes D_1 and D_2 conduct , and voltage at point P is pulled to 0.7V.
- Hence T_2 stops conducting (or is turned OFF) as the base–emitter junction of T_2 is not forward biased.
- When T_2 is turned OFF , the collector voltage at Q_x rises to V_{cc}.
- Since , base–emitter junction of T_3 is forward biased , output Y is pulled up to a high voltage ($\therefore$ Y =1)

Case 1 : When A = 0 B = 1 or A = 1 B = 0

- If either of the inputs are low , then the voltage at point P will again be pulled down to 0.7V.
- This voltage is again not sufficient to switch ON T_2 and hence the whole working is same as that in the previous case.
- So , the output is Y = 1

Case 2 : A = 1 and B = 1

- If A = 1 and B = 1, then both the diodes D_1 and D_2 are not conducting.
- Hence , because of V_{cc}, D_3 starts conducting , which forward biases the base–emitter function of T_2 and T_2 is turned ON.
- When T_2 is turned ON, voltage at Q_x drops down and T_3 is turned OFF.
- Due to this , voltage at Q_y increases so as to turn ON T_4 and T_4 goes into saturation.
- Therefore , the output voltage Y is pulled down to a low voltage.
  Hence Y = LOW

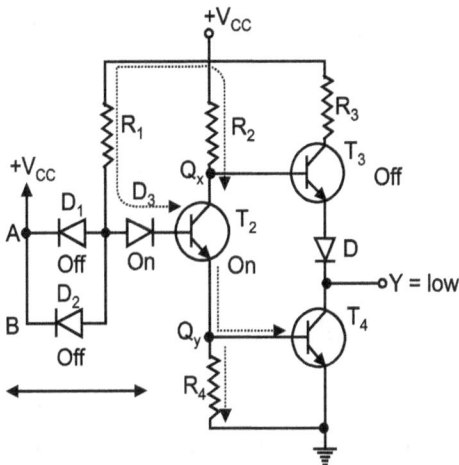

Fig. 1.7 : Equivalent circuit for A = B = 1

1.4.3   3–input TTL NAND Gate

- Fig. 1.8 given below shows a 3 – input TTL NAND gate.
- The working of a 3 – input TTL NAND gate is the same as that of a 2– input TTL NAND gate except that the transistor T_1 has 3 emitters.

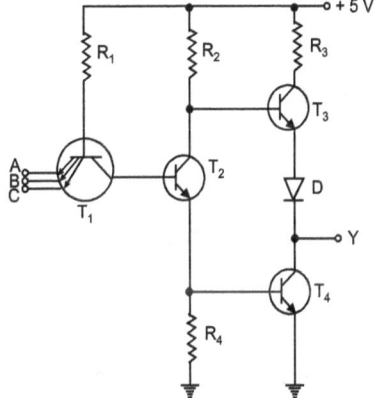

Fig. 1.8 : 3–input TTL NAND gate

1.4.4   Totem–Pole Output

Q. Explain the advantages of Totem pole output in TTL.	**[May 06, 2 M]**
Q. Explain with neat diagrams and compare the different types of output configuration in case of TTL family.	**[Dec. 12, 3 M]**

- The schematic of a typical TTL 7400 NAND gate is shown in Fig. 1.9.
- In this diagram, observe that the output stage consists of two active elements, T_3 and T_4.
- This circuit is designed such that the operation of T_3 and T_4 are complementary, that is when one transistor is ON the other is OFF.

- This configuration with T_4 stacked on top of T_3 is referred to as a **totem – pole** output.

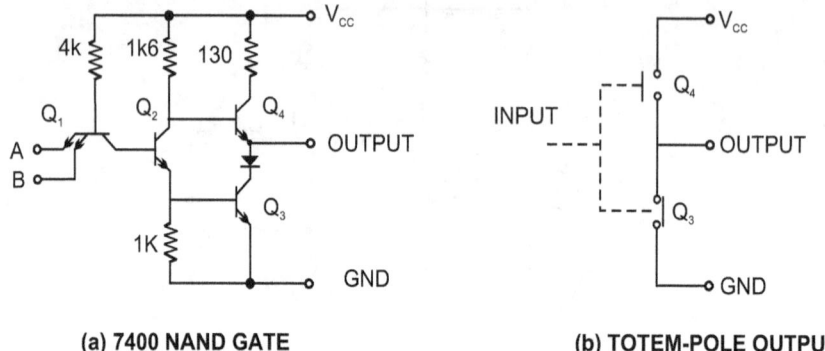

(a) 7400 NAND GATE   (b) TOTEM-POLE OUTPUT

Fig. 1.9 : Schematic of a typical TTL gate

- Also shown in Fig. 1.9 (b) is a simplified schematic of the operation of the totem–pole output. Transistors T_3 and T_4 behave as switches controlled by the INPUT.

- At any time, only one of the two switches is closed while the other is open. In other words, when T_3 is closed, T_4 is open.

- Conversely, when T_3 is open, T_4 is closed. By analyzing this circuit you can follow how the output changes from 0 to 5 volts.

Advantages of Totem – Pole Output

- The main advantage of the totem pole arrangement is that it offers low –output impedance in either of output states (Y = LOW , or Y = HIGH)

- Therefore , any stray capacitance at the output can be charged or discharged very rapidly through this low impedance and hence transitions from one state to the other is very quick at the output.

- Suppose , in the absence of T_3, the collector terminal of T_4 would be connected to $+V_{cc}$ through R_3. As a result , T_4 would need to conduct a fairly large current.

Disadvantages of Totem – Pole output

- The main disadvantage of this type of arrangement is its switching speed.

Explanation

- The transistor T_4 switches OFF slowly than the transistor T_3.

- On account of this , there is a fraction of time (in nanoseconds) , that both the transistor T_3 and T_4 are conducting and therefore, draw a heavy current (30 to 40 mA) from the power supply.

1.4.5 Open–collector output

- Fig. 1.10 (a) shows the schematic of a typical TTL gate with open – collector output, for example, a 7403 NAND gate.

- Observe here that the circuit elements associated with T_4 in the totem–pole circuit is missing and the collector of T_3 is left open – circuited, hence the name **open–collector.**

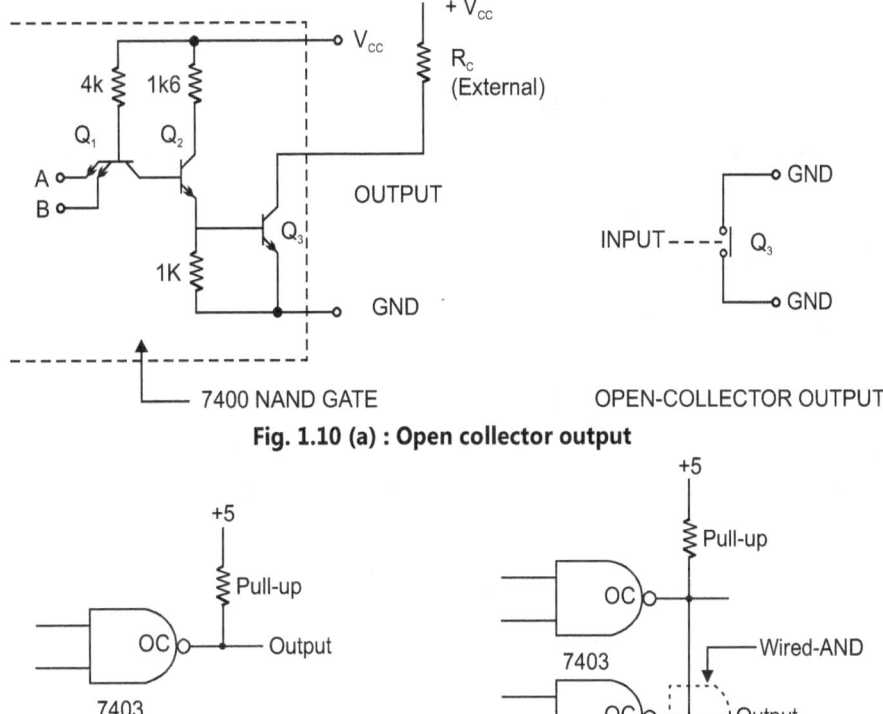

Fig. 1.10 (a) : Open collector output

Fig. 1.10 (b) : Open collector wired OR function

- An open–collector output has **current sinking** capabilities, that is, it can present a logic–LO output. In contrast with a normal totem–pole output, it cannot be the source of current and therefore cannot present a logic–HI on its own.

- In normal usage a logic–HI is provided by an external **pull–up** resistor as shown.

1.4.6 Wired AND operation

Q. Define wired AND connection,	[May 05, 2 M]
Q. Define and explain wired ANDing.	[May 07, Dec. 08, 2M]

Fig. 1.11 (a) shows NAND gates being used to perform AND operation.

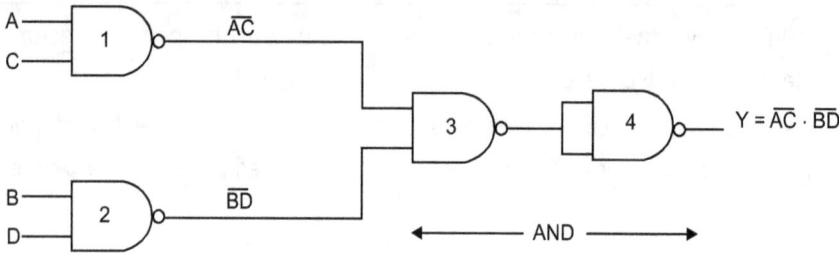

Fig. 1.11 (a) "AND"ing NAND gates

- Therefore, the final Boolean expression is

$$Y = \overline{AC} \cdot \overline{BD}$$

- The same Boolean expression can be obtained by replacing NAND gates 3 and 4 by shorting the $\overline{AC}$ and $\overline{BD}$ signals together.

- When two or more outputs $\left(\overline{AC} \text{ and } \overline{BD} \text{ in this example}\right)$ are tied together then if any one of the outputs goes to low the common output point goes to low. This happens because the transistor T_4 (see Fig. 1.11 (c) gets grounded. The common output will be high only when all outputs are high.

- This is called "wired – AND " ing or outputs. This is shown in Fig. 1.11 (b).

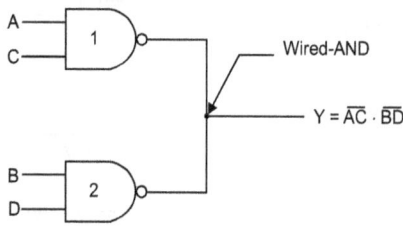

Fig. 1.11 (b) "Wired – AND" ing outputs

- Wired–AND operation is not possible with TTL gates having totem–pole output circuits.

- The wired–And operation of two totem pole TTL gates are shown in Fig. 1.11 (c). Let us assume that the output of gate X is high and gate Y is low. The transistor Q_{4Y} acts as a low resistive load on the transistor Q_{3X}.

- Therefore, the current through Q_{4Y} can be very high (755 mA). The sink current of Q_4 transistor is 16mA. The excess current through Q_{4Y} may damage it. The current through Q_{3X} will be go on increasing where more than two TTL outputs are wired–AND ed.

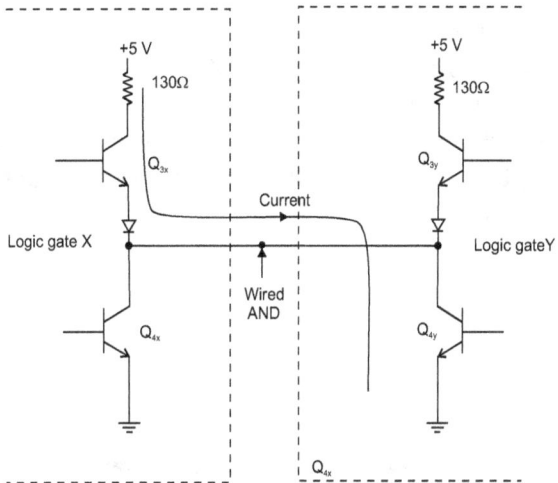

Fig. 1.11 (c) : Wired–AND ing of totem pole outputs

The main advantage of wired– AND operation is that it requires less number of gates.

Open–collector Buffer / Drivers :

- Any logic circuit that is called a *buffer*, a *driver*, or a *buffer/driver* is designed to have a greater output current and /or voltage capability than an ordinary logic circuit. Buffer/driver ICs are available with totem–pole outputs and with open–collector outputs.

- The 7406 is a popular open–collector buffer/driver IC that contains six INVERTERs with open–collector outputs that can sink up to 40 mA in the LOW state. In addition, the 7406 can handle output voltages up to 30 V. This means that the output transistor can be connected to a voltage greater than 5 V.

1.4.7 Tri–state Outputs

Q. What do you mean by tristate logic ? Define and explain tristate logic.

Q. Explain the concept of tristate logic.

- Boolean logic is based on a binary system whereby an output can have one of two states, ON or OFF. What is meant by **tri–state** or **3– state** outputs ? Let us examine the typical totem–pole output once again.

T4	T3	OUTPUT
OFF	ON	0
ON	OFF	1
OFF	OFF	HI – Z
ON	ON	DAMAGING

- Consider all possibilities for T_3 and T_4. The first two conditions show the normal totem–pole operation. If both T_3 and T_4 are ON, maximum current will flow from V_{cc} to GND, possibly damaging the device.
- If both T_3 and T_4 are OFF, the output pin appears to be disconnected from the circuit. The voltage at the output pin is indeterminate and is said to be **floating**. This called the **high impedance** or **Hi–Z state.**

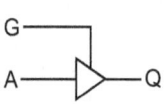

G	A	Q
0	0	HI – Z
0	1	HI – Z
1	0	0
1	1	1

Fig. 1.12 : 74126 bus driver with 3–state output

1.4.8   Other TTL Characteristics

Q. What should be done with the unused inputs of a TTL–NAND gate ?

Q. What should be done with the unused inputs of a TTL–NOR gate ?

(1) Unused Inputs : NAND : If the input is unused i.e. left disconnected then it acts as logic high input. The unconnected input may act as antenna and pick up noise. Hence, it is a good practice to connect unused inputs to V_{cc} through a 1 kΩ resistor. It is also possible to tie the unused input to a used input.

NOR : The unused inputs have to be connected to ground.

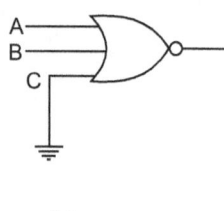

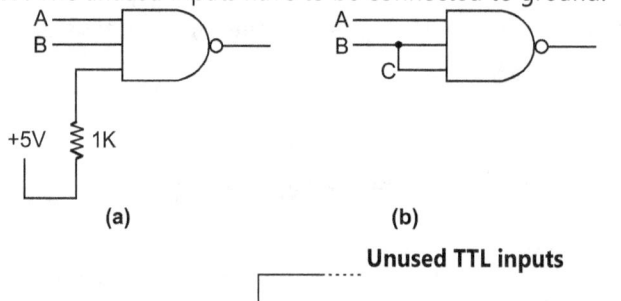

(a)   (b)   (c)

Unused TTL inputs

(a)   UL= 3   (b)   UL= 1

Fig. 1.13

(2) Tied–Together Inputs : When two or more TTL– gate inputs are tied together then the common input will generally have an input loading factor (UL) that is the sum of the input loading factors for each input.

For example NOR gate in the Fig. 1.13 above has 3 UL.

1.5 COMPLEMENTARY METAL-OXIDE-SEMICONDUCTOR (CMOS) CIRCUITS

- The drawbacks of P – MOS and N – MOS families are overcome by the CMOS family.
- The CMOS logic family has both p – channel and n – channel MOSSFETs in the same circuit.
- It is fabricated by connecting a p – channel in series with an n – channel MOSFET.

1.5.1 CMOS Inverter

Q. Explain CMOS Inverter.	**[May 05, 07, 3 M]**
Q. Explain the operation of CMOS inverter.	**[Dec. 08, 3 M]**

- Fig. 1.14 (a) given below shows a CMOS inverter and its equivalent.

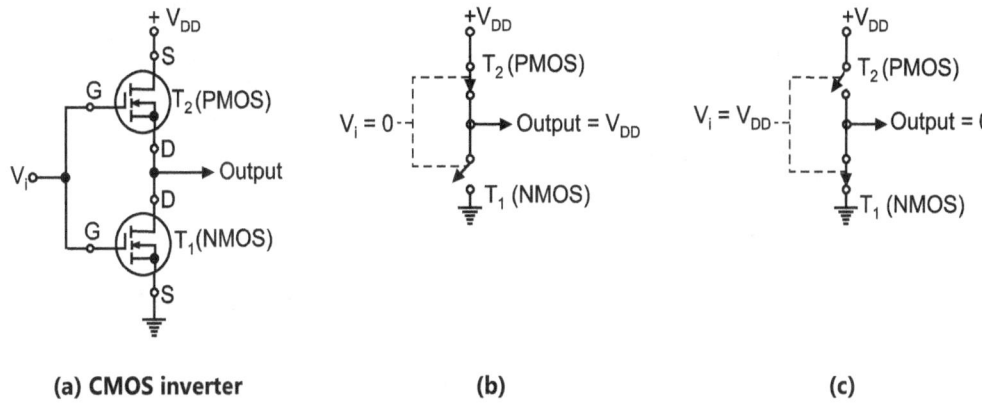

(a) CMOS inverter   **(b)**   **(c)**

Fig. 1.14

- Observe that the drains of both the P–MOS transistor and N–MOS transistor are tied together and the output is taken from the common drain.

- The gates are tied together and the input is given through the common gate.

Case 1 : When V_{in} = 0V (Low)

- When input voltage = 0V , then V_{GS} of transistor T_1 (NMOS) will be 0 volts. Therefore it will not conduct and will be OFF. Fig. 1.4 (b) shows the equivalent circuit.

- V_{GS} of transistor T_2 will be equal to $- V_{DD}$. So , T_2 will be conducting or ON.

- Therefore output Y = HIGH or $V_{out} = V_{DD}$.

Case 2 : When V_{in}=5V (HIGH)

- When input V_{in} = +5V (HIGH) , V_{GS} of T_2 = 5V and hence it would be OFF. Fig. 1.14 (c) shows the equivalent circuit.

- V_{GS} of T_1 = +5V , So , T_1 is ON and conducting. Therefore output (Y = 0) or V_{out} = 0V.

Thus , the above circuit acts as an inverter.

1.5.2 CMOS NAND gate

Q. Explain with a neat circuit diagram the working of 2-input CMOS NAND gate.

[Dec. 04, 09, May 06, 3 M]

Q. Explain with neat diagram, CMOS NAND gate.   **[May 05, 2 M]**

Q. Draw CMOS circuit for NAND gate.

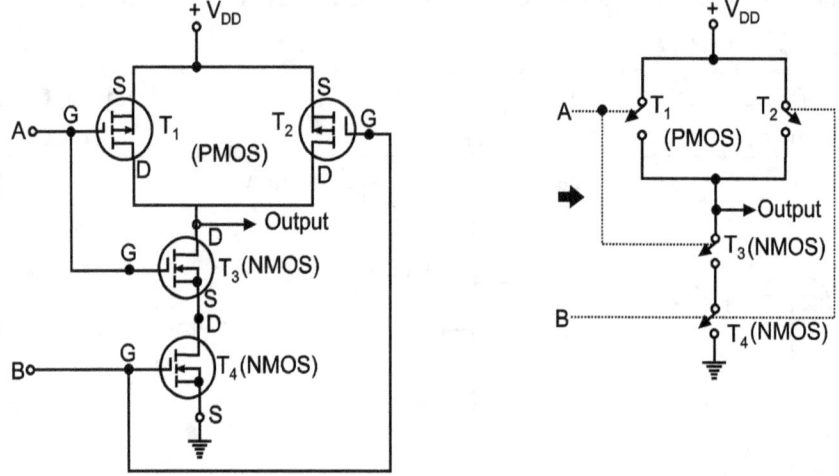

Fig. 1.15 (a) : Shows a CMOS two – input NAND and its equivalent circuit

Case 1 : A = 0 , B = 0 (Fig. 1.16 (a))

- $V_{GS1} = V_{GS2} = -V_{DD} = -5V$, $V_{GS3} = V_{GS4} = 0V$
- Therefore T_1 = ON , T_2 = ON , T_3 = OFF , T_4 = OFF
- $\therefore$ Output Y = 1 or V_{out} = +5V

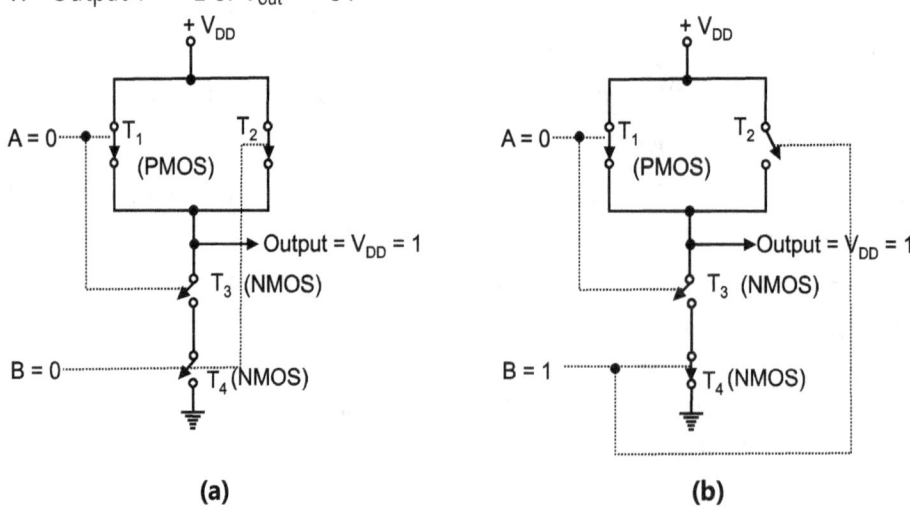

(a)   (b)

Fig. 1.16

Case 2 :   A = 0 , B = 1 (Fig. 1.16 (b))
- $V_{GS1} = -5V$, $V_{GS2} = 0V$, $V_{GS3} = 0V$, $V_{GS4} = +5V$
- ∴ Output Y = 1 or V_{out} = +5V.

Case 3 :   A = 1 , B = 0 (Fig. 1.16 (c))
- $V_{GS1} = 0V$, $V_{GS2} = -5V$, $V_{GS3} = +5V$, $V_{GS4} = 0V$.
- So , T_1 is OFF T_3 is ON, T_2 is ON and T_4 is OFF.
    - ∴   Y =1 or V_{out} = +5V

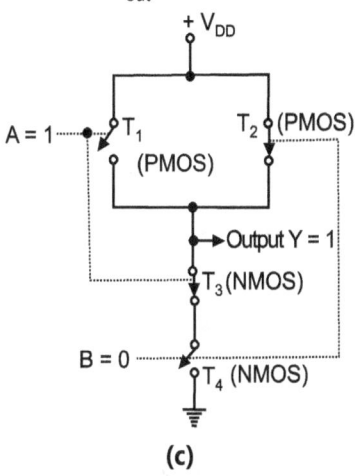

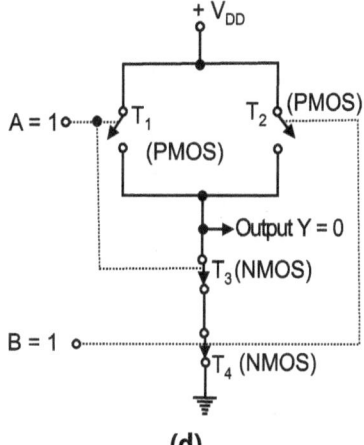

(c)   (d)

Fig. 1.16

Case 4 :   A = 1 , B = 1 Fig. 1.16 (d)
- $V_{GS1} = V_{GS2} = 0V$, $V_{GS3} = V_{GS4} = 5V$
- So , T_1 is OFF , T_3 is ON , T_2 is OFF and T_4 is ON.
    - ∴   Y =0 or V_{out} = 0V

Summary of Operations :

A	B	T_1	T_2	T_3	T_4	V_{out}
0 V	0 V	ON	ON	OFF	OFF	5 V
0 V	5 V	ON	OFF	OFF	ON	5 V
5 V	0 V	OFF	ON	ON	OFF	5 V
5 V	5 V	OFF	OFF	ON	ON	0 V

1.5.3   CMOS NOR gate

Q. Draw and explain briefly the working of 2-input CMOS NOR gate.

[Dec. 04, 05, 06, 07, 08, 12 May 07, 11, 8 M]

Q. Explain with neat diagram CMOS NOR gate.   **[May 05, 10, 5 M]**

Q. Draw CMOS circuit for NOR gate.   **[Dec. 11, 4 M]**

- Fig. 1.17 shows a CMOS 2 – input NOR gate and its equivalent circuits.

- NMOS transistor T_3 and T_4 are connected in parallel and PMOS T_1 and T_2 are connected in series.

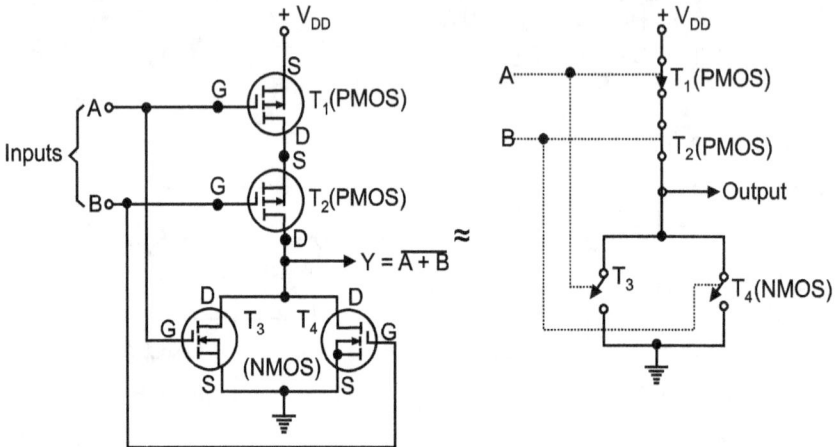

Fig. 1.17

Case 1 : A = 0 , B = 0

- Whenever both the inputs are 0 , then both NMOS are in OFF condition.

- $V_{GS1} = V_{GS2} = -5V$, $V_{GS3} = V_{GS4} = 0V$

  $\therefore \quad T_1 = T_2 = ON \quad T_3 = T_4 = OFF \qquad Y = 1$ or $V_{out} = +5V$.

Case 2 : A = 0 , B = 1

- $V_{GS1} = -5V$, $V_{GS2} = 0V$, $V_{GS3}=0V$ and $V_{GS4}=+5V$ So , T_1 and T_4 are ON , and T_2 and T_3 are OFF.

- Thus , output Y=0 , $V_{out} = 0V$

- Similarly , for the next states (A = 1 , B = 0 and A = 1 , B = 1) either of the NMOS or both the NMOS are ON.

- This provides short circuit path between output Y and ground terminal and the output becomes logic LOW.

  For summary of transistor operations refer to the Truth table below.

A	B	T_1	T_2	T_3	T_4	V_{out}
0 V	0 V	ON	ON	OFF	OFF	5 V
0 V	5 V	ON	OFF	OFF	ON	0 V
5 V	0 V	OFF	ON	ON	OFF	0 V
5 V	5 V	OFF	OFF	ON	ON	0 V

1.5.4 CMOS Characteristics

Q. Explain power dissipation, fan-out of a CMOS IC.

Q. Why CMOS inputs should never be left floating ?

Q. How can static charge damage a CMOS IC ?

1. **Supply Voltage :** The 4000 and 74C series can operate with V_{DD} values ranging from 3 to 15 volts. The 74HC and 74HCT series can operate with voltage values ranging from 2 to 6 volts.

2. **Voltage Levels :** The output of a CMOS is approximately 0V for LOW state and close to 5V for HIGH state.

Generally , the input voltage levels are expressed as percentage of VDD (power supply).

For example $V_{IL(max)}$ = 30% of V_{DD} and

                                   $V_{IH(min)}$ = 70% of V_{DD}

3. **Power Dissipation :**

- For a dc input , power dissipation is extremely low.

- But for a switching circuit , power dissipation increases.

- If V_{DD} = 5V , the dc power dissipation is 2.5 nW per gate.

But if V_{DD} = 10V , then it increases (10nW), which is still too small compared to TTL gates where P_D = 10mW

- Therefore , CMOS devices are preferred for battery operated systems.

- Hence , for low operating frequencies , power dissipation is low and for higher frequencies , power dissipation increases.

4. **Fan Out :**

- The maximum fan – out of a CMOS family is 50 for operating frequency below 1 MHz ($\leq$1MHz).

- This fan – out is limited to 50 as it depends on the propagation delay of each of the gates at the output.

5. **Switching Speed**

- With increase in V_{DD} , the speed of the CMOS gate increases.

- The less the propagation delay , more is the speed of the gate.

- For example :

    For 4000 series – Average t_{pd} = 50ns (V_{DD} = 5V)

                    Average t_{pd} = 25ns (V_{DD} = 10V)

For 74 HC series – t_{pd} = 8ns (V_{DD} = 5V)

    74 AC/ACT series – t_{pd} = 4.7ns (V_{DD} = 5V)

6. Noise Margins

- We know that the noise margins are calculated using –

$$V_{NH} = V_{OH(min)} - V_{IH(min)}$$
$$V_{NL} = V_{IL(max)} - V_{OL(max)}$$

- CMOS ICs are preferred to TTL for operation in noisy environment.

- We know that, if the supply voltage is increased the noise margins in CMOS increases.

7. Unused Inputs

- CMOS inputs should never be left unconnected or floating.

- It there are any unused inputs, they have to be either tied to 0V or V_{DD} power supply or connected to other inputs.

- This is done so that the unused inputs do not get induced voltages due to noise or static charges.

- Such induced voltages may cause overheating and damage the IC permanently.

8. Susceptibility to Static Charge :

- The CMOS gates are prone to static charges because of high input resistance.

- This static charge may induce a high voltage and damage the dielectric insulation between the MOSFET gate and the channel.

- Now – a – days Zener diodes are included on each input to protect the IC from static damage.

1.6 CMOS AND TTL INTERFACING

1.6.1 TTL–to–CMOS Interfacing Techniques

Q. Explain with neat diagram, interface of TTL gate driving CMOS gate.

Q. Draw and justify TTL driving CMOS.   **[Dec. 07, 10, 2 & 4 M]**

Q. Explain with neat diagrams, interface of TTL gate driving CMOS gate.
[May 06, Dec. 06, 08, 09, May 11, Dec. 12, 4 M]

- There are instances wherein the output of a TTL logic gate needs to be used for driving the input of a CMOS gate. Since the voltage–current characteristics and requirements of a TTL gate differ from those of a CMOS gate, it is good practice to use proper interfacial components between them when connecting them to each other. Below are some common techniques used in connecting a TTL gate to a CMOS gate.

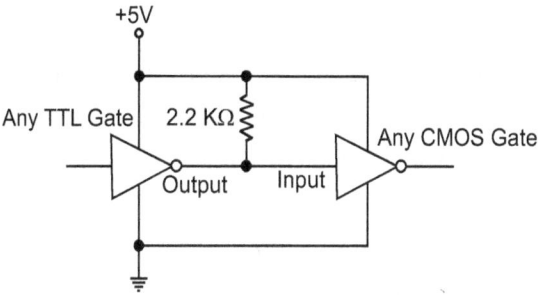

Fig. 1.18 (a) : Interfacing any TTL gate to any CMOS gate using the same power supply (5V)

- When the CMOS gate,that the TTL gate will drive,also uses the same 5–V supply used by the TTL gate, the simple interfacing technique shown in Fig. 1.18 (a) may be employed. Here, a pull–up resistor is just placed between the TTL output and the 5–V supply.

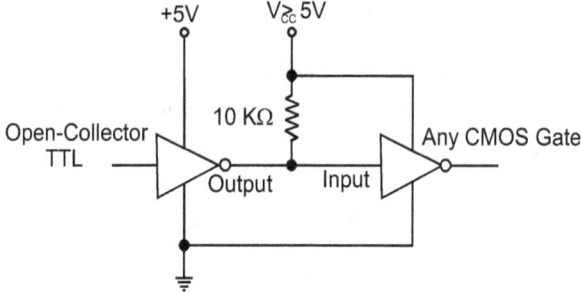

Fig. 1.18 (b) : Interfacing an Open–Collector TTL gate to any CMOS gate using different power supplies

- When the CMOS gate that the TTL gate will drive has a supply voltage that's different from the 5–V supply used by the TTL gate and if the TTL gate has an open collector, the simple interfacing technique shown in Fig. 1.18 (b) may be employed. Here, a 10–K pull–up resistor is just placed between the TTL output and the CMOS gate's supply.

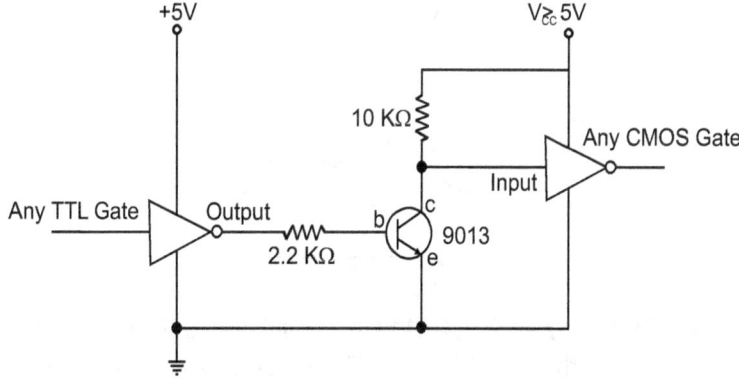

Fig. 1.18 (c) : Interfacing any TTL gate to any CMOS gate using different power supplies

- When the CMOS gate that the TTL gate will drive has a supply voltage that's different from the 5–V supply used by the TTL gate and if the TTL gate does not have an open collector, it would be good to use an NPN transistor to translate the TTL output voltage level to a correct CMOS input voltage level as shown in Fig. 1.18 (c) so as not to overstress the TTL gate.

Important Tips for TTL to CMOS interfacing :

- TTL output thresholds are inconsistent with 74HC, 74C and 40' CMOS inputs.
- When CMOS is run with V_{CC} = 5 V.
- Use an open collector buffer with pullup to 5 V.
- When CMOS uses V_{CC} = 3.3 V (Usually 74HC only)
- Direct connection from TTL to CMOS possible.
- When CMOS uses V_{CC} > 5 V (Usually 4000 or 74C series < use level shifter buffer chip 40109, LTC1045, 14504 or use open collector buffer with pullup to 5 V.

1.6.2 CMOS – to – TTL Interfacing Techniques

Q. Explain with neat diagrams, interface of driving CMOS gate to TTL gate.
[May 06, Dec. 06, 09, 12, May 11, 4 M]
Q. Draw and justify CMOS driving TTL.   **[Dec. 07, 2M, Dec. 10, 4 M]**

There are instances wherein the output of a CMOS logic gate needs to be used for driving the input of a TTL gate. Since the voltage–current characteristics and requirements of a CMOS gate differ from those of a TTL gate, it is good practice to use proper interfacial components between them when connecting them to each other. Below are some common techniques used in connecting a CMOS gate to a TTL gate.

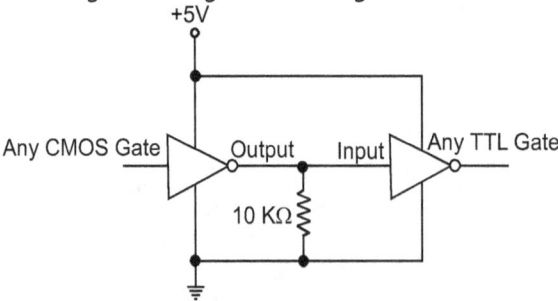

Fig. 1.19 (a) : Interfacing any CMOS gate to any TTL gate using the same power supply (5V)

- When the CMOS gate that will drive the TTL gate also uses the same 5–V supply used by the TTL gate, the simple interfacing technique shown in Fig. 1.19a) may be employed. Here, a pull–down resistor is just between the CMOS gate output and ground.

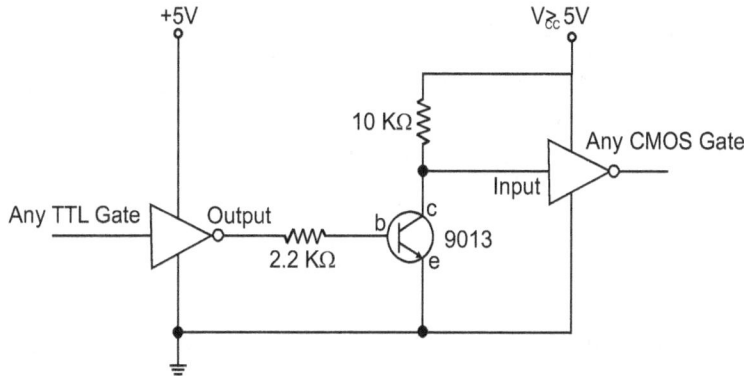

Fig. 1.19 (b) : Interfacing an open–collector TTL gate to any CMOS gate using different power supplies

- When the CMOS gate that will drive the TTL gate has a supply voltage that's different from the 5–V supply used by the TTL gate, it would be good to use an NPN transistor to translate the CMOS output voltage level to correct TTL input voltage level as shown in Fig. 1.19 (b).

- Note that the transistor uses the 5–V TTL supply for its V_{CC}.

- As an alternative to the technique shown in Fig. 1.19 (b) the technique shown in Fig. 1.19 (c) may be employed to connect a CMOS gate to a TTL gate.

- Instead of a transistor, a CMOS buffer (inverting or non–inverting) may be used as long as it is supplied from the 5–V TTL supply. The example in Fig. 1.19 (c) is an inverting buffer, so the input to the TTL gate is an inverted logic of the CMOS output.

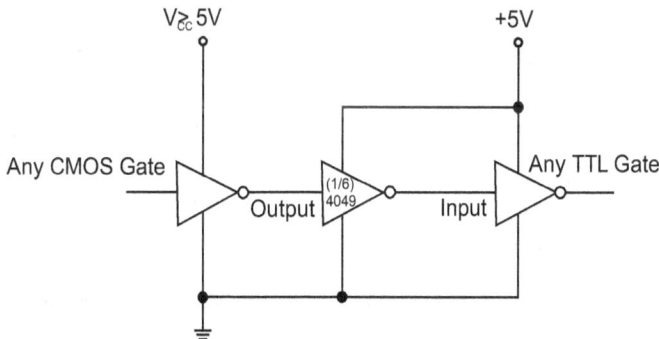

Fig. 1.19 (c) : Interfacing any TTL gate to any CMOS gate using different power supplies

Important Tips for Interfacing CMOS to TTL

- If V_{CC} is + 5V, then one CMOS output can drive one LS TTL input
- CMOS logic levels are close to 0 V or 5 V, so no threshold incompatibility
- If CMOS is run at $V_{CC} \sim 3.3$ V, thresholds are still compatible with TTL
- Sometimes 4000 series or 74 C chips are run at $V_{CC} > 5$ V for improved speed
- Need level–shifter chip to interface to TTL, for example 4049/50, 74C901/2.

1.7   DIFFERENT LOGIC FAMILY SERIES

74AC : A high speed CMOS logic family with CMOS input switching levels and buffered CMOS outputs that can drive ± 24 mA of I_{OH} and I_{OL}.

74ACT : A high speed CMOS logic family with the same buffered CMOS outputs that can drive ± 24 mA of I_{OH} and I_{OL}. This family has a TTL–to–CMOS input buffer stage. The inputs will interface with TTL outputs operating at 5 volts with V_{OH} = 2.4 volts and V_{OL} = 0.4 volts. The devices have the same output buffered structures as the AC family.

74LCX : These devices have a mixed 3 volts–to–5 volts capability for use with applications that have both 3 volts and a 5 volts devices which interface with one another.

74LVX : This family consists of low cost devices with 5 volts tolerant inputs. The devices can receive and output 3 volts or 5 volts.

74LVQ : This family consists of low cost devices designed for 3.3 volts only applications.

74LVT : This family has both high speed and a high output drive. These devices have a + 64 mA / − 32 mA output drive currents. The chips are 5 volts tolerant and are designed to be used with applications that have both 3 V and 5 V devices which interface with one another.

74ALCX : This devices are about the same as the LVT family with out the high drive currents.

74xx : The first TTL family developed. The 74xx family offers a wide variety of logic functions. There are a number of other TTL logic families which offer either higher speed or lower power.

74LXX : This is the Low power version of the TTL family above. The value of the internal device resistors have been increased by a factor of 10x. The family offers 1/10 the power consumption as the previous family, but operates at 1/3 the speed.

74LSXX : This devices adds a Schottky diode between the Base and Collector of the transistor. The Schottky diode prevents the transistor from going into full saturation. So the 74LS family operates at the same speed as the 74 family [10nS] with only 2mW of power dissipation compared to 10mW for 74xx or 1mW for the 74L family [at 33nS].

74SXX : This gains its speed using the same Schottky diode as the 74LS family, but the value of the internal device resistors have been decreased by half the original values of the 74XX family. So, the speed increases [3 nS] and the power consumption also increases [20 mW].

74ALSXX : The advanced LS family offers near same high speed as the 74Sxx family at 4 nS at a power dissipation of only 1mW. Except for the 74SXX family, the 74ALS family out performs the other three TTL families listed. If the design calls for a TTL family which needs to operate at 3 nS, this is the family to use.

74ASXX : If the design needs to operate faster than 3 nS then the 74 AS family should be use. This family is twice as fast as the 74ALS family with a propagation delay of only 1.5 nS. The price is a 7 mW power dissipation.

1.8 COMPARISONS

1.8.1 Comparison of CMOS and TTL

Q. Compare TTL and COMS logic families with respect to :
1. Power dissipation per gate   2. Propagation delay
3. Fig. of merit   4. Fan out.   **[Dec. 05, 06, 8 M]**

Q. Compare COMS and TTL logic families on the basis of :
1. Noise margin   2. Fan out
2. Basic gate   3. Unconnected inputs.
4. Power supply voltage   6. Figure of merit   **[May 07, 4 M, May 11, 8 M]**

Sr. No	Parameter	TTL	CMOS
1.	Device used	Bipolar junction transistor	N – Channel MOSFET and P – channel MOSFET
2.	Operating areas	Transistors are operated in saturation or cut off regions.	MOSFETs are operated as switches. i.e. in the ohmic region or off region.
3.	Supply voltage	Fixed equal to 5 V.	Flexible from 3 V to 15 V.
4.	Low level noise margin	0.4 V	$V_{NL} = 1.45$ V
5.	High level noise margin	0.4 V	$V_{NH} = 1.45$ V
6.	Noise immunity	Less than CMOS	Better than TTL
7.	Propagation delay	10 ns. (Standard TTL)	105 ns (Metal gate CMOS)
8.	Switching speed	Faster than CMOS	Less than TTL
9.	Power dissipation per gate.	10mW	$P_D = 0.1$ mW. Hence used for battery backup applications
10.	Speed power product.	100pJ	10.5pJ
11.	$V_{IH(min)}$	2 V	3.5 V($V_{DD} = 5$ V)
12.	$V_{IL(max)}$	0.8 V	1.5 V
13.	$V_{OH(min)}$	2.7 V	4.95 V
14.	$V_{OL(max)}$	0.4 V	0.05 V
15.	Component density	Less than CMOS since BJT needs more space.	More than TTL since MOSFETs need smaller space while fabricating an IC.

1.8.2   Comparison of TTL, CMOS, ECL, RTL I²L and DCTL

Q. Compare CMOS and ECL logic families with respect to.   **[May 06, 6 M]**

Q. Compare TTL, CMOS and ECL.   **[Dec. 10, 6 M]**

Parameter	TTL	CMOS	ECL	RTL	I²L	OCTL
Fan out	Moderate	Highest	High	Low	Low	Low
Noise margin	Moderate	High	Low	Poor	High	Poor
Circuit complexity	Complex	Moderately complex	Complex	Not complex	Not complex	Not complex
Basic gate	NAND	NAND / NOR	OR/NOR	NOR	NAND	NOR
Components used	Transistors diodes and resistors	MOSFETs	Resistors and Transistors	Resistors and Transistors	Transistors	Resistors and Transistors
Basic gate	NAND	NAND / NOR	OR/NOR	NOR	NAND	NOR

COMBINATIONAL LOGIC DESIGN

2.1 COMBINATIONAL LOGIC DESIGN

2.1.1 Introduction

- Digital circuits or logical circuits are classified into two types : Combinational circuits and sequential circuits.
- Sequential circuits are further divided into two groups : synchronous and asynchronous circuits.
- The following diagram shows the classification of logic circuits.

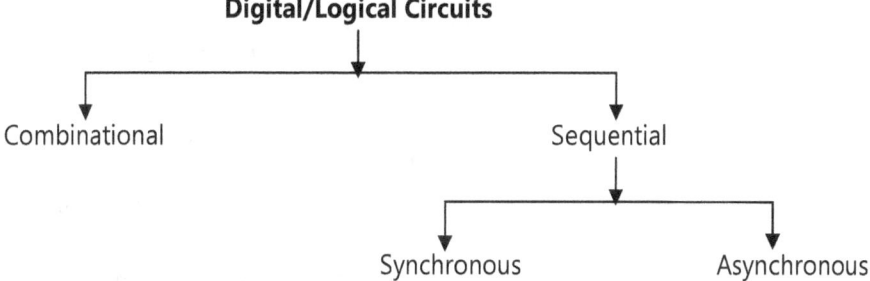

2.1.1.1 Combinational Circuit

Q. Define Combinational Circuit.

- Combinational circuit uses logic gates to implement or satisfy a given Boolean expression.
- The outputs of combinational circuit is a logical function of the input variables.

This can be shown as in Fig. 2.1.

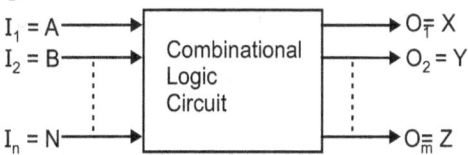

Fig. 2.1 : Block diagram of combinational logic circuit

- The combinational logic circuit has only logic gates and does not require memory. Its operation depends upon the present states of inputs and not on the previous (history) states of the inputs.

2.1.1.2 Sequential Logic Circuit

> **Q.** What are sequential logic circuits?
>
> **Q.** Where are sequential circuits used?

- Sequential circuit is designed using combinational logic circuit and memory elements. There are requirements in digital applications where the output variables depend on the sequence in which the input variables are received.

- For example, counter. A counter circuits count input pulses and hence it has to remember number of input pulses it has received so far.

- This dependency on previous input conditions needs to be stored in memory.

- Combination logic circuit cannot store data and therefore, we require memory elements along with combinational circuit to design sequential logic circuit as shown in Fig. 2.2.

- The output of a sequential logic circuit depends upon the present inputs as well as the last state of inputs and outputs.

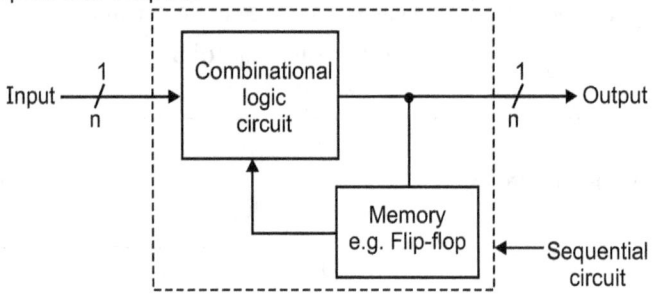

Fig. 2.2 : Block diagram of sequential circuit

- The present state stored in the memory and external inputs are logically evaluated in the combinational block to determine the outputs.

2.1.2 Comparison of Combinational and Sequential Circuit

> **Q.** What is the difference between combinational and sequential circuits?

Combinational Circuit	Sequential Circuit
1. The outputs depend on the combination of inputs.	1. The outputs depend on the past history of inputs as well as the present input states.
2. Memory is not required.	2. Memory is required to store previous states of the inputs.
3. The delay between outputs and inputs is less, so the combinational circuit is faster.	3. Sequential circuit is slower due to propagational delay of additional memory element.

4. Combinational circuits are concurrent in nature.

5. Easier to design.

6. Block diagram :

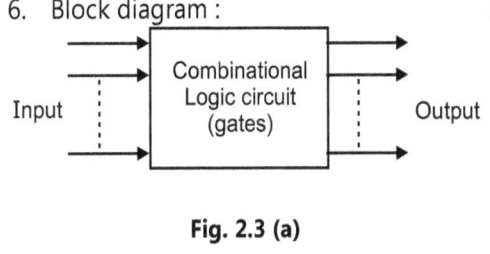

Fig. 2.3 (a)

4. Sequential circuit is not entirely concurrent.

5. Complex to design. Timings can be critical.

6. Block diagram :

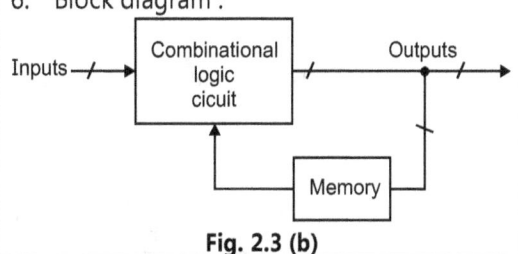

Fig. 2.3 (b)

Sequential Circuits are further classified into two groups :

(A) Synchronous Circuit :

(i) The change in inputs can affect memory element upon the activation of clock signal.

(ii) Memory elements are clocked flip-flops.

(iii) The maximum operational speed of synchronous circuit is governed by the clock speed, which in turn, is decided by the propagation delays of the logic gates.

(B) Asynchronous Circuit :

(i) The change in inputs can occur at any instant of time.

(ii) Memory elements are unclocked flip-flops or time delay elements.

(iii) Asynchronous circuits can operate faster than synchronous circuits because the clock is absent.

2.2 IMPLEMENTING COMBINATIONAL CIRCUIT

- Logic gates are used to design a combinational circuit.

- For example, two AND gates and one OR gate can be used to build a combinational circuit to satisfy Boolean expression. $Y = AB + CD$ as shown in Fig. 2.4.

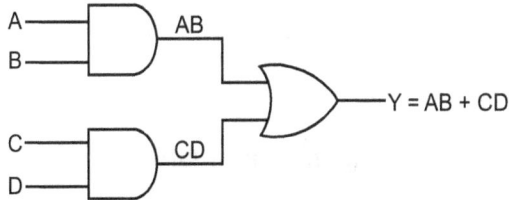

Fig. 2.4 : Combinational circuit for Y = AB + CD

Any combinational circuit can be built using four logics.

(i) AND-OR (Use of inverters allowed).

(ii) OR-AND (Use of inverters allowed).

(iii) NAND-NAND (Inverters implemented using NAND).

(iv) NOR-NOR (Inverters implemented using NOR).

(i) AND-OR Logic :

- When the given Boolean expression is represented by Sum Of Product (SOP) terms then AND-OR logic is used.

- For example,   Product terms

$$P = QR + ST$$

- This can be implemented using AND-OR as shown in Fig. 2.5.

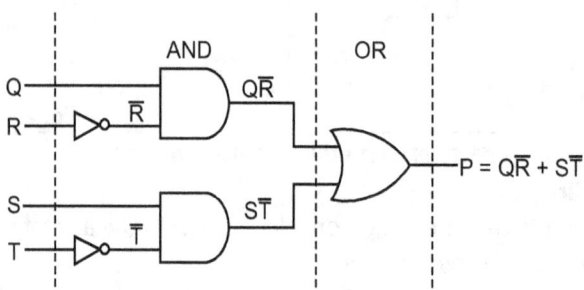

Fig. 2.5 : AND-OR logic

(ii) OR-AND Logic :

- When the Boolean expression is represented by product of sum (POS) terms then OR-AND logic is used.

- For example,   Sum terms

$$X = (A + \bar{B}) \cdot (C + \bar{D})$$

- This can be implemented in OR-AND as shown in Fig. 2.6.

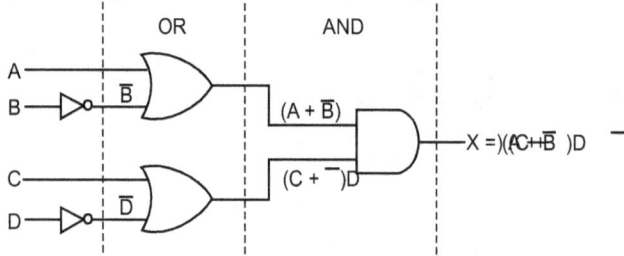

Fig. 2.6 : OR-AND logic

(iii)   NAND-NAND Logic :

- We known that NAND and NOR are universal gates.

- So, any Boolean expression that can be expressed in AND-OR (SOP) or OR-AND (POS) logic can be converted to NAND-NAND or NOR-NOR logic by replacing the basic gates by NAND or NOR gates.

- Following example, Fig. 2.7 shows converting AND-OR logic to NAND-NAND logic.

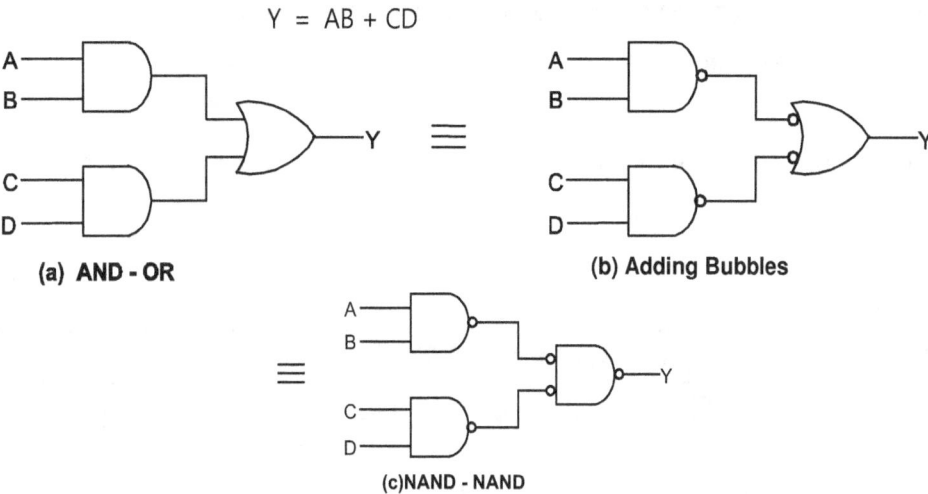

Fig. 2.7 : Converting AND-OR logic to NAND-NAND Logic

Rules to convert AND-OR to NAND-NAND :

(i) Simplify the Boolean expression.

(ii) Express it in Sum-Of-Product (SOP) form.

(iii) Add bubbles on the outputs of each AND and on the inputs to all OR. Draw a NAND gate for each product term.

(iv) Draw a single NAND gate at the second level.

(iv) NOR-NOR Logic :

- Any OR-AND logic can be converted into NOR-NOR logic.

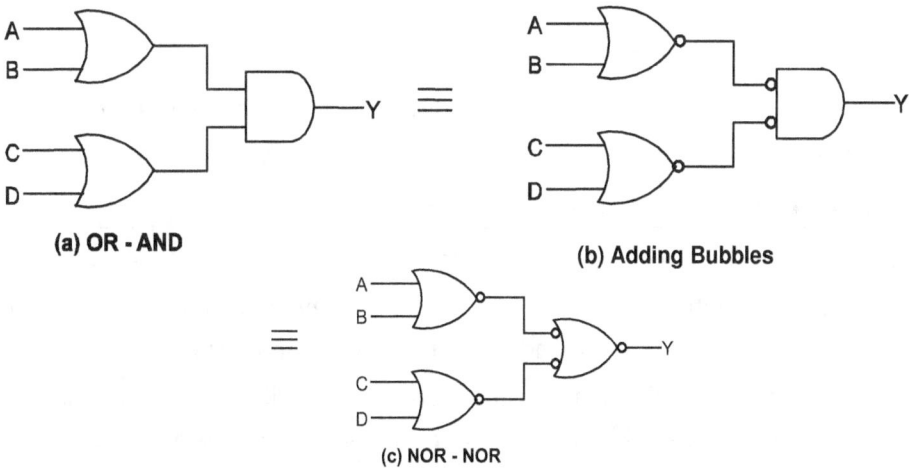

Fig. 2.8 : Converting OR-AND logic to NOR-NOR logic

- **Rules to convert OR-AND logic to NOR-NOR logic (Fig. 2.8) :**

(i) Simplify the Boolean expression.

(ii) Express it in Product Of Sum (POS) form.

(iii) Add bubbles to output of OR and bubbles at input to AND gate. Draw a NOR gate for each sum term.

(iv) Draw a single NOR gate at the second level.

2.3 SUM OF PRODUCTS (SOP) FORM

2.3.1 Standard Terms and Standard (or Canonical) Forms

Q. What is standard or canonical form ?

- The behaviour of the logic circuit can be expressed in standard forms using standard terms.

- If a function is expressed in such a way that each variable is present in each term then it is known as standard form.

2.3.2 Sum Term or Maximum Term (M)

- The output of OR gate is called **sum** term.

- In OR gate, the output is logic '1' for **maximum** number of combinations of inputs.

- So, the output of OR gate is also called **Maximum term** or **Maxterm (M).**

- A sum term of any 'n' variable functions containing all the 'n' literals is called a maxterm. The 'n' variables functions have 2^n maxterms.

- These are denoted as $M_0, M_1, M_2, \ldots M_n$.

- Each variables taking value '0' appears in uncomplemented form in maxterm and each variable taking '1' value appears in complemented form.

2.3.3 Product or Minimum Term (m)

- The output of AND gate is called **product** term.

- In AND gate, the output is logic '1' for **minimum** number of combinations of inputs. So, the output of AND gate is also called '**Minimum term** or **minterm** (m).

- A product term of any 'n' variable functions containing all literals is called a minterm. The 'n' variable functions have 2^n minterms. These are denoted as $m_0, m_1, m_2, \ldots, m_n$.

- In minterms, each variables taking value '1' appears in uncomplemented form.

Table 2.1 : Maxterms and minterms of two-variables

Decimal Equivalent	Variables		Minterms		Maxterms	
	A	**B**	**m_i**	**Notation**	**M_i**	**Notation**
0	0	0	$\bar{A}\bar{B}$	m_0	$A + B$	M_0
1	0	1	$\bar{A}B$	m_1	$A + \bar{B}$	M_1
2	1	0	$A\bar{B}$	m_2	$\bar{A} + B$	M_2
3	1	1	AB	m_3	$\bar{A} + \bar{B}$	M_3

Sum of Products (SOP) Form

- The output of AND-OR gate circuit is called sum-of-products (SOP) form.
- Consider the equation,

$$Y = \bar{A}B + AB$$

- Each term in the equation is called the fundamental minterm. From table mentioned earlier, the output Y can be written as,

$$Y = m_1 + m_3$$
$$= \Sigma\, m_1, m_3$$
$$= \Sigma\, m_i$$

where, $i = 1, 3 = \Sigma\, 1, 3$

- The SOP form can be converted to standard SOP form by ANDing the terms in the expression with terms formed by ORing.
- The variable and its complement which are not present in that term.
- Following steps are followed to convert a given SOP form to standard SOP form :
(i) Write down all the terms.
(ii) If one or more variables are missing in any term, expand that term by multiplying it with the sum of each one of the missing variable and its complement.
For example,

$$Y = AB + \bar{A}\bar{B}C$$

- The variable C is missing in first term. So, multiply the first term by $(C + \bar{C})$.

$$Y = AB\,(C + \bar{C}) + \bar{A}\bar{B}C$$

∴   Standard SOP form is

$$Y = ABC + AB\bar{C} + \bar{A}\bar{B}C$$

(iii) Drop out the redundant terms.

Example 2.1 :

Convert $Y = \bar{A}B + A\bar{C} + \bar{B}C$ into standard SOP form.

Solution :

$$Y = \bar{A}B + A\bar{C} + \bar{B}C$$

$$= \bar{A}B\,(C + \bar{C}) + A\bar{C}\,(B + \bar{B}) + \bar{B}C\,(A + \bar{A})$$

$$= \bar{A}BC + \bar{A}B\bar{C} + A\bar{C}B + A\bar{C}\bar{B} + \bar{B}CA + \bar{B}C\bar{A}$$

$$= \underbrace{\bar{A}BC}_{} + \bar{A}B\bar{C} + A\bar{C}B + A\bar{C}\bar{B} + ABC + \underbrace{\bar{A}\bar{B}C}_{}$$

Redundant terms

$$= \bar{A}BC + \bar{A}B\bar{C} + A\bar{C}B + A\bar{C}\bar{B} + ABC$$

2.4 PRODUCT OF SUMS (POS) FORM

2.4.1 Product-of-Sums (POS) Form

- The output of OR-AND gate circuit is called Product-Of-Sums (POS) form.

Consider the equation,

$$Y = (A + B) \cdot (\bar{A} + B)$$

$$Y = M_0, M_2 = \pi\,(0, 2)$$

where, π stands for the product of maxterms.

- The POS form can be converted to standard POS form by ORing the terms in the expression with terms formed by ANDing the variable and its complement which are not present in that term.

- Following steps are followed to convert a POS form to standard POS form.

(i) Write down all the terms.

(ii) If one or more variables are missing in any sum terms, expand that term by adding the products of each of the missing term and its complement.

(iii) Drop out the redundant terms.

Example 2.2 :

Convert $Y = (A + B) \cdot (A + C) \cdot (B + \bar{C})$ into standard POS form.

Solution : $Y = (A + B) \cdot (A + C) \cdot (B + \bar{C})$

$$= (A + B + C \cdot \bar{C}) \cdot (A + B \cdot \bar{B} + C) \cdot (B + \bar{C} + A \cdot \bar{A})$$

We use $\qquad$ X + YZ = (X + Y) · (X + Z) law to expand the equation.

$$= \underbrace{(A + B + C)}\ \overline{(A + B + \bar{C})}\ (A + C + B)$$

$$\overline{(A + B + C)\ (B + \bar{C} + A)}\ (B + \bar{C} + \bar{A})$$

$$= (A + B + C)\ (A + B + \bar{C})\ (A + \bar{B} + C)$$

$$(\bar{A} + B + \bar{C}) \qquad\qquad (\because \text{ Redundant terms})$$

Example 2.3 :

Simplify the following three variable expression.

$$Y = \pi M\ (1, 3, 5, 7)$$

Solution :

The given boolean expression is in POS from. From the table, we can rewrite the boolean expression as

$$Y = \underset{N_1}{\left(A + B + \bar{C}\right)}\ \underset{N_3}{\left(A + \bar{B} + \bar{C}\right)}\ \underset{N_5}{\left(\bar{A} + B + \bar{C}\right)}\ \underset{N_7}{\left(\bar{A} + \bar{B} + \bar{C}\right)}$$

$$= \left(AA + A\bar{B} + A\bar{C} + BA + B\bar{B} + B\bar{C} + \bar{C}A + \bar{C}B + \bar{C}\bar{C}\right)\left(\bar{A} + B + \bar{C}\right)\left(\bar{A} + \bar{B} + \bar{C}\right)$$

$$= \left(A + A\bar{B} + A\bar{C} + AB + O + B\bar{C}\right)\left(\bar{A} + B + \bar{C}\right)\left(\bar{A} + \bar{B} + \bar{C}\right)$$

$$= \left(A + (1 + \bar{C}) + A\,(\bar{B} + B) + \bar{C}B\right)\left(\bar{A}\,(\bar{B} + B) + \bar{A}\bar{C} + \bar{C}\right)$$

$$= \left(A + A + \bar{C}B\right)\left(\bar{A} + \bar{A}\bar{C} + \bar{C}\right)$$

$$= \left(A + \bar{C}B\right)\left(\bar{A} + \bar{C}\bar{A}\right)\ =\ A\bar{A}\ +\ A\bar{C}\bar{A}\ +\ \bar{C}B\bar{A}\ +\ \bar{C}B\bar{C}\bar{A}$$

$$= 0 + 0 + \bar{C}B\bar{A}\ +\ \bar{C}B\bar{C}\bar{A}\ =\ \bar{A}B\bar{C}\ +\ \bar{A}B\bar{C}$$

$$Y = \bar{A}B\bar{C}$$

2.5 KARNAUGH (K – MAP)

2.5.1 Boolean Algebra Simplification Technique

Q. Why gray code is used in labeling the cells of k-map ?   **[Dec. 05, 2 M, May 10, 4 M]**

- A good digital circuit must have minimum number of logic gates.
- Less number of gates means minimum propagation delay, skew, power dissipation.
- The number of logic gates can be reduced only if the number of terms in the Boolean expression can be reduced.

- There are four methods that are used to simplify or reduce the Boolean equations.
- (i) Algebraic (Boolean Laws, DeMorgan's Theorems).
- (ii) Karnaugh (K) Map.
- (iii) Variable Entered Mapping (VEM).
- (iv) Quine-McCluskey (Q-M) Tabular Method.
- The K-map is the simplest and the most commonly used method.

2.5.2 Reduction of Boolean Equation using K-map

- The K-map method is a systematic approach for simplifying a Boolean expression.
- This method was proposed by Veitch and then modified by Karnaugh, hence it is called Karnaugh map.
- The basis of K-map method is graphical representation of minterms or maxterms in a chart called Karnaugh map (K-map). K-map contains cells.
- Each cell represents one of the 2^n possible product cells that can be formed from n variables.
- Thus, n-variable K-map has 4 cells, 3-variable k-map has 8 cells and 4-variable K-map has 16 cells.
- Product terms are assigned to the cells of a K-map by labelling each row and each column of the map with a variable, with its complements or with a combination of variables and complements. Fig. 2.9 depicts the 2-variable, -variable and 4-variable maps.

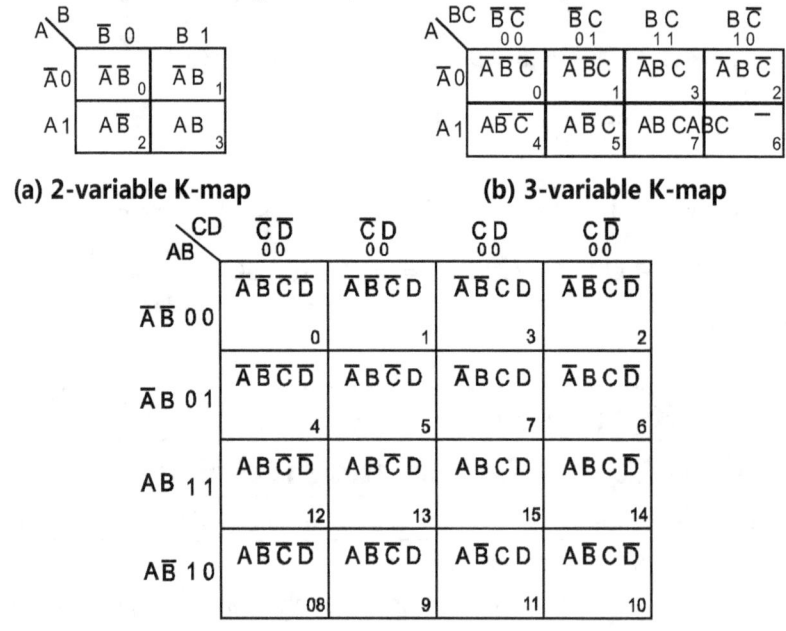

(a) 2-variable K-map   (b) 3-variable K-map

(c) 4-variable K-map

Fig. 2.9

- It is important to note that only one variable changes, when we move from one cell to another along any row or any column.
- Therefore, the third column and the third row in a two-variable K-map have '11' binary representation instead of '10'.
- This peculiar arrangement of K-map has special significance as mentioned below.
- When two inputs change simultaneously then digital circuit output goes in a metastable state.
- Output can swing to either logic '1' or logic '0' state in metastable state.
- This state is to be avoided by prohibiting two inputs from switching simultaneously.
- We know that any logic function can be represented in SOP or POS form. The given Boolean expression can be used to fill entries in the truth table and truth table can be represented on K-map.
- With little practice, it is also possible to fill entries in k-map directly.

2.5.3 Representing SOP Equation on K-map

Example 2.4 :

Plot Boolean expression. $Y = \overline{A}\,\overline{B}CD + \overline{A}B\overline{C}\,\overline{D} + ABCD$

Solution :

(i)   The Boolean expression has four variables, so we use 4-variable K-map.

(ii) Represent each product term by '1' in corresponding cell.

(iii) Note that number of 1's in K-map is equal to the product terms in the given Boolean expression.

(iv) Fill 0's in all other cells.

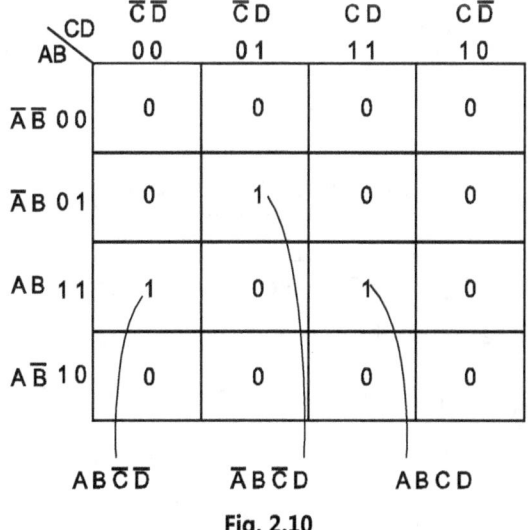

Fig. 2.10

2.5.4 Representing POS Equation on k-map

Example 2.5 :

Plot Boolean expression on a K-map.

$$Z = (X + \bar{Y})(\bar{X} + \bar{Y})$$

Solution :

(i) The Boolean expression has two variables, so we use 2-variable K-map.

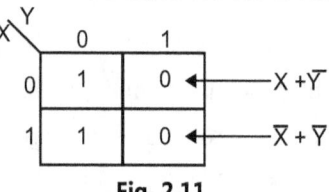

Fig. 2.11

(ii) Represent each sum term by '0' in the corresponding cell.

(iii) Note that number of '0's in K-map is equal to the sum terms in the given Boolean expression.

(iv) Fill '1's in all other cells.

2.5.5 K-map Reduction Techniques

- In K-map minterms are represented by 1's and maxterms are represented by 0's.
- The objective of K-map reduction or simplification technique is to reduce the number of logic gates.
- Once the logic or Boolean expression is plotted on K-map, we use grouping technique to simplify the given Boolean expression as follows :

(a) Grouping Two Adjacent Ones (or Pair) :

- Consider a Boolean expression $Y = ABC + AB\bar{C}$.

  It can be seen from the given Boolean expression that we will require two   three-input AND gates and one two-input OR gate to implement the logic equation.

- Now, if we plot the equation in a 3-variable K-map.

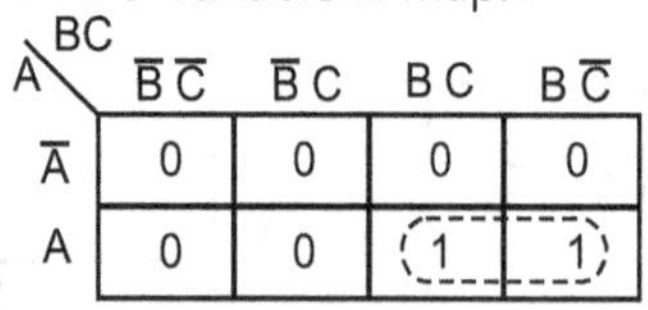

	$\bar{B}\bar{C}$	$\bar{B}C$	BC	$B\bar{C}$
$\bar{A}$	0	0	0	0
A	0	0	1	1

Fig. 2.12 : Grouping on two adjacent ones

- It can be noticed that when the two adjacent 1's are grouped then only one variable

  appears in its complemented and uncomplemented form i.e. C and $\bar{C}$.

$$Y = ABC + AB\bar{C} = AB(C + \bar{C})$$

$$= AB \qquad\qquad (\because C + \bar{C} = 1)$$

- So, these two terms can be combined together to eliminate the variable C.

- Once this third variable is eliminated then it is possible to use two-input AND gate instead of three-input AND.

These adjacent 1's can be also in vertical or any other form as shown in Fig. 2.13.

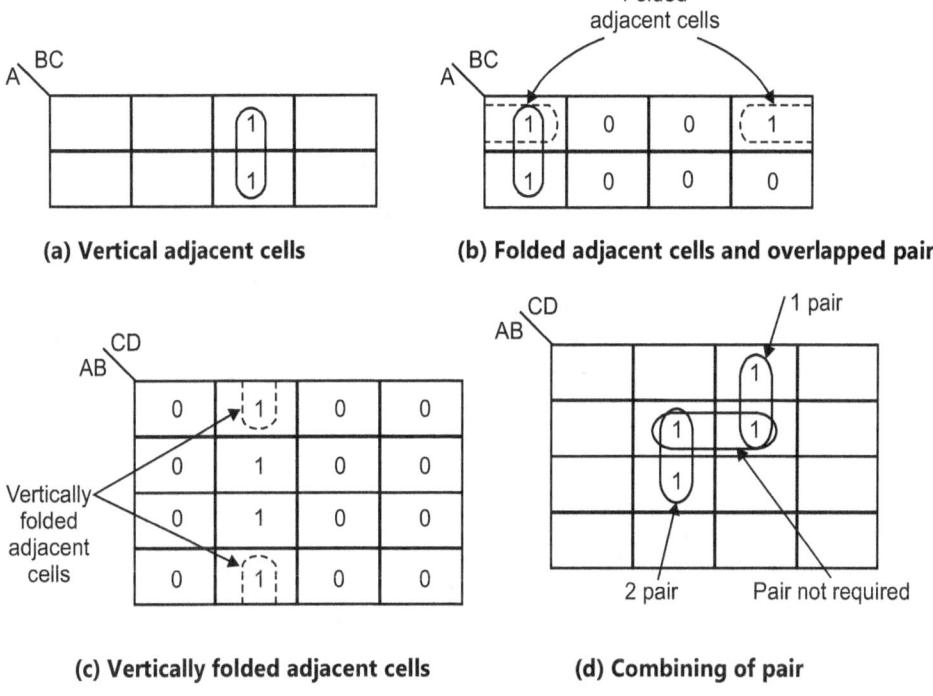

(a) Vertical adjacent cells   **(b) Folded adjacent cells and overlapped pairs**

(c) Vertically folded adjacent cells   **(d) Combining of pair**

Fig. 2.13 : Various Combinations of 1 Pairs

(b) Grouping of Four Adjacent Ones (Quad) :

- We can group four adjacent ones to eliminate two variables out of four variables.

- The several ways to form four adjacent ones or quads are shown in Fig. 2.14.

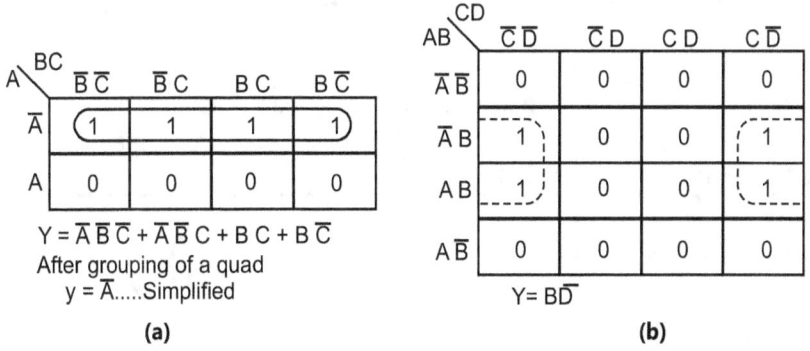

$Y = \overline{A}\,\overline{B}\,\overline{C} + \overline{A}\,\overline{B}\,C + B\,C + B\,\overline{C}$

After grouping of a quad

$y = \overline{A}$.....Simplified

(a)

$Y = B\overline{D}$

(b)

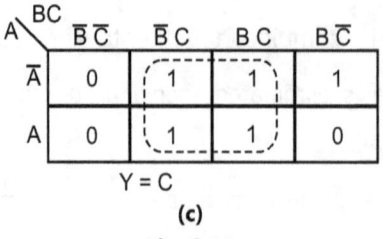

$$Y = C$$

(c)

Fig. 2.14

Example 2.6 :

Minimize the Boolean expression using K-map reduction technique.

$$Y = A\bar{B}C + \bar{A}\bar{B}C + \bar{A}BC + \bar{A}\bar{B}\bar{C} + \bar{A}\bar{B}\bar{C}$$

Solution :

Step 1 : Fill all the minterms in respective cells.

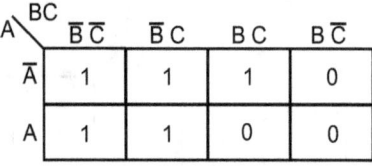

Fig. 2.15 (a)

Step 2 : Group all possible quads and pairs.

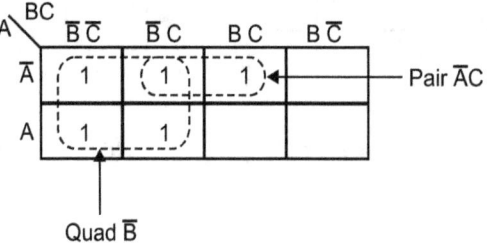

Fig. 2.15 (b)

Step 3 : Write down the Boolean equations representing quads pairs, etc.

In above example, these equations are $\bar{B}$ and $\bar{A}C$.

Step 4 : OR the terms which are generated by groups i.e.

$$Y = \bar{A}C + \bar{B}$$

Step 5 : Compare the number of gates used before K-map simplification.

(three-input AND = 5 numbers; five-input OR = 1 no.) and after k-map simplification (two-input AND = 1 no.; two-input OR = 1 no.).

Example 2.7 :

Design a half-adder and full-adder circuits using K-maps.

Solution :

• Addition is the most basic arithmetic operation in digital circuit.

- The simple addition of two bits has the following truth table.

Truth Table

A	B	Sum	Carry
0	0	0	0
0	1	1	0
1	0	1	0
1	1	0	1

- Note that when both the inputs are 1's then 'sum' is '0' and one carry is generated, similar to decimal addition.

Half-Adder :

- The half-adder has two inputs (A, B) and two outputs (sum, carry).
- The block diagram of half-adder is shown in Fig. 2.16.

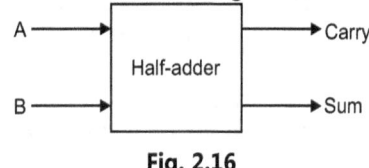

A ———→   ———→ Carry

                    Half-adder

B ———→   ———→ Sum

Fig. 2.16

- When the circuit has two or more outputs, one K-map is plotted for each output.
- The K-maps for half adder are :

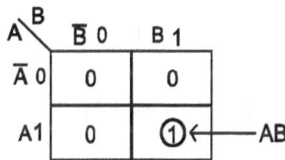

Fig. 2.17 : K-map For Carry

∴   Carry output = AB

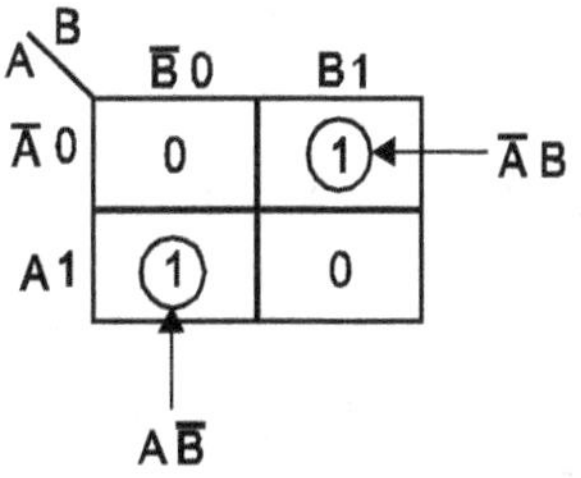

Fig. 2.18 : K-Map for sum output

∴   Sum = $\bar{A}B + A\bar{B}$

= $A \oplus B$

↑

XOR

Half-Adder Circuit :

The half-adder circuit based on above K-map simplifications is shown in Fig. 2.19.

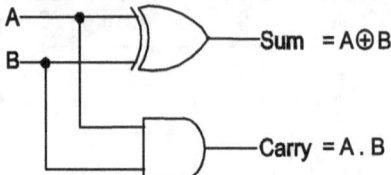

Fig. 2.19 : Half Adder logic diagram

Full-Adder :

- Full-adder has an additional input of previous carry in.
- Full-adder is a combinational circuit that forms the arithmetic sum of three input bits i.e. A, B, C_{in} and produces two outputs, sum, C_{out}.
- The logic block diagram of full adder is shown in Fig. 2.20.

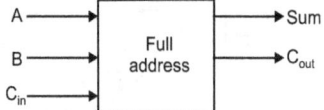

Fig. 2.20 : Block diagram of full-adder

The truth table of full-adder

Inputs			Outputs	
A	B	C_{in}	C_{out}	Sum
0	0	0	0	0
0	0	1	0	1
0	1	0	0	1
0	1	1	1	0
1	0	0	0	1
1	0	1	1	0
1	1	0	1	0
1	1	1	1	1

- Full-adder truth table is plotted on two K-maps corresponding to two outputs, C_{out} and sum.

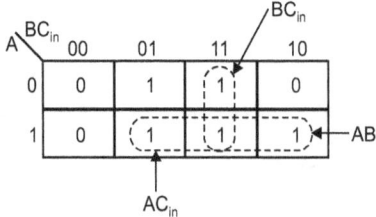

Fig. 2.21 : K-map for C_{out}

$$C_{out} = AB + AC_{in} + BC_{in}$$

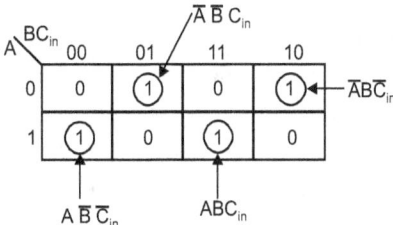

Fig. 2.22 : K-Map for Sum

$$\text{Sum} = \overline{A}\,\overline{B}C_{in} + \overline{A}B\overline{C}_{in} + AB C_{in} + A\overline{B}\,\overline{C}_{in}$$

$$\text{Sum} = \overline{A}\,\overline{B}C_{in} + A\overline{B}\,\overline{C}_{in} + \overline{A}B\overline{C}_{in} + ABC_{in}$$

$$= C_{in}(\overline{A}\,\overline{B} + AB) + \overline{C}_{in}(A\overline{B} + \overline{A}B) = C_{in} \oplus (A \oplus B)$$

- The sum is the XORed output of A, B and C_{in} inputs.

Full-Adder Circuit :

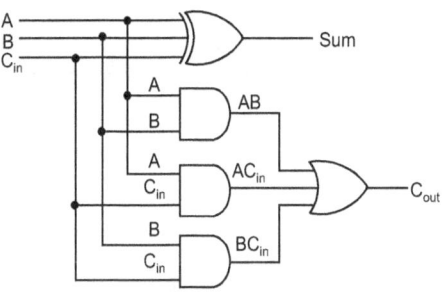

Fig. 2.23 : Full-Adder Logic Diagram

Full-Adder Circuit using Half-Adder :

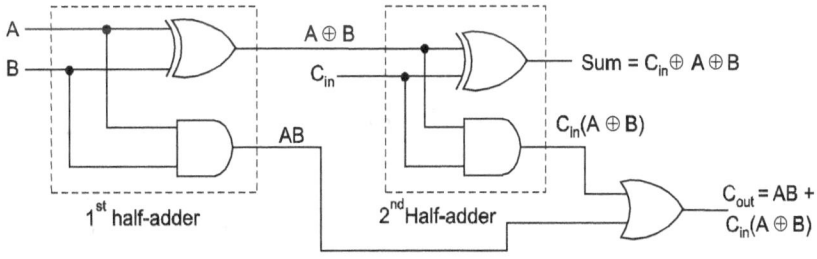

Fig. 2.24 : Full-Adder using Half Adder

For K-map simplification :

$$C_{out} = AB + AC_{in} + BC_{in} = AB + C_{in}(A + B)$$

$$= AB + C_{in}(A\overline{B} + \overline{A}B) = AB + C_{in}(A \oplus B)$$

Therefore, the C_{out} is produced by ORing the carry output of the first adder (AB) with sum of output of the first adder (A ⊕ B).

2.5.6 Don't Care Condition

In some logic circuits, certain input conditions never occur or they are not possible. Therefore, the corresponding output never appears and the output level is not defined. It can be either HIGH or LOW. These output levels are represented as 'Don't Care Conditions' and are indicated by 'X'. Don't care conditions can be used to form groups and hence help in simplifying the Boolean expression. See the example below;

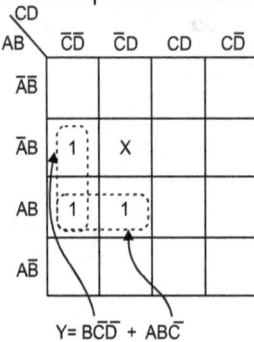
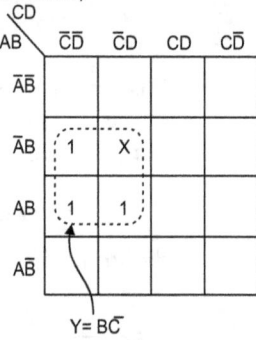

(a) Withoout don't care condition   (b) With don't care condition

Fig. 2.25 :Use of don't care condition in simlifying the boolean expression

Example 2.8 :

Simplify the Bollean expression $Y = \pi M (4,5,6,7,8,12) \cdot d (0,13,15,14)$

Solution : Represent all the maxterms and don't care conditions in the K – map

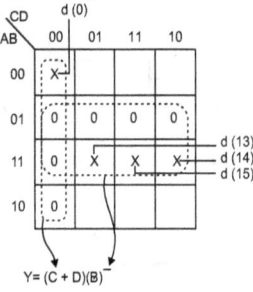

Fig. 2.26

Example 2.9 :

Minimize the given Boolean function $Y = \Sigma m (1,3,5,8,9,11,15) + d (2,13)$

Solution : Represent all the minterms and don't care conditions in the K- map.

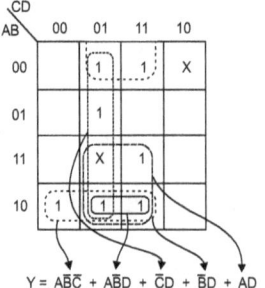

Fig. 2.27

2.6   CODES AND CODE CONVERTERS

2.6.1 Codes

The codes are used to represent the given digital information in particular format. The codes are used to store and transmit the data efficiently. All codes are represented finally as '0' and '1' which computers can understand. There are various types of codes which are enlisted below;

(a) Weighted Code : The weight of digit or bit depends on its position e.g. the weight of 6 in 647 is 600.

(b) Self-complementary Code : Excess-3 code is one example of self- complementary code. In this code, the one's complement of Excess - 3 code is the Excess - 3 code for nine's complement.

(c) Unit Distance Code : There is unit distance between two consecutive codes. e.g. Gray code.

(d) Alphanumerical Code : The binary codes of alphabets, number and special symbols are known as alpha numerical codes. e.g. ASCII (American Standard Code for Information Interchange) code.

(e) Error detecting and Correcting Codes : Special types of codes like parity or Hamming codes are used to detect errors when digital data is transmitted over long distance.

Thus, codes are used to represent binary information and reliable communication. In this chapter we will study three important codes Viz. BCD (Binary Coded Decimal), Gray and seven segment code.

2.6.2 BCD Code

Each digit of decimal number is represented by four bits. For example digit '5' is represented as '0101'. The BCD code is also called as 8-4-2-1 code where 8,4,2 and 1 represent weights of binary symbol in the respective positions. The examples of BCD codes are given below ;

Decimal	4	2	8	6
BCD	0100	0010	1000	0110

BCD code for 0 to 9 digits are given as;

Decimal digit	BCD code
0	0 0 0 0
1	0 0 0 1
2	0 0 1 0
3	0 0 1 1

4	0 1 0 0
5	0 1 0 1
6	0 1 1 0
7	0 1 1 1
8	1 0 0 0
9	1 0 0 1

The remaning 4 digit binary representations i.e. 1010, 1011, 1100, 1101, 1110 and 1111 are invalid BCD codes.

2.6.3 Gray Code

The Gray code is an unweighted code, meaning that the bit positions do not have specific weights. It is four bit numeric code in which decimal numbers 0 to 15 are represented by four bit binary code. Two consecutive codes differ in only one position. Hence, Gray code is also known as unit distance code. Gray codes are used in analog to digital converters but are not suitable for arithmetic operations. The Gray code for the decimal numbers 0 to 15 is given below;

Decimal digit	Gray Code				Decimal digit	Gray Code			
	G_3	G_2	G_1	G_0		G_3	G_2	G_1	G_0
0	0	0	0	0	8	1	1	0	0
1	0	0	0	1	9	1	1	0	1
2	0	0	1	1	10	1	1	1	1
3	0	0	1	0	11	1	1	1	0
4	0	1	1	0	12	1	0	1	0
5	0	1	1	1	13	1	0	1	1
6	0	1	0	1	14	1	0	0	1
7	0	1	0	0	15	1	0	0	0

It may be noted that only one bit of Gray code changes. For example there is only one bit change from 4 to 5.

$$4 \quad 0110$$
$$5 \quad 0111$$

Binary to Gray code conversion : We usually write the binary code of decimal number and then convert into Gray code. The Boolean expressions for converting N bits binary to Gray is

$$G_{N-1} = B_{N-1}$$
$$G_{N-2} = B_{N-1} \oplus B_{N-2}$$

$$G_{N-3} = B_{N-1} \oplus B_{N-1}$$

$$G_2 = B_3 \oplus B_2$$
$$G_1 = B_2 \oplus B_1$$
$$G_0 = B_1 \oplus B_0$$

Example 2.10 :

Find the Gray code of 14.

Solution :

Represent 14 in binary form $\therefore$ 1110

$\therefore$ $B_3 = 1$, $B_2 = 1$, $B_1 = 1$ and $B_0 = 0$

Using binary to Gray conversion Boolean expressions

$$G_3 = B_3 = 1$$
$$G_2 = B_3 \oplus B_2 \quad = 1 \oplus 1 = 0$$
$$G_1 = B_2 \oplus B_1 \quad = 1 \oplus 1 = 0$$
$$G_0 = B_1 \oplus B_0 \quad = 1 \oplus 0 = 1$$

So Gray code of 14 is 1001

Example 2.11 :

Find the Gray code for 11001100

Solution :

$$G_7 = B_7 = 1$$
$$G_6 = B_7 \oplus B_6 = 1 \oplus 1 = 0$$
$$G_5 = B_6 \oplus B_4 = 1 \oplus 0 = 1$$
$$G_4 = B_5 \oplus B_4 = 0 \oplus 0 = 0$$
$$G_3 = B_4 \oplus B_3 = 0 \oplus 1 = 0$$
$$G_2 = B_3 \oplus B_2 = 1 \oplus 1 = 0$$
$$G_1 = B_2 \oplus B_1 = 1 \oplus 0 = 1$$
$$G_0 = B_{12} \oplus B_0 = 0 \oplus 0 = 0$$

$\therefore$ The gray code is 10101010

Gray to Binary code Conversion : The Boolean expressions is find binary code from Gray code are ;

$$B_{N-1} = G_{N-1}$$
$$B_{N-2} = B_{N-1} \oplus G_{N-2}$$

$$B_2 = B_3 \oplus G_2$$
$$B_1 = B_2 \oplus G_1$$
$$B_0 = B_1 \oplus G_0$$

Example 2.12 :

Find the binary code for (1000) Gray.

Solution : $G_3 = 1$, $G_2 = 0$, $G_1 = 0$, $G_0 = 0$

$$B_3 = G_3 = 1$$
$$B_2 = B_3 \oplus G_2 = 1 \oplus 0 = 1$$
$$B_1 = B_2 \oplus G_1 = 1 \oplus 0 = 1$$
$$B_0 = B_1 \oplus G_0 = 1 \oplus 0 = 1$$

∴   The binary code is 1111

2.6.4   Seven Segment code

In many electronic systems seven segments are used for displaying quantities. The binary codes cannot be used to drive seven segment displays. The generalised seven segment display is shown below in Fig. 2.28. It uses seven LED segments. These LED's can be either common - anode connected or common cathode connected.

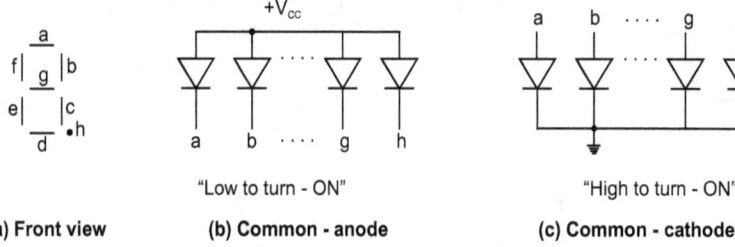

"Low to turn - ON"   "High to turn - ON"

(a) Front view   (b) Common - anode   (c) Common - cathode

Fig. 2.28 : Seven segment display

Table : Common anode seven segment code

Decimal	a	b	c	d	e	f	g	h	Hex code
0 *0*	0	0	0	0	0	0	1	1	03
1 *1*	1	0	0	1	1	1	1	1	5F
2 *2*	0	0	1	0	0	1	0	1	25
3 *3*	0	0	0	0	1	1	0	1	0D
4 *4*	1	0	0	1	1	0	0	1	99
5 *5*	0	1	0	0	1	0	0	1	49
6 *6*	0	1	0	0	0	0	0	1	41
7 *7*	0	0	0	1	1	1	1	1	1F
8 *8*	0	0	0	0	0	0	0	1	01
9 *9*	0	0	0	0	1	0	0	1	09

Table : Common cathode seven segment code

Decimal		a	b	c	d	e	f	g	h	Hex code
0	0	1	1	1	1	1	1	0	0	FC
1	1	0	1	1	0	0	0	0	0	60
2	2	1	1	0	1	1	0	1	0	DA
3	3	1	1	1	1	0	0	1	0	F2
4	4	0	1	1	0	0	1	1	0	66
5	5	1	0	1	1	0	1	1	0	B6
6	6	1	0	1	1	1	1	1	0	BE
7	7	1	1	1	0	0	0	0	0	E0
8	8	1	1	1	1	1	1	1	0	FE
9	9	1	1	1	1	0	1	1	0	F6

2.7 CODE CONVERTERS

2.7.1 Binary to BCD Converter

The truth table of binary to BCD converter is given below;

Decimal digit	Binary Code				BCD Code				
	A	B	C	D	B_4	B_3	B_2	B_1	B_0
0	0	0	0	0	0	0	0	0	0
1	0	0	0	1	0	0	0	0	1
2	0	0	1	0	0	0	0	1	0
3	0	0	1	1	0	0	0	1	1
4	0	1	0	0	0	0	1	0	0
5	0	1	0	1	0	0	1	0	1
6	0	1	1	0	0	0	1	1	0
7	0	1	1	1	0	0	1	1	1
8	1	0	0	0	0	1	0	0	0
9	1	0	0	1	0	1	0	0	1
10	1	0	1	0	1	0	0	0	0
11	1	0	1	1	1	0	0	0	1
12	1	1	0	0	1	0	0	1	0
13	1	1	0	1	1	0	0	1	1
14	1	1	1	0	1	0	1	0	0
15	1	1	1	1	1	0	1	0	1

From the above truth table we write k - maps for all the outputs.

K-map for $B_4 \Rightarrow$

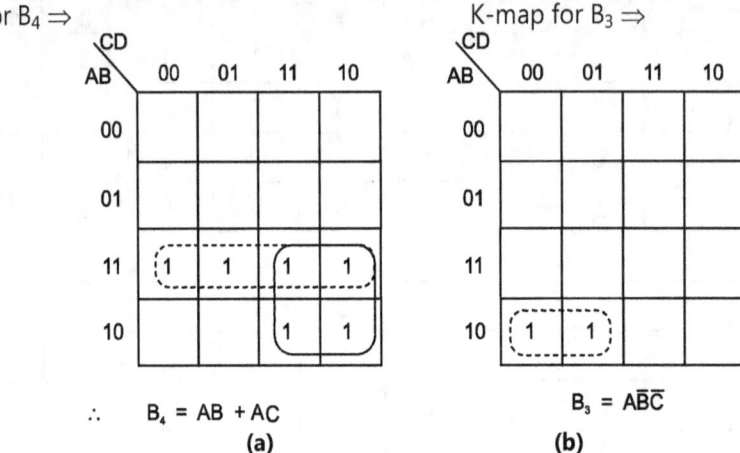

∴ $B_4 = AB + AC$

(a)

K-map for $B_3 \Rightarrow$

$B_3 = A\overline{B}\overline{C}$

(b)

Fig. 2.29

K-map for $B_2 \Rightarrow$

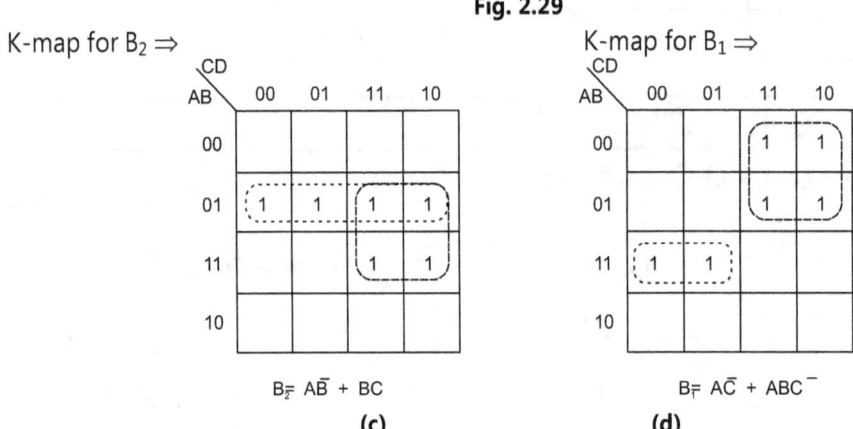

$B_2 = A\overline{B} + BC$

(c)

K-map for $B_1 \Rightarrow$

$B_1 = A\overline{C} + ABC$

(d)

Fig. 2.29

K-map for $B_0 \Rightarrow$

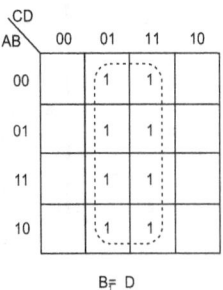

$B_0 = D$

Fig. 2.29 (e)

Therefore, logic diagram for binary to BCD converter is

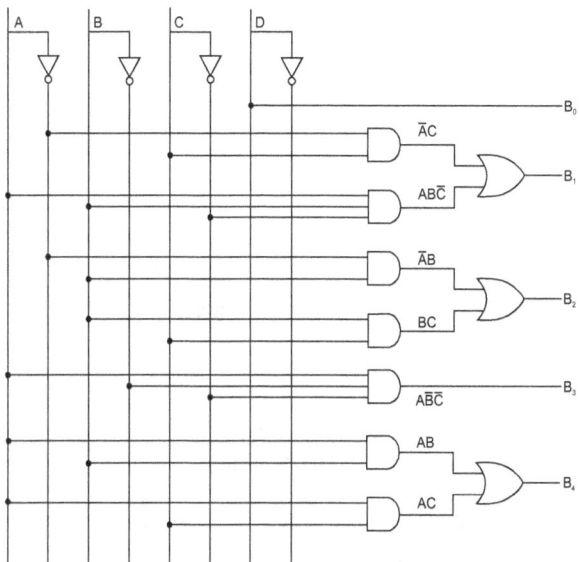

Fig. 2.30 : Logic diagram for binary to bcd converter

2.7.2 BCD to Binary Converter

We write the K-maps for binary outputs considering BCD as inputs. But BCD inputs are 5 bits and hence we will have to write two K– maps for one binary output as shown below. We will map don't care condition 'X' for the input conditions which are not possible

K – Map for A :

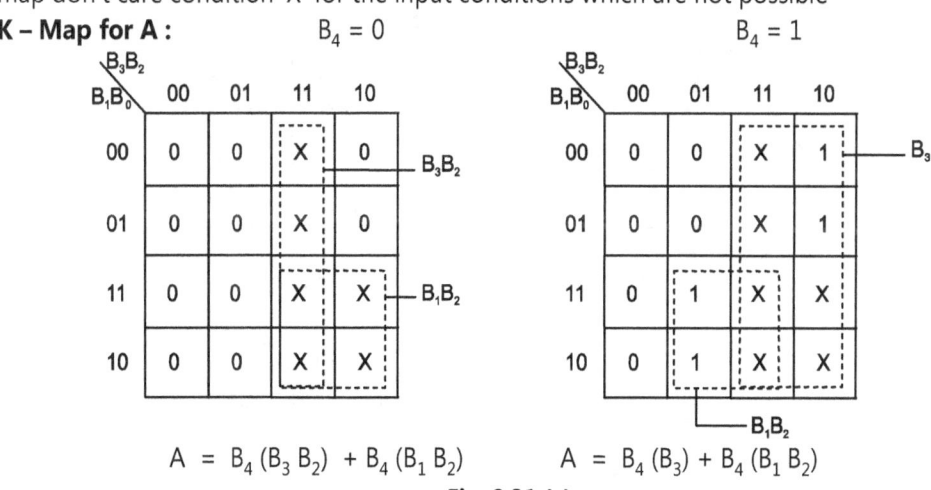

$$A = B_4 (B_3 B_2) + B_4 (B_1 B_2) \qquad A = B_4 (B_3) + B_4 (B_1 B_2)$$

Fig. 2.31 (a)

But $B_4 = 0$ here and we can assume

don't care $x = 0$

$\therefore \ A = 0$ $\qquad \qquad \therefore \ A = B_4 B_3 + B_4 B_1 B_2$

Therefore, the find Bollean expression for A is

$$A = 0 + B_4 B_3 + B_4 B_1 B_2$$

$$A = B_4 B_3 + B_4 B_1 B_2$$

K – map for B :

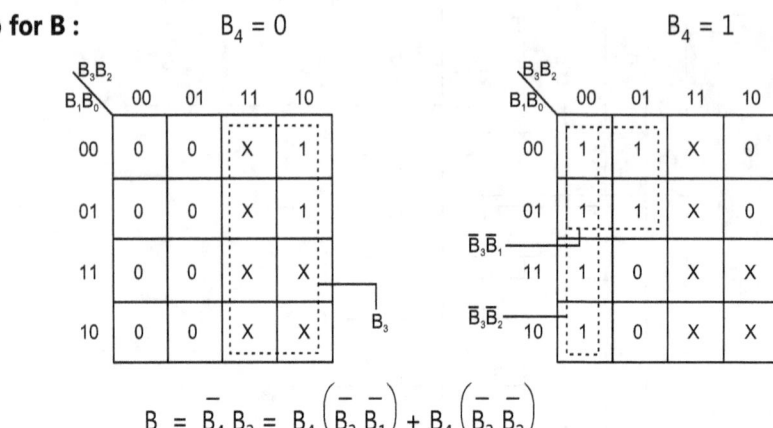

$$B = \bar{B}_4 B_3 = B_4 \left(\bar{B}_3 \bar{B}_1 \right) + B_4 \left(\bar{B}_3 \bar{B}_2 \right)$$

Fig. 2.31 (b)

(Even if B_4 is here we have few high outputs i.e. '1' in k – map $\therefore B = \bar{B}_4 B_3$)

Therefore, the final expression for B is

$$B = \bar{B}_4 B_3 + B_4 \left(\bar{B}_3 \bar{B}_1 \right) + B_4 \left(\bar{B}_3 \bar{B}_2 \right)$$

K – map for C :

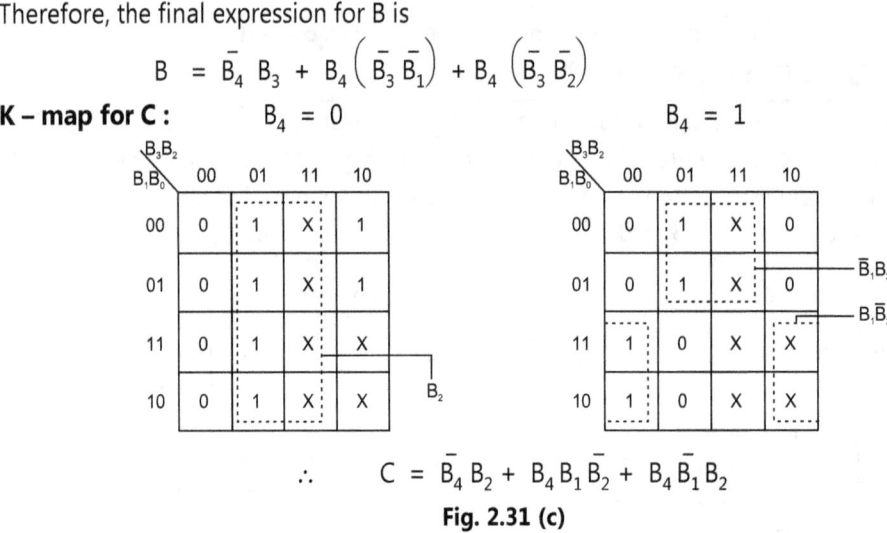

$$\therefore \quad C = \bar{B}_4 B_2 + B_4 B_1 \bar{B}_2 + B_4 \bar{B}_1 B_2$$

Fig. 2.31 (c)

K – map for D :

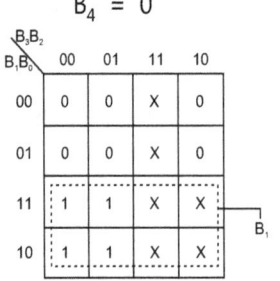

$$\therefore D = \bar{B}_4 B_1 + B_4 \bar{B}_2$$

Fig. 2.31 (d)

K – map for E :

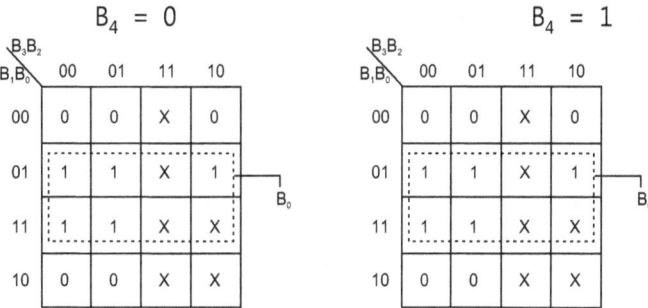

Fig. 2.31 (e)

$$E = \bar{B}_4 B_0 + B_4 B_0 = B_0 \left(\bar{B}_4 + B_4\right) = B_0$$

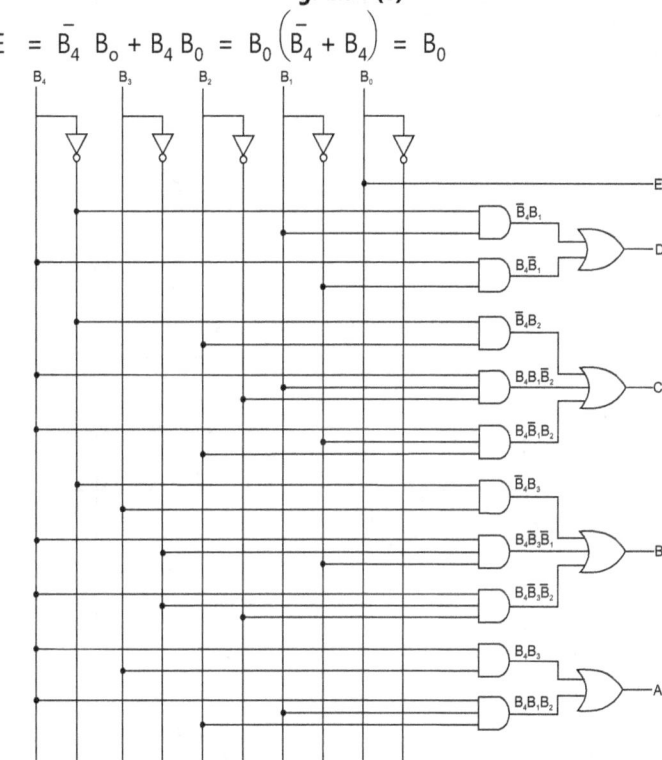

Fig. 2.32 : Logic diagram for bcd to binary coverter

2.7.3 Binary to Gray Code Converter

Q. Design 4-bit binary to gray code converter and implement using logic gate.

[Dec. 04, 7M, Dec. 11, 8 M]

Q. Design and implement a 4-bit binary to gray code converter using discrete gates.

[Dec. 08, 8 M]

The truth table for binary to Gray code converter is given below.

Binary inputs				Gray outputs			
A	B	C	D	G_3	G_2	G_1	G_0
0	0	0	0	0	0	0	0
0	0	0	1	0	0	0	1
0	0	1	0	0	0	1	1
0	0	1	1	0	0	1	0
0	1	0	0	0	1	1	0
0	1	0	1	0	1	1	1
0	1	1	0	0	1	0	1
0	1	1	1	0	1	0	0
1	0	0	0	1	1	0	0
1	0	0	1	1	1	0	1
1	0	1	0	1	1	1	1
1	0	1	1	1	1	1	0
1	1	0	0	1	0	1	0
1	1	0	1	1	0	1	1
1	1	1	0	1	0	0	1
1	1	1	1	1	0	0	0

From the truth table we write k – maps for all the outputs

K – map for G_3 K – map for G_2

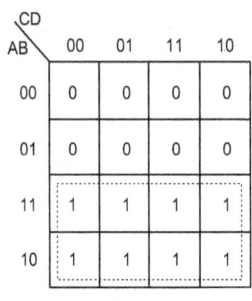

∴ $G_3 = A$ $G_2 = \bar{A}B + A\bar{B} = A \oplus B$

K – map for G_1 K – map for G_0

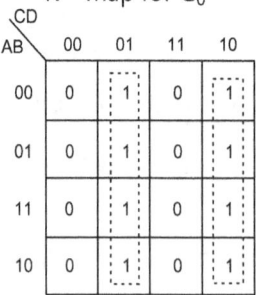

∴ $G_1 = \bar{B}C + B\bar{C} = B \oplus C$ $G_0 = \bar{C}D + C\bar{D} = C \oplus D$

Fig. 2.33

Therefore, logic diagram of binary to Gray code converter.

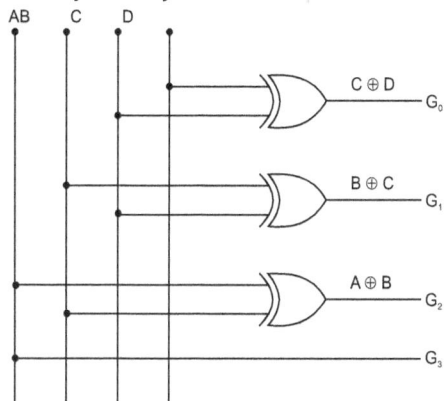

Fig. 2.34 : Logic diagram of binary to gray code converter

2.7.4 Gray to Bindary Code Converter

Q. Design a circuit to convert gray code to binary code.

The k – maps for binary outputs are :

k – map for A   k – map for B

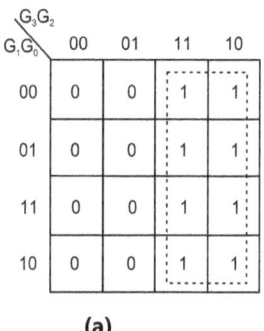

(a)

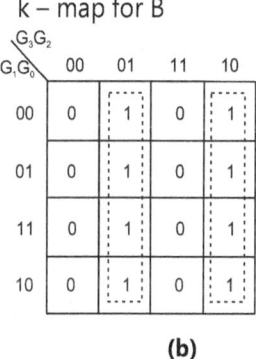

(b)

Fig. 2.35

$$A = G_3$$

$$B = \bar{G_3} G_2 + G_3 \bar{G_2} = G_2 \oplus G_3$$

k – map for C

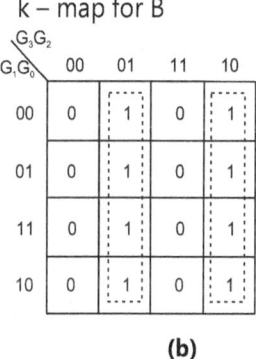

Fig. 2.35 : (c)

$$C = \bar{G}_3\, G_2\, \bar{G}_1 + G_3\, \bar{G}_2\, \bar{G}_1 + \bar{G}_3\, \bar{G}_2\, G_1 + G_3\, G_2\, G_1$$

$$= \bar{G}_1\,(G_3 \oplus G_2) +, G_1\,\left(\overline{G_3 \oplus G_2}\right)$$

$$= (G_3 \oplus G_2 \oplus G_1)$$

$$= (G_1 \oplus B) \text{ because } B = G_2 \oplus G_3$$

K – map for D :

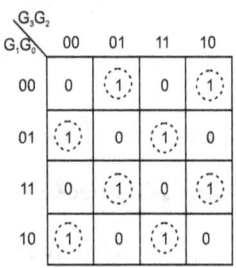

Fig. 2.35 (d)

∴ $D = \bar{G}_3\, G_2\, \bar{G}_1\, G_0 + G_3\, \bar{G}_2\, \bar{G}_1\, \bar{G}_0$

$$+ \bar{G}_3\, \bar{g}_2\, \bar{G}_1\, G_0 + \bar{G}_3\, \bar{G}_2\, G_1\, \bar{G}$$

$$+ G_3\, G_2\, \bar{G}_1\, G_0 + G_3\, G_2\, G_1\, G_0$$

$$+ G_3\, \bar{G}_2\, G_1\, G_0 + G_3\, G_2\, G_1\, G_0$$

After simplifying $D = (G_0 \oplus C)$

Therefore, the logic diagram for Gray to binary code converter is as shown below;

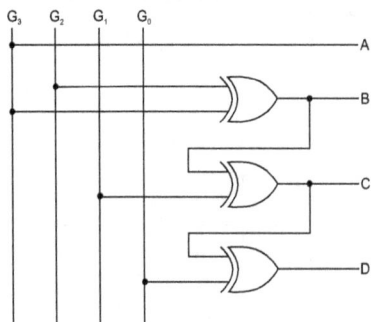

Fig. 2.36 : Logic diagram for gray to binary converter

2.7.5 BCD to Seven Segment Code Converter

(a) Common cathode type seven segment : The truth table for BCD to seven segment (common anode type) is given below.

Decimal	BCD Code				Seven segment code (common anode)							
digit	B_3	B_2	B_1	B_0	a	b	c	d	e	f	g	h
0	0	0	0	0	0	0	0	0	0	0	1	1
1	0	0	0	1	1	0	0	1	1	1	1	1
2	0	0	1	0	0	0	1	0	0	1	0	1
3	0	0	1	1	0	0	0	0	1	1	0	1
4	0	1	0	0	1	0	0	1	1	0	0	1
5	0	1	0	1	0	1	0	0	1	0	0	1
6	0	1	1	0	0	1	0	0	0	0	0	1
7	0	1	1	1	0	0	0	1	1	1	1	1
8	1	0	0	0	0	0	0	0	0	0	0	1
9	1	0	0	1	0	0	0	0	1	0	0	1

From the truth the we write K – maps for seven segment outputs.

K – map a :

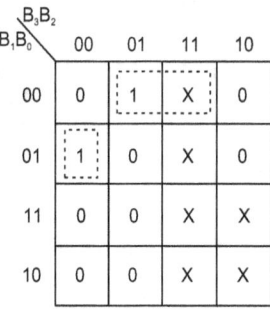

$$a = \bar{B}_1 \bar{B}_0 B_2 + \bar{B}_1 B_0 \bar{B}_3 \bar{B}_2$$

$$\therefore \quad a = \bar{B}_0 \bar{B}_1 B_2 + B_0 \bar{B}_1 \bar{B}_2 \bar{B}_3$$

K – Map for b :

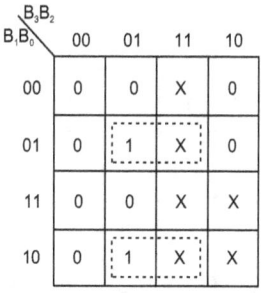

$$b = \bar{B}_1 B_0 B_2 + B_1 \bar{B}_0 B_2$$

$$\therefore \quad b = B_0 \bar{B}_1 B_2 + \bar{B}_0 B_1 B_2$$

K – Map for c :

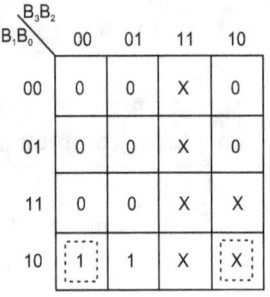

$$c = B_1 \bar{B}_0 \bar{B}_2 = \bar{B}_0 B_1 \bar{B}_2$$

K – Map for d :

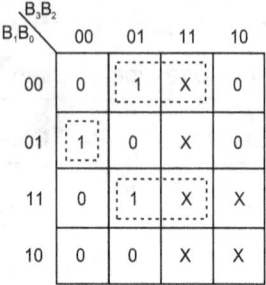

$$d = \bar{B}_1 \ B_0 \bar{B}_3 \ \bar{B}_2 + \bar{B}_1 \ \bar{B}_0 \ B_2 + B_1 B_0 B_2$$

$$\therefore \ d = B_0 \bar{B}_1 \ \bar{B}_2 \ \bar{B}_3 + \bar{B}_0 \ \bar{B}_1 \ B_2 + B_0 B_1 \ B_2$$

K – Map for e :

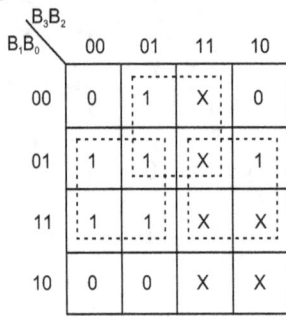

$$e = B_0 + \bar{B}_1 \ B_2$$

K – Map for f :

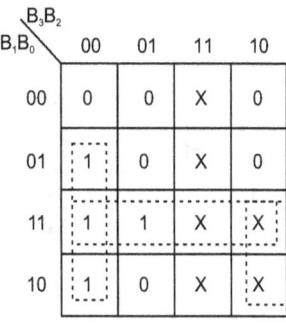

$$f = B_0 B_1 + B_0 \bar{B}_2 \bar{B}_3 + B_1 \bar{B}_2$$

K – Map for g :

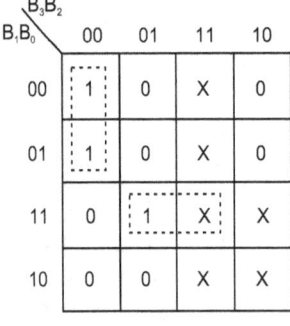

$$g = \bar{B}_1 \ \bar{B}_2 \ \bar{B}_3 + B_0 B_1 \ B_2$$

K – Map for h :

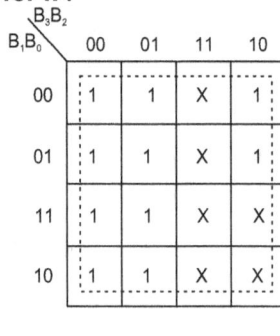

$$h = 1$$

Fig. 2.37

Therefore, the logic diagram for BCD to seven segment common (anode code) converter is

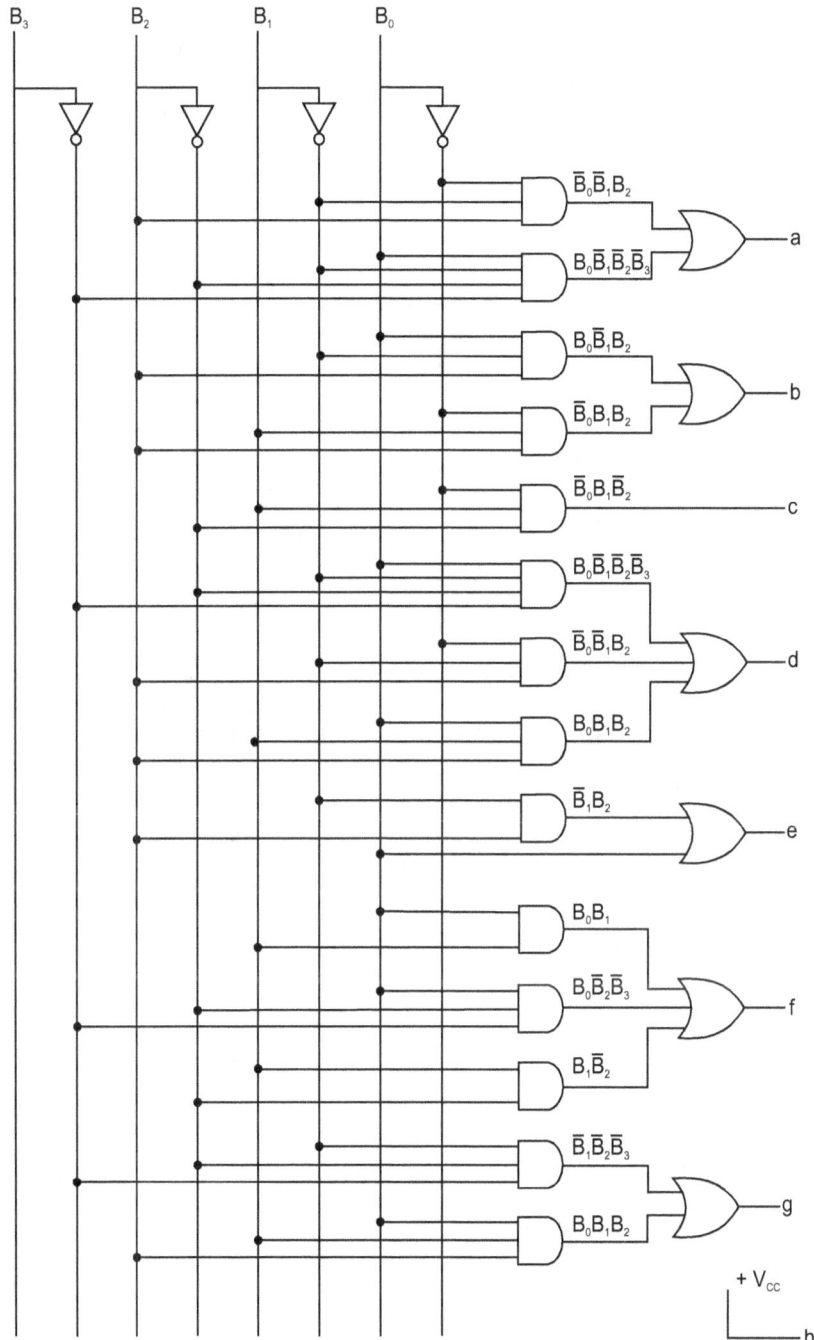

Fig. 2.38 : Logic diagram for BCD to seven segment (common anode) code converter

2.7.6 Common Cathode type Seven Segment

The truth table for common cathode type seven segment outputs is given below;

Decimal	BCD Code				Seven segment code							
digit	B_3	B_2	B_1	B_0	a	b	c	d	e	f	g	h
0	0	0	0	0	1	1	1	1	1	1	0	0
1	0	0	0	1	0	1	1	0	0	0	0	0
2	0	0	1	0	1	1	0	1	1	0	1	0
3	0	0	1	1	1	1	1	1	0	0	1	0
4	0	1	0	0	0	1	1	0	0	1	1	0
5	0	1	0	1	1	0	1	1	0	1	1	0
6	0	1	1	0	1	0	1	1	1	1	1	0
7	0	1	1	1	1	1	1	0	0	0	0	0
8	1	0	0	0	1	1	1	1	1	1	1	0
9	1	0	0	1	1	1	1	1	0	1	1	0

The K – maps for all the seven segment outputs can be written as.

K – map a :   K – Map for b :

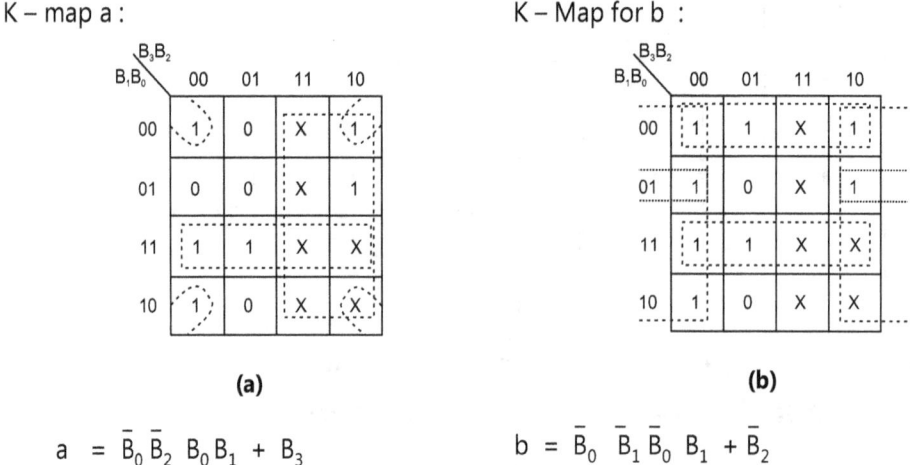

(a)   (b)

$$a = \bar{B}_0 \bar{B}_2 B_0 B_1 + B_3$$ $$b = \bar{B}_0 \bar{B}_1 \bar{B}_0 B_1 + \bar{B}_2$$

K – Map for c :

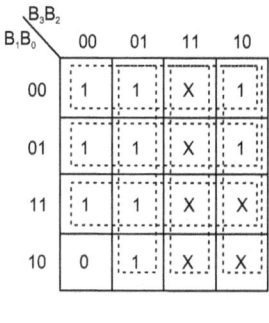

(c)

$$c = B_3 \, B_2 \, \bar{B}_1 + B_0$$

K – Map for d :

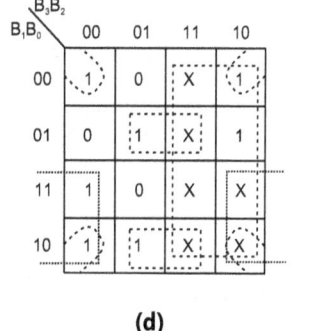

(d)

$$d = \bar{B}_3 + \bar{B}_0 \, \bar{B}_2 + \bar{B}_1 \, \bar{B}_2 + B_0 \, B_1 B_2 + \bar{B}_0 \, b_1 B_2$$

K – Map for e :

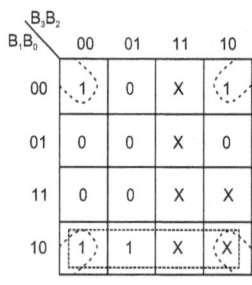

(e)

$$e = \bar{B}_0 \, B_1 + \bar{B}_0 \, \bar{B}_2$$

K – Map for f :

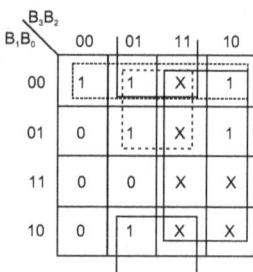

(f)

$$f = B_3 + \bar{B}_1 \, B_2 + \bar{B}_0 \, B_2 + \bar{B}_0 \, \bar{B}_0$$

K – Map for g :

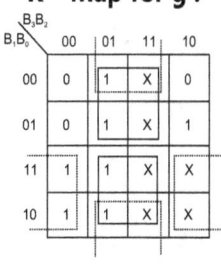

(g)

$$g = B_1 \, \bar{B}_2 + \bar{B}_1 \, B_2 + \bar{B}_0 \, B_2 + B_3$$

K – Map for h :

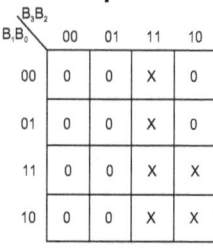

(h)

$$h = 0$$

Fig. 2.39

Therefore, the logic diagram to convert BCD code into seven segment (common cathode) code is;

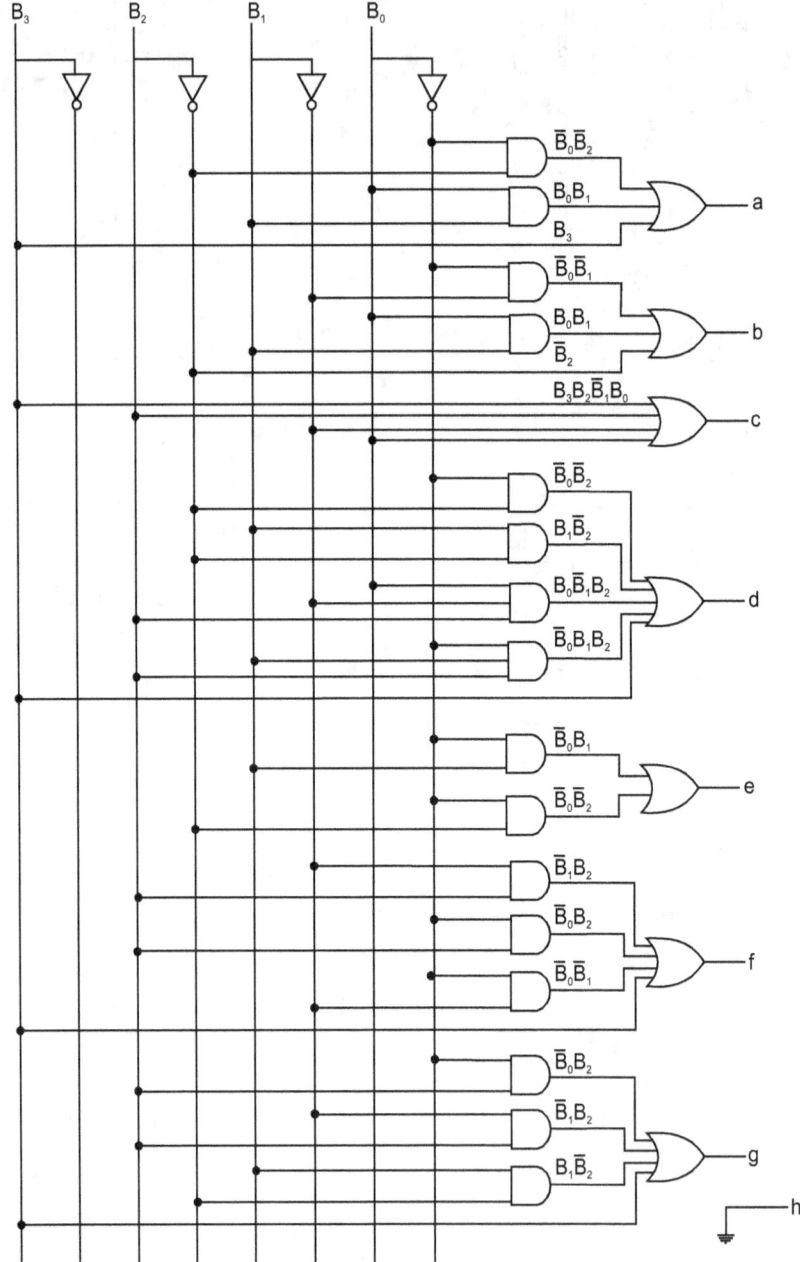

Fig. 2.40 : Logic diagram for BCD to seven segment (common cathode) code converter

2.7.7 BCD to Excess-3 Code Converter

Excess – 3 codes can be obtained from BCD number by adding '3' to it. The input combination 1010, 1011, 1100, 1101, 1110 and 1111 are invalid in BCD to Excess-3 code. The truth table of BCD to Excess – 3 codes is shown below :

BCD code				Excess - 3 code			
A	B	C	D	W	X	Y	Z
0	0	0	0	0	0	1	1
0	0	0	1	0	1	0	0
0	0	1	0	0	1	0	1
0	0	1	1	0	1	1	0
0	1	0	0	0	1	1	1
0	1	0	1	1	0	0	0
0	1	1	0	1	0	0	1
0	1	1	1	1	0	1	0
1	0	0	0	1	0	1	1
1	0	0	1	1	1	0	0

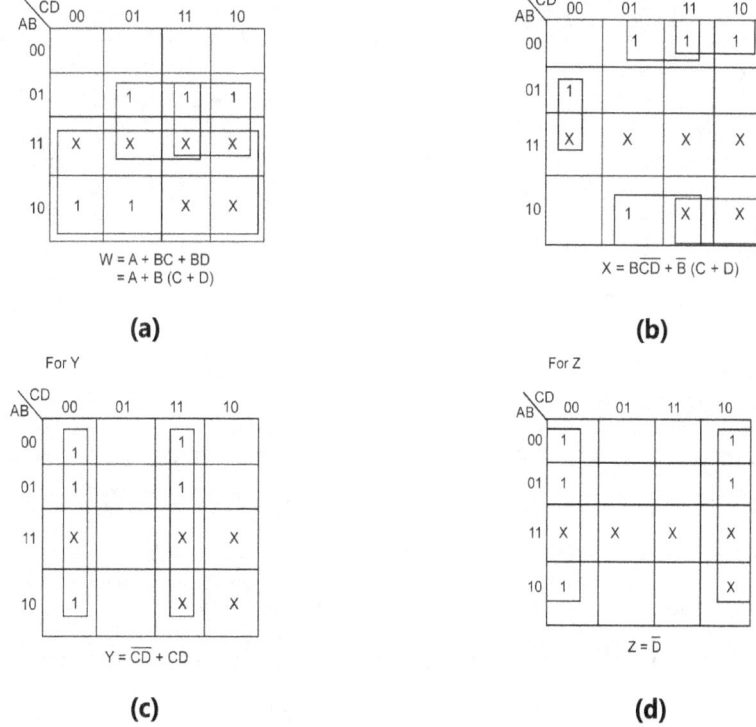

For W

$$W = A + BC + BD$$
$$= A + B (C + D)$$

(a)

For X

$$X = B\overline{CD} + \overline{B} (C + D)$$

(b)

For Y

$$Y = \overline{CD} + CD$$

(c)

For Z

$$Z = \overline{D}$$

(d)

Fig. 2.41

The logic diagram of BCD to Excess- 3 code converter is shown below

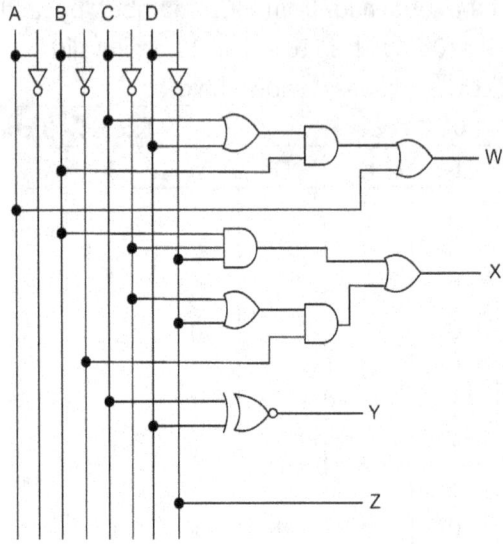

Fig. 2.41 (e)

2.8   OTHER COMBINATIONAL CIRCUITS

2.8.1 Digital Comparators

Q. What is digital comparator.   **[Dec. 11, 2 M]**

Another common and very useful combinational logic circuit is that of the **Digital Comparator** circuit. Digital or Binary Comparators are made up from standard AND, NOR and NOT gates that compare the digital signals at their input terminals and produces an output depending upon the condition of the inputs. For example, whether input A is greater than, smaller than or equal to input B etc.

Digital Comparators can compare a variable or unknown number for example A (A1, A2, A3, ... An, etc) against that of a constant or known value such as B (B1, B2, B3, ... Bn etc) and produce an output depending upon the result. For example, a comparator of 1 – bit, (A and B) would produce the following three output condtioins.

This is useful if we want to compoare two values and produce an output when the condition is achieved. For example, produce an output from a counter when a certain count number is reached. Consider the simple 1 – bit comparator below.

2.8.1.1 1 bit Comparator

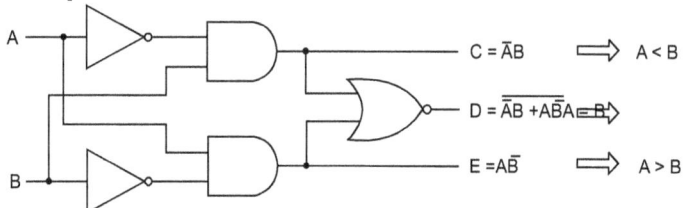

Fig. 2.42 : 1-bit Comparator Circuit

Then the operation of a 1 – bit digital comparator is given in the following

Truth Table :

Inputs		Outputs		
B	**A**	**A > B**	**A = B**	**A < B**
0	0	0	1	0
0	1	1	0	0
1	0	0	0	1
1	1	0	1	0

You may notice two distinct features about the comparator from the above truth table. Firstly, the circuit does not distinguish between either two "0" or two "1"' s as an output A = B is produced when they are both equal, either A = B = "0" or A = B = "1". Secondly, the output condition for A = B resembles that of a commonly avaiblable logic gate, the Exculsive – NOR or Ex – NOR gate giving Q = A B.

Digital comparators actually use Exclusive - NOR gates within their design for comparing the respective pairs of bits in each of the two words with single bit comparators cascaded together to produce Multi – bit comparators so that words can be compared.

For output A < B, K – map is

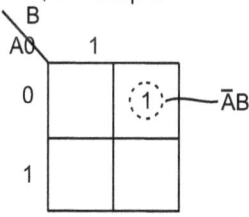

$$\therefore C\ (A < B) = \bar{A}\ B$$

Fig. 2.43 (a)

For output A = B, map – is

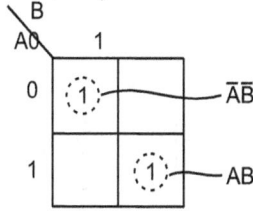

$$\therefore D\ (A = B) = \overline{\bar{A}\ B + A\ \bar{B}}$$

Fig. 2.43 (b)

$$\Rightarrow \bar{A}\ \bar{B}\ +\ AB$$

It's X-NOR implementation is $\overline{\overline{A}B + A\overline{B}}$

For output A > B, K – map is

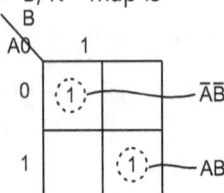

$$\therefore E\,(A > B) = A\overline{B}$$

Fig. 2.43 (c)

2.8.1.2 Two 2 – Bit Binary Comparator

Q. Design and implement 2-bit comparator.	**[Dec. 06, 5 M]**
Q. Design 2-bit comparator using logic.	**[Dec. 09, 8 M]**
Q. Design 2-bit comparator using k-map and implement it.	**[Dec, 12, 8 M]**

- It determines whether one 2 - bit input number is larger than, equal to, or less than the other.
- The circuitry accomplishes this through several logic gates that operate on the principles of Boolean algebra.

Design :

- The first step in the creation of the comparator circuit is the generation of the truth table that lists the input variables, their possible values, and the resulting outputs for each of those values. The truth table used for this experiment is shown in table below.

Inputs				Outputs		
A_1	A_0	B_1	B_0	G	E	L
0	0	0	0	0	1	0
0	0	0	1	0	0	1
0	0	1	0	0	0	1
0	0	1	1	0	0	1
0	1	0	0	1	0	0
0	1	0	1	0	1	0
0	1	1	1	0	0	1
0	1	1	0	0	0	1
1	0	0	0	1	0	0
1	0	0	1	1	0	0
1	0	1	0	0	1	0
1	0	1	1	0	0	1
1	1	0	0	1	0	0
1	1	0	1	1	0	0
1	1	1	0	1	0	0
1	1	1	1	0	1	0

- From the truth table, canonical minterm equations are generated for each output variable. These equations are then simplified to represent as few logic gates as possible. The three minterm equations are simplified to

$$G = A_1 \cdot \bar{B_1} + A_0 \cdot \bar{B_0} \cdot \left(\bar{B_1} + A_1\right)$$

$$E = \overline{(A_1 \oplus B_1) + (A_0 \oplus B_0)}$$

$$L = \bar{A_0} \cdot B_0 \cdot \left(\bar{A_1} + B_1\right) + \bar{A_1} \cdot B_1$$

- The final equations are then used to sketch a circuit schematic for each variable. Once each variable has a schematic, common values are found and the three schematics are combined to create a single circuit diagram shown below;

2 – Bit Comparator :

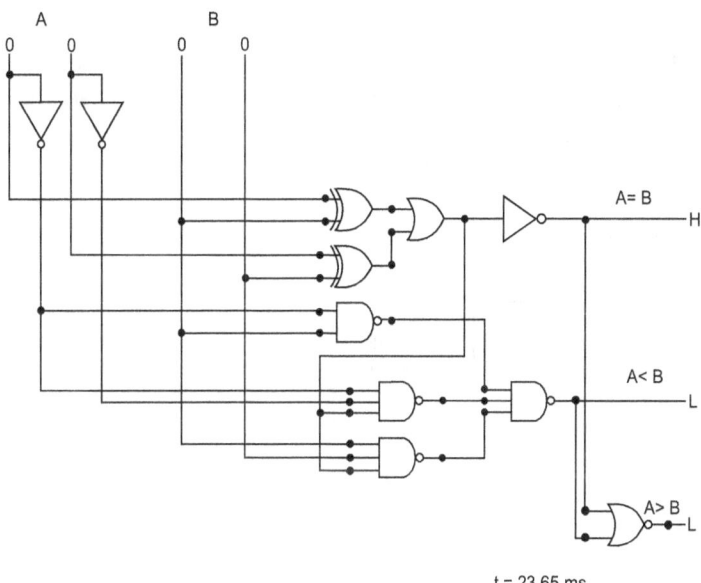

t = 23.65 ms

Fig. 2.44 : 2-bit comparator

2.8.1.3 Magnitude Comparators

- Apart from comparing individual bits, multi – bit comparators can be constructed to compare whole binary or BCD words to produce an output if one word is larger, equal to or less than the other.

- A very good example of this is the 4 - bit **Magnitude Comparator.** Here, two 4 - bit words ("nibbles") are compared to produce the relevent output with one word connected to inputs A and the other to be compared against connected to input B as shown below.

2.8.1.4 4 - bit Magnitude Comparator

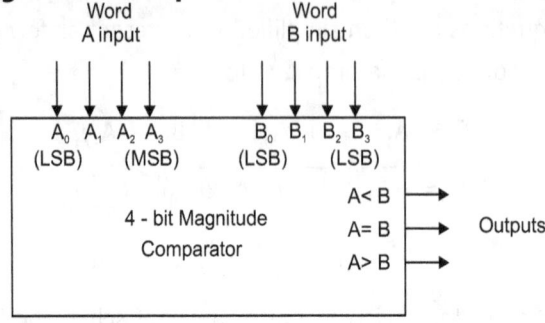

Fig. 2.45 : 4-bit Magnitude Comparator

- Some commercially available Magnitude Comparators such as the 7485 have additional input terminals that allow more individual comparators to be "cascaded" together to compare words larger than 4 - bits with magnitude comparators of "n" - bits being produced.
- These cascading inputs are connected directly to the corresponding outputs of the previous comparator as shown to compare 8, 16 or even 32 - bit words.

2.8.1.5 8 - bit Word Comparator

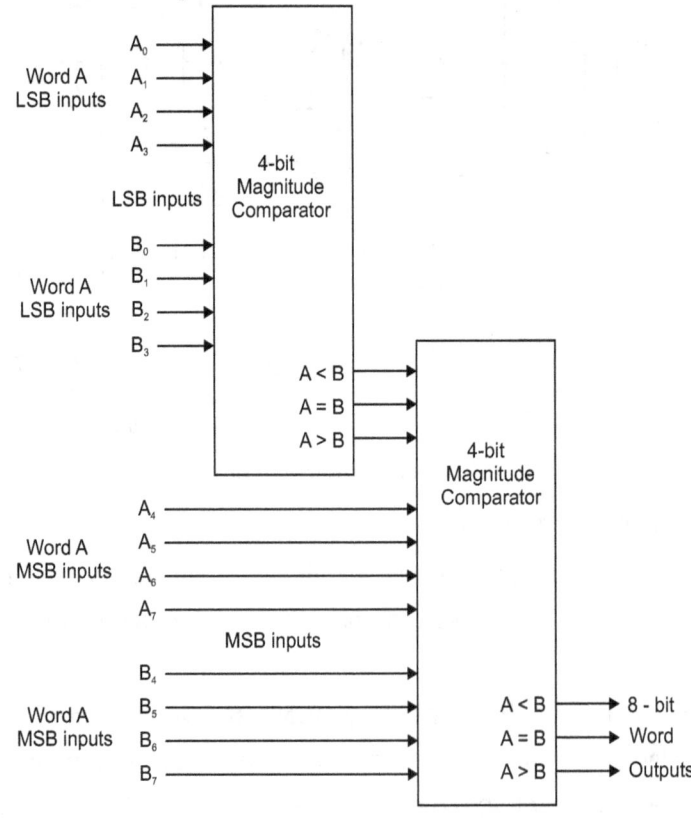

Fig. 2.46 : 8-bit Word Comparator

2.8.2 BCD Adder

> **Q.** Explain with suitable examples rules for BCD addition and design 1 digit BCD adder using IC 74LS83.   **[Dec. 04, 8 M]**

- BCD adder is a combinational arithmetic circuit which performs the addition of two BCD numbers. BCD addition is performed like a binary addition but its result may be a valid BCD code or an invalid BCD code. The invalid BCD code is converted into valid BCD by adding $(0110)_2$ to the result.

2.8.2.1 Algorithm for BCD addition

1. Add two BCD numbers using normal binary addition.
2. Check the result whether it is valid or invalid BCD. (Valid BCD number is ≤ 9).
- If the result is valid BCD, keep the result.
- If the result is invalid BCD, then add $(0110)_2$ or $(6)_{10}$ to get valid BCD output.

Design of a BCD adder :

> **Q.** Design 4-bit BCD adder using binary adder 2c's.   **[May 12, 8 M]**

(a) Let us assume one more signal output denoted by 'invalid – op'. We will have to design a combinational circuit which will generate 'invalid – op' signal from the binary addition signals.

(b) Therefore, if $(B_3 B_2 B_1 B_0)$ and $(A_3 A_2 A_1 A_0)$ are to be added then the output will be $(S_3 S_2 S_1 S_0)$. This addition can be done using a simple binary adder.

(c) We will generate either high 'invalid - op' signal or low 'invalid - op' signal from $(S_3 S_2 S_1 S_0)$. The 'invalid -op' will be high when $(S_3 S_2 S_1 S_0)$ is an invalid BCD code and vice versa. We first write the truth table with C_{out}, S_3, S_2, S_1 and S_0 as inputs and 'invalid-op' as output. The truth table is given below;

C_{out}	S_3	S_2	S_1	S_0	invalid - op	
0	0	0	0	0	0	
0	0	0	0	0	1	
0	0	0	1	0	0	
0	0	0	1	1	0	
0	0	1	0	1	0	
0	0	1	1	0	0	Valid BCD
0	0	1	1	1	0	
0	0	1	1	1	0	
0	1	0	0	0	0	
0	1	0	0	1	0	

0	1	0	1	0	1	
	.		.			
	.		.			Invalid
	.		.			BCD
	.		.			
1	1	1	1	1		

Since, we have five binary inputs we write K – maps as,

K – map for 'invalid - op'

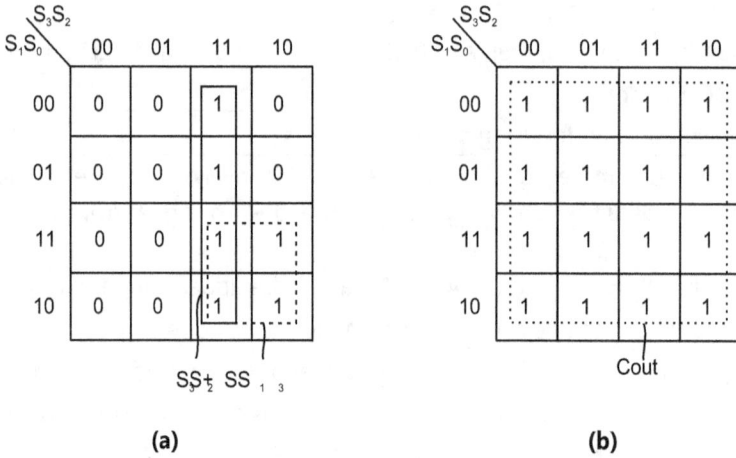

SS₁ + SS
        ₃

(a)   (b)

Fig. 2.47

$\therefore$ invalid - op $= C_{out} + S_1 S_3 + S_2 S_3$

Therefore, the logic circuit to generate a signal i.e. invalid -op to know whether the result of addition of two BCD number is invalid BCD is as shown below;

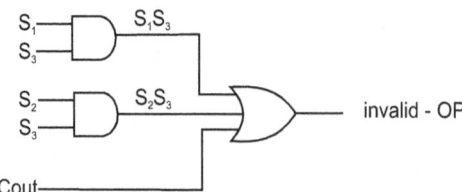

Fig. 2.48 : Logic circuit to generate invalid compact-op signal

(d) When invalid-op signal is 'high' we will add $(0110)_2$ in the answer. Hence, we will require one more binary adder. The complete BCD adder is as shown below ;

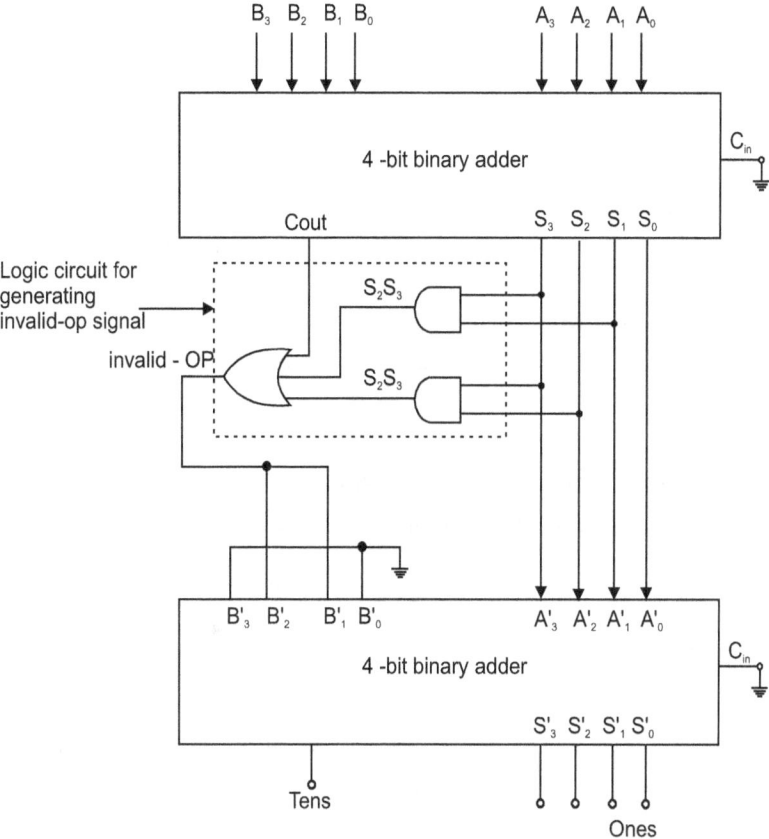

Fig. 2.49 : BCD Adder

Note that if the binary addition of $(B_3 B_2 B_1 B_0)$ and $(A_3 A_2 A_1 A_0)$ is invalid BCD answer then the 'invalid-op' signal will be logic high. Hence, $B_3' B_2' B_1' B_0' = 0110$ which is binary equivalent of decimal 6.

2.8.3 BCD Subtractor using 9's Complement

Alogrithm for 9's complement BCD subtraction

(1) Find the 9's complement of the BCD number which is to be subtracted.

(2) Perform BCD addition. If answer is invalid BCD then convert it into valid BCD by adding $(0110)_2$.

(3) Check the carry.

\# If carry is generated, answer is possible. Add the carry to the answer.

\# If carry is not generated then answer is negative. Find 9's complement of the result.

Design of a BCD Subtractor :

(1) Design of 9's complement circuit :

9's complement = 10 + 1's complement

e.g. 9's complement of 3 = 10 + 1's complement of 3

∴   9's complement of 3 ⇒   1010

$$+\ 1100$$

1 0110

discard carry

∴ 9's complement of 3 is ⇒ 6

We can EXOR gates to find 1's complement and then we use binary adder to add 10. The result of binary addition will be 9's complement.

(2) We use BCD adder circuit to perform BCD addition.

(3) We design a simple combinational circuit to either add carry or add $(0110)_2$ in the BCD addition result.

If C_{out} = 1 then answer is equal to (BCD addition result) + C_{out}

If C_{out} = 0 then answer is equal to (9's complement of BCD addition result)

Therefore, the logic diagram for carrying out BCD subtraction is

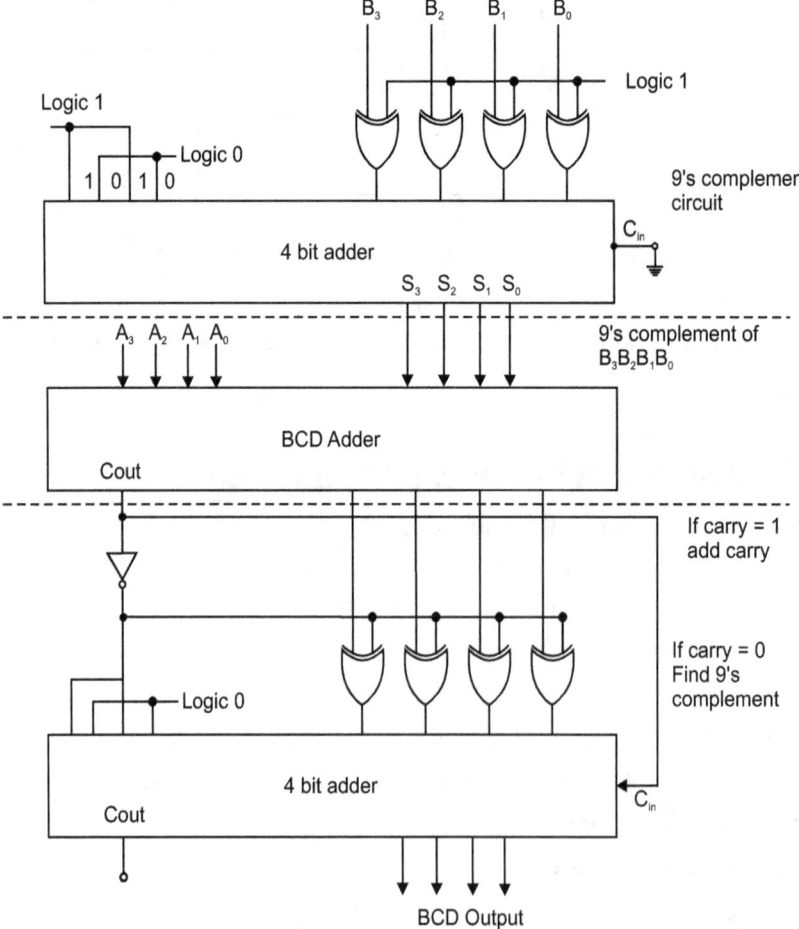

Fig. 2.50 : BCD Subtractor using 9's Complement

2.8.4 Carry Look - Ahead Adder

Q. Briefly explain the operation of look ahead carry generator.   **[Dec. 09, 6 M]**

Q. Explain look ahead carry generator and advantages of the same.

[Dec. 06, 6 M, Dec. 07, 4 M]

Q. Write a short not on look ahead carry generator.   **[May 05, 6 M]**

The delay generated by an N - bit adder is proportional to the length N of the two numbers X and Y that are added because the carry signals have to propagate from one full-adder to the next. For large values of N, the delay becomes unacceptably large so that a special solution needs to be adopted to accelerate the calculation of the carry bits. This solution involves a "look- ahead carry generator" which is a block that simultaneously calculates all the carry bits involved. Once these bits are available to the rest of the circuit, each individual three-bit addition $(X_1 + Y_1 + $ carry–in $(i))$ is implemented by a simple 3 - input XOR gate. The design of the look ahead carry generator involves two Boolean functions named Generate and Propagate. For each input bits pair these functions are defined as :

$$G_i = X_i \cdot Y_i$$
$$P_i = X_i + Y_i$$

The carry bit C-out(i) generated when adding two bits X_i and Y_i is '1' if the corresponding function G_i is '1' or if the C_{out} (i-1) = '1' and the function P_i = '1' simultaneously. In the first case, the carry bit is activated by the local conditions (the values fo X_i and Y_i). In the second, the carry bit is received from the less significant elementary addition and is propagated further to the more significant elementary addition. Therefore, the carry out bit corresponding to a pair of bits X_i and Y_i is calculated according to the equation :

$$\text{carry\_ out } (i) = G_i + P_i \cdot \text{carry \_ in } (i-1)$$

For a four - bit adder the carry -outs are calculated as follows

$$\text{carry\_ out0} = G_0 + P_0 \cdot \text{carry\_in}_0$$

$$\text{carry\_ out1} = G_1 + P_1 \cdot \text{carry\_out}_0 = G_1 + P_1 G_0 + P_1 P_0 \cdot \text{carry\_in}_0$$

$$\text{carry\_ out2} = G_2 + P_2 G_1 + P_2 P_1 G_0 + P_2 P_1 P_0 \cdot \text{carry\_in}_0$$

$$\text{carry\_ out3} = G_3 + P_3 G_2 + P_3 P_2 G_1 + P_3 P_2 P_1 G_0 + P_3 P_2 P_1 \cdot \text{carry\_in}_0$$

The set of equations above are implemented by the circuit below and a complete adder with a look - ahead carry generator is next. The input signals need to propagate through a maximum of 4 logic gate in such an adder as opposed to 8 and 12 logic gates.

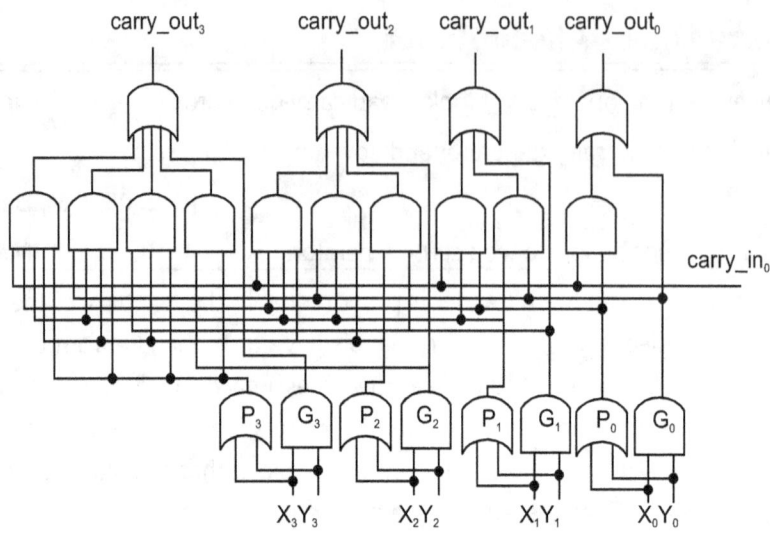

Fig. 2.51 : Carry Look-Ahead Adder – Carry Output

Sums can be calculated from the following equations, where carry _ out is taken from the carry calculated in the above circuit.

$$\text{sum\_out}_0 = X_0 \oplus Y_0 \oplus \text{carry\_out}_0$$

$$\text{sum\_out}_1 = X_1 \oplus Y_1 \oplus \text{carry\_out}_1$$

$$\text{sum\_out}_2 = X_2 \oplus Y_2 \oplus \text{carry\_out}_2$$

$$\text{sum\_out}_3 = X_3 \oplus Y_3 \oplus \text{carry\_out}_3$$

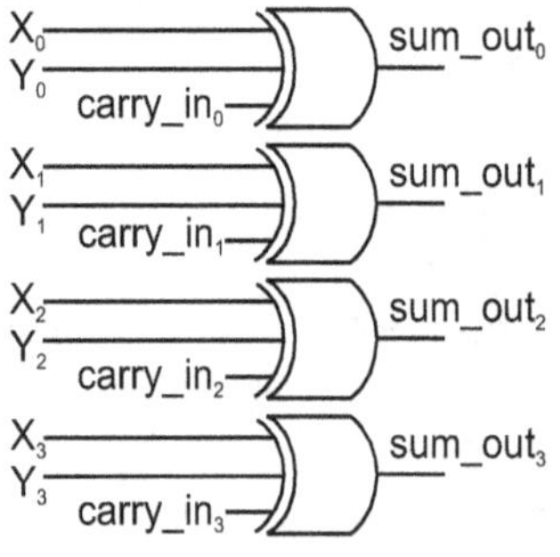

Fig. 2.52 : Carry Look-Ahead Adder – Sum Output

2.8.5 Parity Generator and Checker

Q. Explain the significance of parity bit.   **[May 07, 2 M]**

Parity bit is an extra bit included along with the binary information to detect the errors which might occur during the transmission of the binary information. The combinational logic circuits which generate the parity bit (either even or odd) is called as **'parity generator'**. The total number of ones in the binary information is either even (if even parity generator is used) or odd (if odd parity generator is used). Parity generator circuit is used at the transmission side of the communication channel.

At the receiving end of the communication channel 'parity checker' circuit is used to check the parity of the received information. Parity checker circuit detects whether the received message is corrupted i.e. whether it has error.

IC 74180 is a popular nine input parity generator/checker. It can be used as a parity generator or checker. Its block representation is shown in Fig. 2.53 below :

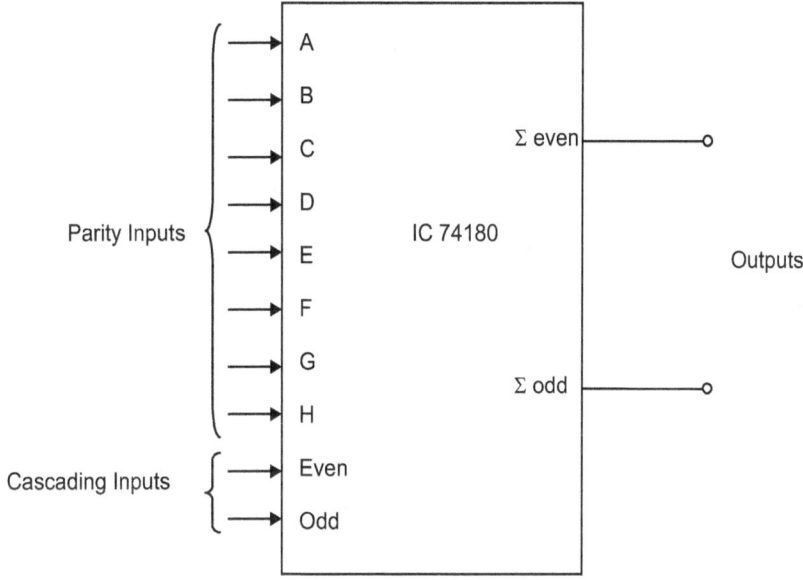

Fig. 2.53

The truth table for IC74180 is given below :

Parity inputs	Cascading Inputs		Outputs	
	Even	Odd	Even	Odd
Even	1	0	1	0
Odd	1	0	0	1
Even	0	1	0	1
Odd	0	1	1	0
X	1	1	1	0
X	0	0	0	0

The working of IC 74180 can be explained with the help of following input conditions.

(a) User wants even parity coding in the message :

\#   Therefore cascading input, "<u>even</u>" should be '1'

\#   If the number of 1's in the input message i.e. in parity inputs (A to H) is even then the IC 74180 will generate a '1' output at it's "$\sum$ even" terminal.

\#   If the number of 1's in the input message (A - H) is odd then the IC 74180 will generate a '1' output at its "$\sum$ even" terminal.

(b) User wants odd parity coding in the message :

\#   Therefore cascading input, "<u>odd</u>" should be '1'.

\#   If the number of 1's in the input message i.e. in parity inputs (A–H) is even then the IC 74180 will generate a '1' at it's "$\sum$ even" terminal output.

\#   If the number of 1's in the input message i.e. in parity inputs (A–H) is odd then the IC74180 will generate a '1' output at its "$\sum$ even" terminal.

A golden rule to understand the working of IC74180 is

Number of 1's in parity inputs (A to H)	Cascading input	Output
Even e.g. (01101100)	'Even' is set to '1'	'$\sum$even' output will be set '1'
Odd e.g. (00010000)	'Odd' is set to '1'	'$\sum$even' output will be set '1'
Odd e.g. (01100010)	'Even' is set to '1'	'$\sum$odd' output will be set '1'
Even e.g. (11111111)	'Odd' is set to '1'	'$\sum$odd' output will be set '1'

Example 2.13 :

Design a 9-bit odd parity generator using IC 74180.

Solution :

Since the user wants odd parity generator hence the cascading input 'odd' should be set to '1' and 'even' input should be reset to '0'.

The logic diagram for 9-bit odd parity generator using IC74180 is shown in Fig. 2.53 below :

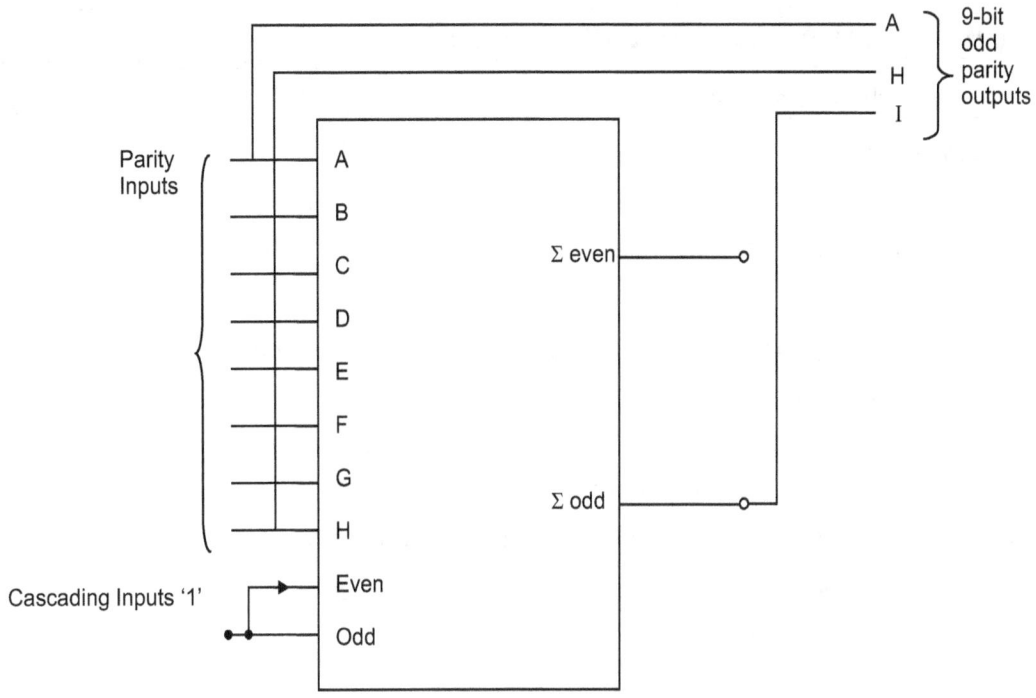

Fig. 2.54 : 9-bit odd parity generator

If the number of 1's in parity inputs (A – H) is even then the output 'Σodd' will be '1'. Thus, total number of 1's in the 9-bit outputs (A – I) will be odd.

If the number of 1's in parity inputs (A – H) is odd then the output 'Σodd' will be '0'. Thus, again total number of 1's in the 9-bit outputs (A – I) will be odd.

Example 2.14 :

Design a 9-bit even parity checker using IC 74180.

Solution :

Since the user wants even parity checker the cascading input 'even' will be connected to 'I' and the cascading input 'odd' will be connected to 'I'.

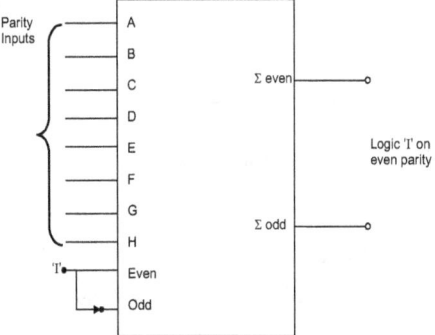

Fig. 2.55 : 9-bit Even Parity Checker

2.9   ARITHMETIC LOGIC UNIT (ALU)

Q. Write short note on ALU.   **[May 05, 6 M, Dec. 06, May 10, Dec. 12, 4 M]**

General Description

The LS181 is a 4 - bit Arithmetic Logic Unit (ALU) which can perform all the possible 16 logic operations on two variables and a variety of arithmetic operations.

Features

- Provides 16 arithmetic operations : add, subtract, compare, double, plus twelve other arithmetic operations.

- Provides all 16 logic operations of two variables : exclusive - OR, compare, AND, NAND, OR, NOR, plus ten other logic operations.

- Full lookahead for high speed arithmetic operation on long words.

    Statistics :   14 inputs; 8 outputs; 61 gates; gate-level schematic

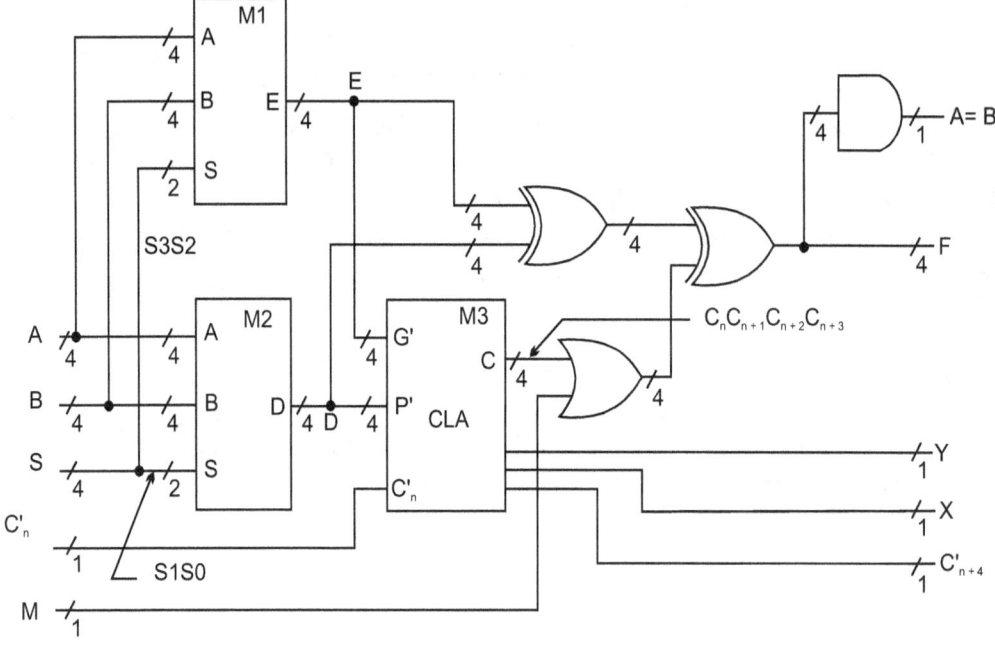

Fig. 2.56 : Functional Block Diagram of ALU

Function Block Diagram : The 74181 can be modeled as shown below in Fig. 2.56 Recognizing the logic that makes up a CLA block — in this case, the circled elements in the gate - level schematic — is the key step in unraveling the secrets of the 74181. The four boxed circuits in the gate-level schematic are represented above by the single module M1 with 4 - bit I/O buses. The second quadruplicated circuit in the 74181 leads to the high- level module M2. The various XOR gates are also grouped into 4 - bit word gates as indicated above. Further analysis shows that the 74181's original designers cleverly constructed the M_1 and M_2 logic so that with input line M = 1, each setting of the S (function select) bus produces one of the 16 possible Boolean functions of the form F (A, B).

Note : The M line above has been logically moved from within the CLA block M3, to after the block. This was done to make module M3 a standard CLA block. The change preserves the function, but does make subtle differences when analyzing, for example, path delays in the two circuits.

Functional Description :

* The ' LS181 is a 4 - bit high speed parallel Arithmetic Logic Unit (ALU). Controlled by the four Function Select inputs (S0 - S3) and the Mode Control input (M), it can perform all the 16 possible logic operations or 16 different arithmetic operations on active HIGH or active LOW operands.

* The Function Table lists these operations when the Mode Control input (M) is HIGH, all internal carries are inhibited and the device performs logic operations on the individual bits as listed. When the Mode Control input is LOW, the carries are enabled and the device performs arithmetic operations on the two 4- bit words. The device incorporates full internal carry look-a-head and provides for either ripple carry between devices using the Cn + 4 output, or for carry look-a-head between packages using the signals P (Carry Propagate) and G (Carry Generate).

* In the ADD mode, P indicates that F is 15 or more, while G indicates that F is 16 or more. In the SUBTRACT mode, P indicates that F is zero or less, while G indicates that F is less than zero. P and G are not affected by carry in. When speed requirements are not stringent, it can be used in a simple ripple carry mode by connecting the Carry output (Cn + 4) signal to the Carry input (Cn) of the next unit. For high speed operation the device is used in conjunction with the 9342 or 93S42 carry lookahead circuit. One carry look-a-head package is required for each group of four 'LS181 devices.

* Carry look-a-head can be provided at various levels and offers high speed capability over extremely long word lengths. The A = B output from the device goes HIGH when all four F outputs are HIGH and can be used to indicate logic equivalence over four bits when the unit is in the subtract mode.

- The A = B output is open - collector and can be wired - AND with other A = B outputs to give a comparison for more than four bits. The A = B signal can also be used with the $C_n + 4$ signal to indicate A > B and A < B. The function Table lists the arithmetic operations that are performed without a carry in. An incoming carry adds a one to each operation. Thus, select code LHHL generates A minus B minus 1 (2's complement notation) without a carry in and generates A minus B when a carry is applied. Because subtraction is actually performed by complementary addition (1's complement), a carry out means borrow; thus a carry is generated when there is no underflow and no carry is generated when there is underflow.

- As indicated, this device can be used with either active LOW inputs producing active LOW outputs or with active HIGH inputs producing active HIGH outputs. For either case the table lists the operations that are performed to the operands labeled inside the logic symbol.

Connection Diagram

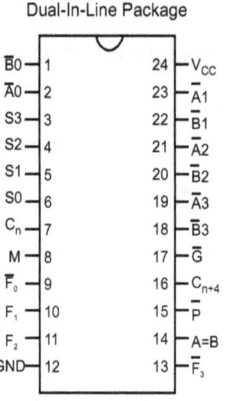

Fig. 2.57

Order Number DM54LS181J, DM54LS181W or DM74LS181N

See Package Number J24A, N24A or W24C

Pin Names	Description
$\overline{A}0 - \overline{A}3$	Operand Inputs (Active LOW)
$\overline{B}0 - \overline{B}3$	Operand Inputs (Active LOW)
S0 - S3	Function Select Inputs

M	Mode Control Input
C_n	Carry Input
$\overline{F0} - \overline{F3}$	Function Outputs (Active LOW)
A = B	Comparator Output
$\overline{G}$	Carry Generate Output (Active LOW)
$\overline{P}$	Carry Propagate Output (Active LOW)
C_{n+4}	Carry Output

Function Table

Mode Select Inputs				Active LOW Operands and F_n Outputs		Active HIGH Operands and F_n Outputs	
				Logic	Arithmetic (Note 5)	Logic	Arithmetic (Note 5)
S3	S2	S1	S0	(M = H)	(M = L) (C_n = L)	(M = H)	(M = L) (C_n = H)
L	L	L	L	$\overline{A}$	A minus 1	$\overline{A}$	A
L	L	L	H	$\overline{AB}$	AB minus 1	$\overline{A+B}$	A + B
L	L	H	L	$\overline{A+B}$	$A\overline{B}$ minus 1	$\overline{A}$ B	$A + \overline{B}$
L	L	H	H	Logic 1	minus 1	Logic 0	minus 1
L	H	L	L	$\overline{A+B}$	A plus $\left(A + \overline{B}\right)$	$\overline{A}$ B	A plus $A\overline{B}$

L	H	L	H	$\bar{B}$	AB plus $\left(A + \bar{B}\right)$	$\bar{B}$	$(A + B)$ plus $A\bar{B}$
L	H	H	L	$\overline{A \oplus B}$	A minus B minus 1	$A \oplus B$	A minus B minus 1
L	H	H	H	$A + \bar{B}$	$A + \bar{B}$	$A\bar{B}$	AB minus 1
H	L	L	L	$\bar{A}\ B$	A plus (A + B)	$\bar{A} + B$	A Plus AB
H	L	L	H	$A \oplus B$	A plus B	$\overline{A \oplus B}$	A plus B
H	L	H	L	B	$A\bar{B}$ plus (A + B)	B	$\left(A + \bar{B}\right)$ plus AB
H	L	H	H	$A + B$	$A + B$	AB	AB minus 1
H	H	L	L	Logic 0	A plus A (Note 4)	Logic 1	A plus A (Note 4)
H	H	L	H	$A\bar{B}$	AB plus A	$A + \bar{B}$	(A + B) plus A
H	H	H	L	AB	$A\bar{B}$ minus A	$A + B$	$\left(A + \bar{B}\right)$ plus A
H	H	H	H	A	A	A	A minus 1

Logic Symbols

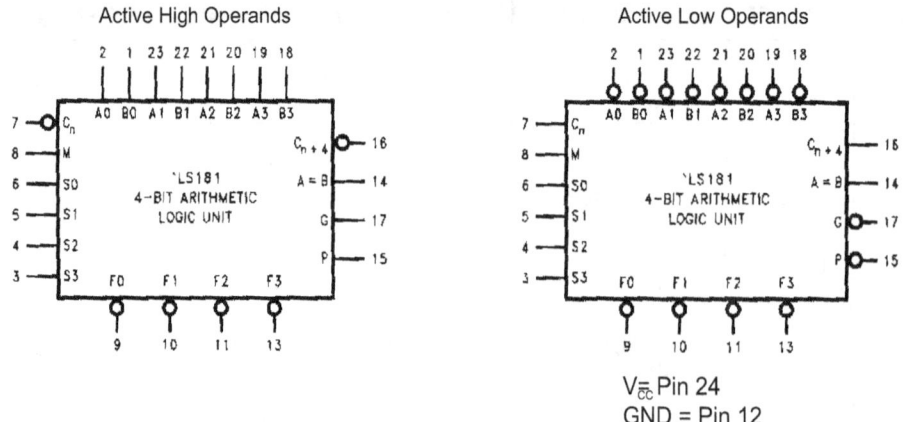

Fig. 2.58

Logic Diagram

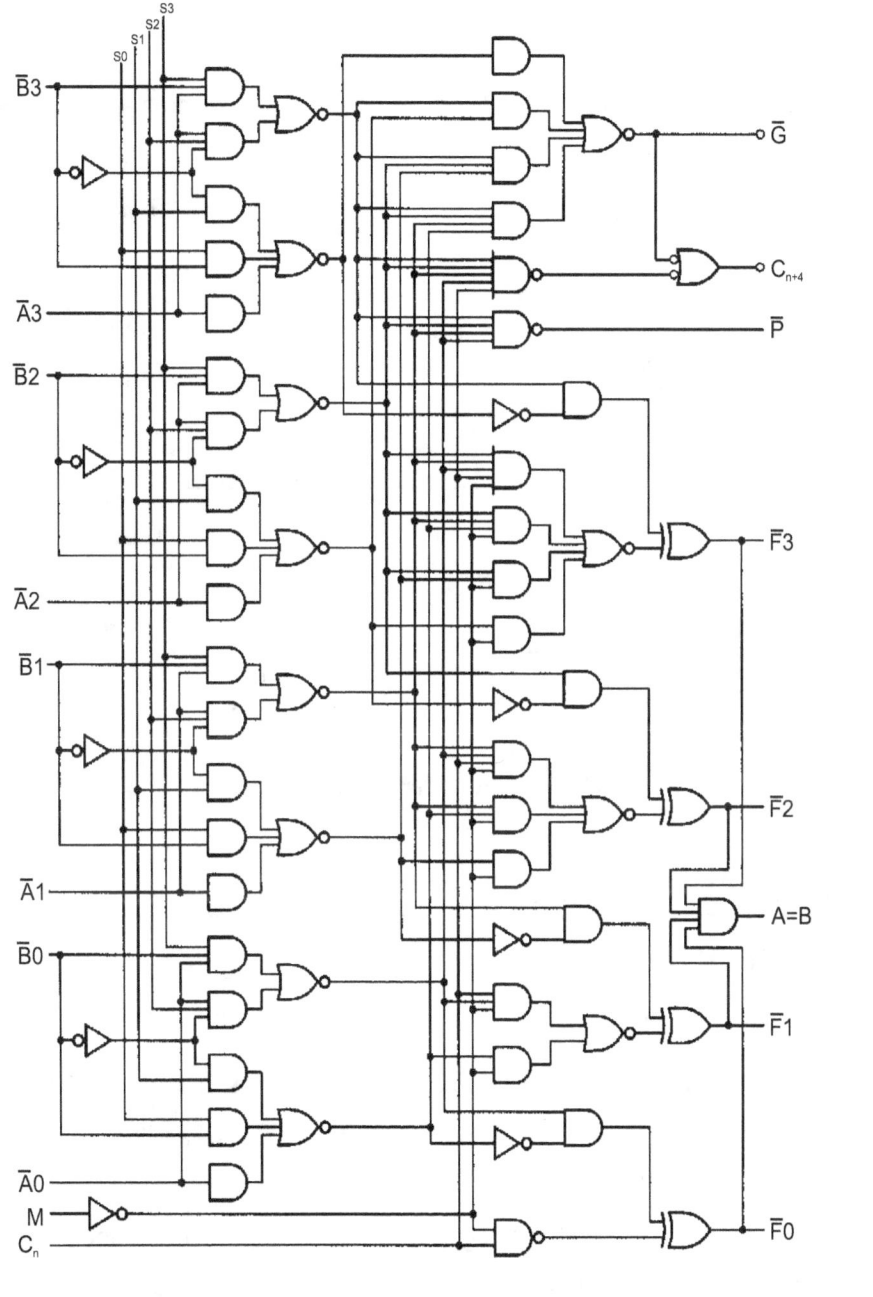

Fig. 2.59

Example 2.20 :

Design a 4 - bit full adder using IC 74181

Solution :

Designing any arithmetic circuit using IC74181 is as easy as selecting proper input signals for the select inputs S_3, S_2, S_1 and S_0.

From the function table we see that from binary addition i.e. 'A plus B' operation the select lines should be

$S_3 = S_0 = $ HIGH   and $S_2 = S_1 = $ LOW

Therefore, 4 bit full adder using IC 74181 is as shown below;

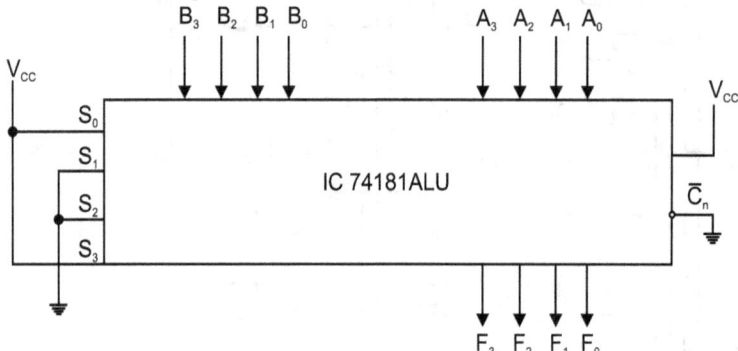

Fig. 2.60 : 4-bit Adder Using 74181

2.10 MULTIPLEXERS AND DEMULTIPLEXERS

2.10.1 Multiplexers

Q. State application of multiplexer.	**[Dec. 04, 06, 2 M]**
Q. What is a multiplexer ?	**[May 05, 2 M]**

• The literal meaning of word 'multiplex' is 'many into one'. A multiplexer circuit may have several inputs and only one output.

• Multiplexer is a special combinational logic circuit which accepts many inputs and allows only one of them to get through to the output at any instance of time.

• Therefore, multiplexer output is a particular data input which is selected with the help of control signal called 'select'.

- Multiplexers are important block of many important digital circuits such as microprocessor and microcontroller. The symbolic representation of multiplexer is shown in Fig. below

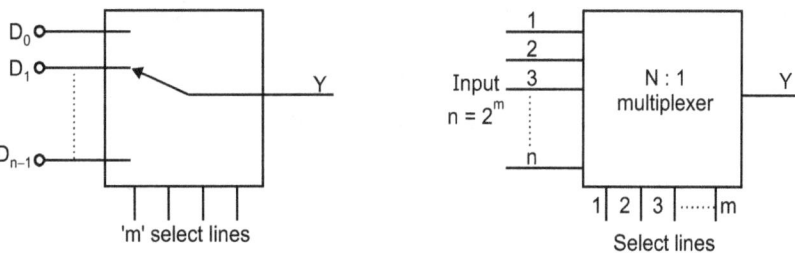

Symbolic Representation of N : 1 Multiplexer

2.10.1.1   2 : 1 Multiplexer

- There are two data inputs D_0 and D_1 in 2 : 1 multiplexer.

- It has only one output. The number of select lines (m) is equal to 1.

- Every multiplexer has one more additional input called 'Enable' or 'Strobe' which is an active low input. This input is always kept at ground potential or logic '0'.

- Fig. 2.61 shows truth table and logic circuit diagram of 2 : 1 multiplexer.

S_0	Y
0	D_0
1	D_1

$$Y = \bar{S_0}D_0 + S_0D_1$$

Fig. 2.61 (a) : Truth Table of 2 : 1 Multiplexer

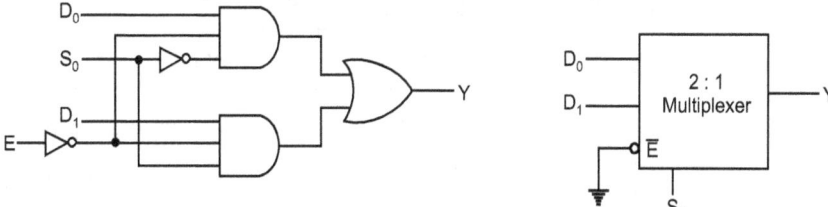

Fig. 2.61 (b) : Logic Circuit of 2 : 1 Multiplexer

2.10.1.2 4 : 1 Multiplexer

- 4 : 1 Multiplexer circuit has four data inputs and one output.

- The number of select lines required to control four data inputs is two.

- These two select lines are called S_0 and S_1.

- The Boolean expression for Y output is,

$$Y_1 = \overline{S_1}\,\overline{S_0}D_0 + \overline{S_1}S_0D_1 + S_1\overline{S_0}D_2 + S_1S_0D_3$$

Fig. 2.62 shows truth table and logic circuit diagram of 4 : 1 multiplexer.

Inputs		Output
S_1	S_0	Y
0	0	D_0
0	1	D_1
1	0	D_2
1	1	D_3

Fig. 2.62 (a) : Truth Table of 4 : 1 Multiplexer

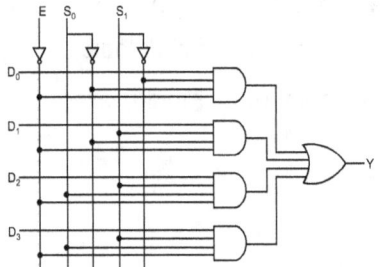

Fig. 2.62 (b) : Circuit Diagram of 4 : 1 Mux

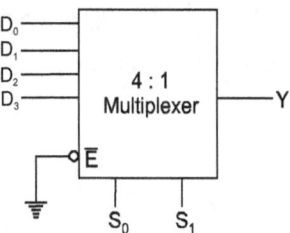

Fig. 2.62 (c) :Block Diagram of 4 : 1 Mux

2.10.1.3 Multiplexer ICs

- The list of popular and commercially available multiplexer ICs.

IC No.	Description	Output/Input
74150	16 : 1 Multiplexer	Inverted input
74151A	8 : 1 Multiplexer	Complementary output
74152	8 : 1 Multiplexer	Inverted input
74153	Dual 4 : 1 Multiplexer	Same as input
74157	Quad 2 : 1 Multiplexer	Same as input
74158	Quad 2 : 1 Multiplexer	Inverted input
74352	Dual 4 : 1 Multiplexer	Inverted input

2.10.1.4 Multiplexer Tree

Fig. 2.63 shows design of 8 : 1 multiplexer using two 4 : 1 multiplexers and one 2 : 1 multiplexer.bbb

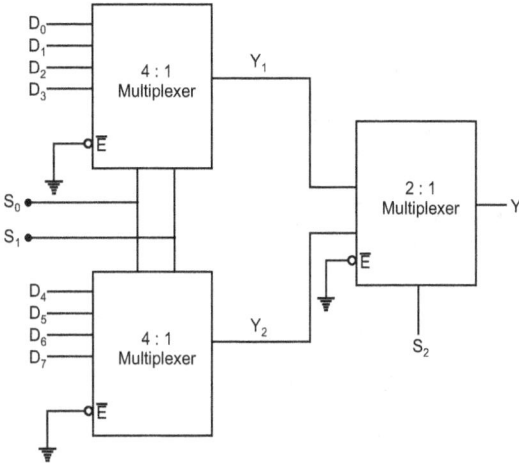

Fig. 2.63 : 8 : 1 Multiplexer

Example 2.16 :

Implement the following expression using a multiplexer

(a)   Y = Σ m (0, 1, 2, 6, 7).

Solution :

Given : Boolean expression is,

Y (A, B, C) = Σ m (0, 1, 2, 6, 7)

It is a three-variable Boolean function and hence a multiplexer will require three select inputs. The inputs of multiplexer corresponding to given minterms are connected to V_{CC}. Other inputs are grounded.

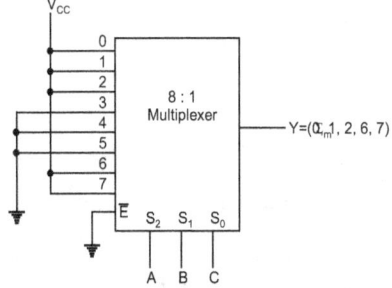

Fig. 2.64

Example 2.17 :

Implement the following Boolean expression $Y = (A + B) (\bar{A} + B + C) (A + \bar{B})$ using multiplexer

Solution : Convert the given Boolean expression into standard POS form

$\therefore$
$$Y = (A + B + C\bar{C}) (\bar{A} + B + C) (A + \bar{B} + C\bar{C})$$

$$= (A + B + C) (A + B + \bar{C}) (\bar{A} + B + C) (A + \bar{B} + C) (A + \bar{B} + \bar{C})$$

But

$$A + B + C = 000 = 0$$

$$A + B + \bar{C} = 001 = 1$$

$$\bar{A} + B + C = 100 = 4$$

$$A + \bar{B} + C = 010 = 2$$

$$A + \bar{B} + \bar{C} = 011 = 3$$

$\therefore$ The Boolean expression becomes

$Y (A, B, C) = \pi M (0, 1, 2, 3, 4)$

Therefore, the inputs corresponding to given maxterms are connected to ground. Other inputs are connected to V_{cc}. The enable pin is grounded.

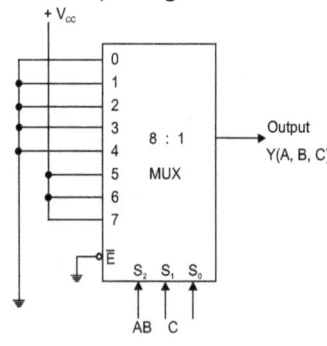

Fig. 2.65

2.10.2   Demultiplexer

Q. What is a Demultiplexer?

- Demultiplexer is a combinational logic circuit having one input and several outputs.

- Demultiplexer means 'One into many'.

- It accepts a single input and sends it to one of the output lines.

- The output line is selected by control or select signals. For n-output demultiplexer, number of select lines is m, where $n = 2^m$.

2.12.2.1 1 : n demultiplexer

- Fig. 2.66 depicts 1 : n demultiplexer.

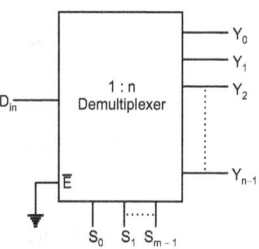

Fig. 2.66 : Block Diagram of 1 : n Demultiplexer

- This 1 : n demultiplexer is also known as binary-to-decimal decoder with binary inputs applied at the select lines, and the decoded output will be obtained on the output line.

- Consider an example 1 : 4 demultiplexer.

- The number of select input lines is 2.

- The truth table of 1 : 4 demultiplexer is given below :

Select Inputs		Outputs			
S_0	S_1	Y_0	Y_1	Y_2	Y_3
0	0	1	0	0	0
0	1	0	1	0	0
1	0	0	0	1	0
1	1	0	0	0	1

- The logic expression for different outputs can be written as,

$Y_0 = \bar{S_0}\bar{S_1}, Y_1 = \bar{S_0}S_1, Y_2 = S_0\bar{S_1}, Y_3 = S_0S_1$

- The logic circuit diagram of 1 : 4 demultiplexer is shown in Fig. 2.67.

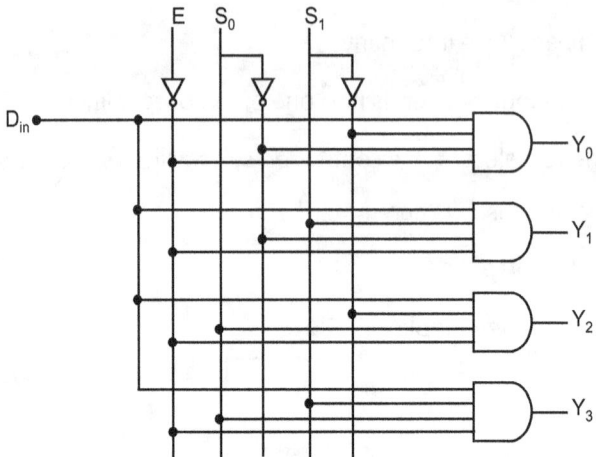

Fig. 2.67 : 1 : 4 Demultiplexer

2.10.2.2 Demultiplexer Tree

- Demultiplexer tree can be built hierarchically by lower hierarchial demultiplexer.
- Many commercially available demultiplexer ICs are listed below.

IC	Description	Output/Input
74139	Dual 1 : 4	Inverted input
74138	Dual 1 : 8	Inverted input
74154	Dual 1 : 16	Same as input

- Let us consider example of implementing 1 : 8 demultiplexer using two 1 : 4 demultiplexers.

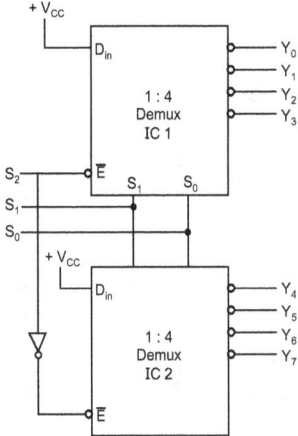

Fig. 2.68 : 1 : 8 Demultiplexer

- Note that 1 : 4 demultiplexer has inverted output. Whenever S_2 is logic '0', the IC_1 is selected and IC_2 is disabled. Depending upon the status of S_1 and S_0 lines the data in will be fed to one of the outputs Y_0, Y_1, Y_2 or Y_3.

- To send the output on Y_4 or Y_5 or Y_6 or Y_7 line, the status of pin S_2 is to be made high. Based on the logic status of S_0 and S_1 the data in will be fed to corresponding output line.

- The truth table of the above $1 : 8$ multiplexer circuit having initial inverted input is given below.

Inputs			Selected IC	Outputs							
S_2	S_1	S_0		Y_7	Y_6	Y_5	Y_4	Y_3	Y_2	Y_1	Y_0
0	0	0	IC1	1	1	1	1	1	1	1	0
0	0	1	IC1	1	1	1	1	1	1	0	1
0	1	0	IC1	1	1	1	1	1	0	1	1
0	1	1	IC1	1	1	1	1	0	1	1	1
1	0	0	IC2	1	1	1	0	1	1	1	1
1	0	1	IC2	1	1	0	1	1	1	1	1
1	1	0	IC2	1	0	1	1	1	1	1	1
1	1	1	IC2	0	1	1	1	1	1	1	1

Example 2.18 :

Design $1 : 16$ demultiplexer using

(a) $1 : 8$ demultiplexer

(b) $1 : 4$ demultiplexer

Solution :

$1 : 8$ demultiplexer is also known as $3 : 8$ decolder. The MSB input S_3 of 4 - bit input i.e. $S_3 S_2 S_1 S_0$ is used to select one of these two $3 : 8$ decoders. S_3 is connected to enable pin.

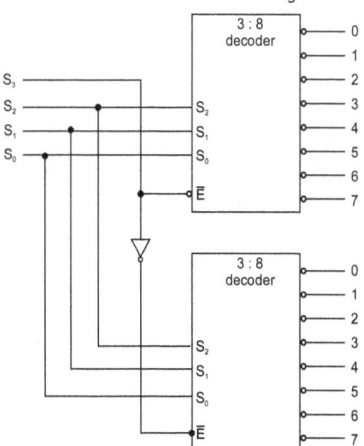

Fig. 2.69 : Demultiplexer using two 1 : 8 demultiplexers

(b)

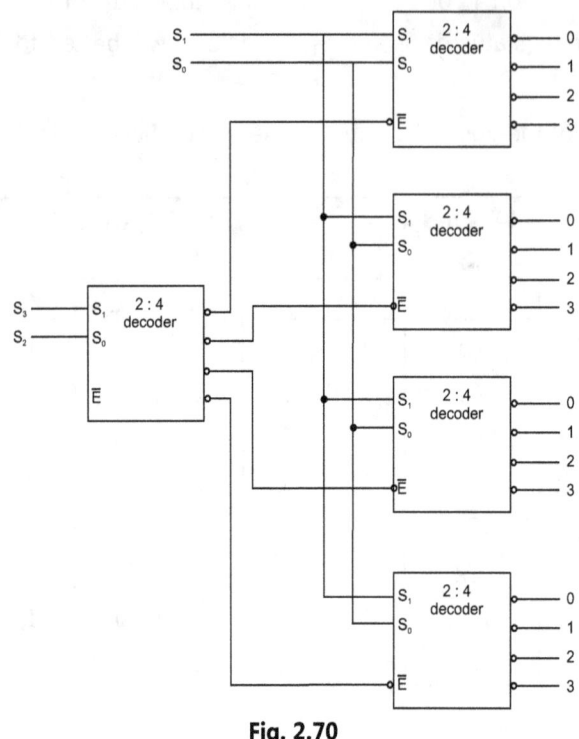

Fig. 2.70

Example 2.19 :

(a) Implement the follwing using 3 : 8 decoder

$$Y_0 (A, B, C) = \Sigma m (0, 1, 2, 4)$$
$$Y_1 (A, B, C) = \Sigma m (1, 3, 5, 7)$$
$$Y_2 (A, B, C) = \Sigma m (4, 5, 6, 7)$$

(b) Design some using NAND gates

Solution :

(a) Since the expressions for Y are in terms of minterms, we use OR gates. Because the outputs of decoder are active low, the inputs to OR gates are inverted.

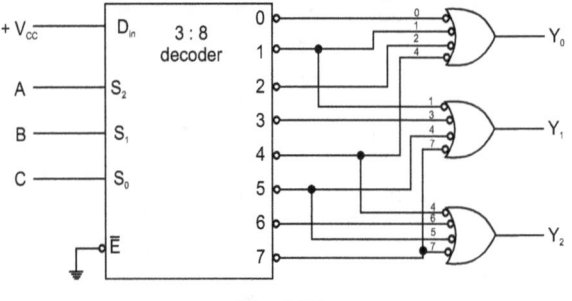

Fig. 2.71

(b) Inverted input OR gate is equivalent to NAND gate.

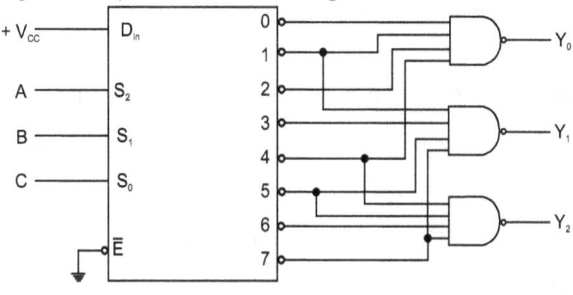

Fig. 2.72

Example 2.20 :

Design full - adder using 3 : 8 decoder

Solution : The truth table of full - adder is

Inputs			Outputs	
A	B	C_{n-1}	S_n	C_n
0	0	0	0	0
0	0	1	1	0
0	1	0	1	0
0	1	1	0	1
1	0	0	1	0
1	0	1	0	1
1	1	0	0	1
1	1	1	1	1

Therefore, the expressions for S_n and C_n are

$$S_n = \Sigma \, m \, (1, 2, 4, 7)$$

$$C_n = \Sigma \, m \, (3, 5, 6, 7)$$

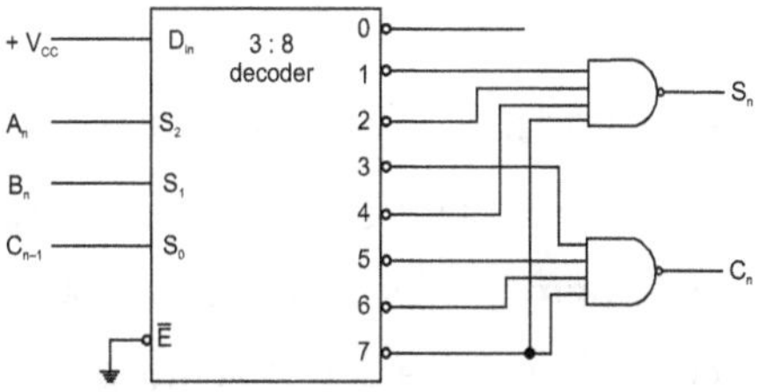

Fig. 2.73 : Full-adder using 3 : 8 decoder

2.11 INTRODUCTION TO QUINE-MC CLUSKEY METHOD

Introduction :

The Quine-McCluskey method is an exact algorithm which finds a minimum cost sum-of-products implementation of a Boolean function. This section introduces the method and applies it to several examples.

There are four main steps in the Quine McCluskey algorithm :

1. Generate Prime Implicants

2. Construct Prime Implicant Table

3. Reduce Prime Implicant Table

    (a) Remove Essential Prime Implicants

    (b) Row Dominance

    (c) Column Dominance

4. Solve Prime Implicant Table.

Note : In step 1, the prime implicants of a function are generated using an iterative procedure. In step 2, a prime implicant table is constructed. The columns of the table are the prime implicants of the function. The rows are minterms of where the function is 1, called ON-set minterms. The goal of the method is to cover all the rows using a minimum of prime implicants.

The reduction step (Step 3) is used to reduce the size of the table. This step has three sub-steps which are iterated until no further table reduction is possible. At this point, the reduced table is either empty or non-empty. If the reduced table is empty, the removed essential prime implicants form a minimum cost solution. However, if reduced table is not empty, the table must be "solved" (Step 4). The table can be solved using either "Petrick's method" or the "branching method". This section focuses on Petrick's method which is used more frequently.

Column Dominance :

• Consider the following Karnaugh map of 4-input Boolean function :

• There are 5 prime implicants, each of which covers 2 ON-set minterms. First, we note that two implicants are essential prime implicants : A'C'D' and ACD. These implicants must be added to the final cover. There are 3 remaining prime implicants. We must pick a minimum subset of these to cover the uncovered ON-set minterms.

- Here is the prime implicant table for the Karnaugh map. The 5 prime implicants are listed as columns, and the 6 ON-set minterms are listed as rows.

	A'C'D	A' BC'	BC'D	ABD	ACD
	(0, 4)	(4, 5)	(5, 13)	(13, 15)	(11, 15)
0	X				
4	X	X			
5		X	X		
11					X
13			X	X	
15				X	X

- We cross out columns A'C'D and ACD and mark them with asterisks, to indicate that these are essential. Each row intersected by one of these columns is also crossed out, because that minterm is now covered. At this point, prime implicant BC'D covers 2 remaining ON-set minterms (5 and 13). However, prime implicant A'BC' covers only one of these (namely, 5), as does ABD (namely, 13). Therefore, we can always use BC'D instead of either A'BC or ABD, since it covers the same minterms. That is BC'D **column-dominates** A'BC, and BC'D **column-dominates** ABD. The dominated prime implicants can be crossed out, and only column BC'D remains.

Row Dominance :

- Consider the following Karnaugh map of a 4-input Boolean function :

There are 4 prime implicants : A'B', C'D, A'D and A'C. None of these is an essential prime implicant. We must pick a minimum subset of these to cover the 5 ON -set Karnaugh. Here is the prime implicants table for the Karnaugh map. The 4 prime implicants are listed as columns, and the 5 ON-set minterms are listed as rows.

	A'B'	C'D	A'D	A'C
	(1, 2, 3)	(1, 5)	(1, 3, 5, 7)	(2, 3, 7)
1	X	X	X	
2	X			X
3	X		X	X
5		X	X	
7			X	X

- Note that row 3 is contained in three columns : A'B', A'D, and A'C. Row 2 is covered by two of these three columns : A'B' and A'C, and row 7 is also covered by two of these three columns : A'D and A'C. In this case, any prime implicant which contains row 2 also contains row 3.

- Similarly, any prime implicant which contains row 7 also contains row 3. Therefore, we can ignore the covering of row 3 : it will always be covered as long as we cover row 2 or row 7. To see this, note that row 3 row dominates row 2, and row 3 **row dominates** row 7. The situation is now the reverse of column dominance : we cross out the dominating (larger) row. In this case, row 3 can be crossed out; it no longer needs to be considered.

- Similarly, row 1 row dominates row 5. Therefore, row 1 can be crossed out. We are guaranteed that row 1 will still be covered, since any prime implicants which covers row 5 will also cover row 1.

Example 2.21 :

Minimize the given Boolean expression

$$F (A, B, C, D) = \Sigma m (0, 2, 5, 6, 7, 8, 10, 12, 13, 14, 15)$$

Solution :

Step 1 : Generate Prime Implicants :

List Minterms

Column I		
0	0000	
2	0010	
8	1000	
5	0101	
6	0110	
10	1010	
12	1100	
7	0111	
13	1101	
14	1110	
15	1111	

Combine Pairs of Minterms from Column I :

A check (√) is written next to every minterm which can combined with another minterm. Two minterms can be combined if there is a change in bit value of only column. Rest all the three columns should have the same bit value. Start with first minterm i.e. '0' and compare it with every other minterm. After comparing it can be seen that '0' can be combined with '2' and '8'. Repeat the same for all other minterms.

	Column I		Column II	
0	0000	√	(0, 2)	00–0
2	0010	√	(0, 8)	– 000
8	1000	√	(2, 6)	0 – 10
5	0101	√	(2, 10)	– 010
6	0110	√	(8, 10)	10 –0
10	1010	√	(8, 12)	1–00
12	1100	√	(5, 7)	01 – 1
7	0111	√	(5, 13)	– 101
13	1101	√	(6, 7)	011 –
14	1110	√	(6, 14)	– 110
15	1111	√	(10, 14)	1–10
			(12, 13)	110–
			(12, 14)	11–0
			(7, 15)	– 111
			(13, 15)	11 – 1
			(14, 15)	111–

Combine Pairs of Products from Column II

	Column I			Column II			Column III	
0	0000	√	(0, 2)	00–0	√	(0, 2, 8, 10)	–0–0
2	0010	√	(0, 8)	–000	√	(0, 8, 2, 10)	–0–0
8	1000	√	(2, 6)	0–10	√	(2, 6, 10, 14)	– 10
5	0101	√	(2, 10)	–010	√	(2, 10, 6, 14)	–10
6	0110	√	(8, 10)	10–0	√	(8, 10, 12, 14)	1–0
10	1010	√	(8, 12)	1–00	√	(8, 12, 10, 14)	1–0
12	1100	√	(5, 7)	–101	√	(5, 7, 13, 15)	–1–1
7	0111	√	(5, 13)	1–01	√	(5, 13, 7, 15)	–1–1
13	1101	√	(6, 7)	011–	√	(6, 7, 14, 15)	–11–
14	1110	√	(6, 14)	–110	√	(6, 14, 7, 15)	–11–
15	1111	√	(10, 14)	1–10	√	(12, 13, 14, 15)	11–
			(12, 13)	110 –	√	(12, 14, 13, 15)	11–
			(12,14)	11–	√		
			(7, 15)	–111	√		
			(13, 15)	11–1	√		

- Column III contains a number of duplicate entries, e.g. (0, 2, 8, 10) and (0, 8, 2, 10). Duplicate entries appear because a product in Column III can be formed in several ways. For example, (0, 2, 8, 10) is formed by combining products (0, 2) and (8, 10) from column II, and (0, 8, 2, 10) (the same product) is formed by combining products (0, 8) and (2, 10).
- Duplicate entries should be crossed out. The remaining unchecked products cannot be combined with other products. These are the prime implicants : (0, 2, 8, 10), (2, 6, 10, 14), (5, 7, 13, 15), (6, 7, 14, 15), (8, 10, 12, 14) and (12, 13, 14, 15); or, using the usual product notation : B'D', CD', BD, BC, AD' and AB.

Step 2 : Construct Prime Implicant Table :

	B'D' (– 0–0)	CD' (– – 10)	BD (– 1–1)	BC (– 11 –)	AD' (1 – – 0)	AB (11 – –)
	(0, 2, 8, 10)	(2, 6, 10, 14)	(5, 7, 13, 15)	(6, 7, 14, 15)	(8, 10, 12, 14)	(12, 13, 14, 15)
0	X					
2	X	X				
5			X			
6		X		X		
7			X	X		
8	X				X	
10	X	X			X	
12					X	X
13			X			X
14		X		X	X	X
15			X	X		X

Step 3 : Reduce Prime Implicant Table :

Iteration 1

(i) Remove Primary Essential Prime Implicants :

	B'D' (*)	CD'	BD (*)	BC	AD'	AB
	(0, 2, 8, 10)	(2, 6, 10, 14)	(5, 7, 13, 15)	(6, 7, 14, 15)	(8, 10, 12, 14)	(12, 13, 14, 15)
(0)0	X					
2	X	X				
(0)5			X			
6		X		X		
7			X	X		
8	X				X	

10	X	X			X	
12					X	X
13			X			X
14		X		X	X	X
15			X	X		X

*   Indicates an essential prime implicant

(0)   Indicates a distinguished row, i.e. a row covered by only 1 prime implicant

- In step 1, primary essential prime implicants are identified. These are implicants which will appear in any solution. A row which is covered by only 1 prime implicant is called a distinguished row. The prime implicant which covers it is an essential prime implicant. In this step, essential prime implicants are identified and removed. The corresponding column is crossed out. Also, each row where the column contains an X is completely crossed out, since these minterms are now covered. These essential implicants will be added to the final solution. In this example, B'D' and BD are both primary essentials.

(ii)   Row Dominance : The table is simplified by removing rows and columns which were crossed out in step (i). (Note : you do not need to do this, but it makes the table easier to read. Instead, you can continue to mark up the original table)

	CD'	BC	AD'	AB
	(2, 6, 10, 14)	(6, 7, 14, 15)	(8, 10, 12, 14)	(12, 13, 14, 15)
6	X	X		
12			X	X
14	X	X	X	X

Row 14 dominates both row 6 and row 12. That is, row 14 has an "X" in every column where row 6 has an "X" (and, in fact, row 14 has "X"s in other columns as well).

Similarly, row 14 has an "X" in every column where row 12 has an "X". Rows 6 and 12 are said to be dominated by row 14.

- A dominating row can always be eliminated. To see this, note that every product which covers row 6 also covers row 14. That is, if some product covers row 6, row 14 is guaranteed to be covered. Similarly, any product which covers row 12 will also cover row 14. Therefore, row 14 can be crossed out.

(iii) Column Dominance :

	CD'	BC	AD'	AB
	(2, 6, 10, 14)	(6, 7, 14, 15)	(8, 10, 12, 14)	(12, 13, 14, 15)
6	X	X		
12			X	X

- Column CD' dominates column BC. That is, column CD, has an "X" in every row where column BC has an "X". In fact, in this example, column BC also dominates column CD', so each is dominated by the other. (Such columns are said to co-dominate each other.) Similarly, columns AD' and AB dominate each other, and each is dominated by the other.

- A dominated column can always be eliminated. To see this, note that every row covered by the dominated column is also covered by the dominating column. For example : C'D covers every row which BC covers. Therefore, the dominating column can always replace the dominated column, so the dominated column is crossed out. In this example, CD' and BC dominate each other, so either column can be crossed out (but not both) Similarly, AD' and AB dominate each other, so either column can be crossed out.

Iteration 2 : (i) Remove Secondary Essential Prime Implicants

	CD' (**)	AD' (* *)
	(2, 6, 10, 14)	(8, 10, 12, 14)
(0) 6	X	
(0) 12		X

** Indicates a secondary essential prime implicant

(0) Indicates a distinguished row

- In iteration 2 and beyond, secondary essential prime implicants are identified. These are implicants which will appear in any solution, given the choice of column-dominance used in the previous steps (if 2 columns co-dominated each other in a previous step, the choice of which was deleted can affect what is an "essential" at this step). As before, a row which is covered by only 1 prime implicant is called a distinguished row. The prime implicant which covers it is a (secondary) essential prime implicant.

- Secondary essential prime implicants are identified and removed. The corresponding columns are crossed out. Also, each row where the column contains an X is completely crossed out, since these minterms are now covered. These essential implicants will be added to the final solution. In this example, both CD' and AD' are secondary essentials.

Step 4 : Solve Prime Implicant Table.

No other rows remain to be covered, so no further steps are required. Therefore, the minimum-cost solution consists of the primary and secondary essential prime implicants B'D', BD, CD' and AD' :   F = B'D' + BD + CD' + Ad'

Example 2.22 :

Minimize the given Boolean expression

$$F (A, B, C, D) = \Sigma m (0, 2, 3, 4, 5, 6, 7, 8, 9, 10, 11, 12, 13)$$

Solution :

Step 1 : Generate Prime Implicants.

Use the method described in earlier example.

Step 2 : Construct Prime Implicants Table.

	A'D'	B'D'	C'D'	A'C	B'C	A'B	BC'	AB'	AC'
0	X	X	X						
2	X	X		X	X				
3				X	X				
4	X		X			X	X		
5						X	X		
6	X			X		X			
7				X		X			
8		X	X					X	X
9								X	X
10		X			X			X	
11					X			X	
12			X				X		X
13							X		X

Step 3 : Reduce Prime Implicant Table.

Iteration 1

(i) Remove Primary Essential Prime Implicants :

There are no primary essential prime implicants : each row is covered by at least two products.

(ii) Row Dominance:

	A'D'	B'D'	C'D'	A'C	B'C	A'B	BC'	AB'	AC'
0	X	X	X						
2	X	X		X	X				
3				X	X				
4	X		X			X	X		
5						X	X		
6	X			X		X			
7				X		X			
8		X	X					X	X
9								X	X
10		X			X			X	
11					X			X	
12			X				X		X
13							X		X

There are many instances of row dominance. Row 2 dominates 3, 4 dominates 5, 6 dominates 7, 8 dominates 9, 10 dominates 11, 12 dominates 13. Dominating rows are removed.

(iii) Column Dominance :

	A'D'	B'D'	C'D'	A'C	B'C	A'B	BC'	AB'	AC'
0	X	X	X						
3				X	X				
5						X	X		
7				X		X			
9								X	X
11					X			X	
13							X		X

Columns A'D', B'D' and C'D' each dominate one another. We can remove any two of them.

Iteration 2

(i) Remove Secondary Essential Prime Implicants

	A'D'**	A'C	B'C	A'B	AC'	AB'	AC'
(0)0	X						
3		X	X				
5				X	X		
7		X		X			
9						X	X
11			X			X	
13					X		X

** indicates a secondary essential prime implicant (0) indicates a distinguished row

Product A'D' is a secondary essential prime implicant; it is removed from the table.

(ii) Row Dominance :

No further row dominance is possible.

(iii) Row Dominance :

No further column dominance is possible.

Step 4 : Solve Prime Implicant Table.

	A'C'	B'C'	A'B	BC'	AB'	AC'
3	X	X				
5			X	X		
7	X		X			
9					X	X
11		X			X	
13				X		X

There are no additional secondary essential prime implicants, and no further row-or column-dominance is possible. The remaining covering problem is called a cyclic covering problem. A solution can be obtained using gone of two methods : (i) Petrick's method or (ii) the branching method. We use Petrick's method below :

Petrick's Method :

- In Petrick's method, a Boolean expression p is formed which describes all possible solution of the table. The prime implicants in the table are numbered in order, from 1 to 6.

  p_1 = A'C, p_2 = B'C, p_3 = A'B, p_4 = BC', p_5 = AB', p_6 = AC'.

For each prime implicant p_i, a Boolean variable p_i is used true whenever prime implicant p_i is included in the solution. Note the difference ! : p_i is an implicant, while p_i is a corresponding.

- Boolean proposition (i.e. true/false statement) which has a true (1) or false (0) value. p_i = 1 means "I select prime implicant p_i for inclusion in the cover," while p_1 = 0 means "I do not select prime implicant p_i for inclusion in the cover.

- Using these p_i variables, a larger Boolean expression p can be formed, which captures the precise conditions for every row in the table to be covered. Each clause in p is a disjunction (OR) of several possible column selections to cover a particular row. The conjunction (AND) of all of these clauses is the Boolean expression p, which describes precisely the conditions to be satisfied for all rows are covered.

- For the above prime implicant table, the covering requirements can be captured by the Boolean equation:

$$p = (p_1 + p_2)(p_3 + p_4)(p_1 + p_3)(p_5 + p_6)(p_2 + p_5)(p_4 + p_6)$$

- If Boolean variable p = 1, each of the disjunctive clauses is satisfied (1), and all rows are covered. In this case, the set of p_is which are 1 indicate a valid cover using the corresponding selection of primes p_is (columns). If p = 0, then at least one disjunctive clause is not satisfied (0), meaning that at least one row is not covered. In this case, the set of P_is which are 1 correspond to a set of selected primes p_i which do not form a valid cover. Note that the above equation is simply a rewriting of the prime implicant table as a Boolean formula : the clasues correspond to the rows.

- In the right expression, the sum $(p_1 + p_2)$ describes the covering requirement for row 3 : product p_1 or p_2 must be included in the solution, in order to cover row 3. Similarly, the sum $(p_3 + p_4)$ describes the covering requirement for row 5 : product p_3 or p_4 must be included to cover row 5. Each sum corresponds to a different row of the table. These, sums are ANDed together, since all such requirement must be satisfied.

  Since p is a Boolean expression, it can be multiplied out into sum of products form :

$$p = p_1 p_4 p_5 + p_1 p_3 p_5 p_6 + p_2 p_3 p_4 p_5 + p_2 p_3 p_5 p_6$$
$$+ p_1 p_2 p_4 p_6 + p_1 p_2 p_3 p_6 + p_2 p_3 p_4 p_6 + p_2 p_3 p_6$$

- Each product describes a solution for the table. Only two products have 3 Boolean variables; the remainder has 4 variables. These two products, $p_1 p_4 p_5$ and $p_2 p_3 p_6$ describe two minimal solutions. The first product describes a solution which includes prime implicants p_1, p_4 and p_5 that is A'C, BC' and AB'. The second product describes a solution using prime implicants p_2, p_3 and p_6; that is B'C, A'B and AC'.

- Both solutions have a minimal number of prime implicants, so either can be used. With either choice, we must include the secondary essential prime implicant, A'D', identified earlier.

- Therefore, the two minimum -cost solutions are :

$$F = A'D' + A'C + BC' + AB'$$
$$F = A'D' + B'C + A'B + AC'$$

◈ ◈ ◈

SEQUENTIAL LOGIC DESIGN

3.0 INTRODUCTION

- Digital circuits are broadly classified into two categories

  (1) Combinational and (2) Sequential.

- In combinational logic circuits, output(s) at any instant of time depends on the present input(s) applied at that instant of time. Though very important, these circuits are only a part of digital systems.

- The other major class is sequential circuits in which the output(s) not only depend on input(s), but also depend upon the past history of input(s).

- The combinational circuits are memoryless circuits while the sequential circuits require memory for storing the past input(s).

- The basic digital memory circuit is known as flip flop. Flip flop is developed from the circuit of cross coupled inverters which is called as one bit memory cell. So we shall start with one bit memory cell.

3.1 ONE BIT MEMORY CELL

- One bit memory cell, as the name suggests can store 'one' bit (logic 0 or logic 1) information.

- It can be built using NAND or NOR gates.

- A one bit memory cell using NAND gates is as shown in Fig. 3.1.

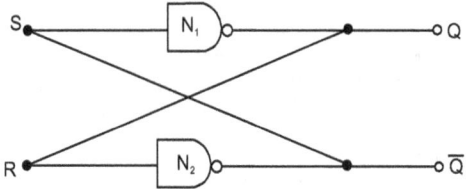

Fig. 3.1 : One bit memory cell

- The above circuit is also known as 'S-R' (Set-Reset) latch.

- This circuit has two stable states : '1 state' (Output Q = 1) and '0 state' (output Q = 0).

- '1 state' is also called as 'set state' and the '0 state' is known as 'reset state'.

- The digital information gets locked or latched in this circuit. Therefore it is known as S-R i.e. set-reset latch.

Operation of the circuit :

- Two NAND gates (N_1 and N_2) are used as inverters. The output of N_1 is connected to the input of N_2 (R) and the output of N_2 is connected to the input of N_1 (S).

- Let us assume that the output of N_1 is logic 1 (Q = 1). This is the input of N_2 i.e. R=1.

  Therefore the output of N_2 becomes logic 0 ($\bar{Q}$ = 0).

- The output of N_2 is the input of N_1 i.e. S become 0 and consequently output of N_1 become 1 (Q=1), which confirms our assumption.

- Let us now assume that the output of N_1 is logic 0 (Q = 0). This is the input of N_2 i.e. R = 0. Therefore the output of N_2 becomes logic 1 ($\bar{Q}$ = 1).

- The output of N_2 is the input of N_1 i.e. S becomes 1 and consequently output of N_1 becomes 0 (Q = 0) which confirms our assumption.

- From above discussion we can conclude that - If the circuit is in 1 state, it continues to remain in this state. Similarly if it is in 0 state, it continues to remain in the same state. This property of the circuit is known as 'memory'. And as this circuit can hold one bit information (either logic 1 or logic 0), it is called as one bit memory cell.

Drawback :

- In the above circuit there is no way to enter the desired digital information. When the power is turned on, the circuit switches to one of the stable states i.e. 1 state or 0 state and it is not possible to predict it.

- To overcome this drawback, a modified circuit with 2 input NAND gates and two additional inverters are used. The desired digital information can be entered in this circuit.

3.2 ONE BIT MEMORY CELL WITH PROVISION FOR ENTERING DATA

- This circuit is with 2 input NAND gates N_1 and N_2; two additional inverters N_3 and N_4 is as shown in Fig. 3.2.

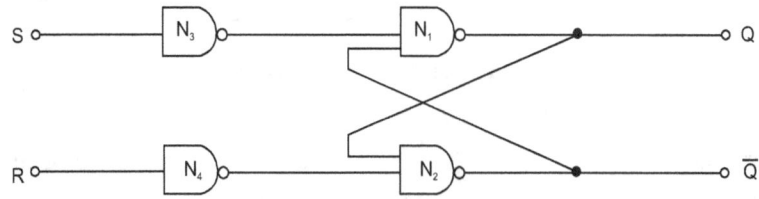

Fig. 3.2 : Memory cell with provision for entering data

- If S = R = 0, the circuit will behave exactly as the previous circuit shown in Fig. 3.2.

- If S = 1 and R = 0 then the output of N_3 will be 0 and the output of N_4 will be 1. As one of the inputs of N_1 is 0, its output will be certainly 1 (Q = 1).

- When Q become 1, both inputs of N_2 become 1 causing its output to go low ($\bar{Q}$ = 0). This is known as 1 state or set state of the circuit, which is achieved with the input pattern S = 1 and R = 0.

- If S = 0 and R = 1, then the output of N_4 will be 0 and the output of N_3 will be 1. As one of the inputs of N_2 becomes 0, its output will be certainly 1 ($\bar{Q}$ = 1).

- When $\bar{Q}$ becomes 1, both inputs of N_1 become 1 causing its output to go low (Q = 0). This is known as 0 state or reset state of the circuit which is achieved with the input pattern S = 0 and R = 1.

- In this way, user can enter desired information in the one bit memory cell.

- Uptil now we have seen that the outputs Q and $\bar{Q}$ are always complementary. If we apply the input S = 1 and R = 1, then the output of N_3 and N_4 become 0. This makes one input of both N_1 and N_2 as 0, which in turn cause both outputs Q and $\bar{Q}$ to become 1.

- Both Q and $\bar{Q}$ getting same state is not allowed and therefore the condition of inputs S = R = 1 is prohibited.

3.3   EDGE TRIGGERED FLIP FLOPS

Q. What are edge triggered Flip Flops?

- S-R flip flop and JK flip flop are known as level triggered flip flops as their output changes according to applied inputs as long as clock is present.

- As these flip flops respond when CLK=1 they are further called as positive level triggered flip flops.

- We know that level triggered JK flip flop has the drawback of race around condition. And to overcome that drawback we use master slave JK flip flop which is called as pulse triggered flip flop.

- In a pulse triggered flip flop like MSJK flip flop, output changes according to applied inputs, when a pulse is applied at the clock input. The state of this flip flop changes at the negative transition of the clock.

- Thus, in MSJK flip flop the race around condition is eliminated as the fed back output is blocked at the master when the CLK = 0.

- But in certain systems there is a possibility that the inputs of flip flop may change during the presence of the clock pulse. This causes uncertainty in the output of flip flop. This uncertainty can be eliminated by using edge triggered flip flops.
- In edge triggered flip flops output changes according to applied inputs only at the positive or negative edge of the clock pulse.
- Based on the type of edge there are two types of edge triggered flip flops :

  (1) positive edge triggered and (2) negative edge triggered.
- In case of positive edge triggered flip flop output changes only when the clock pulse changes from 0 to 1. While in case of negative edge triggered flip flop output responds only when the clock pulse changes from 1 to 0. The positive and negative edge of the clock is shown in Fig. 3.3.

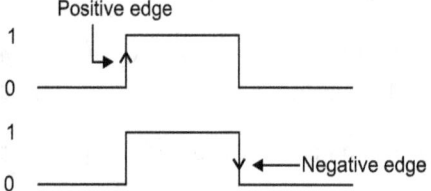

Fig. 3.3 : Positive and negative edge of the clock

- Thus, the state of the flip flop changes during very short interval of time in which clock changes from 0 to 1 or 1 to 0 and the uncertainty in the output gets completely eliminated.
- The logic symbol of positive edge triggered and negative edge triggered JK flip flop is shown in Fig. 3.4.

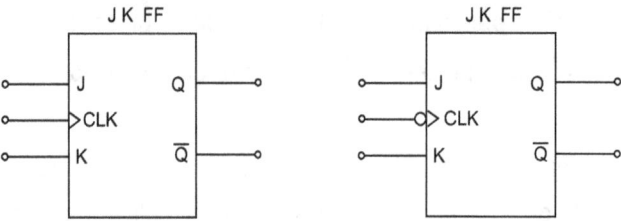

(i) Positive edge triggered   **(ii) Negative edge triggered**

Fig. 3.4 : Edge triggered JK flip flop

- Note that the logic symbol of negative edge triggered JK flip flop is same as that of MSJK flip flop without preset and clear inputs.
- Also in case of positive edge triggered JK flip flop bubble is absent.

3.4 CLOCKED S-R FLIP-FLOP

Q. Explain clocked S-R flip-flop.

- It is often required to enter the desired digital information in the memory cell, in synchronism with a train of pulses known as clock. The circuit of clocked S-R flip flop is as shown in Fig. 3.5.

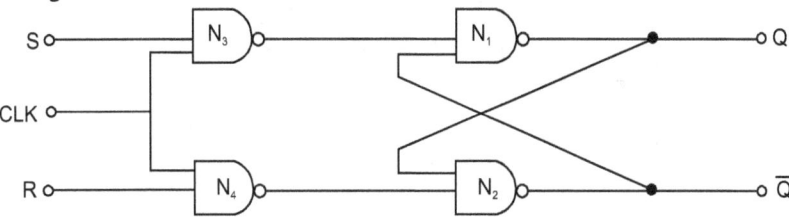

Fig. 3.5 : Clocked S-R. flip flop

- In above circuit, when CLK = 0, output of both N_3 and N_4 is certainly 1. In this case, both S and R inputs have no effect on output Q.

- When CLK = 1, the operation of this circuit is exactly the same as that of Fig. 3.5.

- For S = R = 0, then output Q does not change i.e. if it is 0 it remains 0 and if it is 1, it remains 1. Thus, there is no change in the output for this input condition.

- For S = 1 and R = 0, the output Q becomes 1 as explained in the section 3.2. This is known as the set state of the circuit.

- For S = 0 and R = 1 the output Q becomes 0 as explained in the section 3.2. This is known as the reset state of the circuit.

- For S = R = 1, both the outputs Q and $\bar{Q}$ try to become 1 which is not allowed and therefore this input condition is prohibited.

- Thus, the above circuit responds to S and R inputs, only when CLK = 1.

- The operation of the circuit for CLK = 1 can be tabulated as shown in table 3.1.

Table 3.1

Inputs		Output
S	R	Q
0	0	No change
0	1	0 (Reset)
1	0	1 (Set)
1	1	Prohibited

- If we represent Q_n as the output of present state of the circuit and S_n, R_n as the inputs of the present state, then Q_{n+1} becomes the output of the next state of the circuit.
- The above table 3.1 can be redrawn in terms of present state and next state as table 3.2

Table 3.2 : Truth table of S-R flip flop

Inputs		Output
S_n	R_n	Q_{n+1}
0	0	Q_n
0	1	0
1	0	1
1	1	Prohibited

- The table 3.2 is the truth table of clocked S-R flip flop.
- The truth table of a flip flop is also referred to as the characteristic table as it specifies the operational characteristic of the flip flop.
- Logic symbol of clocked S-R flip flop is as shown in Fig. 3.6

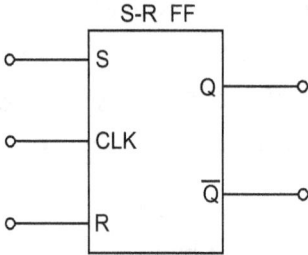

Fig 3.6 : Logic symbol of clocked S-R flip flop

3.5 CLOCKED S-R FLIP FLOP WITH PRESET and CLEAR INPUTS

Q. Explain clocked S-R flip flop with preset and clear inputs.

- The circuit of clocked S-R flip flop shown in Fig. 3.7 switches to either set state or reset state when the power is turned on i.e. the state of the circuit is uncertain.
- In many applications it is required to define the initial state of the flip flop when the power is turned on.

- This is accomplished by using the preset and clear inputs.

- Preset and clear inputs are known as asynchronous inputs as they do not work in synchronism with the clock.

- Clocked S-R flip flop with preset and clear inputs can be obtained by using N_1 and N_2 NAND gates as 3 input gates as shown in Fig. 3.7

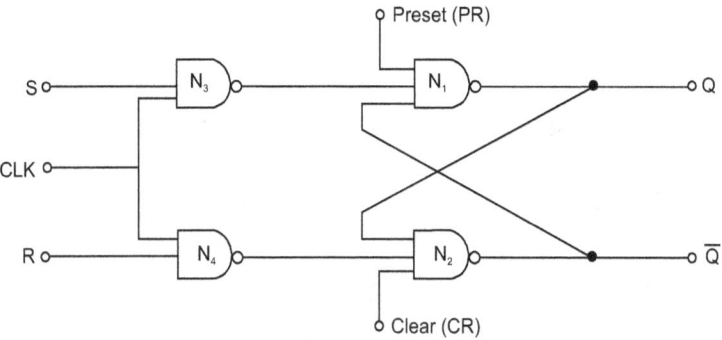

Fig. 3.7 Clocked S-R flip flop with preset and clear inputs.

- In When PR = CR = 1, above circuit operates in accordance with the truth table of clocked S-R flip flop given in table 3.2.

- When CR = 0 and PR = 1, one of the inputs of N_2 is 0, therefore its output is certainly high ($\bar{Q}$ = 1). Consequently all three inputs of N_1 are high which make Q = 0.

- Thus, CR = 0 resets or clears the flip flop.

- Similarly when CR = 1 and PR = 0, one of the inputs of N_1 is 0, therefore its output is certainly high (Q = 1). Consequently all three inputs of N_2 are high which make $\bar{Q}$ = 0. Thus, PR = 0 sets the flip flop.

- Both preset and clear inputs are known as active low inputs as they perform the intended operation of setting or clearing the flip flop, when they are low.

- Once the desired initial state of the flip flop is achieved using preset and clear inputs, these inputs are connected to logic 1 while the normal operation of the flip flop takes place.

- The condition PR = CR = 0 must not be used, since this leads to an uncertain state.
- The logic symbol of this flip flop is as shown in Fig. 3.8. Preset and clear inputs are shown as bubbled inputs indicating that they are active low inputs.

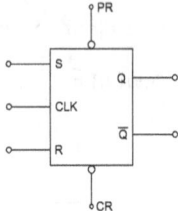

Fig 3.8 : Logic symbol of clocked S-R flip flop with preset and clear inputs.

3.6 JK FLIP FLOP

Q. Explain JK flip flop with clear and present inputs.

- We know that in case of clocked S-R flip flop, for the input condition S = R = 1 both the outputs Q and $\bar{Q}$ try to become 1, which is not allowed and therefore this input condition is prohibited.
- This drawback can be eliminated by converting S-R flip flop into a JK flip flop.
- The data input J is ANDed with $\bar{Q}$ to obtain S input and the data input K is ANDed with Q to obtain R input as shown in Fig. 3.9

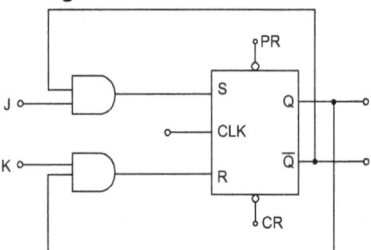

Fig. 3.9 : JK flip flop constructed using S-R flip flop

- When J = K = 0, output of both AND gates is 0. Therefore, S and R both become 0. So next state output Q_{n+1} remains same as that of present state output Q_n.
- When J = 0 and K = 1, the output of upper AND gate is 0, so S = 0. If the present state output Q_n = 0, the output of lower AND gate is also 0 and R becomes 0. For the input condition S = R = 0 the next state output remains unchanged. But if the present state output Q_n = 1, the output of lower AND gate becomes 1 i.e. R becomes 1. With S = 0 and R = 1 input combination the next state output Q_{n+1} is reset. Thus for J = 0 and K = 1 input condition, irrespective of the present state Q_n, the next state output Q_{n+1} be is 0 i.e. the flip flop is reset.

- Similarly for J = 1 and K = 0 input condition, the next state output Q_{n+1} is certainly 1 i.e. the flip flop is set.

Race around condition

> **Q.** Explain race around condition in a flip-flop.   **[May 07, 4 M]**
>
> **Q.** How can a race around condition be eliminated in a flip flop?

- The race around condition occurs for the input combination J = K = 1.
- Let us assume that initially the output Q is 0. With this the output of lower AND gate becomes 0 and upper AND gate becomes 1. Therefore S becomes 1 and R becomes 0. This input combination of S-R causes output Q to become 1.Thus the output changes from 0 to 1 after the time interval Δt equal to the propagation delay through AND gate and S-R flip flop. Now we have J = K = 1 and output Q = 1.
- After another time interval Δt, the output Q will change back to 0 and the cycle repeats till CLK=1.
- At the end of the clock pulse the output Q is uncertain and this situation is known as race around condition. It is shown in Fig. 3.10.

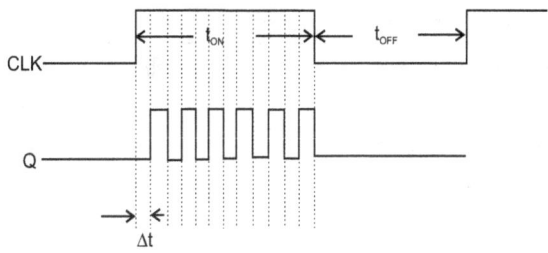

Fig. 3.10 : Timing diagram showing race around condition

- The race around condition can be eliminated if t_{ON} is made smaller than the propagation delay Δt.
- It can also be eliminated using the master slave JK (MSJK) flip flop.
- The operation of JK flip flop can be expressed with the truth table 3.3.

Table 3.3 Truth table of JK flip flop

Inputs		Output
J_n	K_n	Q_{n+1}
0	0	Q_n
0	1	0
1	0	1
1	1	$\bar{Q}_n$

- The logic symbol of JK flip flop is shown in Fig. 3.11.

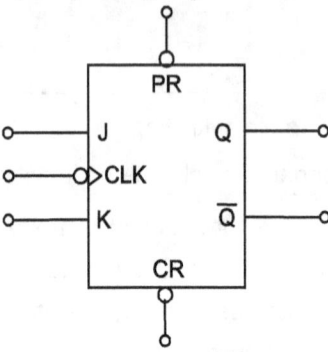

Fig. 3.11 : Logic symbol of JK flip flop

3.7 MASTER SLAVE JK (MSJK) FLIP FLOP

Q. Explain the operation of a master-slave JK flip-flop and show how the race around condition is eliminated in it ?	**[May 10, 8 M]**
Q. Discuss methods to avoid race around condition in JK flip-flop.	**[Dec. 07, 4 M]**
Q. How can race around condition be avoided ?	**[Dec. 08, 09, 3 M]**

- Master slave JK flip flop is a cascade of two S-R flip flops as shown in Fig. 3.12
- As shown in Fig. 3.12, outputs of slave are fed back to the inputs of master. Also clock is directly applied to the master while it is inverted and then applied to the slave.
- When CLK=1, the master is enabled and the slave is disabled. The outputs of master Q_m

  and $\bar{Q}_m$ respond to the inputs J and K according to the table 3.3. As long as CLK=1, Q

  and $\bar{Q}$ outputs do not change as the slave is disabled and therefore the fed back inputs of master also do not change.

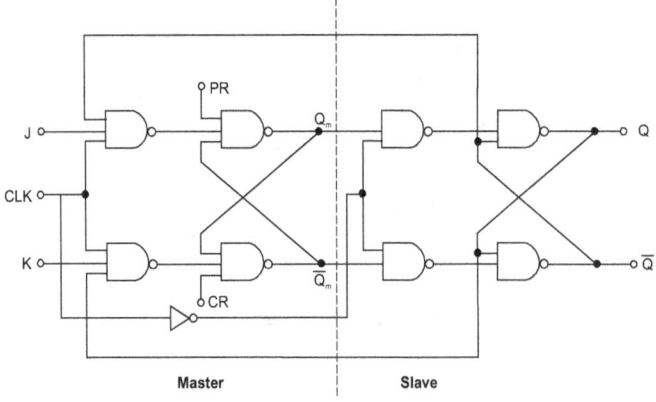

Fig. 3.12 : Master slave JK flip flop

- When CLK= 0, the slave is enabled and the master gets disabled. The outputs Q and $\bar{Q}$ change according to the outputs of the master Q_m and $\bar{Q}_m$. As long as CLK = 0, Q_m and $\bar{Q}_m$ outputs do not change as the master is disabled and therefore Q and $\bar{Q}$ outputs also retain their new values.

- Thus the race around condition gets eliminated.

- The state of the master slave JK flip flop shown in Fig. 3.12, changes at the negative transition of the clock pulse.

- The logic symbol of master slave JK flip flop is shown in Fig. 3.13.

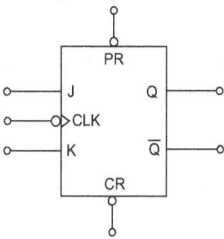

Fig. 3.13 : Logic symbol of MSJK flip flop

- The symbol '>' at the CLK input indicates that output changes when the clock makes a transition.

- The bubble indicates that the output changes when there is a negative transition of the clock (i.e. when the clock changes from 1 to 0).

3.8   D FLIP FLOP

Q. Justify name 'delay' for D-flip flop giving truth table.   **[May 07, 2 M]**

- It has only one input called as data input (D).

- It is also known as data flip flop or delay flip flop.

- If we use only middle two rows of the truth table of S-R flip flop or JK flip flop we obtain D flip flop.

- The middle two rows of both truth tables indicate that the two inputs S, R or J, K are always complement of each other.

- Thus a D flip flop can be constructed from S-R flip flop or JK flip flop by connecting a NOT gate in between the two inputs as shown in Fig. 3.14.

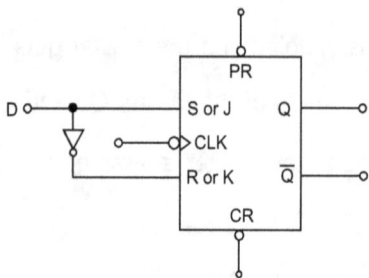

Fig. 3.14 : D flip flop using S-R flip flop or JK flip flop

- The truth table of D flip flop is as shown in table 3.4.

Table 3.4 : Truth table of D flip flop

Input	Output
D_n	Q_{n+1}
0	0
1	1

- Here D_n represents the present state input and Q_{n+1} represents the next state output.

- From truth table, it is clear that output is same as that of input therefore it is known as 'data' flip flop.

- The input data appears at the output at the end of the clock pulse. Thus transfer of data from input to the output is delayed by clock pulse and hence it is also called as 'delay' flip flop.

- The logic symbol of D flip flop is shown in Fig. 3.15.

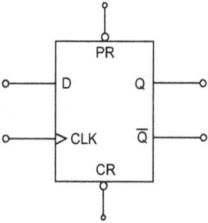

Fig. 3.15 : Logic Symbol of D flip flop

3.9 T FLIP FLOP

Q. Justify 'toggle' for T-flip-flop giving truth table and wave forms.   **[May 07, 2 M]**

- It has only one input called as toggle input (T). It is known as toggle flip flop.

- If we use the first and last row of the truth table of JK flip flop, we obtain T flip flop.

- The first and last row of the truth table of JK flip flop indicate that the J and K inputs are identical.
- Thus, a T flip flop can be constructed from JK flip flop, just by connecting J and K input terminals together as shown in Fig. 3.16.

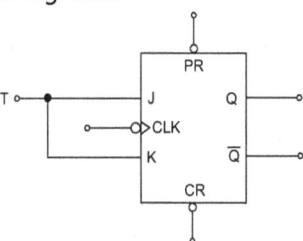

Fig. 3.16 : T flip flop using JK flip flop.

- The truth table of T flip flop is as below.

Table 3.5 Truth table of T flip flop

Input	Output
T_n	Q_{n+1}
0	Q_n
1	$\bar{Q}_n$

- Here T_n represents the present state input, Q_n represents the present state output and Q_{n+1} represents the next state output.
- From truth table it is clear that, for T = 1, it acts as toggle switch. The output Q changes for every active transition of the clock signal. Therefore it is called as toggle flip flop.
- S-R flip flop can not be converted into T flip flop since S = R = 1 input condition is not allowed.
- The logic symbol of T flip flop is shown in Fig. 3.17.

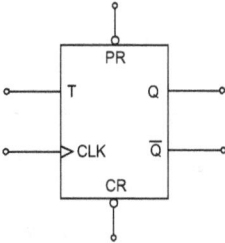

Fig. 3.17 : Logic symbol of T flip flop

3.10 EXCITATION TABLE OF FLIP FLOP

- In the design of sequential circuits, it is often required to find input conditions so that desired next state of the circuit is obtained from the present state of the circuit.

- These input conditions can be obtained using the excitation table of a flip flop.

- The truth table of a flip flop specifies its operational characteristic while the excitation table of a flip flop gives an idea regarding the present input conditions along with present state, to obtain the desired next state.

- Construction of excitation table is discussed below.

3.10.1 Excitation table of S-R flip flop

- Let the present state of the S-R flip flop be $Q_n = 0$ and the desired next state be $Q_{n+1} = 0$.

- As there is no change in the state of the flip flop (present state and next state is same), from the first row of the truth table of S-R flip flop we obtain the input condition as $S_n = 0$ and $R_n = 0$.

- Similarly from the third row of the truth table of S-R flip flop, it is clear that whatever may be the present state, the next state of the flip flop is certainly 0 for the input condition $S_n = 0$ and $R_n = 1$.

- By combining these two input conditions we conclude that, S_n input must be 0 while R_n input can be 0 or 1 i.e. R_n input can be X (don't care), to obtain next state $Q_{n+1} = 0$ from the present state $Q_n = 0$. This gives first row of the excitation table of S-R flip flop.

- Similarly input conditions can be found for remaining three combinations of present state and next state. The excitation table is given in table 3.6.

Table 3.6 : Excitation table of S-R flip flop

Present State	Next State	Flip flop inputs	
Q_n	Q_{n+1}	S_n	R_n
0	0	0	X
0	1	1	0
1	0	0	1
1	1	X	0

3.10.2   Excitation table of JK, D and T Flip Flop

- In the similar manner excitation table of JK, D and T flip flops can be prepared by using their truth tables. Table 3.7, table 3.8 and table 3.9 are the excitation table of JK, D and T flip flop respectively.

Table 3.7 : Excitation table of JK flip flop

Present State	Next State	Flip flop input	
Q_n	Q_{n+1}	S_n	R_n
0	0	0	X
0	1	1	X
1	0	X	1
1	1	X	0

Table 3.8 : Excitation table of D flip flop

Present State	Next State	Flip flop input
Q_n	Q_{n+1}	D_n
0	0	0
0	1	1
1	0	0
1	1	1

Table 3.9 : Excitation table of T flip flop

Present State	Next State	Flip flop inputs
Q_n	Q_{n+1}	T_n
0	0	0
0	1	1
1	0	1
1	1	0

Example 3.1 :

Refer Fig. 3.18(a) and determine the Q output waveform if the flip flop starts out RESET.

[PU 04, 2 M]

Solution :

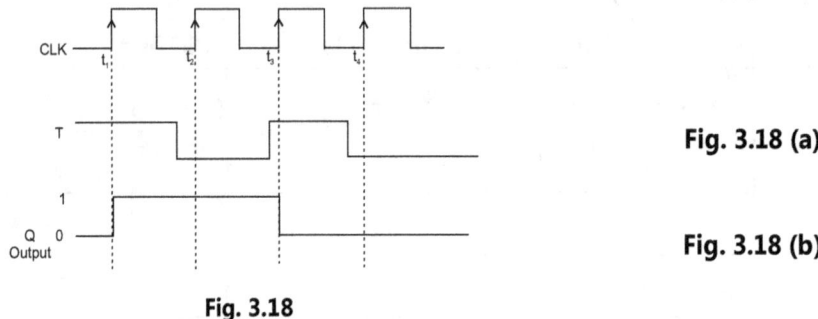

Fig. 3.18 (a)

Fig. 3.18 (b)

Fig. 3.18

- As shown in figure 3.18 (a) the flip flop is positive edge triggered, therefore the output Q can change only at positive edge of the clock i.e. at instants t_1, t_2, t_3 and t_4 as shown.

- It is given that flip flop starts out RESET. Therefore Q = 0 at instant just before t_1.

- At t_1, T=1, therefore Q toggles and becomes 1

- At t_2, T=0, therefore there is no change in Q, it is equal to 1.

- At t_3, T=1, therefore Q toggles and becomes 0

- At t_4, T=0, therefore there is no change in Q, it is equal to 0.

Example 3.2 :

The D input and single clock pulse are shown in figure 3.19 compare the resulting Q output for: positive edge triggered flip flop, negative edge triggered flip flop and pulse triggered master slave flip flops. The flip flops are initially RESET.

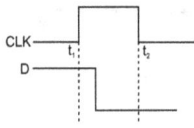

Fig. 3.19

Solution :

- As shown in figure 3.20 positive edge of the clock occurs at t_1 and negative edge of the clock occurs at t_2. The output Q_1, Q_2 and Q_3 for the positive edge triggered, negative edge triggered and pulse triggered flip flop respectively is as shown.

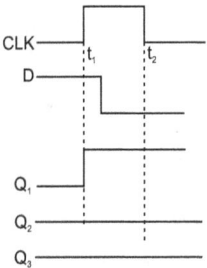

Fig. 3.20

- It is given that the flip flops start out RESET, therefore $Q_1 = Q_2 = Q_3 = 0$ for the instant just before t_1.

- At t_1, positive edge triggered flip flop output can change and at t_2 negative edge triggered as well as pulse triggered flip flop output can change.

- At t_1, D=1 therefore Q_1 changes to 1 and remains 1 thereafter.

- At t_2, D=0 therefore Q_2 and Q_3 do not change. They remain 0 throughout as shown in figure 3.20.

Example 3.3 :

Prepare the truth table for the circuit shown in figure 3.21 and show that it acts as T type flip flop.

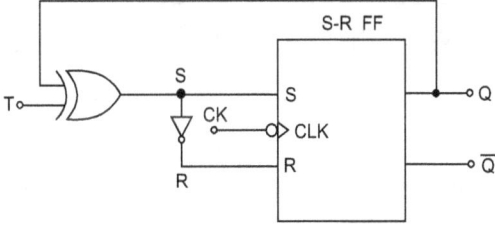

Fig. 3.21

Solution :

- Let us assume that initially Q=0 and T=0. Therefore output of EX-OR is also 0- which leads S=0 and R=1. From the truth table of S-R flip flop, for this input condition, next state output is 0. This gives first row of the truth table for the circuit.

- Now let us assume that Q=1 and T=0.Therefore output of EX-OR is 1 which leads S = 1 and R = 0. From the truth table of S-R flip flop for this input condition, next state output is 1. This gives second row of the truth table for the circuit.

- Proceeding in a similar manner, we can obtain the remaining two rows of the truth table. The complete truth table is given in table 3.10.

Table 3.10

Data Input	Present State	Next State
T	Q_n	Q_{n+1}
0	0	0
0	1	1
1	0	1
1	1	0

- From the first two rows of the table 3.10, it is clear that when T=0, the next state output Q_{n+1} is same as that of present state output Q_n. From the last two rows of the table 3.10, it is clear that, when T=1, the next state output Q_{n+1} is complement of the present state output Q_n. this can be represented in a tabular form as shown in table 3.11

Table 3.11

Data input	Next state output
T_n	Q_{n+1}
0	Q_n
1	$\bar{Q}_n$

- The table 3.11 is the truth table of T type flip flop. Thus, the given circuit is same as that of T type flip flop.

Example 3.6 :

If $\bar{Q}$ output of a D type flip flop is connected to D input, it acts a toggle switch. State whether True or False? Justify your answer.

Solution :

If $\bar{Q}$ output of a D type flip flop is connected to D input it acts as a toggle switch - True.

It is as shown in figure 3.23.

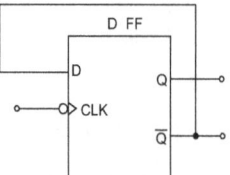

Fig. 3.22

- Initially assume that Q=0. Therefore $\bar{Q}$ =1 and D=1. Upon application of clock pulse, Q become 1 according to the truth table of D type flip flop. This makes $\bar{Q}$ =0 and D=0. With the application of next clock pulse, again Q becomes 0 and the cycle repeats.
- Thus, the output Q switches in between 0 and 1 with the application of successive clock pulses. It acts as a toggle switch.

3.11 FLIP FLOP CHARACTERISTICS

- Flip flop is the basic element of sequential circuits. It can store 1 bit information.
- The two outputs of flip flop, Q and $\bar{Q}$ are always complementary.
- Flip flop has two stable states. In one stable state, Q=1 which is known as set state or 1 state while in another stable state, Q=0 which is known as reset state or 0 state.
- Flip flop can be triggered in three different ways-level, pulse and edge.
- The data inputs of the flip flops such as S, R, J, K, T or D are synchronous inputs i.e. they work in synchronism with the clock signal.
- Flip flops also have asynchronous inputs like preset or clear which give the desired initial state of the flip flop.

3.12 CONVERSION OF FLIP FLOPS

- In the earlier sections we have discussed the conversion of S-R flip flop to JK flip flop, JK flip flop to D flip flop and JK flip flop to T flip flop based on their operations using truth table.
- Now we will study the conversion technique for carrying out all these conversions. It is based upon the block diagram as shown in Fig. 3.23.

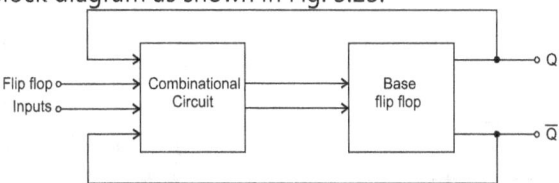

Fig. 3.23 : Block diagram used for flip flop conversion.

- Base flip flop shown in the Fig. 3.23 is the flip flop to be converted. Here we need to design a combinational circuit for converting the base flip flop into desired one.
- For designing the combinational circuit we have to use the excitation tables of both, base flip flop and desired flip flop. From that we construct a truth table with desired flip flop data inputs, present state Q, as inputs and base flip flop data inputs as outputs.
- Then we write separate k-maps for individual outputs and obtain the simplified expressions. Based on these expressions we get the combinational circuit required for conversion.

Example 3.5 :

Convert S-R flip flop to JK, T and D flip flop

Solution : (1) S-R to JK conversion :

- Here the base flip flop is S-R and desired flip flop is JK.

- We first construct a truth table in which inputs are - desired flip flop data inputs i.e. J, K and present state Q. In the truth table outputs are - based flip flop data inputs i.e. S,R.

- Using the excitation table of both flip flops we construct the truth table 3.10.

- The first row of excitation table of JK flip flop for Q=0 is JK=0X. Therefore in the truth table for first two rows we get inputs as JK=00 and JK=01 for Q=0.

- The first row of excitation table of S-R flip flop for Q=0 is S-R=0X. Therefore in the truth table for first two rows we get the outputs as S-R=OX.

- Proceeding in this manner we obtain the truth table 3.10.

- In this table cell number for the k-map is also written so that it becomes easy while representing the truth table in the k-map.

- Figures in the right bottom corner of k-map cell indicate the cell numbers.

Table 3.12 : Truth table for S-R to JK conversion.

Cell no.	Desired FF data inputs		Present state	Base FF data inputs	
	J	K	Q	S	R
0	0	0	0	0	×
2	0	1	0	0	×
4	1	0	0	1	0
6	1	1	0	1	0
3	0	1	1	0	1
7	1	1	1	0	1
1	0	0	1	×	0
5	1	0	1	×	0

- Now we write sepate k-maps for S and R outputs according to the cell numbers.

(1) For S $\Rightarrow$

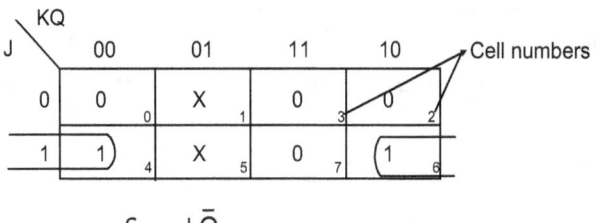

$$\therefore \quad S = J\bar{Q} \qquad \qquad ...\,3.1$$

(2) For R $\Rightarrow$

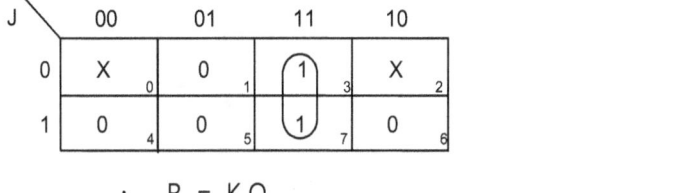

$$\therefore \quad R = KQ \qquad \qquad ...\,3.2$$

- From the expressions 3.1 and 3.2 it is clear that we require combitional circuit consisting of two 2-input AND gates for the conversion. The resulting conversion diagram is as shown in Fig. 3.24.

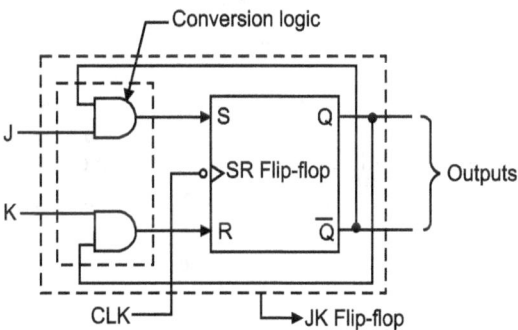

Fig. 3.24

(2) S-R to T conversion :

- It is not possible to convert S-R flip flop to T flip flop as the input condition S = R = 1 is not allowed.

(3) S-R to D conversion :

- Using the directions given for S-R to JK conversion we construct the truth table 3.13 for S-R to D conversion.

Table 3.13 : Truth table for S-R to D conversion.

Cell No	Desired FF data input	Present State	Base FF Data inputs	
	D	Q	S	R
0	0	0	0	×
2	1	0	1	0
1	0	1	0	1
3	1	1	×	0

- k map for S ⇒

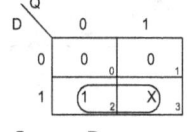

$$\therefore \quad S \; = \; D \qquad\qquad\qquad ... 3.3$$

- k map for R ⇒

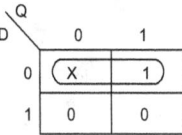

$$\therefore \quad R \; = \; \bar{D} \qquad\qquad\qquad ... 3.4$$

- From the expressions 3.3 and 3.4 it is clear that we require combinational circuit consisting of one NOT gate for the conversion. The resulting conversion diagram is as shown in Fig. 3.25.

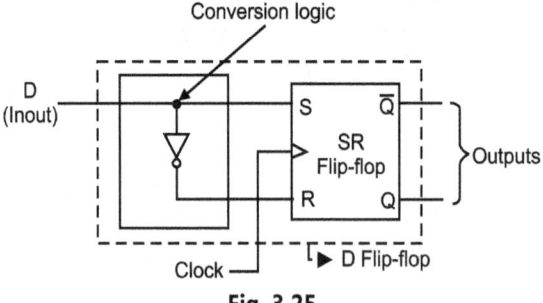

Fig. 3.25

Example 3.6 :

Convert JK flip flop into T and D flip flop

Solution : (1) JK to T conversion :

- Construct the truth table 3.14 for JK to T conversion.

Table 3.14 : Truth table for JK to T conversion

Cell No	Desired FF data input	Present State	Base FF data input	
	T	Q	J	K
0	0	0	0	×
2	1	0	1	×
3	1	1	×	1
1	0	1	×	0

- k maps for J ⇒

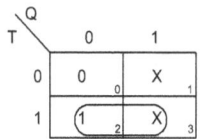

$$\therefore \ J \ = \ T \qquad\qquad\qquad ... 3.5$$

- k maps for K ⇒

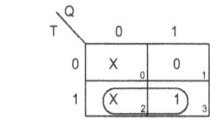

$$\therefore \ K \ = \ T \qquad\qquad\qquad ... 3.6$$

- From the expression 3.5 and 3.6 it is clear that J and K inputs are to be connected together to get the single T input, for the conversion. The resulting conversion diagram is as known in Fig. 3.26.

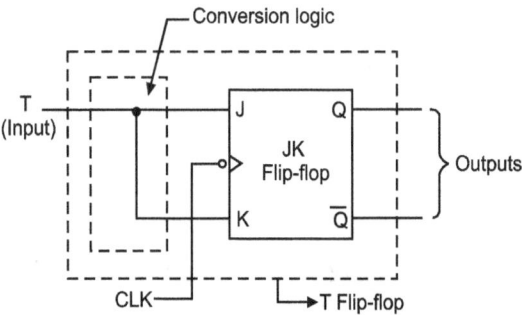

Fig. 3.26 : Logic diagram for conversion of JK FF to TFF

(2) JK to D conversion :

- Construct the truth table 3.15 for JK to D conversion.

Table 3.15 : Truth table for JK to D conversion.

Cell No	Desired FF data input	Present State	Base FF data input	
	D	Q	J	K
0	0	0	0	×
2	1	0	1	×
1	0	1	×	1
3	1	1	×	0

- k map for J=>

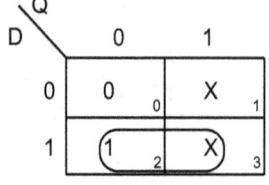

$$\therefore \quad J \quad = \quad D \qquad \qquad ... 3.7$$

- k map for K=>

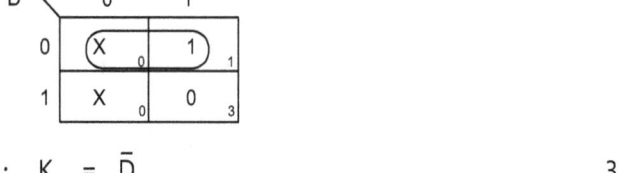

$$\therefore \quad K \quad = \quad \bar{D} \qquad \qquad ... 3.8$$

- From the expression 3.7 and 3.8, it is clear that we require combinational circuit consisting of one NOT gate for the conversion. The resulting conversion diagram is as shown in Fig. 3.27.

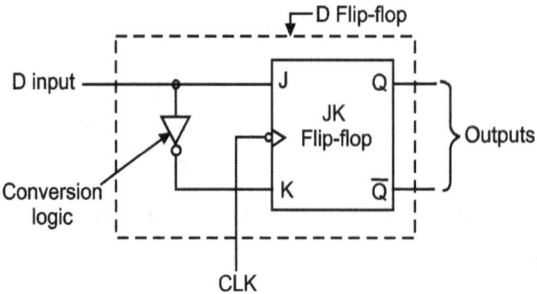

Fig. 3.27 : Logic diagram for conversion from JK FF to D FF

3.13 COUNTERS

- A circuit that counts electrical pulses, applied as input to it is known as counter.

- In practice, these circuits are used as event counters i.e. to count number of events occurred. Electrical pulses are generated corresponding to the occurance of an event and these pulses are given as input to the counters.

- A counter with n flip flops has 2^n possible states. Therefore a three bit up counter can count from 0 to 7 while a four bit down counter can count from 15 down to 0.

- A n bit counter is built with n flip flops. Therefore a three bit counter circuit has three flip flops.

- Number of distinct states in the operation of counter is known as modulus of that counter and that counter is called as mod 2^n counter. In case of three bit counter, the number of distinct states is $2^3 = 8$. Therefore modulus of three bit counter is 8 and it is also called as modulo 2^3 that is modulo 8 or simply mod 8 counter.

- Counters are broadly classified into two categaries-1) Asynchronous counters and 2) synchronous counters. All the flip flops are clocked simultaneously for synchronous counters while external clock input is applied to one flip flop and output of previous stage is connected as clock input of next stage in case of asynchronous counters.

- Based on output sequence the counters are also classified into three categaries-1) Up counter 2) Down counter and 3) Up/down counter

- Up counter- If the decimal equivalent of the counter output increases with successive clock pulses, it is called as up counter. For example in a three bit up counter output goes from 0 to 7.

- Down counter- If the decimal equivalent of the counter output decreases with successive clock pulses, it is called as down counter. For example in a four bit down counter output goes from 15 down to 0.

- Up/down counter- A counter which can count in any direction ie. up or down, depending upon direction control input is called as up/down counter.

3.13.1 Difference between Synchronous and Asynchronous Counters

Q. State the difference between synchronous and asynchronous counters.

[May 07, 2 M, Dec. 07, 4 M]

- All the flip flops are clocked simultaneously in case of synchronous counters. In case of asynchronous counters, external clock is applied to one flip flop and for the remaining flip flops. Output of previous stage is connected as clock input of next stage.
- Synchronous counters are faster than asynchronous counters.
- Synchronous counters can be designed for any count sequence while asynchronous counters can be designed to generate straight binary sequences in up or down directions.
- Design of asynchronous counters is simpler as compared to that of synchronous counters.
- Asynchronous counters can be implemented with only MSJK and T type of flip flop while synchronous counters can be implemented with any type of flip flop.

3.14 DESIGN OF ASYNCHRONOUS COUNTER

- Asynchronous counters are also known as ripple counters.
- In these counters all the flip flops are not clocked simultaneously.
- They are slower than synchronous counters.
- They are designed to generate straight binary sequences in up or down directions.
- Their design is simpler as compared with synchronous counter. We shall discuss the design of asynchronous counters in the following examples.

Example 3.7 :

Design and implement 3-bit asynchronous up counter using flip flops and explain with output waveforms.

Solution :

- For the implementation of 3-bit counter, three flip flops are required.
- The number of distinct states in the operation of this counter is 2^3 = 8. Therefore, it is also called as mod-8 counter.
- In case of 3-bit up counter, the output goes from 0 to 7.
- Let Q_2, Q_1 and Q_0 be the outputs of the three flip flops used for the design. The count sequence is as shown in the table 3.16.

Table 3.16 : Count sequence of 3-bit up counter

Q_2	Q_1	Q_0	State of the counter
0	0	0	0
0	0	1	1
0	1	0	2
0	1	1	3
1	0	0	4
1	0	1	5
1	1	0	6
1	1	1	7

- From the table 3.16 it is clear that the output Q_0 of the least significant flip flop changes for every clock pulse applied to it. So it can be implemented using a T type flip flop with $T_0 = 1$.

- Also, the output Q_1 changes from 0 to 1 or 1 to 0, only when in the corresponding states Q_0 changes from 0 to 1. So it can be implemented using a T-type flip flop with $T_1 = 1$ and Q_0 is connected as its clock input.

- Similarly the output Q_2 changes only when Q_1 changes from 0 to 1. So it can be implemented using a T-type flip flop with $T_2 = 1$ and Q_1 is connected as its clock input. This completes the design and the resulting circuit is as shown as Fig. 3.24.

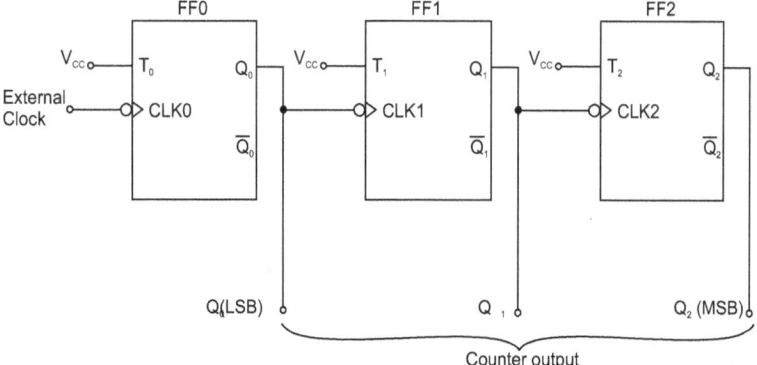

Fig. 3.28 : 3-bit ripple up counter

- The waveforms of the outputs are shown in Fig. 3.29.

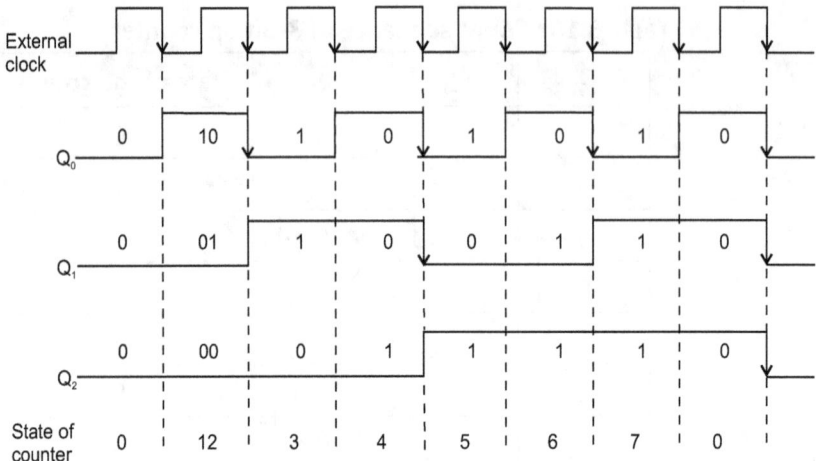

Fig. 3.29 : Waveforms/Timing diagram of 3 bit ripple up counter

- From the waveform of external clock and Q_0, it is clear that two clock periods are required for the completion of one cycle of Q_0. Therefore, clock frequency is twice to that of Q_0 output. In other words the Q_0 is the divide by 2 ($\div$ 2) output with respect to clock frequency. Similarly Q_1 is the divide by 4 ($\div$ 4) output and Q_2 is divide by 8 ($\div$ 8) output with respect to clock frequency.

- Therefore this mod - 8 counter is also known as divide by 8 ($\div$ 8) counter.

Example 3.8 :

Design 3 bit down ripple counter. Draw waveforms.

Solution :

- 3 bit ripple down counter requires three flip flops. The counter output goes from 7 down to 0. The count sequence is as shown in table 3.17.

Table 3.17 : Count sequence of 3-bit down counter.

Q_2	Q_1	Q_0	State of the counter
1	1	1	7
1	1	0	6
1	0	1	5
1	0	0	4
0	1	1	3
0	1	0	2
0	0	1	1
0	0	0	0

- Just like previous example, the least significant stage can be implemented using T flip flop with $T_0 = 1$.

- Output Q_1 changes whenever there is 0 to 1 transition of Q_0, in the corresponding states. So we can realise it with a flip flop which is positive edge triggered. The Q_0 output needs to be connected to the clock input and $T_1 = 1$.

- When Q_0 makes transition from 0 to 1, $\bar{Q}_0$ changes from 1 to 0. So we can realise the second stage by using a negative edge triggered flip flop as shown in Fig. 3.30 with $T_1 = 1$. $\bar{Q}_0$ output needs to be connected as clock input.

- Similarly, the most significant stage can be realised with a negative edge triggered T flip flop with $T_2 = 1$ and $\bar{Q}_1$ connected as its clock input. This completes the design and the resulting circuit is as shown in Fig. 3.30. Also the waveforms of the outputs are shown in Fig. 3.31.

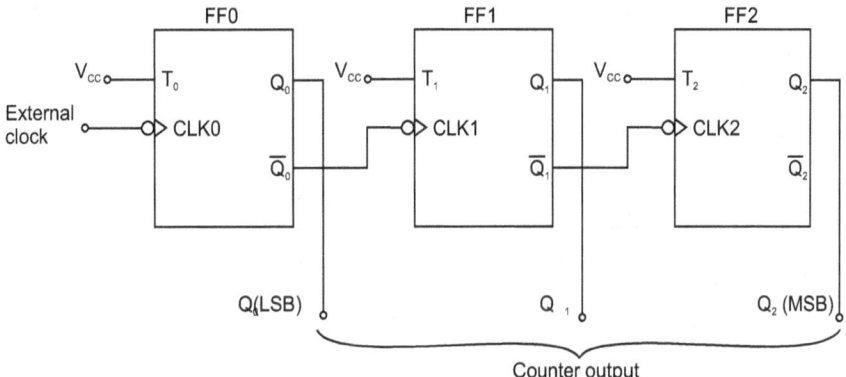

Fig. 3.30 : 3 bit ripple down counter

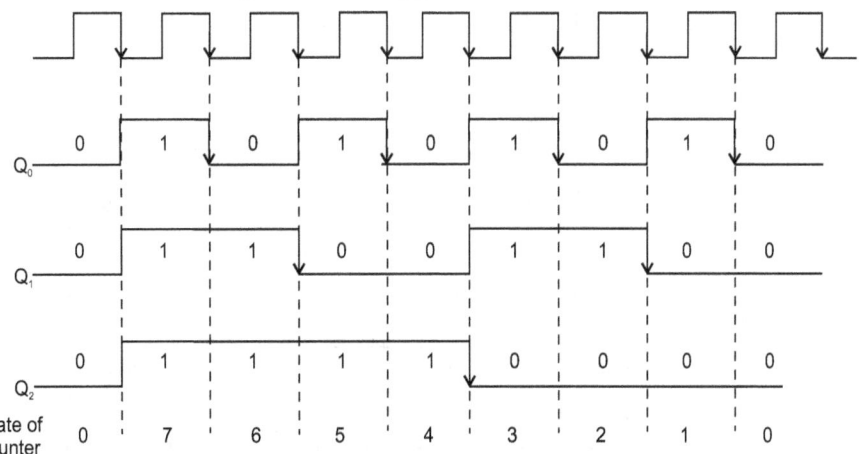

Fig. 3.31 : Waveforms/timing diagram of 3 bit ripple down counter

Example 3.9 :

Design a 4-bit binary Up/Down ripple counter with a control for Up/Down counting. Also draw timing diagram.

Solution :

- From example 3.8, we know that for a ripple up counter Q output of the preceeding stages are to be connected to the clock inputs of next stages.

- We know that for a ripple down counter $\overline{Q}$ outputs of preceeding stages are to be connected to the clock input of next stages.

- Therefore to design a Up/Down counter, AND-OR gates are used between flip flops as shown in Fig. 3.32.

- The upper AND gates are enabled when UP/Down input is at logic 1 which connect Q outputs to the inputs. While the lower AND gates are enabled when UP/Down input is 0 which connect $\overline{Q}$ outputs to the clock inputs. For 4-bit counter, 4 four flip flops are required.

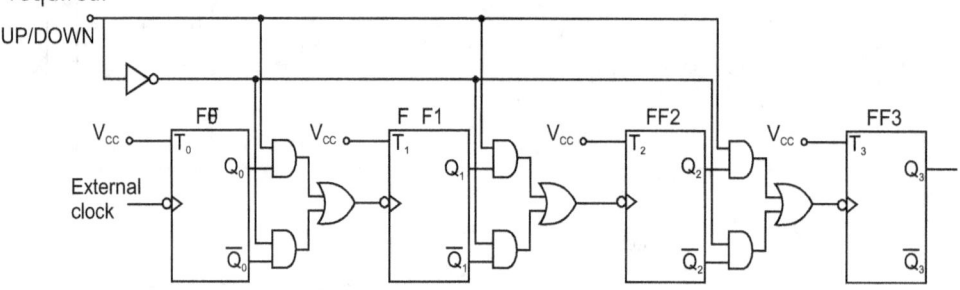

Fig. 3.32 : 4-bit ripple Up/Down counter.

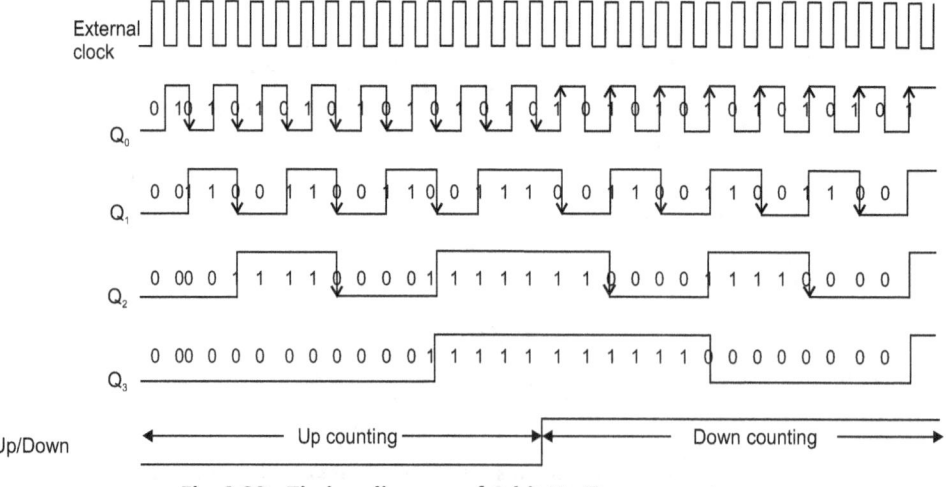

Fig. 3.33 : Timing diagram of 4-bit Up/Down counter

Example 3.10 :

A certain counter is being pulsed by a 256 kHz clock signal. The output frequency from the last flip flop is 2 kHz : (i) Determine the mod of counter (ii) Determine the counting range.

Solution :

- Input clock frequency is 256 kHz and the output frequency from last flip flop is 2 kHz.

- Therefore it is divide by (256/2=128) counter ($\div$ 128).

- As it is a divide by 128 counters, the modulus of counter is also 128. Therefore it is a mod-128 counter.

- The counting range in case of up counter will be from 0 to 127 i.e. the binary output will go from 0000000 to 1111111.

- Similarly, the counting range in case of down counter will be from 127 down to 0 ie. the binary output will go from 1111111 to 0000000.

Example 3.11 :

For the ripple counter shown in Fig. 3.34 below, show the complete timing diagram for eight clock pulses.

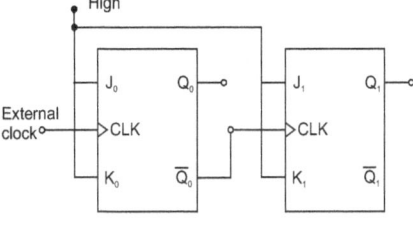

Fig. 3.34

Solution :

- The waveforms are shown in Fig. 3.35.

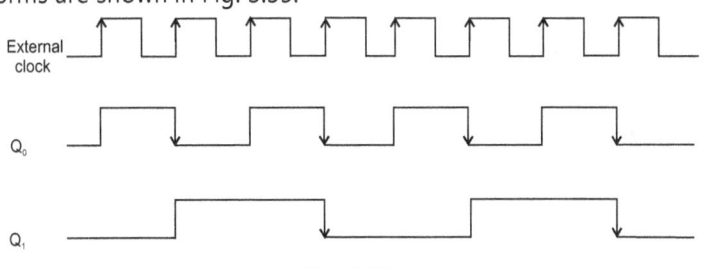

Fig. 3.35

- Here instead of T flip flop, a positive edge triggered JK flip flop is used but J and K inputs are connected together to V_{CC} therefore it becomes a T flip flop with $T_0 = T_1 = 1$.

- The Q_0 output toggles with respect to every positive edge of the clock as shown in the waveform.

- It is shown in the circuit that, $\bar{Q}_0$ output is connected as clock input of the next flip flop which is a positive edge triggered flip flop. Therefore, Q_1 toggles whenever $\bar{Q}_0$ makes transition from 0 to 1 or Q_0 makes transition from 1 to 0 as shown in the waveform.

- From the waveforms, it is clear that the above circuit is a 2 bit ripple up counter.

Example 3.12 :

Design 1-bit counter using S-R flip flop.

Solution :

- 1 bit counter has 2^1 distict states in its operation (mod 2 counter) i.e. the output toggles between 0 and 1 with the application of successive clock pulses. The circuit of 1 bit counter using S-R flip flop is shown in Fig. 3.36. This circuit is also called as S-R toggle switch.

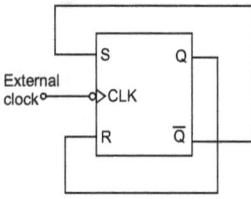

Fig. 3.36

Example 3.13 :

Design BCD ripple counter.

Solution :

- We know that, binary coded decimal (BCD) is in the range from 0 to 9. Therefore modulus of counter is 10.

i.e. $2^n \geq 10$ ...3.9

- For N = 1, N = 2 and N = 3 the inequality 3.9 is not satisfied.

- Putting N=4 in the inequality 3.9 we get,

$$2^4 \geq 10$$
$$\Rightarrow \quad 16 \geq 10$$

- The inequality is satisfied. Therefore for the implementation of BCD counter four flip flops are required.

- Here we shall design a up counter, for which we require four T flip flops with the T inputs connected to V_{CC}. Also Q_0, Q_1 and Q_2 outputs are connected as the clock inputs of the respective next stages.

- In BCD counter the state $Q_3 Q_2 Q_1 Q_0$ = 1010 should not occur i.e. when Q_3 and Q_1 both become 1, at the same instant the counter should be resetted. Therefore we require a 2 input NAND gate as reset logic for BCD counter. The resulting circuit diagram is shown in Fig. 3.37.

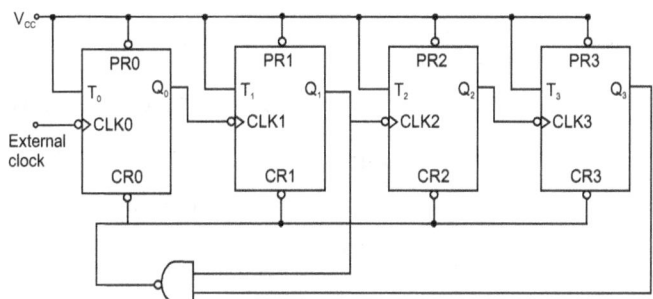

Fig. 3.37 : BCD ripple up counter

3.14.1 Draw backs of ripple counter

Q. Design mod 5 ripple up counter using a 3 bit ripple counter.	**[Dec. 11, 6 M]**
Q. Explain the problem of glitches in asynchronous counter circuits and solution for the same.	**[Dec. 07, 4 M]**
Q. Explain problems faced by ripple counter.	**[Dec. 05, 6 M]**

- Observe the timing diagram of 3 bit ripple up counter shown in Fig. 3.29.

- Upon application of clock pulse, the count sequence proceeds from 7 to 0. That is the output changes from $Q_2 Q_1 Q_0$ = 111 to $Q_2 Q_1 Q_0$ = 000.

- This change from 111 to 000 does not take place simultaneously. As shown in Fig. 3.28 external clock applied to FF0 will change the output Q_0 from 1 to 0 first. Further the 1 to 0 change in Q_0 acts as trigger for FF1 and its output also change from 1 to 0. Now this 1 to 0 transition in Q_1 triggers FF2 to change its output from 1 to 0. In this manner the next state 000 is obtained from the present state 111.

- As explained above, the carry ripples through the circuit, like the ripple in water. Therefore asynchronous counters are known as ripple counters.

- Let us assume that each flip flop shown in Fig. 3.28 has propogation delay of 50 nS duration, the output Q_0 will change from 1 to 0. After another 50 nS duration Q_1 will change from 1 to 0, i.e. after 50 + 50 = 100 ns duration since the clock pulse is applied to FF0. Similarly FF2 will take separate 50 ns duration for the change from 1 to 0. So Q_2 will change after 50+50+50=150 nS duration since the clock pulse is applied to FF0.

- This time period will increase as the numbers of flip flops are increased. This limits the frequency of operation of ripple counters.

- In short, 3 bit ripple up counter requires 150 ns duration to change from state 111 to 000 while synchronous counter all the flip flops are clocked simultaneously, it takes 50 ns duration for the same change. Also this duration is constant for any number of flip flops.

- Thus asynchronous counters are slower than synchronous counters.

- Another drawback of asynchronous counters is that they can generate straight binary sequences in up or down direction while synchronous counters can be designed for any count sequence.

- Also we have to use JK or T flip flops only in the design of asynchronous counters.

3.15 DESIGN OF SYNCHRONOUS COUNTER

- In synchronous counter all the flip flops are clocked simultaneously. Therefore it is faster in operation.

- It can be designed for any count sequence which need not be always straight binary.

- For the design of synchronous counter, first find out the number of flip flops required.

- Then prepare a table consisting of present state, next state and determine the flip flop inputs which must be present to obtain the next state using the excitation table of the flip flop.

- Prepare k-map for each flip flop input and obtain the simplified expressions from which complete the circuit diagram.

Example 3.14 :

Design 3-bit synchronous counter using JK flip flop and explain.   **[Dec. 2006, 8 M]**

Solution :

- We know that for 3 bit counter three flip flops are required.

- The table consisting of present state, next state and the required inputs of flip flop is as shown in table 3.18. Here Q_2, Q_1 and Q_0 represent the present state variables with Q'_2 Q'_1 and Q'_0 represent the next state variables.

Table 3.18

Present state			Next state			Flip flip inputs					
Q_2	Q_1	Q_0	Q'_2	Q'_1	Q'_0	J_2	K_2	J_1	K_1	J_0	K_0
0	0	0	0	0	1	0	×	0	×	1	×
0	0	1	0	1	0	0	×	1	×	×	1
0	1	0	0	1	1	0	×	×	0	1	×
0	1	1	1	0	0	1	×	×	1	×	1
1	0	0	1	0	1	×	0	0	×	1	×
1	0	1	1	1	0	×	0	1	×	×	1
1	1	0	1	1	1	×	0	×	0	1	×
1	1	1	0	0	0	×	1	×	1	×	1

- Observe the first row of the table 3.18. Present state is Q_2 Q_1 Q_0 = 0 0 0 and next state Q'_2 Q'_1 Q'_0 = 0 0 1. For flip flop 2, $Q_2 = Q'_2 = 0$. Therefore, from first row of excitation table of JK flip flop we get the J_2 K_2 input combination as 0 X.

- Similarly for flip flop 1 as $Q_1 = Q'_1 = 0$, the J_1 K_1 input combination is 0 X.

- For flip flop 0, present state = Q_0 = 0 while the next state = Q'_0 =1. Therefore from the second row of excitation table of JK flip flop we get J_0 K_0 input combination as 1 X.

- This completes the first row of the table 3.18. Proceeding in a similar manner, the remaining rows of the table are completed.

- Now we represent each individual input in a k map and obtain the simplified expressions.

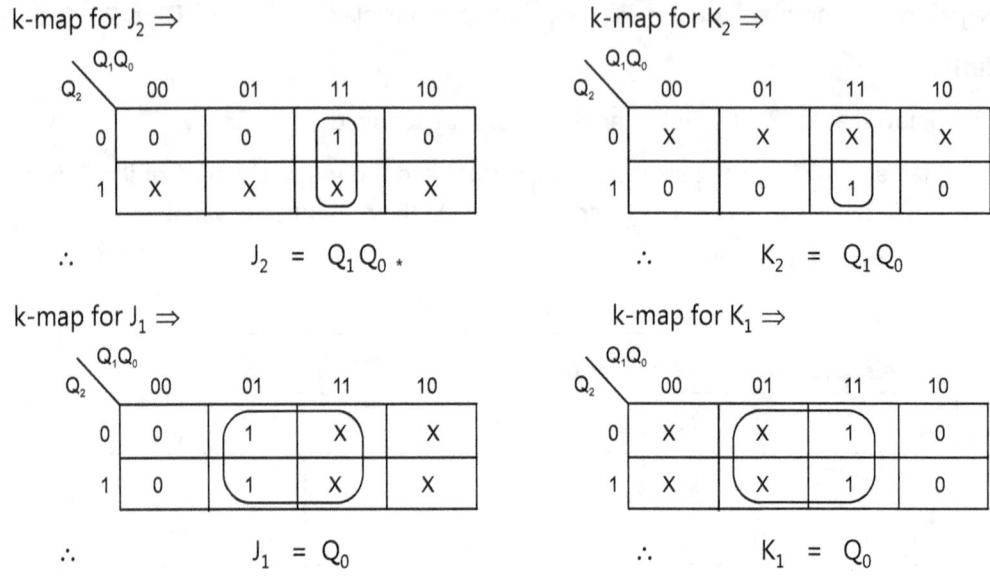

k-map for J_2 $\Rightarrow$

$\therefore \qquad J_2 = Q_1 Q_0$ *

k-map for K_2 $\Rightarrow$

$\therefore \qquad K_2 = Q_1 Q_0$

k-map for J_1 $\Rightarrow$

$\therefore \qquad J_1 = Q_0$

k-map for K_1 $\Rightarrow$

$\therefore \qquad K_1 = Q_0$

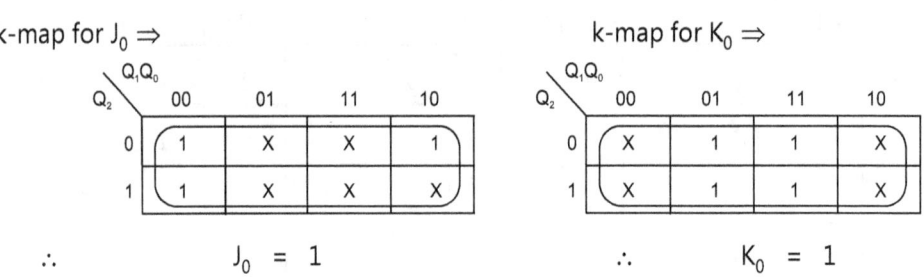

k-map for J_0 $\Rightarrow$

$\therefore \qquad J_0 = 1$

k-map for K_0 $\Rightarrow$

$\therefore \qquad K_0 = 1$

- Based on above expressions, the resulting circuit diagram is drawn in Fig. 3.34.

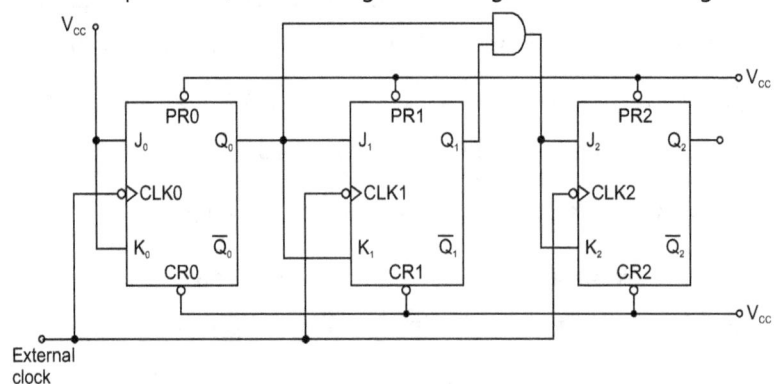

Fig. 3.38 : 3 - bit synchronous up counter.

Example 3.15 :

Design and implement synchronous BCD counter using T flip flops.   **[Dec. 2005, 8 M]**

Solution :

- We know that a BCD counter requires four flip flops.

- BCD counter is a truncated counter. In BCD up counter 0 to 9 are used states while 11 to 15 are unused states. Next state of unused state is unknown. Let it be don't care. Therefore the corresponding flip flop input is also don't care.

- The table 3.19 consist of present state, next state and the required input of flip flop.

Table 3.19

Present state				Next state				Flip flip input			
Q_3	Q_2	Q_1	Q_0	Q'_3	Q'_2	Q'_1	Q'_0	T_3	T_2	T_1	T_0
0	0	0	0	0	0	0	1	0	0	0	1
0	0	0	1	0	0	1	0	0	0	1	1
0	0	1	0	0	0	1	1	0	0	0	1
0	0	1	1	0	1	0	0	0	1	1	1
0	1	0	0	0	1	0	1	0	0	0	1
0	1	0	1	0	1	1	0	0	0	1	1
0	1	1	0	0	1	1	1	0	0	0	1
0	1	1	1	1	0	0	0	1	1	1	1
1	0	0	0	1	0	0	1	0	0	0	1
1	0	0	1	0	0	0	0	1	0	0	1

- Now we represent each individual input in a k-map and obtain the simplified expressions.

k-map for T_3 ⇒

k-map for T_2 ⇒

∴ $T_3 = Q_3 Q_0 + Q_2 Q_1 Q_0$ ∴ $T_2 = Q_1 Q_0$

k-map for $T_1 \Rightarrow$

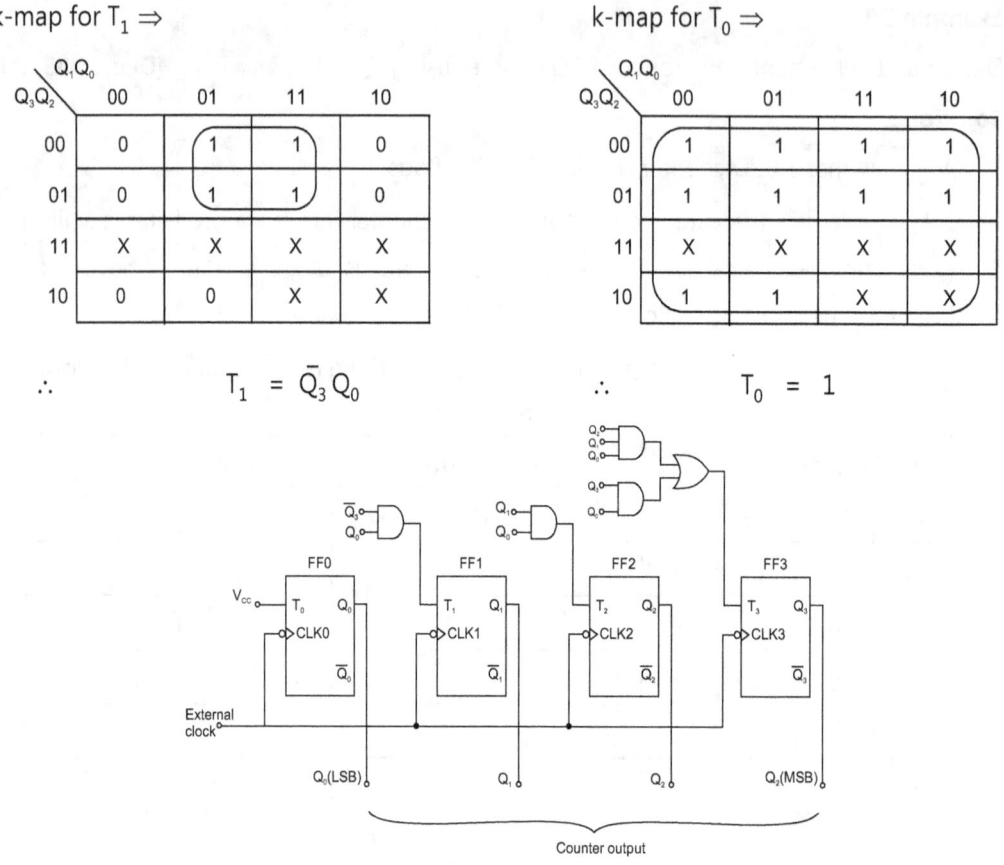

k-map for $T_0 \Rightarrow$

$\therefore \qquad\qquad T_1 = \bar{Q}_3 Q_0 \qquad\qquad\qquad \therefore \qquad\qquad T_0 = 1$

Fig. 3.39

Based on the above expressions the resulting circuit diagram is shown in Fig. 3.39.

Example 3.16 :

Design mod-12 synchronous counter using D flip flop.

Solution :

- For the implementation of MOD-12 counter four D flip flops are required.

- It is also a truncated counter. 0 to 11 are used states while 12 to 15 are unused states.

- Next state of unused state is unknown. Let it be don't care. Therefore the corresponding flip flop input is also don't care.

- The table 3.20 consist of present state, next state and the required input of flip flop.

Table 3.20

Present state				Next state				Flip flip input			
Q_3	Q_2	Q_1	Q_0	Q'_3	Q'_2	Q'_1	Q'_0	D_3	D_2	D_1	D_0
0	0	0	0	0	0	0	1	0	0	0	1
0	0	0	1	0	0	1	0	0	0	1	0
0	0	1	0	0	0	1	1	0	0	1	1
0	0	1	1	0	1	0	0	0	1	0	0
0	1	0	0	0	1	0	1	0	1	0	1
0	1	0	1	0	1	1	0	0	1	1	0
0	1	1	0	0	1	1	1	0	1	1	1
0	1	1	1	1	0	0	0	1	0	0	0
1	0	0	0	1	0	0	1	1	0	0	1
1	0	0	1	1	0	1	0	1	0	1	0
1	0	1	0	1	0	1	1	1	0	1	1
1	0	1	1	0	0	0	0	0	0	0	0

- Now we represent each individual input in a k-map and obtain the simplified expressions.

k-map for $D_3 \Rightarrow$ k-map for $D_2 \Rightarrow$

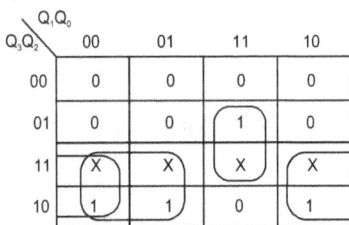   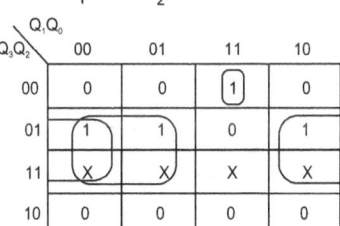

$$D_3 = Q_3\bar{Q}_1 + Q_3\bar{Q}_0 + Q_2Q_1Q_0$$ $$D_2 = Q_2\bar{Q}_1 + Q_2\bar{Q}_0 + \bar{Q}_3\bar{Q}_2Q_1Q_0$$

k-map for $D_2 \Rightarrow$ k-map for $D_0 \Rightarrow$

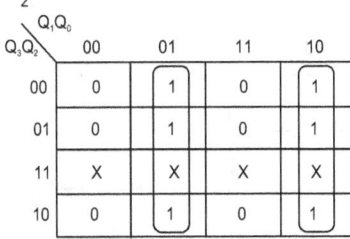   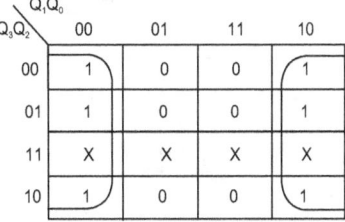

$$D_1 = \bar{Q}_1Q_0 + Q_1\bar{Q}_0 = Q_1 \oplus Q_0$$ $$D_0 = \bar{Q}_0$$

- Based on above expressions the resulting circuit diagram is shown in Fig. 3.40.

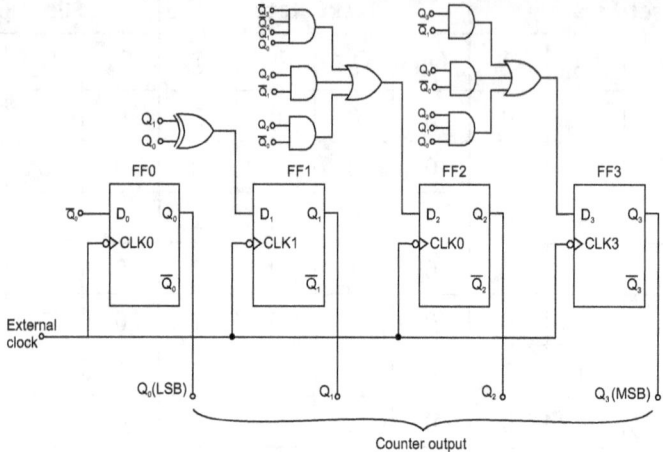

Fig. 3.40

Example 3.17 :

Design synchronous counter using D flip flop for the sequence as shown in Fig. 3.41.

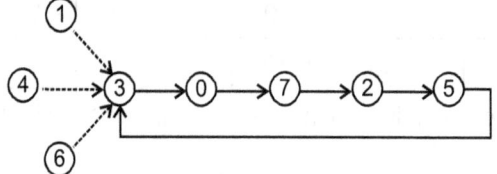

Fig. 3.41

Solution :

- From Fig. 3.41, it is clear that number of states are 8. Therefore three D flip flops are required to design the counter.

- The table 3.21 consist of present state, next state and the required input of flip flop.

Table 3.21

Present state			Next state			Flip flip input		
Q_2	Q_1	Q_0	Q'_2	Q'_1	Q'_0	D_2	D_1	D_0
0	0	0	1	1	1	1	1	1
0	0	1	0	1	1	0	1	1
0	1	0	1	0	1	1	0	1
0	1	1	0	0	0	0	0	0

1	0	0	0	1	1	0	1	1
1	0	1	0	1	1	0	1	1
1	1	0	0	1	1	0	1	1
1	1	1	0	1	0	0	1	0

- As shown in Fig. 3.41, for present state 3 next state is 0, similarly for present state 0 next state is 7 etc. Based on this, the table 3.21 is prepared.

- Also in this counter, 3, 0, 7, 2 and 5 are called as used states while 1, 4, and 6 are called as 'unused states'.

- For every unused state the next state assigned is 9, used state. Therefore we can say that this circuit is designed to avoid lock out condition.

- Now we represent each individual input in k-map and obtain the simplified expressions.

k-map for $D_2 \Rightarrow$

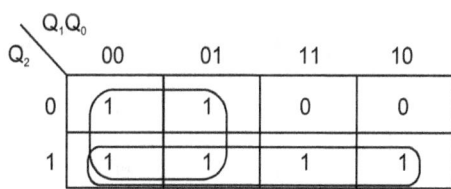

$$D_2 = \bar{Q}_2\, \bar{Q}_0$$

k-map for $D_1 \Rightarrow$

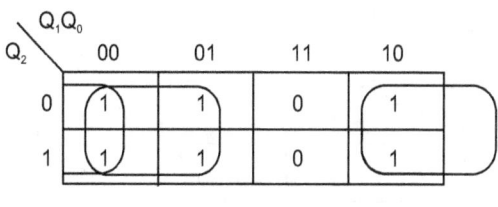

$$D_1 = \bar{Q}_1 + \bar{Q}_2$$

k-map for $D_0 \Rightarrow$

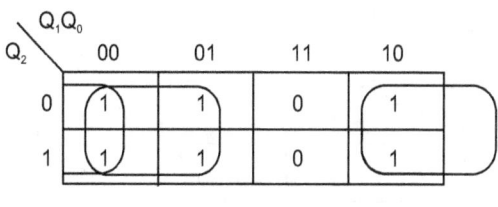

$$D_0 = \bar{Q}_1 + \bar{Q}_0$$

- Based on above expressions, the resulting circuit diagram is shown in Fig. 3.42.

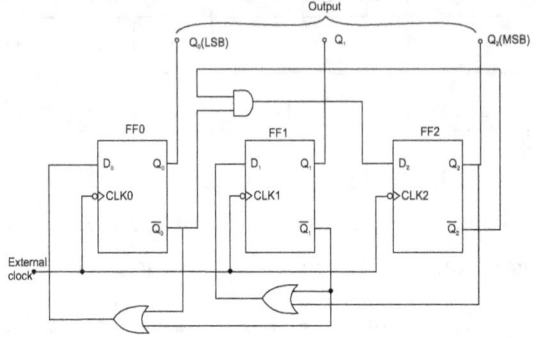

Fig. 3.42

Example 3.18 :

Using JK flip flops design a synchronous counter that has the following sequence.

---------- $0 \rightarrow 2 \rightarrow 5 \rightarrow 6 \rightarrow 0$ --------

Unused states 1, 3, 4, 7 must always go to 0 on the next clock pulse.

Solution :

- From the given sequence it is clear that number of states are 8. Therefore three JK flip flops are required to design the counter.

- The table consist of present state, next state and the required inputs of the flip.

Table 3.22

Present state			Next state			Flip flip inputs					
Q_2	Q_1	Q_0	Q'_2	Q'_1	Q'_0	J_2	K_2	J_1	K_1	J_0	K_0
0	0	0	0	1	0	0	×	1	×	0	×
0	0	1	0	0	0	0	×	0	×	×	1
0	1	0	1	0	1	1	×	×	1	1	×
0	1	1	0	0	0	0	×	×	1	×	1
1	0	0	0	0	0	×	1	0	×	0	×
1	0	1	1	1	0	×	0	1	×	×	1
1	1	0	0	0	0	×	1	×	1	0	×
1	1	1	0	0	0	×	1	×	1	×	1

- Now we represent each individual input in a k-map and obtain the simplified expressions.

k-map for $J_2 \Rightarrow$ k-map for $K_2 \Rightarrow$

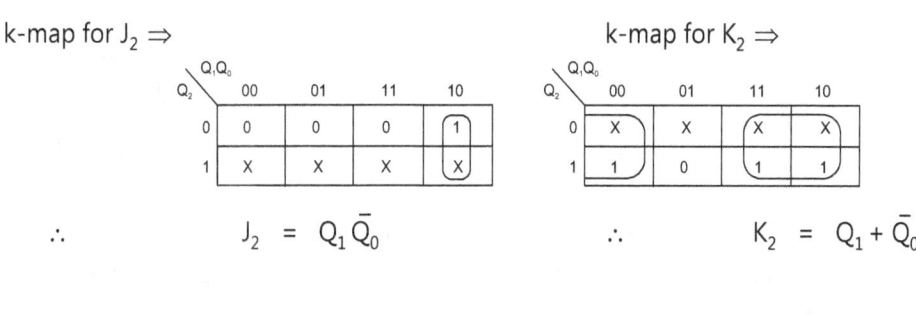

$$\therefore \quad J_2 = Q_1 \bar{Q}_0 \qquad\qquad\qquad \therefore \quad K_2 = Q_1 + \bar{Q}_0$$

k-map for $J_1 \Rightarrow$ k-map for $K_1 \Rightarrow$

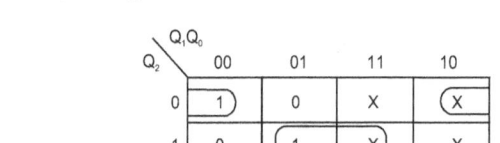 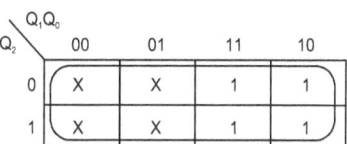

$$\therefore \ J_1 = \bar{Q}_2 \bar{Q}_0 + Q_2 Q_0 = \overline{Q_2 \oplus Q_0} \qquad\qquad \therefore \qquad K_1 = 1$$

k-map for $J_0 \Rightarrow$ k-map for $K_0 \Rightarrow$

$$\therefore \quad J_0 = \bar{Q}_2 Q_1 \qquad\qquad\qquad \therefore \quad K_0 = 1$$

Based on above expressions the resulting circuit diagram is shown in Fig. 3.43.

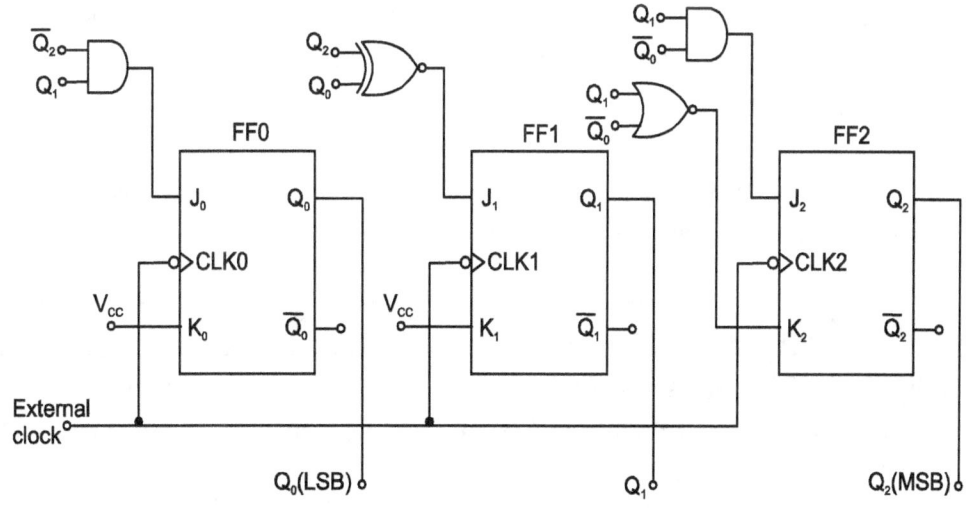

Fig. 3.43

3.15.1 Unused states and lock out condition

Q. Describe lock out condition.	**[May 07, 2 M]**
Q. Comment on : Lock out condition.	**[Dec. 06, 2 M]**

Unused states :

• In example 3.18, 1, 3, 4 and 7 states are known as unused states, while 0, 2, 5 and 6 states are known as used states. Upon application of successive clock pulses the counter output goes from 0 to 2, 2 to 5, 5 to 6, 6 to 0 and then the cycle repeats. Therefore these are known as used states.

• Counter output never goes to 1, 3, 4 and 7 states, therefore they are known as unused states.

Lock out condition :

• If the counter output goes to unused state and the next state of it is also another unused state and it repeats again and again so that counter never goes to used state, then that counter is said to be in lock out condition.

• In example 3.20 suppose the counter goes to unused state 1 and upon application of successive clock pulses it goes through a series of unused states as shown below.

$$1 \rightarrow 3 \rightarrow 4 \rightarrow 7$$

Then it is said that the counter is in lock out condition.

• If the counter goes into lock out condition, then it becomes useless as it can not generate correct output.

• Lock out condition can be avoided by assigning next state as used state, for every unused state. So whenever counter finds itself in one of the unused state then upon application of clock pulse automatically it will come to the used state and will produce the correct output.

• In example 3.20 the counter is designed to avoid lock out condition as for every unused state 1, 3, 4 and 7 the next assigned state is 0, which is a used state.

3.16 REGISTERS

Registers are used for storing digital information.

• We know that, a flip flop can store 1 bit information, therefore it is also known as 1 bit register.

• The basic building block of the register is flip flop. A n-bit register consist of n flip flops.

- D flip flop is used for the construction of registers. S-R flip flop and JK flip flop converted into D flip flop are also used in registers.

- Registers are the inherent part of the architecture of any microprocessor or microcontroller. For example Intel's 8086 microprocessor consist of various 16-bit registers like AX, BX, CX, DX etc.

3.16.1 Modes of operation of registers

- There are four modes of operation of registers which depend upon the way in which data is written into and read from the registers.

- The data can be written into and read from the registers in two different ways-

  (1) serial and (2) parallel.

- If the read or write operation is performed bit by bit then it becomes serial mode while if it is performed with all bits simultaneously then it becomes parallel mode.

- Serial mode requires a number of clock pulses equal to the number of bits to be written into or read from the register. But has the advantage that, it requires single line for the write or read operation.

- Parallel mode requires no clock pulse for read or write operation (asynchronous loading). So it is faster than serial mode. But has the dis-advantage that, it requires a number of lines equal to number of bits in the register for write or read operation.

- Based on the serial or parallel technique of read or write operation, the four modes of operation of registers are as below.

  (1)   Serial in serial out (SISO)

  (2)   Serial in parallel out (SIPO)

  (3)   Parallel in serial out (PISO) and

  (4)   Parallel in parallel out (PIPO)

3.17 SHIFT REGISTER

> **Q.** Explain modes of operation of shift register.   **[May 07, 4 M]**
>
> **Q.** Draw the logical diagram of 4-bit shift register. Explain how shift register right operation is performed.

- In case of serial write or serial read operation with register the data bits are shifted from one flip flop to another with the application of clock pulses. Such register is known as shift register.

- Thus, in case of shift registers either read, write or both operations are performed in a serial manner.
- There are three modes of operation of shift registers.
  - (1) Serial in serial out (SISO)
  - (2) Serial in parallel out (SIPO) and
  - (3) Parallel in serial out (PISO)
- A 4-bit shift register using D flip flops is shown in Fig. 3.44.

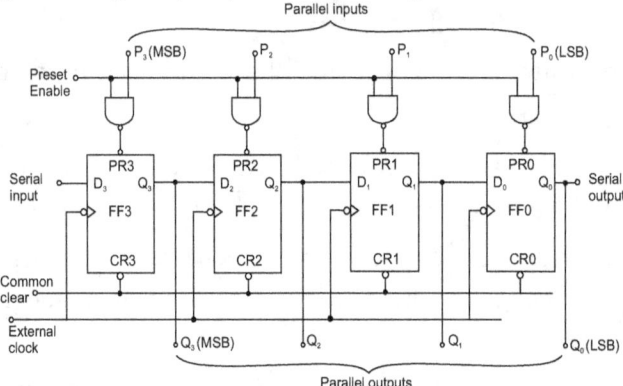

Fig. 3.44 : 4 bit shift register

- Serial in, serial out, parallel in and parallel out operation of the circuit shown in Fig. 3.42 is explained here with a data word 1101.

(1) Serial in

- First all flip flops are cleared (resetted) by connecting common clear terminal to ground. Therefore $Q_3 = Q_2 = Q_1 = Q_0 = 0$. Then for normal operation the clear input of all flip flops is disabled by connecting it to V_{cc}. Also preset enable is connected to ground so that the preset input of all flip flops is disabled.
- The data word is applied at the serial input in a bit by bit fashion.
- At start the LSB of the data word is applied at the serial input. Upon application of clock pulse the output of FF3 becomes 1 while all other outputs remain same. Therefore, $Q_3 = 1$ and $Q_2 = Q_1 = Q_0 = 0$.
- Now the input corresponding to next bit (0) is applied and upon application of second clock pulse, the flip flop outputs becomes, $Q_3 = 0$ $Q_2 = 1$ $Q_1 = 0$ and $Q_0 = 0$.
- Similarly, the input corresponding to each bit is applied till the MSB and the bits go on shifting from left to right upon application of successive clock pulses as shown with the waveforms, in the Fig. 3.45. After the fourth clock pulse the outputs of the flip flops are, $Q_3 = 1$ $Q_2 = 1$ $Q_1 = 0$ and $Q_0 = 1$.

- In this way the data word 1101 gets stored in the register. It requires four clock pulses to store the data.

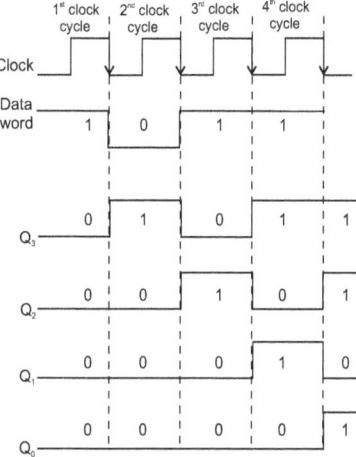

Fig. 3.45 : Waveforms of shift register for data word 1101

(2) Serial out :

- The stored information in shift register can read in serial or parallel form. The data in serial form is obtained at Q_0 output which is known as serial output.

- Upon application of clock pulses the data will get shifted in the right direction and can read bit by bit at Q_0. The number of clock pulses required will be same as the number of bits.

- Thus, for reading the word 1101 serially, it will require four clock pulses.

(3) Parallel in :

- To write the data in parallel form, preset input of the flip flops is used. Initially all flip flops are cleared using common clear input.

- The preset input of all flip flops can be enabled by applying logic 1 at the preset enable input. Therefore one of the input of NAND gates is at logic 1.

- The data to be entered is applied at the parallel inputs as shown in Fig. 3.43. For storing data 1101, it is applied at parallel inputs in the following manner.

$$P_3 = 1, P_2 = 1, P_1 = 0 \text{ and } P_0 = 1$$

- When the parallel input is 1, both inputs of NAND gate become 1, therefore its output is 0. This logic 0 is applied at the active low preset input of the flip flop and the output of the corresponding flip flop becomes 1. i.e. 1 gets stored in that flip flop.

- When the parallel input is 0, one of the inputs of the NAND gates becomes 0, therefore its output is 1. We know preset is active low input of the flip flop, so it gets deactivated. There is no change in the output of flip flop.

- In this way, the data word 1101 gets loaded in the register.

- This method of entering data through preset input of the flip flop is known as asynchronous loading which require no clock pulse.

- Data can be entered in parallel form synchronously by applying individual bits at the D inputs of flip flops directly. This method requires one clock pulse for loading. It is called as synchronous loading.

(4) Parallel out :

- Data in parallel form is available at individual output of the flip flops Q_3 ,Q_2 ,Q_1 and Q_0 and can be read directly without need of any clock pulse.

- Further in parallel form, the data can be read any number of times while in serial form it can be read only once as the data gets shifted out of register and the register becomes empty.

3.18 BI-DIRECTIONAL SHIFT REGISTER

Q. Draw the logical diagram of 4-bit bidirectional shift register. Explain shift left and right shift operation.   **[Dec. 08, 8 M]**
Q. Draw 4-bit bidirectional shift register.   **[May 07, 4 M]**
Q. Draw the circuit and explain the function of 4-bit bidirectional shift register. Draw the waveform.   **[May 08, 8 M]**
Q. Explain with the help of neat diagram, the operation of 4-bit bi-directional shift register how to load delta word ABCD = 1101 in the same using shift left mode.   **[Dec. 04, 8 M]**

- We know that, the register in which upon application of clock pulses data gets shifted from one flip flop to another are known as shift registers.

- In a shift register, with the successive clock pulses when the data gets shifted in right direction, it is known as right shift register.

- Similarly when the data gets shifted in left direction with the application of clock pulses, it is known as left shift register.

- The register in which data can be shifted in both, left direction and right direction is called as bi-directional shift register.

- The diagram of 4-bit bi-directional shift register is as shown in Fig. 3.46.

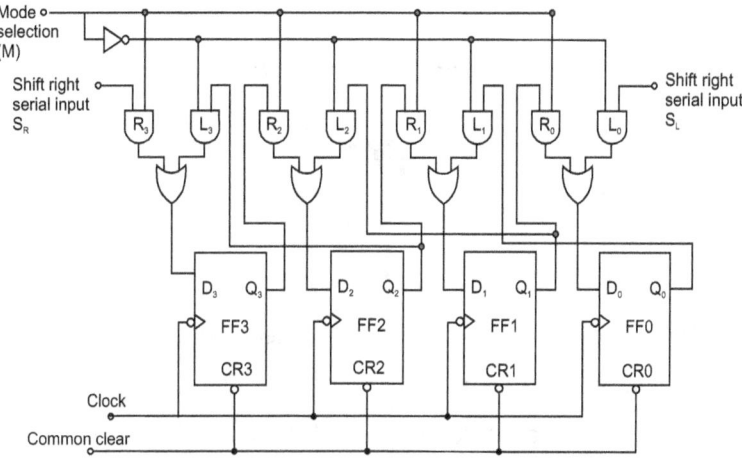

Fig. 3.46 : 4-bit bi-directional shift register

- When the mode selection input M=1, the bidirectional shift register acts as a right shift register. The AND gates R_3 ,R_2 ,R_1 and R_0 are enabled.

- When the mode selection input M=0, the bidirectional shift register acts as a left shift register. The AND gates L_3, L_2, L_1 andL_0 get enabled.

- For right shift operation, the data bits are applied at the shift right serial input S_R. As R_3 AND gate is enabled, the data appears at the D_3 input of FF3. Also as R_2, R_1 and R_0 AND gates are enabled, Q_3 output gets connected to D_2 input, Q_2 output gets connected to D_1 input and Q_1 output gets connected to D_0 input.

- Similarly for left shift operation (M = 0) the data bits are applied at the shift left serial input S_L. As L_0 AND gate is enabled, the data appears at the D input of FF0. Also as L_1, L_2, and L_3 AND gates are enable, Q_0 output gets connected to D_1 input. Q_1 output gets connected to D_2 input and Q_2 output gets connected to D_3 input.

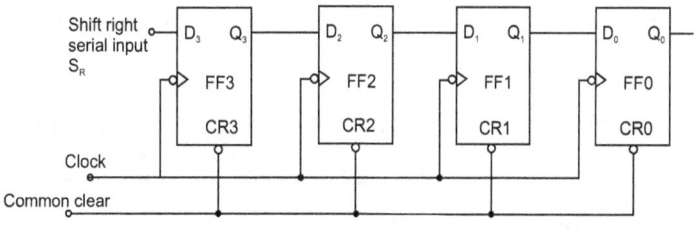

Fig. 3.47

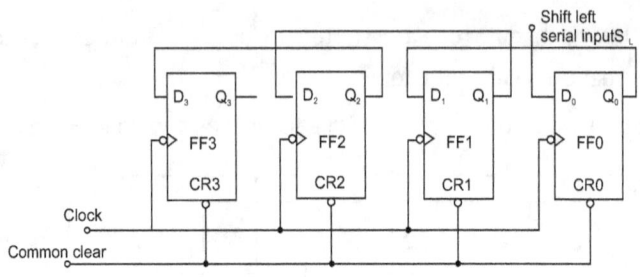

Fig. 3.48

- The shift left mode of the bidirectional shift register shown in Fig. 3.48 is explained here for the data word 1011.

- All the flip flops are cleared first using common clear input.

- In shift left mode, the MSB of the data word is applied at the shift left serial input S_L. Mode selection input is connected to ground. Therefore, the L_0, L_1, L_2 and L_0 AND gates are enabled. Through the AND gate L_0 and associated OR gate, the MSB appears at the D_0 input of the flip flop FF0. Upon application of the clock pulse the MSB gets stored in FF0.

- Similarly input corresponding to each bit is applied till the LSB and the bits go on shifting to left through the L_1, L_2 and L_3 AND gates upon application of successive clock pulses.

- At the end of the second clock pulse the outputs of flip flops are-

  $Q_3 = 0, Q_2 = 0, Q_1 = 1$ and $Q_0 = 0$

- At the end of the third clock pulse,

  $Q_3 = 0, Q_2 = 1, Q_1 = 0$ and $Q_0 = 1$

- At the end of the fourth clock pulse,

  $Q_3 = 1, Q_2 = 0, Q_1 = 1$ and $Q_0 = 1$

- Thus, the desired data 1011 gets stored in the register. The corresponding waveforms are shown in Fig. 3.49.

- Instead of using D flip flop, JK flip flop or S-R flip flop can be used for the construction of the bidirectional shift register. In this case, we need to convert first the JK flip flop or S-R flip flop into D flip flop.

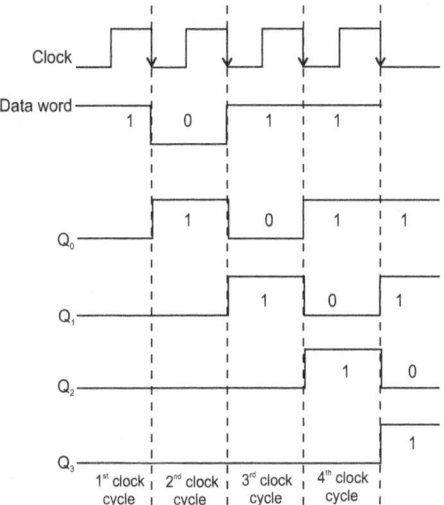

Fig. 3.49 : Waveforms of bi-directional shift register for data word 1011

3.19 UNIVERSAL SHIFT REGISTER

Q. Draw neat circuit diagram of 3-bit bi-directional shift register using J-K flip-flop and explain its operation. **[Dec. 06, 6 M]**

Q. Draw and explain the operation of 3-bit bidirectional shift register. **[Dec. 09, 4 M]**

Q. Explain with the help of neat diagram the operation of a 3-bit universal shift register.
[Dec. 05, 8 M]

- A register which can be operated in all four possible modes of operation (SISO, SIPO, PISO and PIPO) and is also a bidirectional register, is known as universal shift register. A 3 bit universal shift register is shown in Fig. 3.50.

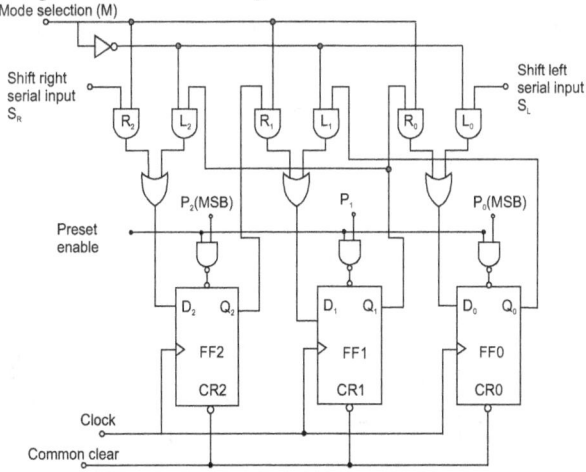

Fig. 3.50 : 3 bit universal shift register

- As shown in Fig. 3.50 the positive edge triggered flip flops are used.

3.20 APPLICATIONS OF SHIFT REGISTERS

Q. State various applications of shift register.   **[May 05, 3 M]**

- Mainly shift registers are used for storage of data. Besides that other important applications are-

1. Serial to Parallel Conversion

Q. Explain how shift register is used as serial to parallel converter.   **[May 10, 2 M]**

- In many applications it is required that the data must be in parallel form. In such cases, the available data in serial form can be converted into parallel form using serial in parallel out (SIPO) shift register as shown in Fig. 3.51.

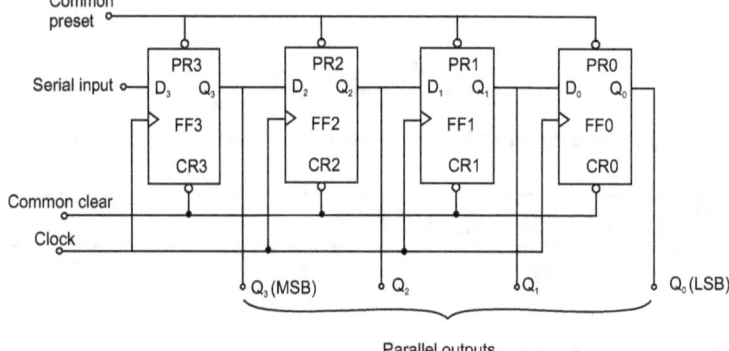

Fig. 3.51 : SIPO register

2. Parallel to Serial Conversion

Q. Explain how shift register is used as parallel to serial converter.   **[May 10, 2 M]**

- In many applications it is required that the data must be in serial form. In such cases, the available data in parallel form can be converted into serial form using parallel in serial out (PISO) shift register as shown in Fig. 3.52.

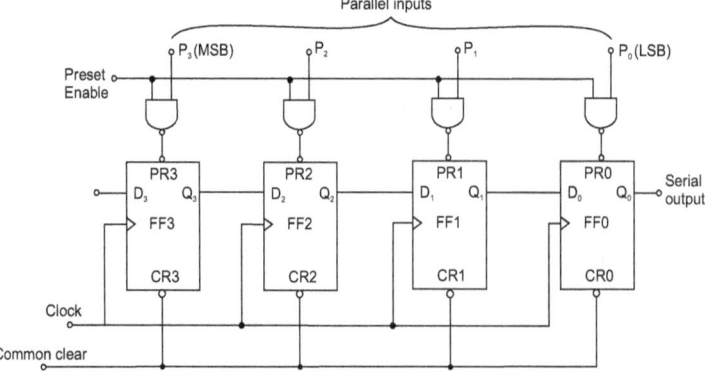

Fig. 3.52 : PISO register

3, Division and Multiplication by Two

- A binary number can be divided by two by shifting it one stage to right and inserting 0 at the MSB position. For example a binary number $1010 = (10)_{10}$ when shifted 1 bit to the right we get $0101 = (5)_{10}$ i.e. it gets divided by two.

- In shifting right, the LSB is lost which causes an error of 0.5 in case of an odd number. For example a binary number $0101 = (5)_{10}$ when shifted 1 bit to the right we get $0010 = (2)_{10}$.

- Similarly a binary number can be multiplied by two by shifting it one stage to left. But in this case, before shifting the MSB must be 0

  For example a binary number $0011 = (3)_{10}$ when shifted 1 bit to the left we get $0110 = (6)_{10}$ i.e. it gets multiplied by two. But when a binary number $1000 = (8)_{10}$ is shifted 1 bit to the left, we get $0000 = (0)_0$ which is a wrong result as the MSB $= 1$ before shifting.

- The other important applications of shift registers are ring counter, Johnson counter and sequence generator which are discussed separately.

3.21 RING AND TWISTED RING COUNTER

- Another important applications of shift register are (1) ring counter and (2) Johnson counter

3.21.1   Ring counter

Q. Explain how shift register is used as ring counter ?   **[May 10, 12, 4 M]**

- The shift register acts as ring counter, if the serial output is connected back to the serial input as shown in Fig. 3.53.

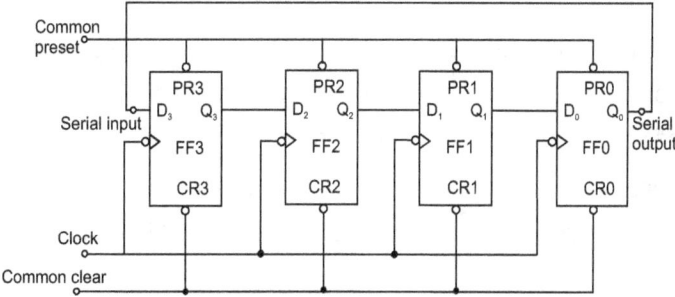

Fig. 3.53 : Ring counter

- Let us consider the initial state of the circuit as $Q_3 Q_2 Q_1 Q_0 = 1000$.

- The output of each flip flop after every clock pulse will be as shown in the table 3.23.

Table 3.23

Clock pulse Number	Q_3	Q_2	Q_1	Q_0
Initially	1	0	0	0
1	0	1	0	0
2	0	0	1	0
3	0	0	0	1
4	1	0	0	0

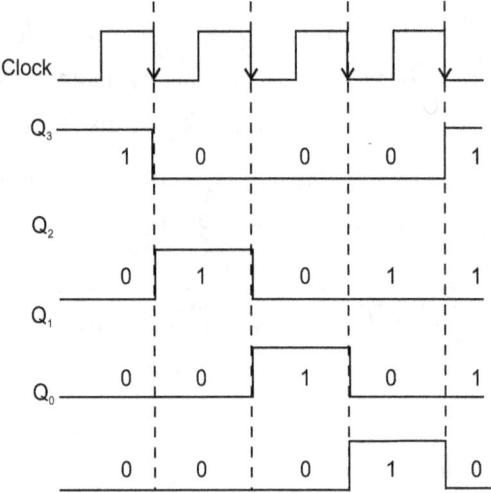

Fig. 3.54 : Waveforms of ring counter

- The n-bit ring counter counts n clock pulses, therefore the circuit shown in Fig. 3.54 counts four clock pulses.

- From table 3.23 it is clear that the number of distinct states in the operation of this counter is four. Therefore, it is a mod - 4 counter. In general n-bit ring counter is mod- n counter. The waveforms are as shown in Fig. 3.54.

- From the waveforms it is clear that, frequency of pulses obtained at any output is equal to frequency of clock pulses divided by four. Therefore this counter is a divide by four ($\div$ 4) counter.

- In general n-bit ring counter is a divide by n ($\div$ n) counter.

- The outputs Q_3, Q_2, Q_1 and Q_0 are sequential non-overlapping pulses which can be used to excite the stepper motor.

3.21.2 Johnson Counter

Q. Explain how shift register are used as twisted ring counter ?   **[May 12, 4 M]**

Q. Design Johnson's counter using 2-bit shift register. Draw waveform.

[May 07, Dec. 08, 4 M]

- It is also known as twisted ring counter or moebius counter.

- The shift register acts as a Johnson counter if the $\overline{Q}_0$ output is connected to the serial input as shown in Fig. 3.55.

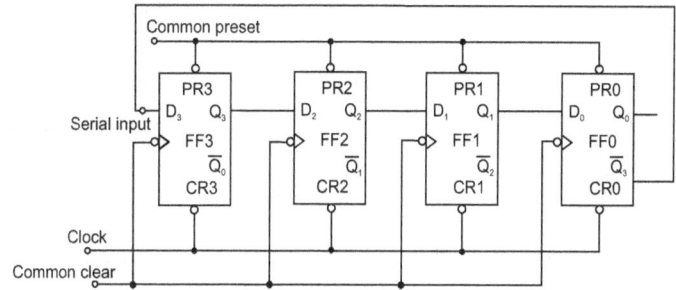

Fig. 3.55 : Johnson counter

- Initially all the flip flops are cleared using the common clear input ie. the initial state of the circuit is $Q_3 Q_2 Q_1 Q_0$ = 0000.

- The output of each flip flop after clock pulse will be as shown in the table 3.24.

Table 3.24

Clock pulse Number	Q_3	Q_2	Q_1	Q_0
Initially	0	0	0	0
1	1	0	0	0
2	1	1	0	0
3	1	1	1	0
4	1	1	1	1
5	0	1	1	1
6	0	0	1	1
7	0	0	0	1
8	0	0	0	0

- From table 3.24 it is clear that the number of distinct states in the operation of this counter is eight. Therefore it is a mod 8 counter. In general, every n-bit Johnson counter is a mod 2n counter. The waveforms are as shown in Fig. 3.56.

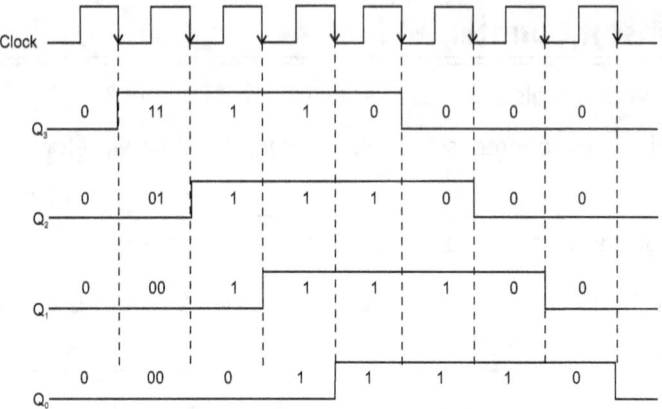

Fig. 3.56 : waveforms of Johnson counter

- As shown in Fig. 3.56 square waveforms are obtained at each flip flop output.
- Also for completion of one cycle, each output requires eight clock pulses therefore it is a divide by 8 ($\div$ 8) counter.
- In general, n-bit Johnson counter is a divide by 2n ($\div$ 2n) counter.

Example 3.19 :

How many flip flops are required to implement each of the following in a Johnson counter configuration : (i) mod 10 (ii) mod 16

Solution :

- We know that a n-bit Johnson counter is a mod 2n countrer where n is the number of flip flops used in counter.

(i) For mod 10 counter,

$$2n = 10$$

$$\therefore \quad n = 5$$

Five flip flops are required, and

(ii) For mod 16 counter.

$$2n = 16$$

$$\therefore \quad n = 8$$

Eight flip flops are required.

Example 3.20 :

Design Johnson counter using 3.-bit shift register.

Draw waveforms

Solution :

- A 2-bit Johnson counter can be designed using two flip flops. When the output of FF0 is connected to the D_1 input of FF1 as shown in Fig. 3.57 we get the 2 bit Johnson counter.

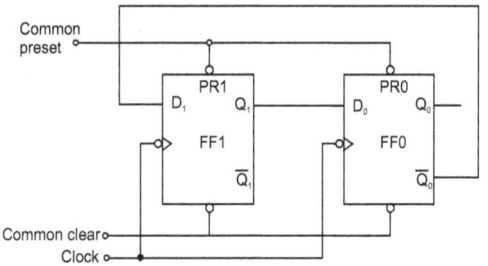

Fig. 3.57 : 2-bit Johnson counter

- The waveforms are shown in Fig. 3.58.

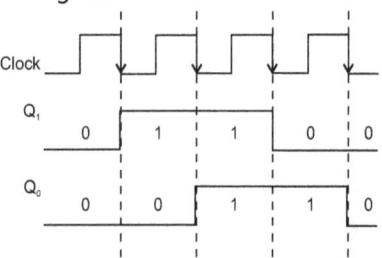

Fig. 3.58 : Waveforms of 2-bit Johnson counter

3.22 SEQUENCE GENERATOR

- Sequence generator circuits can be built with shift registers or flip flops. The two methods are discussed here.

3.22.1 Sequence generator using shift registers

- A circuit that generates prescribed sequence of bits upon application of clock pulses is known as sequence generator.

- For this type of sequence generator shift register is used as the basic building block. The block diagram of it is as shown in Fig. 3.59.

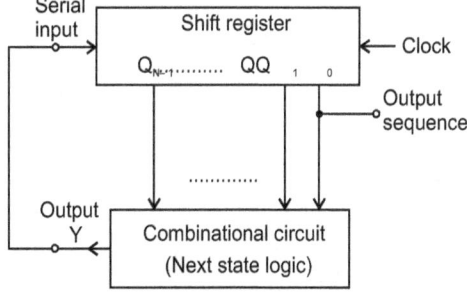

Fig. 3.59 : Block diagram for sequence generator

- As shown in Fig. 3.59, a serial in parallel out (SIPO) shift register is used.

- Depending upon requirement outputs of one or more flip flops of the shift register are connected as input to the combinational circuit which is also known as next state logic. Further the output Y of the combinational circuit is connected as the serial input of the shift register.
- Here main task is to design the combinational circuit that decides the serial input of the flip flop.
- The desired bit pattern (output sequence) is available at the individual output of all flip flops.
- The design procedure is as below.

1. Decide minimum number of flip flops N in the shift register from the length of the sequence L using the relationship.

$$L \leq 2^N - 1 \tag{... (3.10)}$$

2. Write down the desired sequence under the output of flip flop corresponding to the MSB of the shift register and delay it by one or more clock pulses till the LSB. Write the states of the circuit and check all states are distinct or not.

3. If any state is repeating, increase the count of flip flops by one and repeat the above procedure till distinct states are obtained.

4. Prepare the column of output Y and then represent it in a k-map to get the simplified expression.

5. Build the combinational circuit from the simplified expression and connect its output as serial input of shift register.

Example 3.21 :

Design and implement the following sequence generator using shift register.

------ 1010 ------

Solution :

- The length of the given sequence is two. Therefore minimum number of flip flops N can be obtained from equation 3.11

$$L \leq 2^N - 1$$

$$\text{For } N = 1; \ 2 \leq 2^1 - 1$$

The inequality is not satisfied

$$\text{For } N = 2; \ 2 \leq 2^2 - 1$$

The inequality is satisfied.

Therefore number of flip flops required = N= 2

- Now we prepare the state table 3.25.

Table 3.25

Q_1	Q_0	State of the circuit
1	0	2
0	1	1

- The desired sequence is written under the output Q_1 (MSB) and is delayed by one clock pulse for Q_0 (LSB). As shown the states of the circuit are distinct, therefore the given sequence generator can be implemented using two flip flops.
- Now we prepare another table 3.26 showing the state of the circuit and output Y of the combinational circuit.

Table 3.26

State of circuit	Q_1	Q_0	Y
2	1	0	0
1	0	1	1
2	1	0	0

- As shown in Fig. 3.60 the output Y of the combinational circuit is connected as the serial input of the shift register. In this example, output Y is to be connected to D_1 input of FF1. The output Y applied at D_1 will become Q_1 after application of the clock pulse. Therefore whatever state of Q_1 is required during the next clock cycle, the same must be generated by the combinational circuit during the present clock cycle.
- Based on this, the column for output Y is completed. In the second row of table 3.26, $Q_1 = 0$ therefore, in the first row of column Y, 0 is written as indicated with arrow. Similarly, in the second row of column Y, 1 is written.
- Now we prepare a k-map for Y in terms of Q_1 and Q_0,

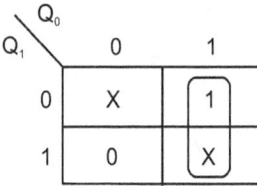

$\therefore$ $Y = Q_0$

- As other two combinations of Q_1, Q_0 such as 00 and 11 do not occur, 'X' is written in the corresponding cell of k-map.
- Based on the above expression the block diagram is shown in the Fig. 3.60.

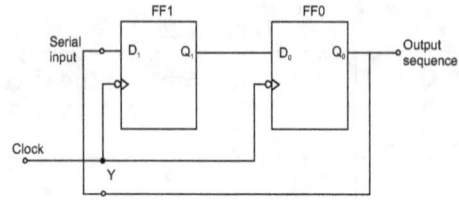

Fig. 3.60

- As $Y = Q_0$, combinational circuit is a simple connection between output Q_0 and serial input D_1. The desired output sequence is available at both outputs Q_1 and Q_0 with the application of successive clock pulses.

Example 3.22 :

Design sequence generator using Shift register to generate sequence 1101.

Solution :

- The length of the given sequence is four. Therefore minimum number of flip flops N can be obtained from the equation.

$$L \leq 2^N - 1$$

- Putting N = 2,

$$4 \leq 2^2 - 1$$

The inequality is not satisfied.

Putting N = 3,

$$4 \leq 2^3 - 1$$

The inequality is satisfied

Therefore, number of flip flops required = N = 3.

- Now we prepare the state table 3.27

Table 3.27

Q_2	Q_1	Q_0	State of the circuit
1	1	0	6
1	1	1	7
0	1	1	3
1	0	1	5

- The desired sequence is written under the output Q_2 (MSB) and is delayed by one clock pulse upto Q_0 (LSB). As shown, the states of the circuit are distinct, therefore the given sequence generator can be implemented using three flip-flops.
- Prepare table 3.28 which shows the state of the circuit and output Y of the combinational circuit.

Table 3.28

State of circuit	Q_2	Q_1	Q_0	Y
6	1	1	0	1
7	1	1	1	0
3	0	1	1	1
5	1	0	1	1

- From table 3.28, the k-map for output Y is prepared.

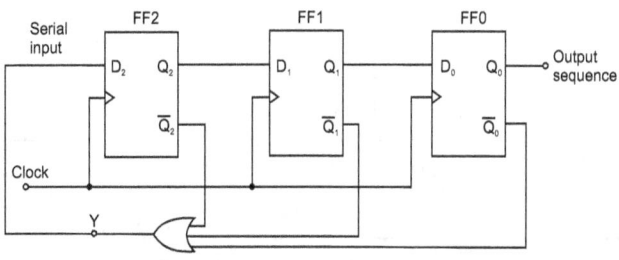

$$ \therefore \qquad Y = \bar{Q}_2 + \bar{Q}_1 + \bar{Q}_0 $$

- Based on the above expression, the block diagram is shown in Fig. 3.61.
- As shown in Fig. 3.61, the combinational circuit consists of 3 input OR gate and its output Y is connected to the serial input D_2 of the shift register. The desired output sequence is available at any of the outputs Q_2, Q_1 and Q_0 with the application of successive clock pulses.

Fig. 3.61

3.22.2 Sequence Generator using Flip-Flops

> **Q.** Design a sequence generator to generate the following sequence 10110.
>
> **[May 12, 4 M]**
>
> **Q.** Design pulse train generator using shift register to generate the following pulse. 10110   **[Dec. 12, 8 M]**
>
> **Q.** Design and implement the following sequence generator using shift register ...1010...   **[Dec. 06, 4 M]**
>
> **Q.** Design a pulse train generator using a shift register for the following pulse train ...1000 110...   **[May 12, 10 M]**

- The sequence generator using flip flops is same as that of design of a synchronous counter.
- The sequence generator using flips flops can be designed to avoid the lock out condition by assigning the next state as used state for every unused state.

Example 3.23 :

Design the circuit to generate the sequence :

$$0 \to 2 \to 5 \to 4 \to 7 \to 3.$$

Solution :

- From the given sequence it is clear that three flip flops are required for the implementation of the circuit. We shall use D flip flop for the design of the circuit.
- First the table 3.29 consisting of present state of the circuit, next state of the circuit and flip flop input is prepared using the excitation table of D flip flop as shown

Table 3.29

Present state			Next state			Flip flop input		
Q_1	Q_2	Q_0	Q'_1	Q'_2	Q'_0	D_1	D_2	D_0
0	0	0	0	1	0	0	1	0
0	0	1	0	0	0	0	0	0
0	1	0	1	0	1	1	0	1
0	1	1	0	0	0	0	0	0
1	0	0	1	1	1	1	1	1
1	0	1	1	0	0	1	0	0
1	1	0	0	0	0	0	0	0
1	1	1	0	1	1	0	1	1

- We now prepare the k-maps for individual input of flip flops and obtain the simplified expressions.

k-map for $D_2 \Rightarrow$

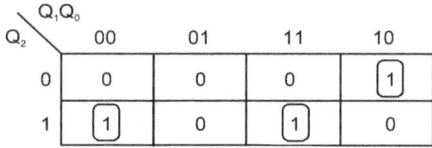

Q_2 \ Q_1Q_0	00	01	11	10
0	0	0	0	[1]
1	[1]	1]	0	0

k-map for $D_1 \Rightarrow$

Q_2 \ Q_1Q_0	00	01	11	10
0	[1]	0	0	0
1	1	0	[1]	0

$\therefore \qquad D_1 = Q_2 \bar{Q}_1 + \bar{Q}_2 Q_1 \bar{Q}_0$

$\therefore \qquad D_1 = \bar{Q}_1 \cdot \bar{Q}_0 + Q_2 Q_1 Q_0$

k-map for $D_0 \Rightarrow$

Q_2 \ Q_1Q_0	00	01	11	10
0	0	0	0	[1]
1	[1]	0	[1]	0

$\therefore \quad D_0 = Q_2 \bar{Q}_1 \bar{Q}_0 + Q_2 Q_1 Q_0 + \bar{Q}_2 Q_1 \bar{Q}_0$

- Based on the above expressions the block diagram can be constructed as shown in Fig. 3.62.

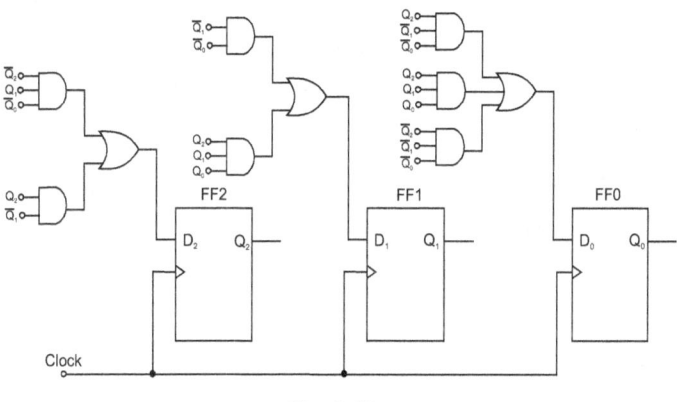

Fig. 3.62

3.23 CLOCK SKEW

Q. Define clock skew.

Q. What are the causes of clock skew?

- Clock skew is a phenomenon in which the clock signal arrives at different components at different times.

- It can be caused by many different things such as :

1. Connecting logic gates to the clock inputs of flip-flops for the clock enable circuit.

2. Wire interconnect length.

3. Temperature variations.

4. Material imperfections and

5. Differences in input capacitance of clock inputs of devices using the clock.

- Clock skew becomes an important issue in the design of circuits operating at higher clock frequencies.

- For proper functionality of the circuit it must be avoided or minimized as much as possible.

3.24 EFFECT ON SYNCHRONOUS DESIGN

Q. Explain effect on synchronous design.

- Consider for example, a circuit that counts digit 1 in a binary number. The circuit consist of a shift register and a counter which are clocked from the same source. The binary number is loaded in the shift register and its LSB is checked for the digit 1. The counter is incremented only when the digit 1 is present at the LSB position of the shift register. The content of the register are then shifted to right by one bit position and the cycle repeats till MSB.

- Suppose the clock skew is present in this circuit so that the clock signal arrives at the shift register earlier than the counter.

- It may cause the shift register to be shifted before the value of its LSB is used to cause the counter to increment.

- This in turn will produce wrong result for the count of 1s in a binary number.

Clock Enable Circuits :

- In many circuits, an enable input is used to prevent a flip-flop from changing its stored value when an active clock edge occurs. It can be implemented as with the circuit as shown in Fig. 3.63.

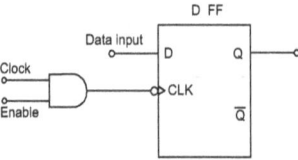

Fig. 3.63

- For the circuit shown in Fig. 3.59 if Enable = 0, AND gate is disabled. In this case, the content of the flip-flop are unaltered as the clock signal does not reach to the flip-flop.

- The content of the flip-flop get changed according to the data input when Enable = 1 which enables the AND gate and the clock signal reaches the flip flop.

- Consider a sequential circuit that has many flip flops and some of which have an Enable input as shown in Fig. 3.64. In such circuit, the flip flops without Enable input will observe changes in the clock signal slightly earlier than the flip flops that have the Enable input.

- Thus, the clock signal arrives at different times at different flip flops which causes the problem of clock skew.

- The clock skew can be avoided with the use of 2 : 1 multiplexer instead of AND gate as shown in Fig. 3.64.

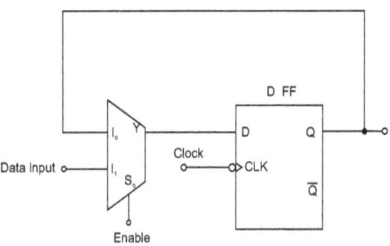

Fig. 3.64

- For the circuit shown in Fig. 3.60 clock signal is independent of the Enable input. Therefore all the flip flops with or without Enable input will get the clock signal simultaneously and the problem of clock skew will not arise.

- Also the stored value of the flip flop does not change as long as the Enable = 0 as channel I_0 of the 2 : 1 multiplexer gets selected and output Q is connected to the input D of the flip flop.

- The content of the flip flop get changed according to the data input when Enable = 1 as channel I_1 of the 2 : 1 multiplexer gets selected.

- The problem of clock skew can be minimized with the use of carefully designed networks of wires to distribute the clock signal to the flip flops. Example of such network is as shown in Fig. 3.65.

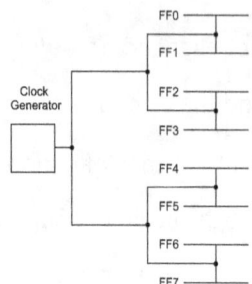

Fig. 3.65

- Flip flops (FF0 to FF7) is shown in the Fig. 3.65. Here the length of the wire between the clock input of each flip flop and the clock generator is same for all flip flops, therefore the clock signal reaches to all the flip flops at the same time which minimizes the problem of clock skew.

STATE MACHINES

4.1 INTRODUCTION

Q. Draw and explain the block diagram of sequential circuit.

- In many applications it is required to generate digital outputs in accordance with the sequence in which the input signals are applied.

- Thus, these applications require that the outputs to be generated are not only dependent on present input conditions. The outputs also depend upon the past history of these inputs.

- The past history is provided by storing it in memory elements and providing a feedback from the output back to the input.

- Such circuits are known as sequential circuits. Block diagram of a sequential circuit is shown in Fig. 4.1.

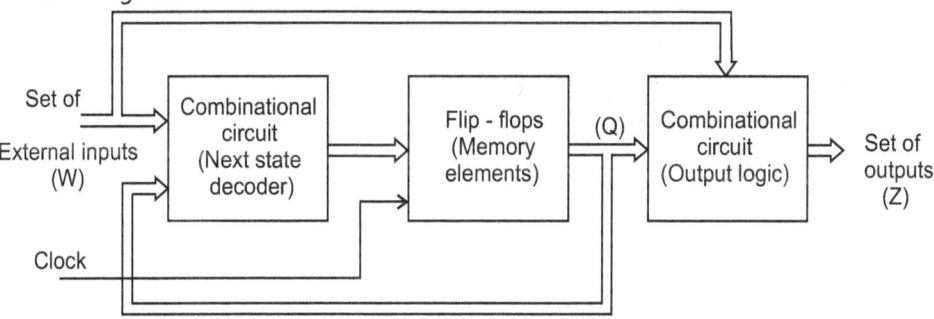

Fig. 4.1 : Block diagram of sequential circuit

- As shown in above Fig. 4.1, the circuit accepts a set of external inputs W and produces a set of outputs Z.

- The values of the outputs of the flip–flops are known as the state Q of the circuit.

- Upon application of clock pulse, the flip flop outputs change their state (circuit goes to next state).

- As shown in Fig. 4.1 the next state of the circuit is decided by the combinational circuit (next state decoder) that provides the inputs to the flip–flops.

- The combinational logic that provides the inputs to the flip–flops, derives its input from two sources (1) set of external inputs (W) and (2) the present state Q of the circuit (outputs of the flip–flops).
- Thus, changes in state depend upon the external inputs as well the present state of the circuit.
- As shown in Fig. 4.1, the outputs of the sequential circuit are generated by another combinational circuit (output logic). The outputs are generated from the present state Q of the circuit and the set of primary inputs W.
- Sequential circuits are also known as finite state machines (FSMs) as the functional behaviour of these circuits can be represented using finite number of states.
- Sequential circuits are broadly classified into two categories :
  (1) Moore type sequential circuits and   (2) Mealy type sequential circuits.

4.2 MOORE AND MEALY MACHINES

Q. Explain Moore circuit with example.	**[Dec. 10, 12, 4 M]**
Q. Explain the difference between Mealy and Moore machine with suitable example.	
	[Dec. 09, 6 M]
Q. Write a short on : Mealy machine Vs Moore machine.	**[Dec. 04, 6 M]**
Q. Explain Mealy circuit with example.	**[May 12, 4 M]**

- Though the outputs of a sequential circuits always depend on the present state Q it is not necessary that the outputs are always dependent on set of external inputs W.
- Based on this, the sequential circuits are classified into these two types.
- In moore machines, the set of outputs Z, depends only on the present state Q of the circuit. Thus, the connection from external inputs to output logic block in Fig. 4.1 is not required. The modified block diagram is as shown in Fig. 4.2

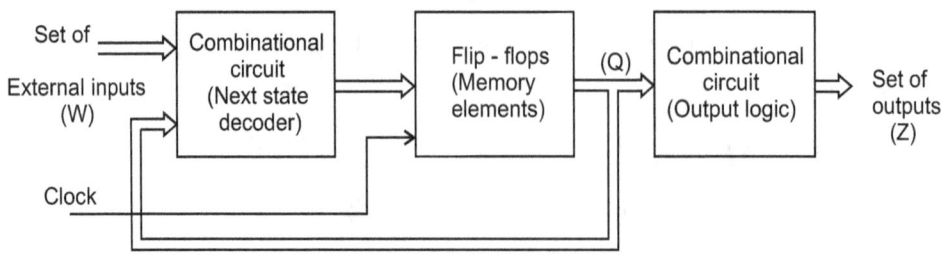

Fig. 4.2 : Block diagram of moore machine

- The block diagram of Fig. 4.1 is the block diagram of Mealy machine. Thus in Mealy machines, the set of outputs Z depends on both, the present state Q of the circuit and the set of primary inputs W.

- The block diagram of Mealy machine is redrawn in Fig. 4.3.

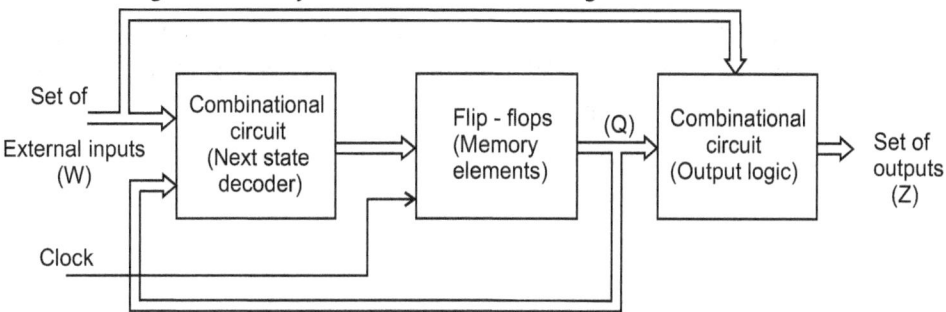

Fig. 4.3 : Block diagram of mealy machine

4.3 STATE DIAGRAM

Q. Explain state diagram.   **[May 05, 06, 11, Dec. 08, 10, 2 M]**

- Behavior of a sequential circuit can be described in different ways. The simplest method uses the pictorial representation known as state diagram.

- In the state diagram the states of the circuits are shown as nodes or circles and the transitions between states are shown as arcs.

- Consider for example, the design of sequential circuit with following conditions.

  (1) The circuit has single input W and single output Z.

  (2) If for two successive clock pulses input W is 1 then the output Z is 1 otherwise it is 0.

  We shall draw the state diagram first, for this example.

- Before we draw the state diagram we must decide, how many states are needed and which transitions are possible from one state to another.

- To start, we select one state as the starting state, also known as reset state. This is the state in which the circuit should enter when the power is turned on or a reset signal is applied. Let this state be 'a'.

- When in state 'a', as long as the input W = 0 , the circuit should remain in the same state. When input W = 1, the circuit should recognize this and move to a different state. Let this state be 'b'.

- In both states 'a' and 'b', the output Z = 0 as the input W is not equal to 1 for two successive clock pulses.

- When in state 'b', the circuit should move back to state 'a' if input W = 0 while it should move to another state if input W = 1. Let this state be 'c'.
- As for two successive clock cycles input W = 1, when the circuit goes to state 'c' output Z becomes 1.
- When in state 'c' the circuit should remain in the same state as long as input W = 1 keeping the output Z = 1. When W = 0, the circuit should move back to state 'a'. Thus this machine requires three states i.e. a, b, and c.
- Based on above discussion, the state diagram is drawn as show in Fig. 4.4.

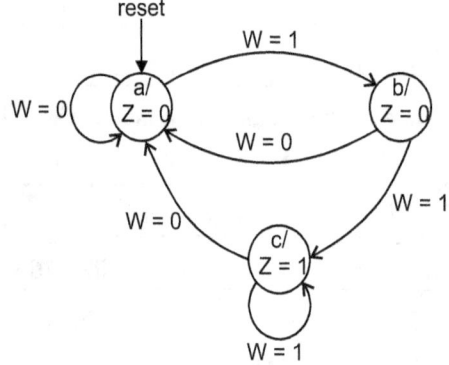

Fig. 4.4 : State diagram

- In the state diagram of Fig. 4.4., three nodes are shown representing three states, whose names are written inside the nodes. Besides that, the status of output is also written inside the node itself.
- Node 'a' represents the starting or reset state and the circuit enters into it upon application of reset input or when power is turned on. In this state Z = 0, therefore inside node 'a' it is written a/Z = 0.
- The circuit remains in state 'a' as long as W = 0, it shown with an arc which is starting and terminating at the same node and the arc is labelled with input condition W = 0.
- When W = 1 the circuit moves to state 'b'. In the state diagram it is shown with an arc which starts at node 'a' and terminates at node 'b' and is labelled as W = 1.
- Similarly, when in state 'b' if the input W = 0 the circuit goes back to state 'a'. It is shown with an arc originating at node 'b' and terminating at node 'a' and labelled as W = 0.
- In this way, the state diagram is completed. As shown in Fig. 4.4., the state diagram is a pictorial representation and it describes the behaviour of the sequential circuit. It uses nodes and arcs for the representation.

4.4 STATE TABLE

Q. Write short note on state table.   **[Dec. 06, May 10, 2 M]**

Q. What is meant by a state table ?   **[May 05, Dec. 09, 1 M]**

- We know that the state diagram provides a description of the behavior of a sequential circuit.
- But to proceed for the implementation of the circuit, it is required to translate the information contained in the state diagram into table known as state table.
- We shall construct the state table for the example discussed in section 4.3
- When the circuit is in state 'a' it goes to state 'b' if the input W = 1 otherwise it remains in state 'a' as long as input W = 0. Also output Z = 0 in state a. This gives the first line of the state table. Similarly the remaining two lines of the state table are completed for the present states 'b' and 'c' respectively. The resultant state table is as drawn in table 4.1.

Table 4.1

Present State	Next state		Output
	W = 0	W = 1	Z
a	a	b	0
b	a	c	0
c	a	c	1

- Thus state table gives all transitions from each present state to the next state for different values of input. It also specifies the output for each present state.

4.5 STATE ASSIGNMENT

Q. Write short note on state assignment.   **[Dec. 06, May 10, 2 M]**

Q. Explain state assignment.   **[Dec. 10, May 11, Dec. 12, 2 M]**

- In the next step, towards the implementation of the circuit it is required that each state to be represented with the combinations of state variables.
- For two states one state variable is required as the two values of one state variable (0 and 1) can be used to represent each of the two states.
- Similarly for four states two state variables are required. The four different combinations of the two state variables (00, 01, 10 and 11) can be used to represent each of the four states.
- Further each state variable is implemented with a flip flop.

- For the example discussed in section 4.3 there are three states, therefore at least two state variables are required for the realization of each state.

- There are four combinations of the two state variables (00, 01, 10 and 11). Each state ('a', 'b', and 'c') can be represented with one of the four combinations of state variables. One possible assignment can be 'a' = 00 'b' = 01 and 'c' = 10.

- Based on this assignment we can prepare a truth table, in which each entry in the column of present state and next state of the state table is replaced with the above combinations of state variables.

- For this example, there are two state variables, therefore two flip-flops are required. Let u_1 and u_0 be the outputs of the two flip–flops. From the block diagram of sequential circuit shown in Fig. 4.1, it is clear that the outputs of the flip - flops represent present state of the circuit. Therefore '$u_1 \, u_0$' become the present state variables. These are denoted with small case letters.

- Similarly as shown in Fig. 4.1 the outputs of the combinational circuit (next state decoder) decide the inputs of the flip–flops which in turn decide the next state of the circuit. Let these be next state variables denoted with the upper case letters as 'U_1, U_0'.

- The truth table with present state variables and next state variables is as drawn in table 4.2.

Table 4.2

Present State	Next state		Output
	W = 0	W = 1	Z
$u_1 \, u_0$	$U_1 \, U_0$	$U_1 \, U_0$	
00	00	01	0
01	00	10	0
10	00	10	1

- The above table 4.2 is known as state assignment table.

- Thus, state assignment table is the modified version of the state table, in which each state is replaced with the combinations of present state variables and next state variables.

- The above table 4.2 does not have the appearance of a normal truth table as there are two separate columns for each value of W for the next state. A simplified table in terms of input W and present state variables '$u_1 \, u_0$' is as drawn in table 4.3.

Table 4.3

Input	Present state		Next state	
W	u_1	u_0	U_1	U_0
0	0	0	0	0
0	0	1	0	0
0	1	0	0	0
0	1	1	×	×
1	0	0	0	1
1	0	1	1	0
1	1	0	1	0
1	1	1	×	×

- As shown in table 4.3 for the present state combination u_1u_0 = 11 the next state is $U_1 U_0$ = XX.

- Out of the four combinations of two state variables we have used only three corresponding to the three states 'a', 'b' and 'c'. As the fourth combination 11 is not used, the next state of it is assumed to be don't care.

- Also in the table 4.3 output Z is absent as the example which we are discussing is of Moore type, in which then output is dependent only on the present state of the circuit and it is not a function of present input.

- The table 4.3 becomes useful when we write the flip flop inputs and k – maps for them before the implementation.

4.6 IMPLEMENTATION

Q. Give the implementation details of sequential circuit.

- So we have discussed the different phases of sequential circuit design such as construction of state diagram, state table and state assignment table with respect to one example.

- The last step of it is the implementation.

- For the implementation first we need to decide the type of flip - flop to be used.

- Then using the excitation table of the desired flip-flop we need to construct the truth table.

- Now each column of the flip - flop input is required to represent in a separate k - map and obtain the simplified expression.

- Based on the simplified expressions, the circuit diagram for the given finite state machine (FSM) can be drawn.

- Let us use JK flip–flop for the implementation of the sequential circuit which we discussed in the last sections.

- Using the excitation table of the JK flip–flop we construct the truth table 4.4,

Table 4.4

Input	Present state		Next state		Flip–flop Inputs			
W	u_1	u_0	U_1	U_0	J_1	K_1	J_0	K_0
0	0	0	0	0	0	×	0	×
0	0	1	0	0	0	×	×	1
0	1	0	0	0	×	1	0	×
0	1	1	×	×	×	×	×	×
1	0	0	0	1	0	×	1	×
1	0	1	1	0	1	×	×	1
1	1	0	1	0	×	0	0	×
1	1	1	×	×	×	×	×	×

- Now we prepare separate k-maps for the flip–flop inputs and obtain the simplified expressions.

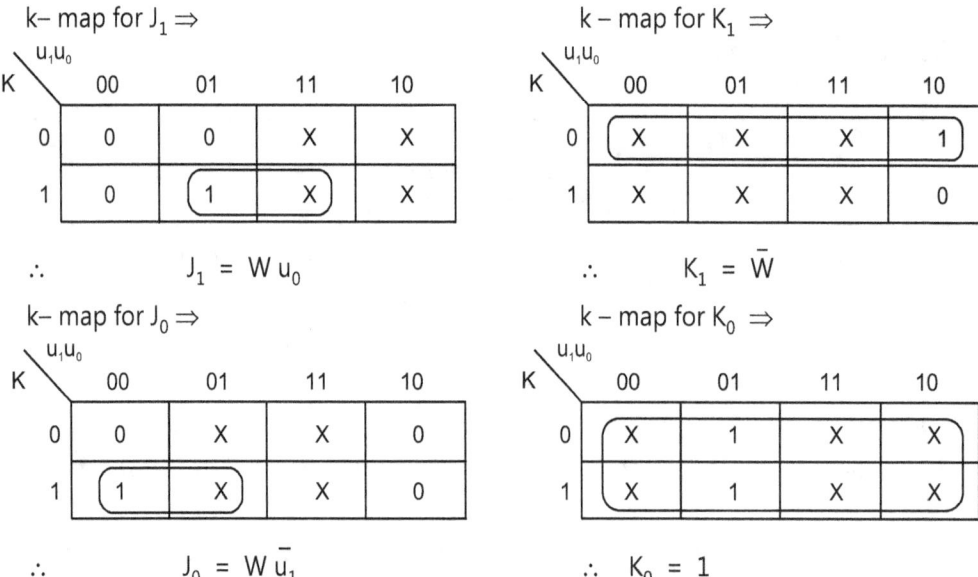

k– map for J_1 ⇒

K \ u_1u_0	00	01	11	10
0	0	0	X	X
1	0	1	X	X

∴ $J_1 = W u_0$

k– map for J_0 ⇒

K \ u_1u_0	00	01	11	10
0	0	X	X	0
1	1	X	X	0

∴ $J_0 = W \bar{u}_1$

k – map for K_1 ⇒

K \ u_1u_0	00	01	11	10
0	X	X	X	1
1	X	X	X	0

∴ $K_1 = \bar{W}$

k – map for K_0 ⇒

K \ u_1u_0	00	01	11	10
0	X	1	X	X
1	X	1	X	X

∴ $K_0 = 1$

- As it is a Moore type machine, output is dependent only on the present state of the circuit as shown in table 4.2. It is redrawn as table 4.5.

Table 4.5

Present state		Output
u_1	u_0	Z
0	0	0
0	1	0
1	0	1
1	1	$\times$

- Now we prepare a two variable k -map for output and obtain the simplified expression.

  k - map for Z

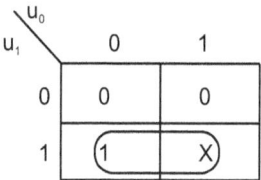

∴ $Z = u_1$

- Based on the above expressions we construct the circuit diagram as shown in Fig. 4.5

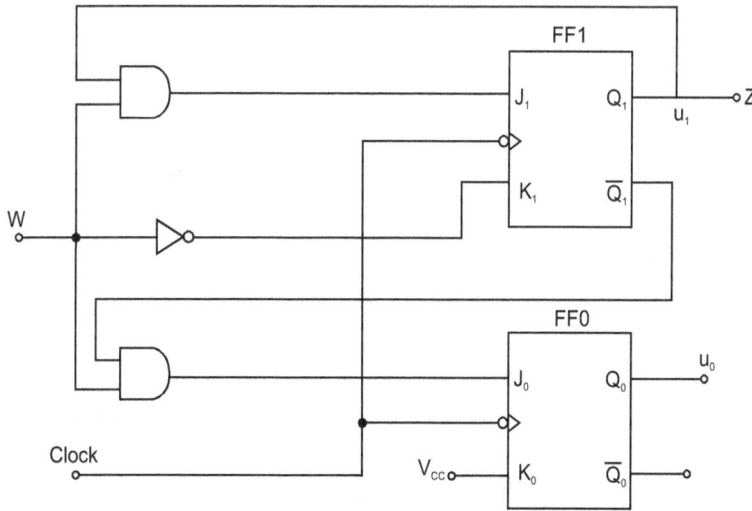

Fig. 4.5

4.7 STEPS TO DESIGN SEQUENTIAL CIRCUIT

Q. Give the detail steps to design sequential circuit.   **[May 06, 07, 4 M]**

- In the design of a sequential circuit the following steps are involved :

(1) The state diagram, which describes the behaviour of the sequential circuit is drawn first.

(2) The information contained in the state diagram is then translated into a table known as state table.

(3) Further each state is represented with the combinations of state variables i.e. state assignment is done and based on that the state assignment table is prepared.

(4) Next, using the excitation table of the flip flop which is to be used for the implementation, a truth table is constructed.

(5) Each flip-flop input is represented in a separate k-map and the simplified expressions are obtained.

(6) Based on the simplified expressions, the circuit diagram is constructed.

4.8 DESIGN OF MEALY TYPE MACHINE

- In the previous sections we discussed the design of a Moore type machine in which each state has specific values of the output signals associated with it.

- Now we shall study the Mealy type machine in which the output is decided by the present state of the circuit and the present input applied to the circuit.

Example 4.1 :

Design a sequential circuit that generates output $Z = 1$ in the same clock cycle when a second occurance of the input $W = 1$ is detected.

Solution :

- The design steps that we follow for a Mealy machine are similar to the Moore machine. We first prepare the state diagram.

- To start, we select one state as the starting state which is also known as reset state. This is the state in which circuit should enter when the power is turned on or a reset signal is applied. Let this state be 'a'.

- When in state 'a', as long as input $W = 0$ the circuit should remain in the same state producing an output $Z = 0$. When input $W = 1$, the circuit should recognize this first occurrence and move to a different state. Let this state be 'b'.

- When in state 'b' with input $W = 1$, the circuit should detect the second occurrence of 1 and produce the output $Z = 1$ remaining in the same state. Thus as long as the circuit is in state 'b' and the input $W = 1$, the output $Z = 1$.

- When the input W = 0, the output Z should become 0 and the circuit should come back to state 'a'.
- Thus, the machine requires two states i.e. 'a' and 'b'. Based on above discussion, the state diagram is drawn as shown in Fig. 4.6

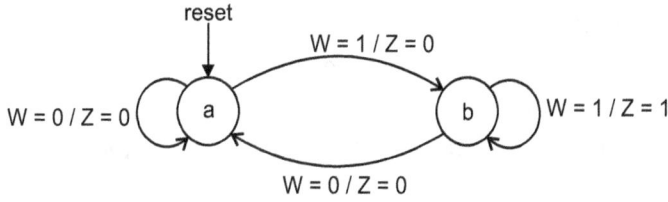

Fig. 4.6

- In the state diagram of Fig. 4.6 two nodes are shown representing the two states whose names are written inside the nodes.
- Node 'a' represents the starting or reset state and the circuit enters into it upon application of reset input or when power is turned on.
- The circuit remains in state 'a' as long as input W = 0 and the output Z = 0. This is indicated with an arc which is starting and terminating at the same node and the arc is labelled as W = 0 / Z = 0.
- When input W = 1, the output Z is still 0 but the machine moves to state 'b'. This is shown with an arc starting at node 'a' and terminating at node 'b' with label W = 1/ Z = 0.
- In state 'b', the output is Z = 1 when the input W = 1 and the circuit remains in the same state. This is shown by an arc starting and terminating at state 'b' with label W = 1/Z = 1.
- But when input W = 0 in state 'b' the circuit goes back to state 'a' producing output Z = 0. It is shown by an arc which starts at state 'b' and terminates at state 'a' and is labelled as W = 0 / Z = 0.
- Comparing the two state diagrams for Moore machine and Mealy machine shown in Fig. 4.4 and 4.6 respectively we can note that in case of Moore machine the output is specified inside the node itself while in case of Mealy machine the output is specified on the arcs.
- Now we translate the information contained in the state diagram into the state table 4.6.

Table 4.6

Present state	Next State		Output	
	W = 0	W = 1	W = 0	W = 1
a	a	b	0	0
b	a	b	0	1

- As there are only two states, one state variable is required for the representation of the states.
- The state variable has two possible values 0 and 1. Let the state assignment be, 'a' = 0 and 'b' = 1.
- Based on this assignment we now prepare a truth table in which each entry in the column of present state and next state of the state table is replaced with the above assignment.
- We know, one state variable can be implemented with single flip–flop. Let u and U be the present state and the next state of the flip–flop. The state assignment table is as drawn in table 4.7,

Table 4.7

Present state	Next State		Output	
u	U		Z	
	W = 0	W = 1	W = 0	W = 1
0	0	1	0	0
1	0	1	0	1

- Let D flip–flop is to be used for the implementation. Now we prepare a truth table 4.8 from the state assignment table and the excitation table of D flip–flop.

Table 4.8

Input	Present state	Next state	Output	Flip–flop input
W	u	U	Z	D0
0	0	0	0	0
0	1	0	0	0
1	0	1	0	1
1	1	1	1	1

- Now we prepare a k-map for the flip–flop input D_0 and output Z to obtain the simplified expression.

k - map for D_0 ⇒   k - map for ⇒

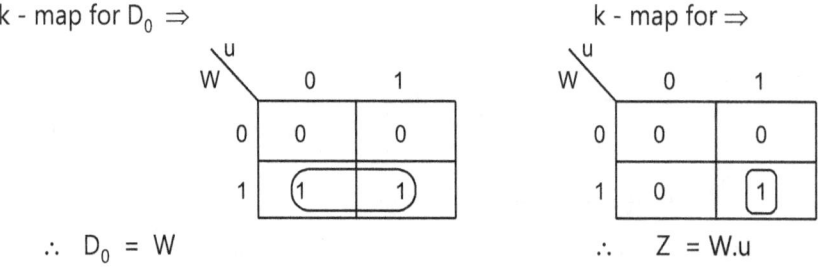

∴ $D_0 = W$ ∴ $Z = W.u$

- Based on the above expressions we construct the circuit diagram as shown in Fig. 4.7.

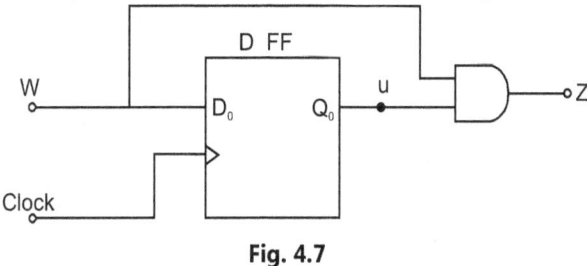

Fig. 4.7

4.9   DIFFERENCE BETWEEN MOORE AND MEALY MACHINE

Q. Compare Moore and Mealy circuit.	**[May 07, Dec. 07, 2 M]**

(1) The block diagram of Moore type machine is as shown in Fig. 4.8

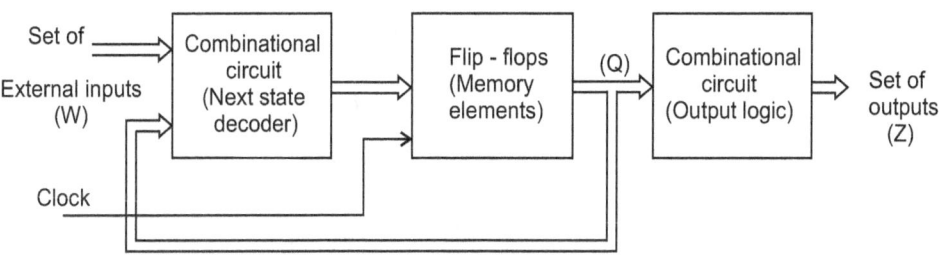

Fig. 4.8

The block diagram of Mealy type machine is as shown in Fig. 4.9.

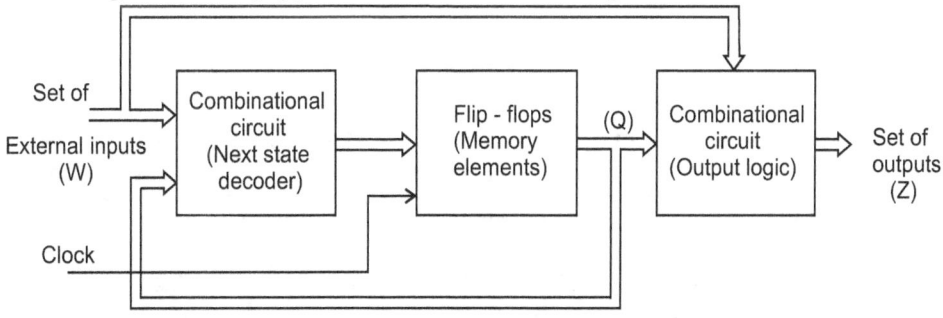

Fig. 4.9

(2) From the Fig. 4.8 and 4.9 it is clear that the output of a Moore machine is dependent only on the present state of the circuit while the output of a Mealy machine is dependent upon the present state of the circuit and the present input applied.

(3) In the state diagram of Moore machine, output is specified inside the node while in the state diagram of Mealy machine output is specified as the label of an arc.

(4) In the state diagram, of Moore machine, the label of the arc is only input while in the state diagram of Mealy machine the label of the arc is input/ output.

(5) For the sequence detector of Moore type machine the number of states are equal to length of the sequence plus 1, while for the sequence detector of Mealy type machine the number of states are exactly equal to the length of the sequence. For example, to detect sequence 11 of length 2, a Moore machine requires $2 + 1 = 3$ states while a Mealy machine requires only 2 states.

(6) There is greater flexibility in the design of Mealy type machines as compared with the Moore type machines.

(7) Due to additional flexibility the Mealy type machines result in simple circuits as compared with the Moore type machines.

Example 4.2 :

Design the sequential circuit using JK flip–flops for state diagram shown in Fig. 4.10.

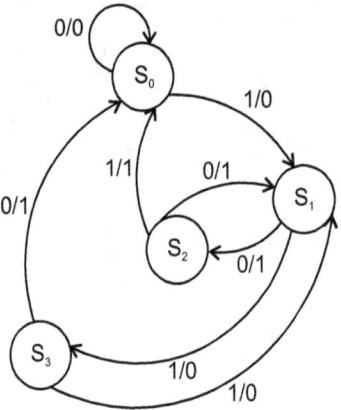

Fig. 4.10

Solution : We first prepare a state table 4.9 from the state diagram shown in Fig. 4.10.

Table 4.9

Present State	Next State		Output	
	W = 0	W = 1	W = 0	W = 1
S_0	S_0	S_1	0	0
S_1	S_2	S_3	1	0
S_2	S_1	S_0	1	1
S_3	S_0	S_1	1	0

- As shown in table 4.9, there are four states. Therefore two state variables are required for the representation of the states.

- Four possible combinations of the two state variables are 00, 01, 10 and 11. One possible assignment is shown in table 4.10

Table 4.10

Name of State	Assignment
S_0	00
S_1	01
S_2	10
S_3	11

- Based on the assignment shown in table 4.10 we prepare a state assignment table 4.11

Table 4.11

Present state	Next State		Output	
	W = 0	W = 1	W = 0	W = 1
$u_1 u_0$	$U_1 U_0$	$U_1 U_0$	Z	Z
00	00	01	0	0
01	10	11	1	0
10	01	00	1	1
11	00	01	1	0

- As shown in table 4.11 U_1, U_0 are the next state variables and u_1, u_0 are the present state variables.
- From the table 4.11 and excitation table of JK flip– flop the truth table 4.12 is prepared.

Table 4.12

Input	Present State		Next state		Flip–flop Inputs				Output
W	u_1	u_0	U_1	U_0	J_1	K_1	J_0	K_0	Z
0	0	0	0	0	0	×	0	×	0
0	0	1	1	0	1	×	×	1	1
0	1	0	0	1	×	1	1	×	1
0	1	1	0	0	×	1	×	1	1
1	0	0	0	1	0	×	1	×	0
1	0	1	1	1	1	×	×	0	0
1	1	0	0	0	×	1	0	×	1
1	1	1	0	1	×	1	×	0	0

- Now we represent the flip–flop inputs and output into separate k - maps and obtain simplified expressions.

k – map for $J_1 \Rightarrow$ k – map for $K_1 \Rightarrow$

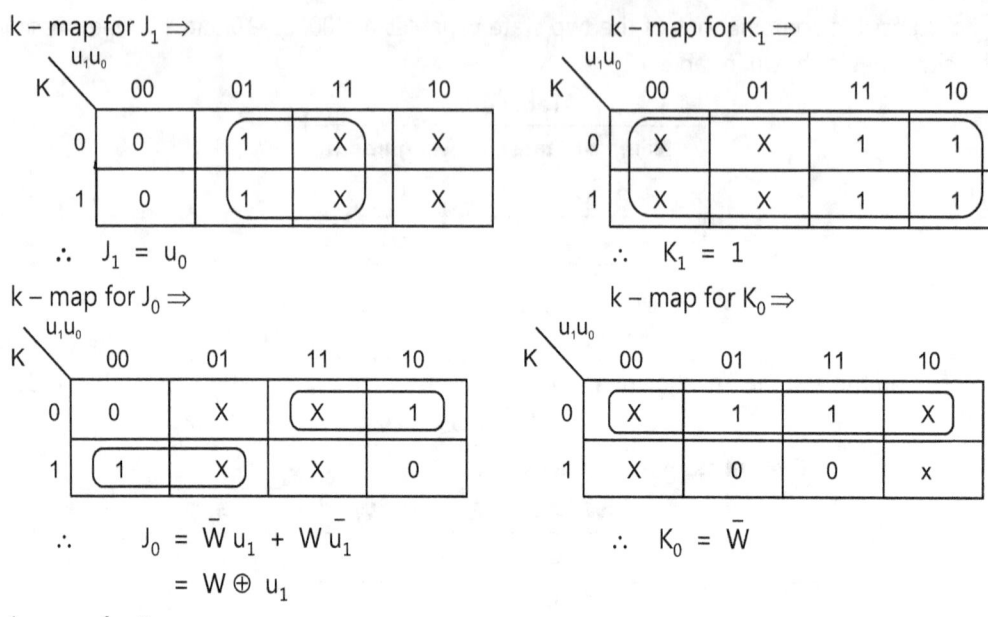

$\therefore \quad J_1 = u_0$ $\therefore \quad K_1 = 1$

k – map for $J_0 \Rightarrow$ k – map for $K_0 \Rightarrow$

$\therefore \qquad J_0 = \bar{W} u_1 + W \bar{u}_1$ $\therefore \quad K_0 = \bar{W}$

$\qquad = W \oplus u_1$

k – map for Z

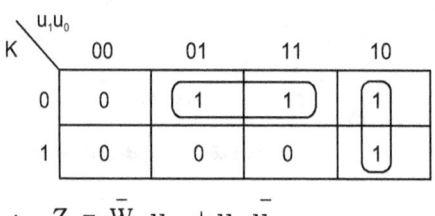

$\therefore \quad Z = \bar{W} u_0 + u_1 \bar{u}_0$

- Based on the above expressions we construct the circuit diagram as shown in Fig. 4.11.

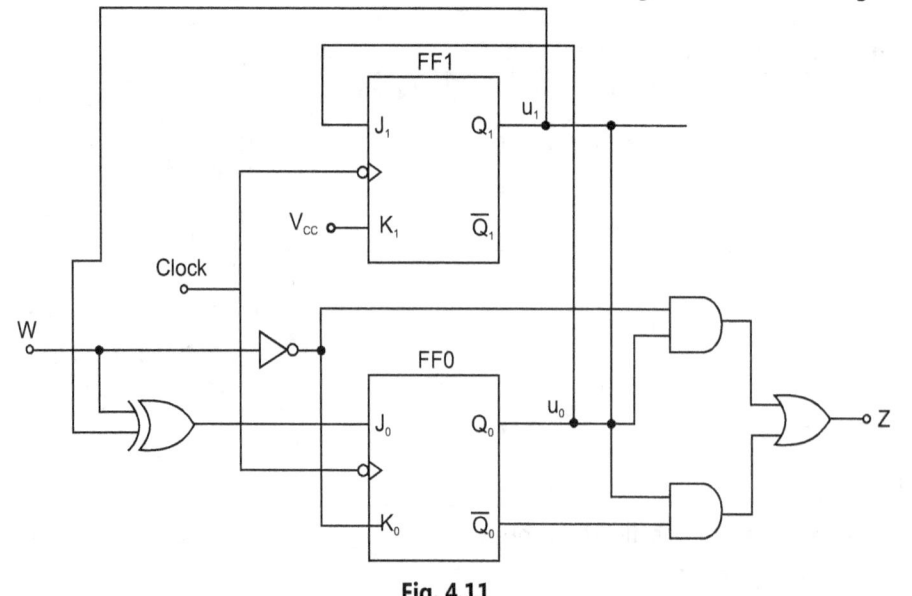

Fig. 4.11

4.10 SEQUENCE DETECTOR

Q. Give steps of designing sequence generator or sequence detector.	**[May 07, 4 M]**
Q. Give steps to design the sequence detector.	**[Dec. 06, 4 M]**

- The circuit which detects the occurrence of a particular pattern of the input applied to it, is known as sequence detector.

- The sequential circuit which we discussed in example 4.1 is a sequence detector. It detects the sequence 11 of input W.

- The design steps for a sequence detector are same as that of the design steps for a sequential circuit as sequence detector is an example of sequential circuit. The design steps are given in section 4.7.

- As there are finite numbers of states in the operation of sequence detector, it is a finite state machine (FSM) and it can be of types – Moore or Mealy.

- The output of the sequence detector becomes 1 when the entire sequence is detected.

Example 4.3 :

Draw state diagram and state table for sequence detector to detect sequence 110.

[PU 2007, 4M]

Solution :

- As the type of machine is not specified we shall design Moore type machine.

- We select one state as the starting state (reset state). The circuit should enter in this state when the power is turned on or a reset signal is applied. Let this state be 'a'. It can be shown with a node and name of the state is specified inside the node. Also the output Z = 0 is also specified inside the node.

- When in state 'a' as long as the input W = 0 the circuit should remain in the same state. It can be shown with an arc starting and terminating at same state 'a' with label W = 0.

- In state 'a' when the input W = 1 the circuit should recognize this as the first bit of the sequence to be detected and make transition to another state say 'b'. It can be shown with an arc starting at node 'a' and terminating at node 'b' with label W = 1.

- When the circuit is in state 'b' the output Z = 0 as only the first bit of the sequence is detected and not the entire sequence. As in earlier case, there are two possibilities of the input. For input W = 0 the input sequence becomes 10 and comparing it with the first two bits of desired sequence the circuit can neither proceed to the next state (as the sequence is not 11) nor it can remain in the same state (as the last input is 0 and not 1). Therefore, the circuit goes back to state 'a'. It can be shown with an arc from 'b' to 'a' with label W = 0. For input W = 1, the input sequence become 11 which is exactly similar to the first two bits of the sequence to be detected. Therefore, the circuit moves to the next state say 'c' and it can be shown with an arc from 'a' to 'c' with label W = 1.

- Proceeding in this manner upto the state 'd' we can construct the state diagram for the sequence detector as shown in Fig. 4.12

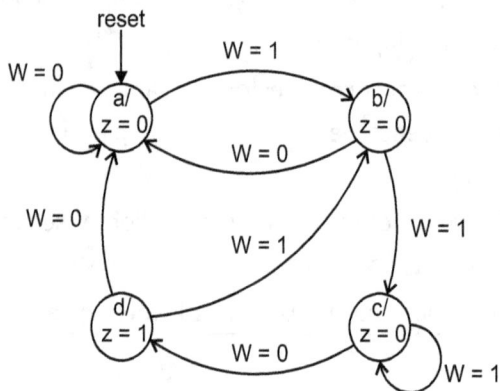

Fig. 4.12

- As shown in Fig. 4.12, there are four states as the length of the sequence to be detected is three. The output Z = 1 in state 'd'.

- The information contained in the state diagram of Fig. 4.12 can be represented in tabular form as shown in the state table 4.13.

Table 4.13

Present State	Next State		Output
	W = 0	**W = 1**	
a	a	b	0
b	a	c	0
c	d	c	0
d	a	b	1

- As shown in Fig. 4.12, when the circuit enters state 'd' output Z = 1 , as the sequence 110 has been detected. When instate 'd' if the input W = 0 then the circuit moves to the reset state 'a' and will start detecting the new sequence. If the input W = 1 then the circuit moves to the state 'b' and we say that the circuit has already started detecting the new sequence and the first bit of it has been detected.

Example 4.4 :

Draw the state diagram, write state transition table and design Moore state machine using D flip– flop to detect the given sequence 1011   **[PU 2008, 8M]**

Solution :

- The length of the sequence to be detected is four so there are five states in the Moore type machine.

Let W be the input and Z be the output of the circuit.

- As in the previous example 4.3 we select the starting state 'a' in which the circuit enters when the power is turned on or reset signal is applied.

- If input W = 1 then the circuit moves to the next state 'b' otherwise it remains in the same state.

- When in state 'b' the circuit moves to the next state 'c' if the input W = 0. For input W = 1 it remains in the same state 'b' and waits for next input 0 so that it can move to the next state 'c'.

- When in state 'c' the circuit moves to the next state 'd' if the input W = 1. For input W = 0 the input sequence so far is 100. Comparing it with first three bits of desired sequence i.e. 101 we say that the circuit can not proceed to the next state 'd' for input W = 0.

- Now we compare the last two inputs so far i.e. 0 with the first two bits of the desired sequence. As it is not matching we say that the circuit can not remain in same state 'c'.

- Now we compare the last input i.e. 0 with the first bit of the desired sequence . As it is also not matching we say that the circuit can not go back to state 'b'.

- The only option is to go back to state 'a'. Thus, when in state 'c' and the input W = 0 the circuit goes back to state 'a'.

- In a similar manner the behaviour of the circuit can be describesd for the remaining two states 'd' and 'e'. Based on that the state diagram is constructed as shown in Fig. 4.13.

- As shown in Fig. 4.13 in states 'a', 'b', 'c' and 'd' the output Z is 0 as the entire sequence is not detected in these states. While as the sequence is detected in state 'e' the output Z = 1.

- When in state 'e' if the input W = 0 the input sequence so far is 10110. Comparing last two inputs of this sequence with the first two bits of the desired sequence, we find a match. Therefore, the circuit goes to state 'c' from state 'e' with W = 0 as shown. Here we can say that the circuit starts detecting the input sequence 1011 second time while the first time detection is in progress. Similarly the circuit moves to state 'b' from state 'e' with input W = 1.

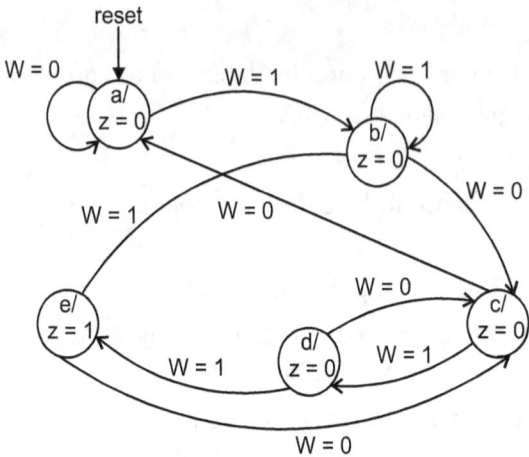

Fig. 4.13

- The information contained in the state diagram of Fig. 4.13 can be represented in tabular form as shown in state table 4.14 which is also known as state transition table.

Table 4.14

Present state	Next State		Output
	W = 0	**W = 1**	
a	a	b	0
b	c	b	0
c	a	d	0
d	c	e	0
e	c	b	1

- As the number of states are five at least three state variables are required for the representation of the states.

- Eight possible combinations of the three state variables are from 00 to 111. One possible assignment is shown in table 4.15.

Table 4.15

Name of State	Assignment
a	000
b	001
c	010
d	011
e	100

- Based on the assignment shown in table 4.15 we prepare state assignment   table 4.16.

Table 4.16

Present State			Next state						Output
			W = 0			W = 1			
u_2	u_1	u_0	U_2	U_1	U_0	U_2	U_1	U_0	Z
0	0	0	0	0	0	0	0	1	0
0	0	1	0	1	0	0	0	1	0
0	1	0	0	0	0	0	1	1	0
0	1	1	0	1	0	1	0	0	0
1	0	0	0	1	0	0	0	1	1

- As shown in table 4.16, U_2, U_1, U_0 are the next state variables and u_2, u_1, u_0 are the present state variables.

- Now, we represent the column of output Z in the k-map and obtain the simplified expression.

k - map for Z $\Rightarrow$

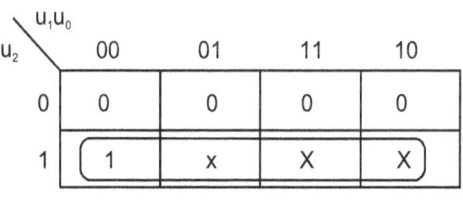

$$\therefore \ Z \ = \ U_2$$

- As shown in table 4.15, the remaining combinations of the state variables from   101 to 111 are not used. Therefore the output Z for those combinations is shown don't care in the k - map.

- From the table 4.16 and the excitation table of D flip flop the truth table 4.17 is prepared.

Table 4.17

Input	Present State			Next State			Flip flop Inputs		
W	u_2	u_1	u_0	U_2	U_1	U_1	D_1	D_1	D_0
0	0	0	0	0	0	0	0	0	0
0	0	0	1	0	1	0	0	1	0
0	0	1	0	0	0	0	0	0	0

0	0	1	1	0	1	0	0	1	0
0	1	0	0	0	1	0	0	1	0
0	1	0	1	×	×	×	×	×	×
0	1	1	0	×	×	×	×	×	×
0	1	1	1	×	×	×	×	×	×
1	0	0	0	0	0	1	0	0	1
1	0	0	1	0	0	1	0	0	1
1	0	1	0	0	1	1	0	1	1
1	0	1	1	1	0	0	1	0	0
1	1	0	0	0	0	1	0	0	1
1	1	0	1	×	×	×	×	×	×
1	1	1	0	×	×	×	×	×	×
1	1	1	1	×	×	×	×	×	×

- For the unused combinations of the state variables, the next state as well as flip inputs are don't care as shown in table 4.17.

- Now we represent the flip–flop inputs in the k - maps and obtain the simplified expressions.

k - map for D_2 ⇒ 　　　　　　　　　　　　　　　k - map for D_1 ⇒

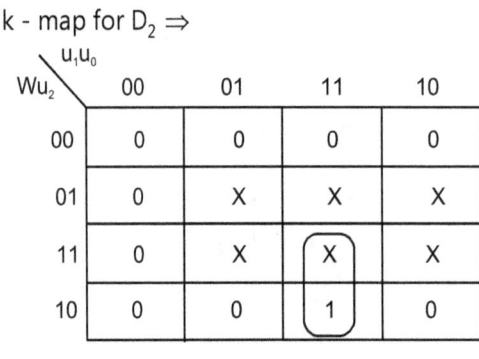

∴ 　　　$D_2 = = Wu_1u_0$

∴ $D_1 = \overline{W}u_2 + \overline{W}\ u_0 + W u_1\ \bar{u}_0$

∴ $D_1 = \overline{W}\ (u_2 + u_0) + Wu_1\bar{u}_0$

k - map for $D_0 \Rightarrow$

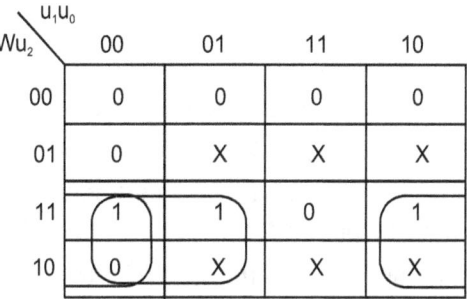

∴ $\qquad D_0 = W\bar{u}_1 + W\bar{u}_0$

∴ $\qquad D_0 = W\left(\bar{u}_1 + \bar{u}_0\right)$

- Based on the above expressions we construct the circuit diagram as shown in Fig. 4.14

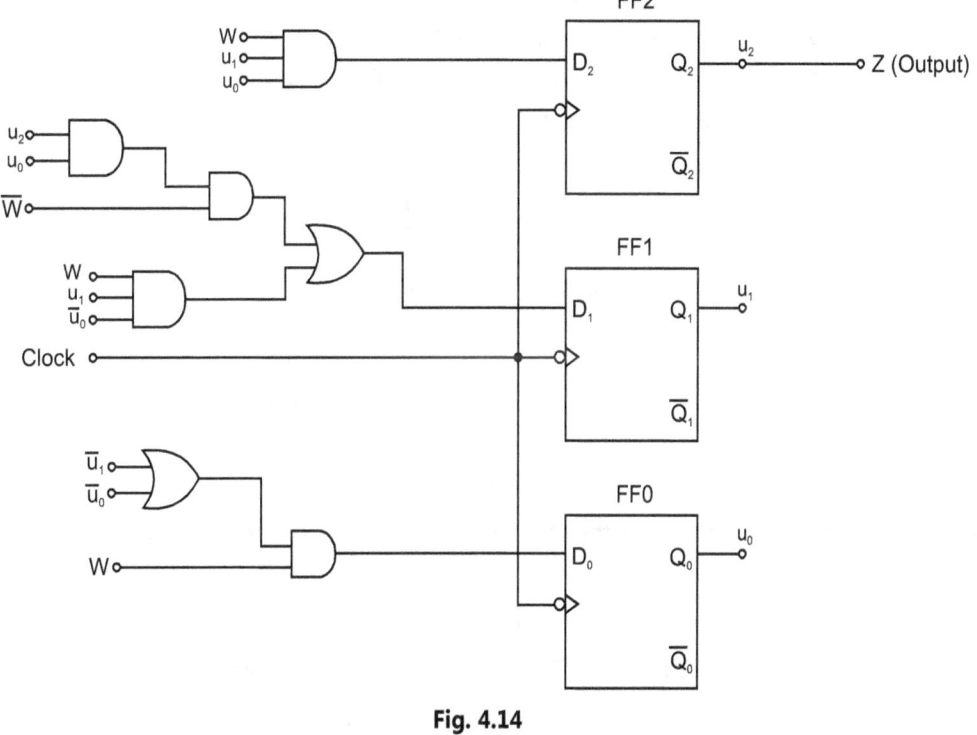

Fig. 4.14

Example 4.5 :

Design a sequence detector to detect the following sequence using JK flip–flops : .... 110 .... (Use Mealy machine)   **[PU 2004 - 10 M)**

Solution :

- The length of the sequence to be detected is three, so there are three states in the Mealy type machine.
- Let W be the input and Z be the output of the circuit.
- As in the earlier examples, we select the starting state 'a' in which the circuit enters when the power is turned on or reset signal is applied.
- If input W = 1, then the circuit moves to the next state 'b', otherwise it remains in the same state. In both cases the output Z = 0.
- When in state 'b' the circuit moves to the state 'c' if the input W = 1. For input W = 0 it goes back to the state 'a'. Again in both cases the output Z = 0.
- When in state 'c' if the input W = 1, the circuit remains in the same state 'c' and waits for next input 0. So that the desired sequence is detected. In this case, output Z = 0.
- When in state 'c' if the input W = 1 the circuit remains in the same state 'c' and waits for next 0 so that the desired sequence is detected. In this case output Z = 0.
- When in state 'c', if the input W = 0, the output Z = 1 as the desired sequence is dected. The circuit goes back to state 'a' and will start detecting the new sequence.
- The state diagram is as shown in Fig. 4.15

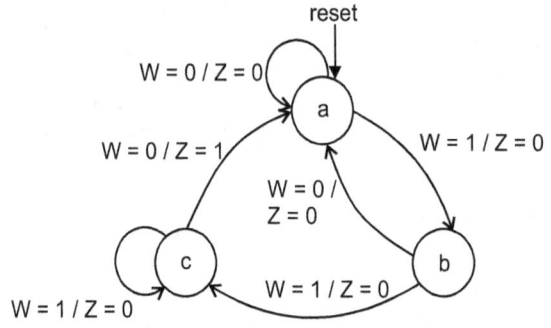

Fig. 4.15

- The information contained in the state diagram of Fig. 4.15 can be represented in tabular form as shown in state table 4.18

Table 4.18

Present State	Next State		Output	
	W = 0	W = 1	W = 0	W = 1
a	a	b	0	0
b	a	c	0	0
c	a	c	1	0

- As the number of states are three, at least two state variables are required for the representation of the states.
- Four possible combinations of the two state variables are 00, 01, 10 and 11. One possible assignment is shown in table 4.19

Table 4.19

Name of State	Assignment
a	00
b	01
c	11

- As indicated in table 4.19 the combination 10 is not used for this particular assignment. The assignment may vary therefore we say that the possible assignment is as shown.
- Based on the assignment shown in table 4.19 we prepare state assignment table 4.20

Table 4.20

Present state	Next State		Output	
	W = 0	W = 1	W = 1	W = 0
$u_1 u_0$	$U_1 U_0$	$U_1 U_0$	Z	Z
00	00	01	0	0
01	00	11	0	0
11	00	11	1	0

- From table 4.20 and the excitation table of JK flip–flop the truth table 4.21 is prepared.
- For the unused combination of the state variable (10), the next state, inputs of the flip–flops and output of the circuit are don't care as shown in table 4.21.
- As shown in table 4.21, $U_1 U_0$ are the next state variables and u_1, u_0 are present state variables.

Table 4.21

Input	Present State		Next State		Flip–flop inputs				Output
W	u_1	u_0	U_1	U_0	J_1	K_1	J_0	K_0	Z
0	0	0	0	0	0	×	0	×	0
0	0	1	0	0	0	×	×	1	0
0	1	0	×	×	×	×	×	×	×

0	1	1	0	0	×	1	×	1	1
1	0	0	0	1	0	×	1	×	0
1	0	1	1	1	1	×	×	0	0
1	1	0	×	×	×	×	×	×	×
1	1	1	1	1	×	0	×	1	0

- Now we represent the flip– flop inputs and the output in the separate k - maps and obtain the simplified expressions.

k - map for $J_1 \Rightarrow$ k - map for $K_1 \Rightarrow$

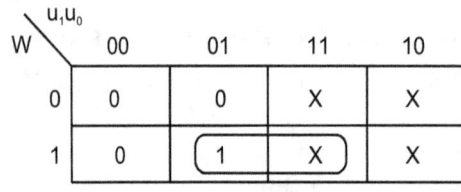

$\therefore \qquad J_1 = Wu_0$

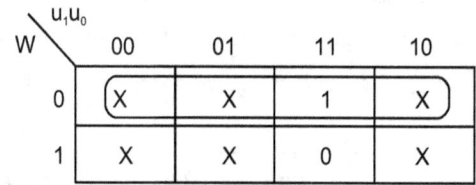

$\therefore \quad K_1 = \overline{W}$

k - map for $J_0 \Rightarrow$ k - map for $K_0 \Rightarrow$

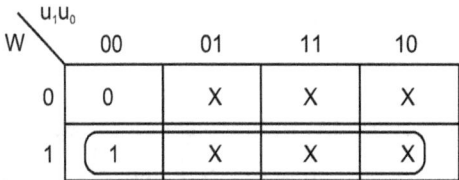

$\therefore \qquad J_0 = W$

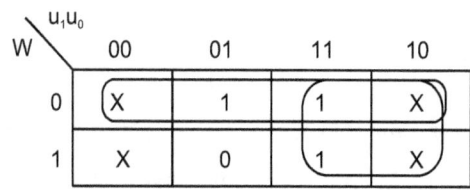

$\therefore \quad K_0 = \overline{W} + u_1$

k - map for $Z \Rightarrow$

W \ u_1u_0	00	01	11	10
0	0	0	1	X
1	0	0	0	X

$\therefore \qquad Z = \overline{W}\, u_1$

- Based an above expressions we construct the circuit diagram as shown in Fig. 4.16

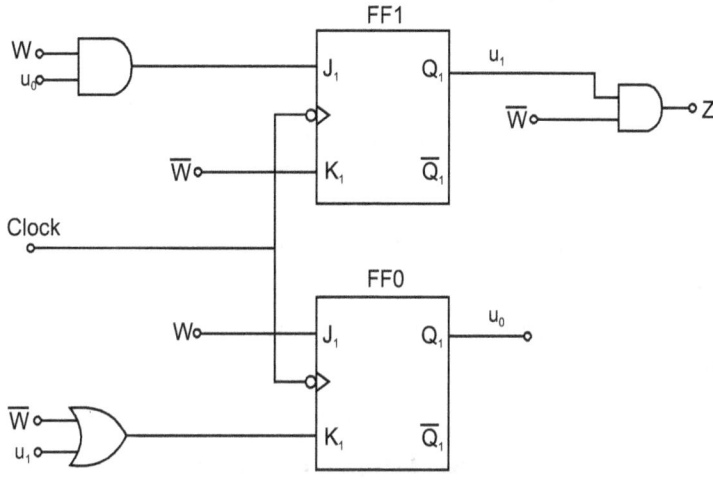

Fig. 4.16

4.11 COUNTER

- Synchronous counters is an example of finite state machine in which outputs are taken directly from the flip–flops.

- The design steps for a counter are same as that of the design steps for a sequential circuit. The only difference is that the column of output is not required.

- The output of the circuit is same as that of the present state of the circuit.

- Thus counters are the Moore type machines.

Example 4.6 :

Design a synchronous counter that goes through following states :

...... 0 – 4 – 2 – 6 – 1 – 5 – 3 – 7 – 0 – 4 ......

The output of the counter is represented by the outputs of the flip–flops.

Solution :

- There are eight district states in the operation of the counter.

- Let 'a', 'b', 'c', 'd', 'e', 'f', 'g', and 'h' be the states associated with each count 0, 1, 2, 3, 4, 5, 6, and 7 respectively.

- The state diagram is as shown in Fig. 4.17.

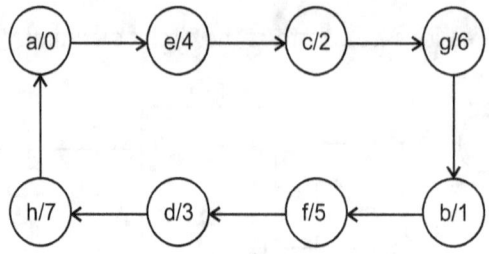

Fig. 4.17

- The information contained in the state diagram of Fig. 4.17 can be represented in tabular form as shown in state table 4.22.

- In the table 4.22 the column of output is absent as the present state of the circuit represents output.

Table 4.22

Present State	Next state
a	e
b	f
c	g
d	h
e	c
f	d
g	b
h	a

- For eight district states, three state variables are required. We go for the straight binary assignment as mentioned earlier i.e. 'a' is represented as 000 and like wise 'h' is represented as 111.

- We shall design the counter using D flip–flops and three D flip–flops are required for the implementation.

- Let U_2, U_1, U_0 be the next state variables which are the inputs D_2, D_1, D_0 respectively of the D flip–flops.

- Let u_2, u_1, u_0, u be the present state variables which also represent the output of the circuit.

- From the state table 4.22 and the excitation table of D flip–flop a truth table 4.23 is prepared.

Table 4.23

Present State			Next State			Flip flop Inputs		
t_2	t_1	t_0	T_2	T_1	T_0	D_2	D_1	D_0
0	0	0	1	0	0	1	0	0
0	0	1	1	0	1	1	0	1
0	1	0	1	1	0	1	1	0
0	1	1	1	1	1	1	1	1
1	0	0	0	1	0	0	1	0
1	0	1	0	1	1	0	1	1
1	1	0	0	0	1	0	0	1
1	1	1	0	0	0	0	0	0

- Now we represent the flip–flop inputs in the k - maps and obtain simplified expressions.

k - map for $D_2 \Rightarrow$ k - map for $D_1 \Rightarrow$

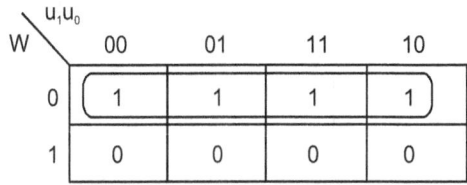

$\therefore$ $D_2 = \bar{u}_2$ $\therefore$ $D_1 = \bar{u}_2 u_1 + u_2 \bar{u}_1$

$\therefore$ $D_1 = u_2 \oplus u_1$

k - map for $D_0 \Rightarrow$

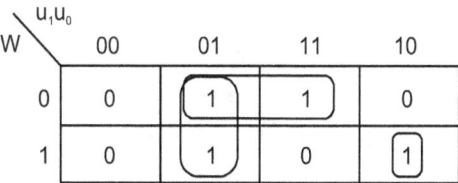

$\therefore$ $D_0 = \bar{u}_2 u_0 + \bar{u}_1 u_0 + u_2 u_1 \bar{u}_0$

$\therefore$ $D_0 = u_0 \left(\bar{u}_2 + \bar{u}_1 \right) + u_2 u_1 \bar{u}_0$

- Using De Morgan's theorem,

$$D_0 = u_0 \left(\overline{u_2 \cdot u_1} \right) + u_2 u_1 \bar{u}_0$$

- Let
  $$u_2 \cdot u_1 = x$$

  $\therefore$
  $$D_0 = u_0 \, \bar{x} + x \cdot \bar{u}_0$$

  $\therefore$
  $$D_0 = u_0 \oplus x$$

- Putting the value of x we get,
  $$D_0 = u_0 \oplus u_2 \cdot u_1$$

- Based on above expressions we construct the circuit diagram as shown in Fig. 4.18.

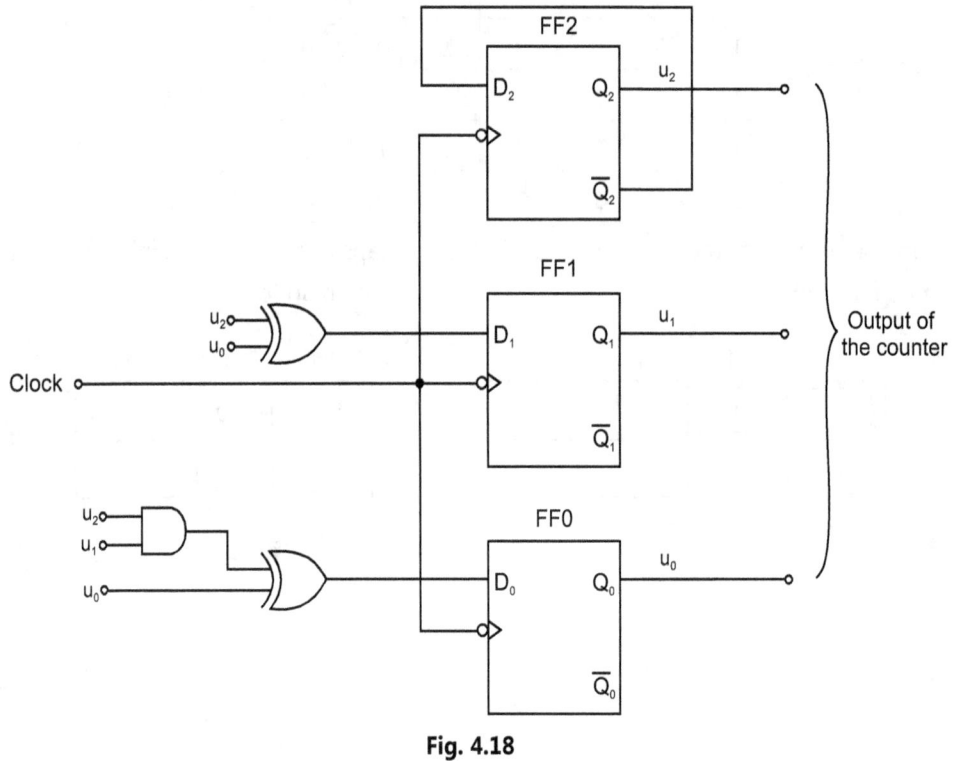

Fig. 4.18

Example 4.7 :

Design 2 - bit synchronous up counter. Draw the state diagram, write state table and design the machine using T flip–flop.

Solution :

- There are four distinct states in the operation of 2 - bit up counter as it goes through the states 0, 1, 2, and 3.

- Let 'a', 'b', 'c', and 'd' be the names of the states associated with each count 0, 1, 2, and 3 respectively.

- The state diagram is as shown in Fig. 4. 19

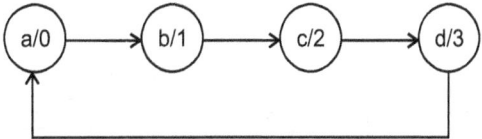

Fig. 4.19

- The state diagram in Fig. 4.19 can be translated into the state table 4.24. The column of output is absent as the present state of the circuit represents output.

Table 4.24

Present State	Next State
a	b
b	c
c	d
d	a

- For four district states, two state variables are required. We go for the straight binary assignment as mentioned earlier. i.e. 'a' is represented as 00 and like wise 'd' is represented as 11.
- The counter is to be designed using T flip flops and two T flip–flops are required.
- Let U_1, U_0 the next state variables, which are the inputs T_1, T_0 respectively of the T flip–flops.
- Let u_1, u_0 be the present state variables which also represent the output of the circuit.
- From the state table 4.24 and the excitation table of T flip flop a truth table 4.25 is prepared.

Table 4.25

Present State		Next State		Flip–flop Inputs	
U_1	U_0	U_1	U_0	T_1	T_0
0	0	0	1	0	1
0	1	1	0	1	1
1	0	1	1	0	1
1	1	0	0	1	1

- Now we represent the flip-flop inputs in the k - maps and obtain simplified expressions.

k - map for $T_1 \Rightarrow$ k - map for $T_0 \Rightarrow$

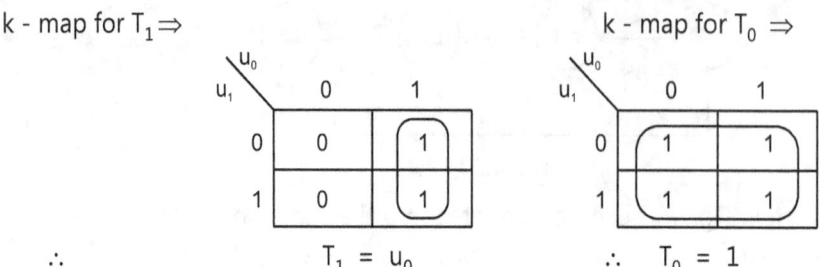

$\therefore \qquad T_1 = u_0 \qquad\qquad \therefore \quad T_0 = 1$

Based on above expressions we construct the circuit diagram as shown in Fig. 4.20.

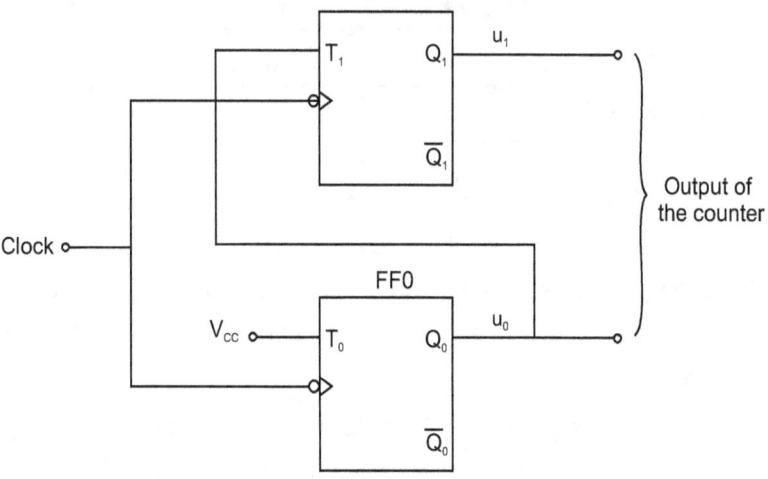

Fig. 4.20

4.12 SEQUENCE GENERATOR

Q. Describe steps of sequence generator.

- A circuit that generates output as per the prescribed sequence in synchronism with a clock is referred to as sequence generator.

- Sequence generator is also an example of finite state machine in which outputs are taken directly from the flip–flops.

- Sequence generator is nothing but a synchronous counter. For example, suppose a sequence generator generate the following sequence.

$$3 \rightarrow 2 \rightarrow 1 \rightarrow 0$$

then from sequence we can say that, it is a 2 - bit down counter.

- Example 4.6 is a type of sequence generator.

- Therefore, the design steps for a sequence generator are same as that of the design steps for a counter and in these designs also, the column of output is not required.

- The output of the circuit is same as that of the present state of the circuit. Thus, sequence generators are also Moore type machines.

Example 4.8 :

Design sequence generator to generate sequence $1 \rightarrow 9 \rightarrow 2 \rightarrow 7 \rightarrow 3 \rightarrow 6$ using JK flip–flop.   **[PU 2007 - 8M]**

- As per the given sequence to be generated there are six distinct states in the operation of the machine.

- Let 'a', 'b', 'c', 'd', 'e', and 'f' be the states associated with each digit of the given sequence. Therefore, when in state 'a' the circuit generates output 1 and like wise when in state 'f' it generates output 6.

- The state diagram is as shown in Fig. 4.21

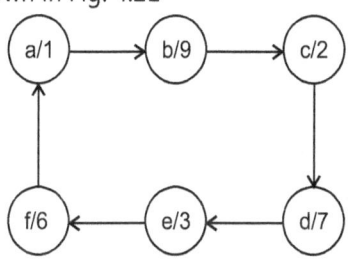

Fig. 4.21

- The state diagram in Fig. 4.21 can be translated into the state table 4.26. The column of output is absent as the present state of the circuit represents output.

Table 4.26

Present State	Next State
a	b
b	c
c	d
d	e
e	f
f	a

- As shown in Fig. 4.21 in state 'b' the circuit generates output 9. The binary equivalent of 9 is 1001. Therefore four state variables are required to design the circuit.

- For each digit of the given sequence we carry out the assignment as the binary equivalent of the digit. Therefore for state 'a' the assignment is 0001 and for state 'f' it is 0110.

- There are sixteen possible combinations of the four state variables out of which only six are used. Therefore for every unused combination the next state and the flip–flop inputs are don't care.

- Let U_3, U_2, U_1, U_0 be the next state variables and u_3, u_2, u_1, u_0 be the present state variables.

- From the table 4.26 and the excitation table of JK flip–flop, a truth table 4.27 is prepared.

Table 4.27

Present State				Next State				Flip–flop Inputs							
u_3	u_2	u_1	u_0	U_3	U_2	U_1	U_0	J_3	K_3	J_2	K_2	J_1	K_1	J_0	K_0
0	0	0	0	×	×	×	×	×	×	×	×	×	×	×	×
0	0	0	1	1	0	0	1	1	×	0	×	0	×	×	0
0	0	1	0	0	1	1	1	0	×	1	×	×	0	1	×
0	0	1	1	0	1	1	0	0	×	1	×	×	0	×	1
0	1	0	0	×	×	×	×	×	×	×	×	×	×	×	×
0	1	0	1	×	×	×	×	×	×	×	×	×	×	×	×
0	1	1	0	0	0	0	1	0	×	×	1	×	1	1	×
0	1	1	1	0	0	1	1	0	×	×	1	×	0	×	0
1	0	0	0	×	×	×	×	×	×	×	×	×	×	×	×
1	0	0	1	0	0	1	0	×	1	0	×	1	×	×	1
1	0	1	0	×	×	×	×	×	×	×	×	×	×	×	×
1	0	1	1	×	×	×	×	×	×	×	×	×	×	×	×
1	1	0	0	×	×	×	×	×	×	×	×	×	×	×	×
1	1	0	1	×	×	×	×	×	×	×	×	×	×	×	×
1	1	1	0	×	×	×	×	×	×	×	×	×	×	×	×
1	1	1	1	×	×	×	×	×	×	×	×	×	×	×	×

- Now we represent the flip–flop inputs in the k - maps and obtain simplified expressions.

k - map for $J_3 \Rightarrow$

u_3u_2 \ u_1u_0	00	01	11	10
00	X	1	0	0
01	X	X	0	0
11	X	X	X	X
10	X	X	X	X

$\therefore \qquad J_3 = \bar{u}_1$

k - map for $K_3 \Rightarrow$

u_3u_2 \ u_1u_0	00	01	11	10
00	X	X	X	X
01	X	X	X	X
11	X	X	X	X
10	X	1	X	X

$\therefore \qquad K_3 = 1$

k - map for $J_2 \Rightarrow$

u_3u_2 \ u_1u_0	00	01	11	10
00	X	0	1	1
01	X	X	X	X
11	X	X	X	X
10	X	0	X	X

$\therefore \qquad J_2 = u_1$

k - map for $K_2 \Rightarrow$

u_3u_2 \ u_1u_0	00	01	11	10
00	X	X	X	X
01	X	X	1	1
11	X	X	X	X
10	X	X	X	X

$\therefore \quad K_2 = 1$

k - map for $J_1 \Rightarrow$

u_3u_2 \ u_1u_0	00	01	11	10
00	X	0	X	X
01	X	X	0	0
11	X	X	X	X
10	X	1	X	X

$\therefore \qquad J_1 = u_3$

k - map for $K_1 \Rightarrow$

u_3u_2 \ u_1u_0	00	01	11	10
00	X	X	0	0
01	X	X	0	1
11	X	X	X	X
10	X	X	X	X

$\therefore \quad K_1 = u_2 \, \bar{u}_0$

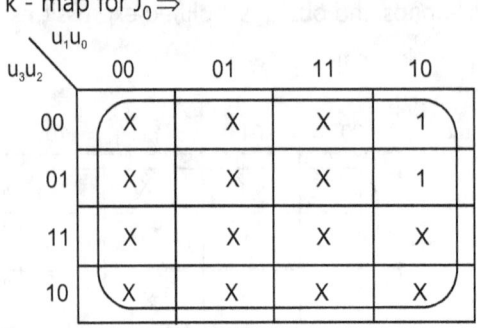

k - map for $J_0 \Rightarrow$

k - map for $K_0 \Rightarrow$

$$\therefore \quad J_0 = 1$$

$$\therefore \quad K_0 = u_3 + u_3\, u_1$$
$$\therefore \quad K_0 = u_3\, (1 + u_1)$$
$$\therefore \quad K_0 = u_3$$

- Based on above expressions we construct the circuit diagram as shown in Fig. 4.22.

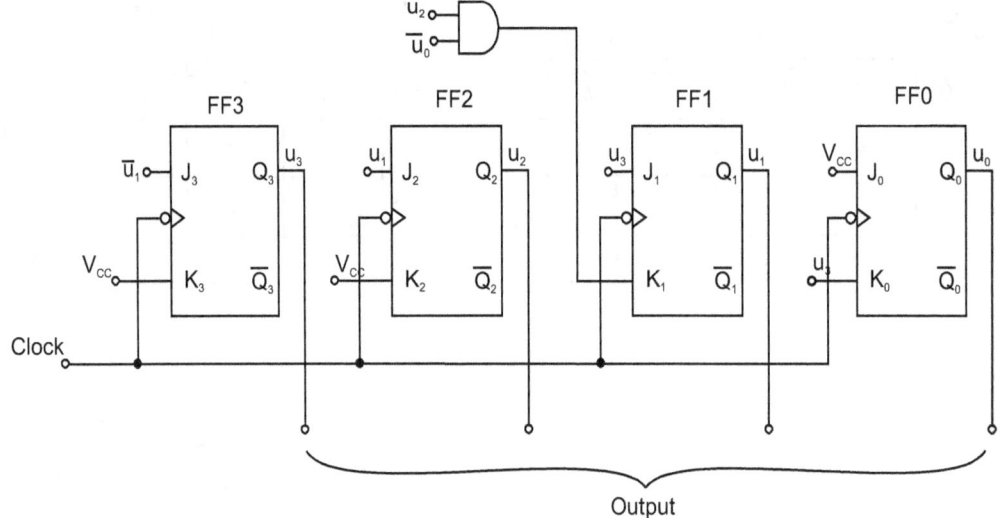

Output

Fig. 4.22

Example 4.9 :

Design mod - 8 up counter for the condition that there exist an input signal W, and if W = 1 the count is incremented by one otherwise it remains same.

- As the modulus of counter is eight, there are same number of district states in the operation of it.

- Let 'a', 'b', 'c', 'd', 'e', 'f', 'g', and 'h' be the names of the states associated with each count 0, 1, 2, 3, 4, 5, 6, and 7 respectively.

- It is given that the count is incremented by one if the input W = 1. Thus the transition from state 'a' to state 'b', state 'b' to state 'c' and so on is possible only when W = 1. Otherwise the circuit remains in the same state.

- Thus it is required that, in each state the status of W must be checked and accordingly the next state is decided.

- The state diagram is as shown in Fig. 4.23

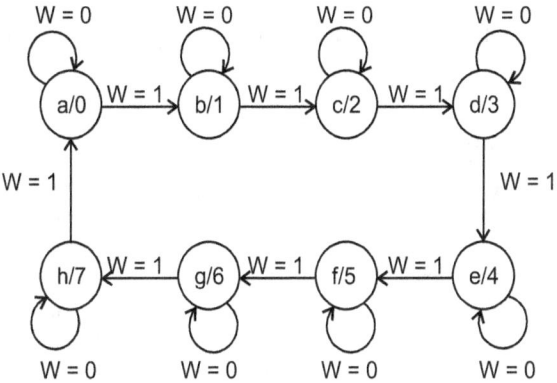

Fig. 4.23

- The state diagram in Fig. 4.23 can be translated into the state table 4.28. The column of the output is absent as the present state of the circuit represents output.

Table 4.28

Present State	Next State	
	W = 0	**W = 1**
a	a	b
b	b	c
c	c	d
d	d	e
e	e	f
f	f	g
g	g	h
h	h	a

- For eight district states, three state variables are required. We go for the straight binary assignment i.e. 'a' is represented as 000 and like wise h is represented as 111.
- We shall design the counter using D flip–flops and three D flip–flops are required.
- Let U_2, U_1, U_0 be the next state variables which are the inputs D_2, D_1, D_0 respectively of the D flip–flops.
- Let u_2, u_1, u_0 be the present state variables which also represent the output of the circuit.
- From the table 4.28 and the excitation table of D flip–flop, a truth table 4.29 is prepared.

Table 4.29

Input	Present State			Next State			Flip flop Inputs		
W	u_2	u_1	u_0	U_2	U_1	U_0	D_2	D_1	D_0
0	0	0	0	0	0	0	0	0	0
0	0	0	1	0	0	1	0	0	1
0	0	1	0	0	1	0	0	1	0
0	0	1	1	0	1	1	0	1	1
0	1	0	0	1	0	0	1	0	0
0	1	0	1	1	0	1	1	0	1
0	1	1	0	1	1	0	1	1	0
0	1	1	1	1	1	1	1	1	1
1	0	0	0	0	0	1	0	0	1
1	0	0	1	0	1	0	0	1	0
1	0	1	0	0	1	1	0	1	1
1	0	1	1	1	0	0	1	0	0
1	1	0	0	1	0	1	1	0	1
1	1	0	1	1	1	0	1	1	0
1	1	1	0	1	1	1	1	1	1
1	1	1	1	0	0	0	0	0	0

- Now we represent the flip–flop inputs in the k-maps and obtain simplified expressions.

k - map for $D_2 \Rightarrow$

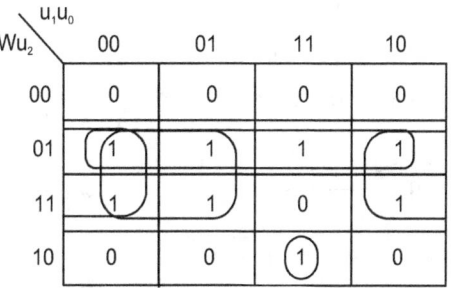

$\therefore \qquad D_2 = \bar{W}\, u_2 + u_2\bar{u_1} + u_2\, \bar{u_0} + W\, \bar{u_2}\, u_1\, u_0$

$\therefore \qquad D_2 = u_2\left(\bar{W} + \bar{u_1} + \bar{u_0}\right) + \bar{u_2} \cdot (W\, u_1\, u_0)$

$\therefore \qquad D_2 = u_2\left(\overline{W \cdot u_1\, u_0}\right) + \bar{u_2}\, (W\, u_1\, u_0)$

$\therefore \qquad D_2 = u_2 \oplus W\, u_1\, u_0$

k - map for $D_1 \Rightarrow$

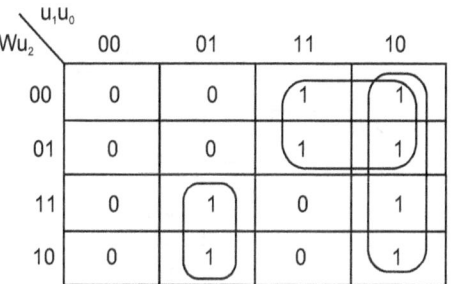

$\therefore \qquad D_1 = u_1\, \bar{u_0} + \bar{W}\, u_1 + W\, \bar{u_1}\, u_0$

$\therefore \qquad D_1 = u_1\left(\bar{u_0} + \bar{W}\right) + \bar{u_1} \cdot (W \cdot u_0)$

$\therefore \qquad D_1 = u_1\left(\overline{u_0 \cdot W}\right) + \bar{u_1}\, (u_0 \cdot W)$

$\therefore \qquad D_1 = u_1 \oplus u_0 \cdot W$

k - map for $D_0 \Rightarrow$

Wu_2 \ u_1u_0	00	01	11	10
00	0	1	1	0
01	0	1	1	0
11	1	0	0	1
10	1	0	0	1

$$\therefore \qquad D_0 = W \, \overline{u_0} + \overline{W} \, u_0$$

$$\therefore \qquad D_0 = W \oplus u_0$$

∴ Based on expressions we construct the circuit diagram as shown in Fig. 4.24

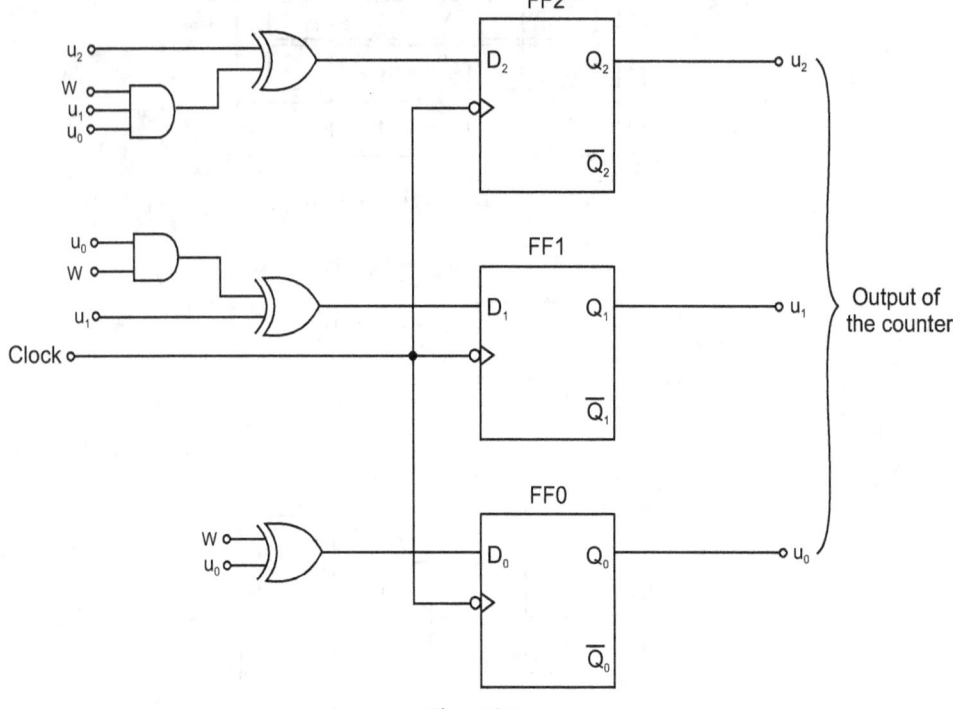

Fig. 4.24

4.13 STATE REDUCTION

Q. What is the advantage of state reduction in the design of sequential circuits ?
[May 05, Dec. 09, 2 M]
Q. Write short note on rules for state reduction.   **[Dec. 06. 08, May 10, 11, 2 M]**

- In the design of sequential circuits, the number of states is an important parameter.

- Based on the count for states, we decide the number of state variables required to represent the individual states.

- One state variable requires one flip–flop for implementation, therefore number of flip–flops required for a circuit is dependent upon the number of states.

- Thus, the hardware requirement of a circuit is decided by the number of states.

- Sometimes if may be possible to reduce the number of states which is known as state reduction. It results in reduction of flip–flops (hardware) and cost.

- The state reduction is possible if redundant states are present. The redundant states are also known as equivalent states.
- Two states are redundant, if all possible combinations of inputs generate exactly same output and next state.
- When two states are redundant one of them can be removed directly.
- Consider the state diagram of a Mealy model as shown in Fig. 4.25.

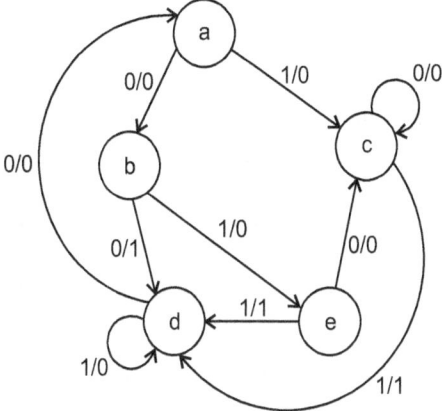

Fig. 4.25

- The state diagram in Fig. 4.25 can be translated into the state table 4.30.

Table 4.30

Present state	Next State		Output (Z)	
	W = 0	W = 1	W = 0	W = 1
a	b	c	0	0
b	d	e	1	0
c	c	d	0	1
d	a	d	0	0
e	c	d	0	1

- As shown in table 4.30 there are five states which require three state variables for the representation. Thus, three flip–flops are required for the implementation.
- In table 4.30 states 'c' and 'e' are redundant states, as they produce exactly same next state and output for the two combinations of input W.
- Therefore one of the two states 'c' and 'e' can be eliminated. We eliminate the state 'e'.
- Thus, 'e' is replaced by 'c' wherever it occurs and new, reduced state table 4.31 is prepared.

Table 4.31

Present state	Next State		Output (Z)	
	W = 0	W = 1	W = 0	W = 1
a	b	c	0	0
b	d	c	1	0
c	c	d	0	1
d	a	d	0	0

- As shown in table 4.31, there are only four states which can be represented with two state variables. Thus two flip–flops are required for the implementation.
- Thus by using state reduction, in this example we reduced hardware by one flip–flop.

Example 4.10 :

Design a clocked sequential circuit using D flip flop for the following state diagram using state reduction technique.   **[PU 2008 - 10 M]**

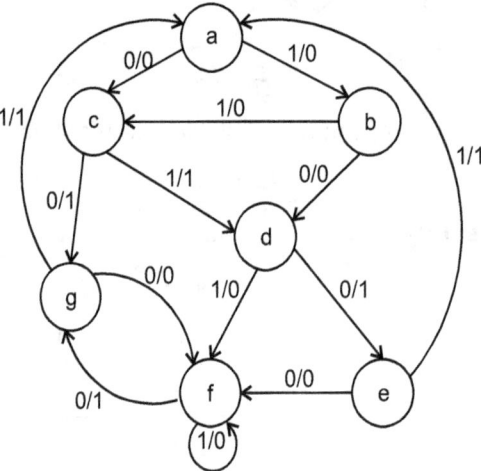

Fig. 4.26

Solution :

- The state diagram in Fig. 4.26 can be translated into the state table 4.32.

Table 4.32

Present State	Next State		Output (Z)	
	W = 0	W = 1	W = 0	W = 1
a	c	b	0	0
b	d	c	0	0

c	g	d	1	1
d	e	f	1	0
e	f	a	0	1
f	g	f	1	0
g	f	a	0	1

- In table 4.32, states 'e' and 'g' are redundant states, as they produce exactly same next state and output for the two combinations of input W.
- Therefore, one of the two states 'e' and 'g' can be eliminated. We eliminate the state 'g'.
- Thus 'g' is replaced by 'e' wherever if occurs and new, reduced state table 4.33 is prepared.

Table 4.33

Present State	Next State		Output (Z)	
	W = 0	W = 1	W = 0	W = 1
a	c	b	0	0
b	d	c	0	0
c	e	d	1	1
d	e	f	1	0
e	f	a	0	1
f	e	f	1	0

- In table 4.33, states 'd' and 'f' are redundant states, as they produce exactly same next state and output.
- Therefore one of the states 'd' and 'f' can be eliminated. We eliminate state 'd'.
- Thus 'd' is replaced by 'f' wherever it occurs and another new, reduced state table 4.34 is prepared.

Table 4.34

Present State	Next State		Output (Z)	
	W = 0	W = 1	W = 0	W = 1
a	c	b	0	0
b	f	c	0	0
c	e	f	1	1
e	f	a	0	1
f	e	f	1	0

- As the number of states are five, at least three state variables are required for the representation of the states.

- Eight possible combinations of the three state variables are from 000 to 111. One possible assignment is shown in table 4.35.

Table 4.35

Name of state	Assignment
a	000
b	001
c	010
e	011
f	100

- Based on the assignment shown in table 4.35, we prepare state assignment table 4.36.

Table 4.36

Present state			Next state						Output	
			W = 0			W = 1			W = 0	W = 1
u_2	u_1	u_0	U_2	U_1	U_0	U_2	U_1	U_0	Z	Z
0	0	0	0	1	0	0	0	1	0	0
0	0	1	1	0	0	0	1	0	0	0
0	1	0	0	1	1	1	0	0	1	1
0	1	1	1	0	0	0	0	0	0	1
1	0	0	0	1	1	1	0	0	1	0

- As shown in table 4.36, T_2, T_1, T_0 are the next state variables and u_2, u_1, u_0 are the present state variables.

- From the table 4.36 and excitation table of D flip–flop, the truth table 4.37 is prepared.

- For the unused combinations of the state variables such as 101, 110, and 111, the next state and input of flip–flops are don't care as shown in table 4.37.

Table 4.37

Input	Present state			Next state			Flip flop inputs			Outputs
W	U_2	U_1	U_0	T_2	T_1	T_0	D_2	D_1	D_0	Z
0	0	0	0	0	1	0	0	1	0	0
0	0	0	1	1	0	0	1	0	0	0
0	0	1	0	0	1	1	0	1	1	1
0	0	1	1	1	0	0	1	0	0	0
0	1	0	0	0	1	1	0	1	1	1
0	1	0	1	×	×	×	×	×	×	×
0	1	1	0	×	×	×	×	×	×	×
0	1	1	1	×	×	×	×	×	×	×
1	0	0	0	0	0	1	0	0	1	0
1	0	0	1	0	1	0	0	1	0	0
1	0	1	0	1	0	0	1	0	0	1
1	0	1	1	0	0	0	0	0	0	1
1	1	0	0	1	0	0	1	0	0	0
1	1	0	1	×	×	×	×	×	×	×
1	1	1	0	×	×	×	×	×	×	×
1	1	1	1	×	×	×	×	×	×	×

- Now we represent the flip–flop inputs and the output in the separate k - maps and obtain simplified expressions.

k - map for $D_2 \Rightarrow$

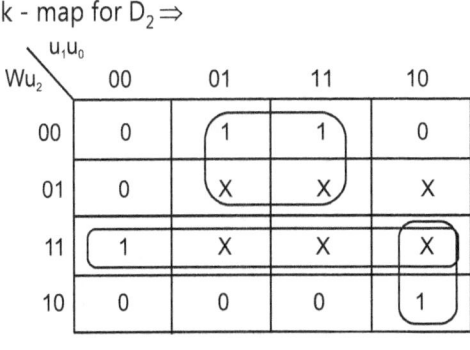

$$\therefore \quad D_2 = Wu_2 + \bar{W}u_0 + Wu_1\bar{u}_0$$

k - map for $D_1 \Rightarrow$

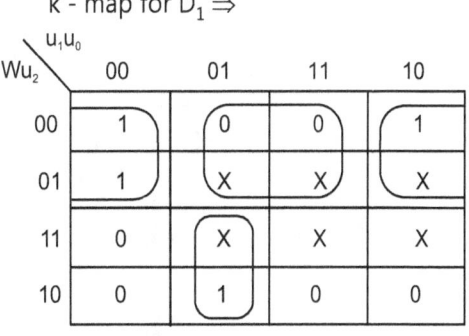

$$\therefore \quad D_1 = \bar{W}\bar{u}_0 + W\bar{u}_1u_0$$

k - map for $J_0 \Rightarrow$

Wu$_2$ \ u$_1$u$_0$	00	01	11	10
00	0	0	0	1
01	1	X	X	X
11	0	X	X	X
10	1	0	0	0

$$\therefore \ D_0 = W\bar{u}_2\,\bar{u}_1\,\bar{u}_0 + \bar{W}\,u_2 + \bar{W}\,u_1\,\bar{u}_0$$

k - map for $K_0 \Rightarrow$

Wu$_2$ \ u$_1$u$_0$	00	01	11	10
00	0	0	0	1
01	1	X	X	X
11	0	X	X	X
10	0	0	1	1

$$\therefore \ Z = \bar{W}u_2 + Wu_1 + u_1\,\bar{u}_0$$

- Based on above expressions we construct the circuit diagram as shown in Fig. 4.27.

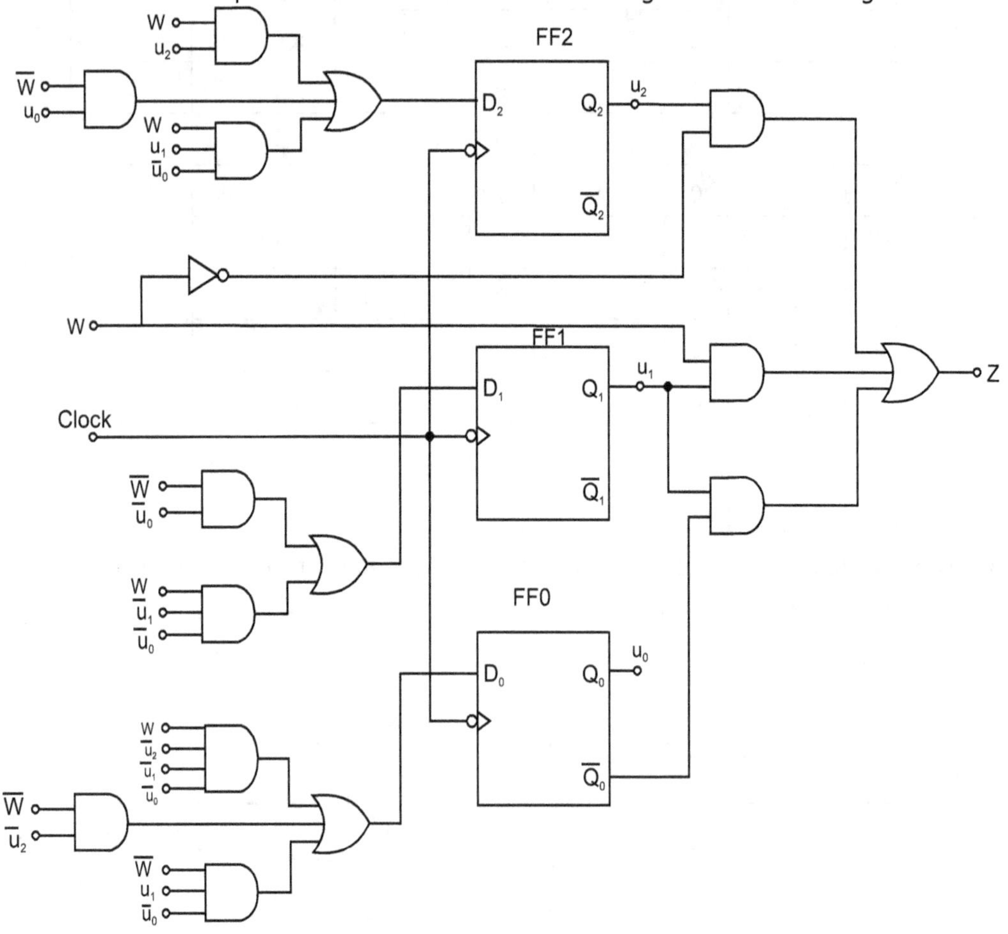

Fig. 4.27

PROGRAMMABLE LOGIC DEVICES AND SEMICONDUCTOR MEMORIES

5.1 INTRODUCTION

- The technological growth in digital design has increased complexity of the system to a large extent. Also, size, power and speed are the major factors in the design aspect. Therefore, there is a need to study different programmable logic devices.

5.2 PROGRAMMABLE LOGIC DEVICES (PLDS)

Q. What is a PLD ? **[2 M]**

- Programmable logic devices (PLD) are standard ICs that are available in standard configurations.

- They are special type of ICs which can be programmed by the users as per their requirements.

- PLDs are configured (programmed) to create a part, customized to a specific application and so they also belong to family of Application Specific Integrated ICs (ASICs).

- PLDs use different technologies to allow programming of the device.

5.2.1 Types of PLDS

- Simple Programmable Logic Devices (SPLDs)
- Complex Programmable Logic Devices (CPLDs)
- Field Programmable Gate Arrays (FPGAs)

5.2.2 Simple Programmable Logic Devices (SPLDS)

- Again, Simple Programmable Logic Devices used are,
- Programmable logic Arrays (PLAs)
- Programmable Array Logic (PAL)
- Generic Array Logic (GAL)
- SPLD's are smallest and consequently the least expensive form of the programmable logic. These PLDs have lesser power consumption, fewer IC count and are more reliable than discreet logic designs.

5.2.3 Need of Programmable Logic Devices

Q. Explain the advantages of PLD ?   **[Dec. 04, 3 M]**

Programmable logic provides many advantages, as listed below.

1. Programmable logic saves valuable board space, or real estate power and debug time, which can lower cost.
2. It also increases performance and design security. There is a security fuse, which can be used to protect proprietary intellectual property.
3. Integration increases design reliability because there are fewer dependencies on the interconnection of devices.
4. Greatest advantage of programmable logic is flexibility. If there are changes in the design, we can modify the connections inside programmable logic devices, without making and breaking connections. This will save additional NRE costs and lost time to market.
5. Programmable logic allows you to use design tools that help you to automate the process. The real work in programmable logic design process is in producing the design description from the design specification. The rest of the steps are automated with software. The design description can be captured in a number of languages, including VHDL/VERILOG or ABEL. The output of the software is a fuse map that is used to program a device.

5.3   PROGRAMMABLE LOGIC ARRAYS (PLAS)

Q. Explain PLA with the help of neat diagram.   **[Dec. 10, 2 M]**
Q. What is the difference between a masked PLA and FPLA ? How is the size of PLA specified ?   **[Dec. 05, 8 M]**

The first PLDs were Programmable Logic Arrays (PLAs). A programmable logic array device contains basically an array of AND-OR functions whose configuration is done by the user.

5.3.1 Architecture of PLA

The block diagram for internal architecture of PLA is shown in Fig. 5.1.

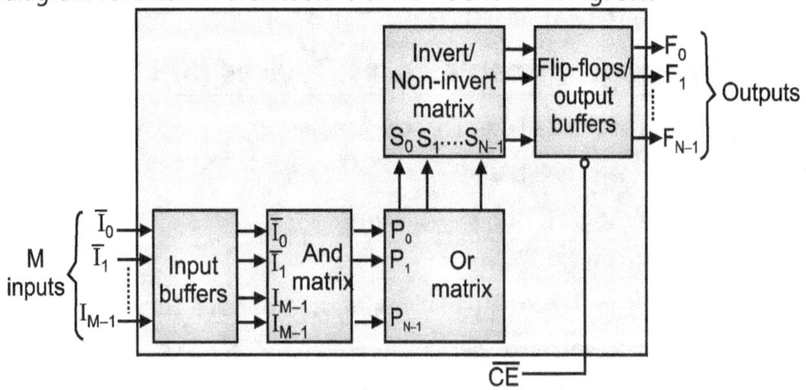

Fig. 5.1 : Block diagram of PLA device

- A PLA consists of two level AND – OR circuits on a single chip. The number of AND and OR gates and their inputs are fixed for a given PLA chip. The AND gates provide the product terms and OR gates ORs their product terms and generates a SOP (sum of products) expression.

Input buffer

- Input buffer produces inverted as well as non-inverted inputs at the output as shown in Fig. 5.2 for one input. There are similar buffers for each one of the M inputs. Input buffers are required to limit loading of the sources that drive the inputs.

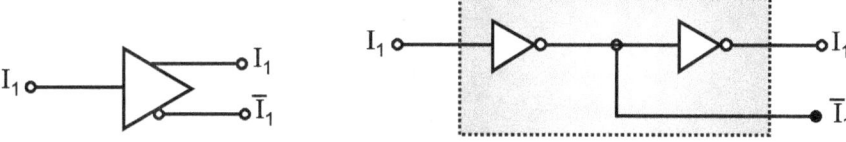

Fig. 5.2 : Input Buffers

5.3.2 AND Matrix

- An AND matrix is used to form product terms. A typical AND matrix is shown in Fig. 5.3

- It has n AND gates with outputs P_0 to P_{n-1} and 2M inputs (I_0 to I_{M-1} and I0 to $\overline{I}_{M-1}$) for each AND gate. Nichrome fuse link is connected in series with each diode. All the links are closed in an unprogrammed PLA device and logic 0 is stored.

- Each AND gate generates one product term which is given by

$$P = I_0 \cdot \overline{I_0} \cdot I_1 \cdot \overline{I_1} \ldots I_{m-1} \cdot \overline{I}_{m-1}$$

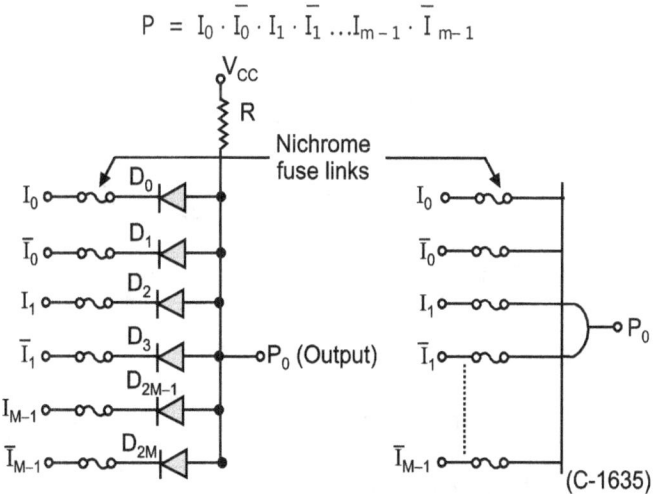

Fig. 5.3 : An AND Matrix

- By using a programmer device, unwanted links are opened, to generate required product term.

The gate representation for P_0 output is shown in Fig. 5.4.

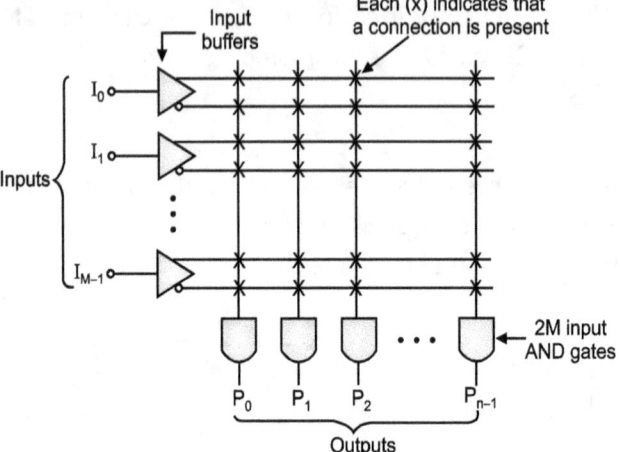

Fig. 5.4 : An AND Matrix

5.3.3 OR matrix

- The OR matrix is used to produce the logical sum of the product terms (outputs of AND matrix). Fig. 5.5 shows an OR matrix using transistor. An OR gate consists of parallel connected transistors with a common emitter load. S_0 to S_{n-1} are the outputs of an OR matrix.

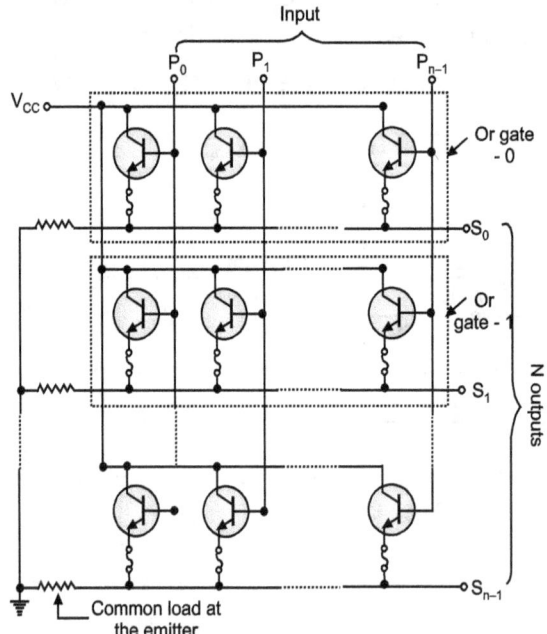

Fig. 5.5

- All the fuse links are closed in an unprogrammed device. The S_0 output is given by

$$S_0 = P_0 + P_1 + \cdots P_{n-1}$$

- The unwanted fuse links can be opened to generate required sum terms.

For example, if P_0 and P_1 fuse links are closed and all others are blown off (opened) for the output S_0, then $\qquad S_0 = P_0 + P_1$

- The logic symbol for one OR gate is shown in Fig. 5.6.

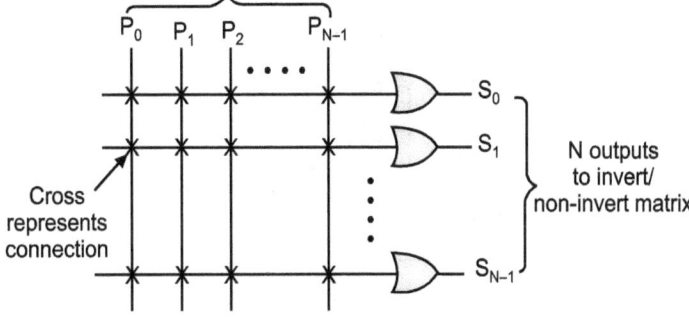

Fig. 5.6 : An OR matrix

5.3.4 Invert/Non-Invert matrix

- This is a programmable buffer. This is used to generate active low or active high outputs. Typical circuits for this operation are shown in Fig. 5.7.

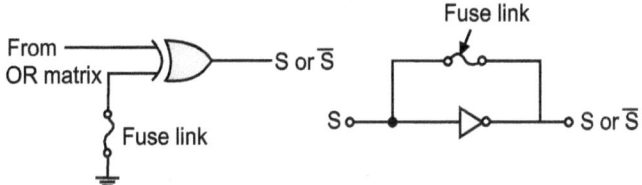

Fig. 5.7 : Inverting /Non-inverting buffer

- When fuse link is closed, the output is S and output is $\overline{S}$ when fuse is blown off (opened).

Output buffer : To increase the driving capability of the PLA, output buffers are required. Usually, the outputs are TTL compatible. Fig. 5.8 shows the three-state output buffers.

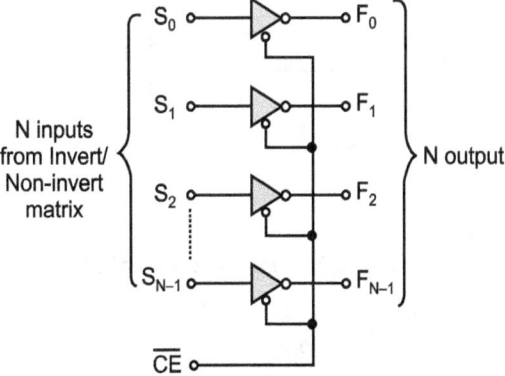

Fig. 5.8 : Output buffers

5.3.5 Output through flip-flop and Buffers

- The output of the OR gate can be connected to the input of flip-flops. The device output can be available through tristate buffers as shown in Fig. 5.9. The PLA device with Output flip-flops and Buffers are suitable for state machine application.

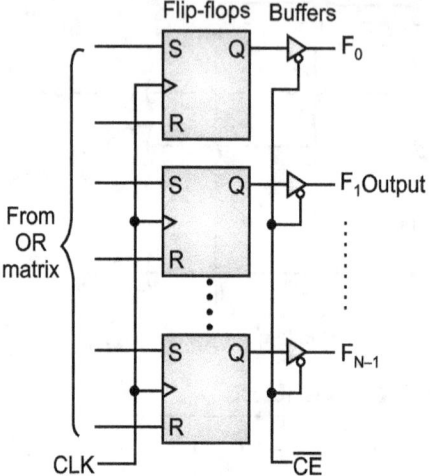

Fig. 5.9 : Output through flip-flop

The PLA can be represented by AND and OR arrays as shown in Fig. 5.10.

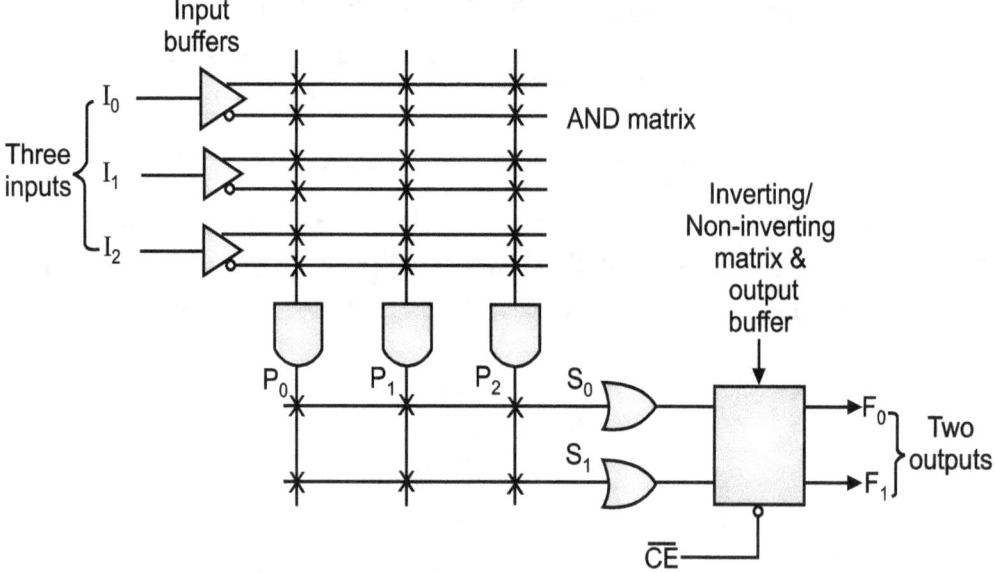

Fig. 5.10 : Representation of PLA

- A PLA device can be programmed similar to the programming of ROM. For a mask programmable device, the data pattern is to be specified by the customer. The appropriate masks are designed by the manufacturers and the data pattern is built in during the manufacturing process.

- An FPLA (Field Programmable Logic Array) has its entire nichrome links intact at the time of manufacturing. The unwanted links are electrically open circuited during programming. The links to be opened are accessed by applying voltages at the inputs and outputs of the device. The FPLAs are not reprogrammable.

5.3.6 Circuit Realization using PLA

Example 5.1 :

Implement BCD to gray code converter using PLA.   **[May 08, 8M May 11, 9M]**

Solution :

The following table shows BCD numbers and their equivalent gray code.

Truth Table 5.1

BCD Code				Gray Code			
D_3	D_2	D_1	D_0	G_3	G_2	G_1	G_0
0	0	0	0	0	0	0	0
0	0	0	1	0	0	0	1
0	0	1	0	0	0	1	1
0	0	1	1	0	0	1	0
0	1	0	0	0	1	1	0
0	1	0	1	0	1	1	1
0	1	1	0	0	1	0	1
0	1	1	1	0	1	0	0
1	0	0	0	1	1	0	0
1	0	0	1	1	1	0	1

The K-Maps for the above truth table can be made as follows:

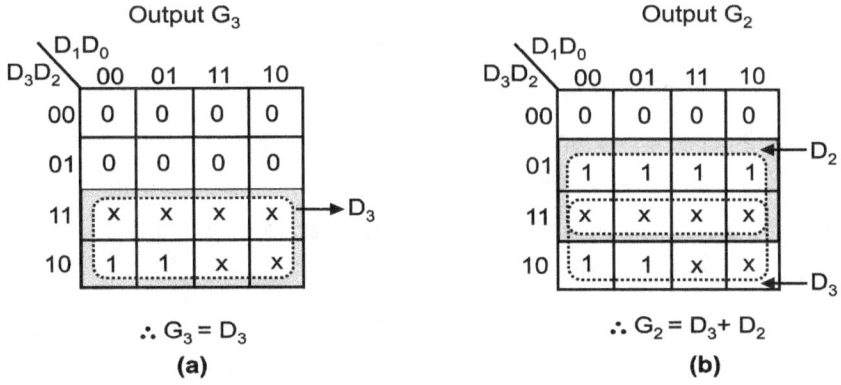

$\therefore G_3 = D_3$

(a)

$\therefore G_2 = D_3 + D_2$

(b)

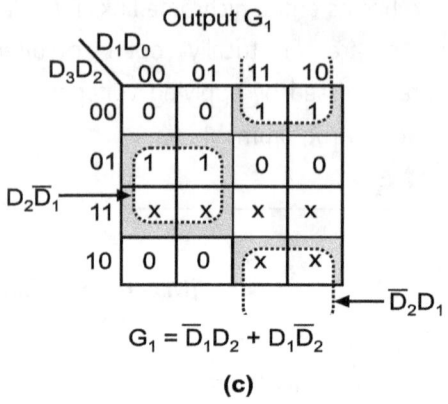

$G_1 = \overline{D}_1 D_2 + D_1 \overline{D}_2$

(c)

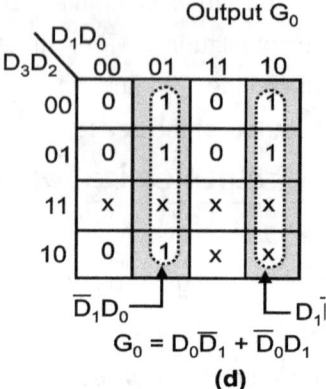

$G_0 = D_0 \overline{D}_1 + \overline{D}_0 D_1$

(d)

Fig. 5.11

From the table, we can get

$$G_3 = D_3$$
$$G_2 = D_2 \oplus D_3 = \overline{D_2} D_3 + D_2 \overline{D_3}$$
$$G_1 = D_1 \oplus D_2 = \overline{D_1} D_2 + D_1 \overline{D_2}$$
$$G_0 = D_0 \oplus D_1 = \overline{D_0} D_1 + D_0 \overline{D_1}$$

PLA with 4 inputs, 7 product terms and 4 outputs is shown in Fig. 5.12.

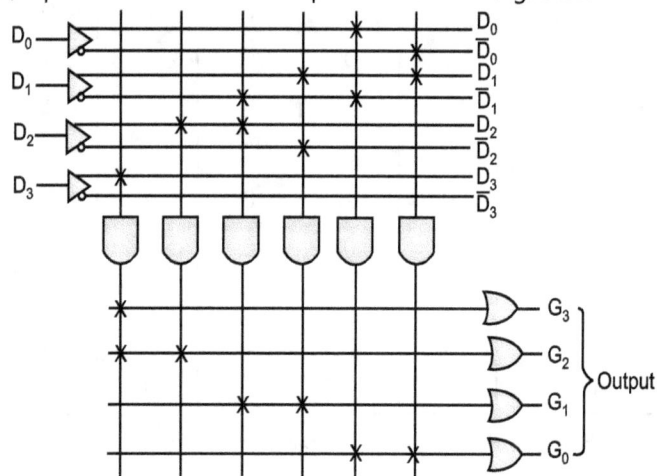

Fig. 5.12 : PLA realization

The AND-OR array equivalent of K-maps is shown in Fig. 5.12.

From Fig. 5.12, it can be observed that PLA utilizes less space as compared to ROM. A more better way of utilization of empty space in PLA can be done by allowing two or more input lines to share the same column, or to let the product lines share the same row or by both. This sharing is known as folding.

In PLA, both AND and OR arrays are programmable. Hence PLA devices are more flexible than PAL devices. Thus the same AND output can be sent to any number of OR gates.

Example 5.2 :

Implement the following output function using suitable PLA

   f (A, B, C, D) = Σ m (3, 4, 5, 7, 10, 14, 15)

Solution :

To implement a combinational circuit using PLA, first we need to convert the function in their sum of products form. Also, we can find the common product terms among the k-maps of the outputs.

K – map is

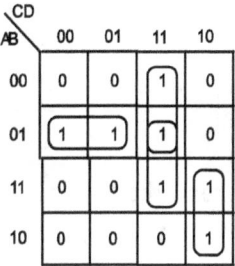

Fig. 5.13

$$f (A, B, C, D) = \bar{A} B \bar{C} + \bar{A} C \bar{D} + BCD + AC\bar{D}$$

Now, in the above equation, there are 4 product terms. Therefore, we need minimum 4 inputs, 1 output and 4 product terms.

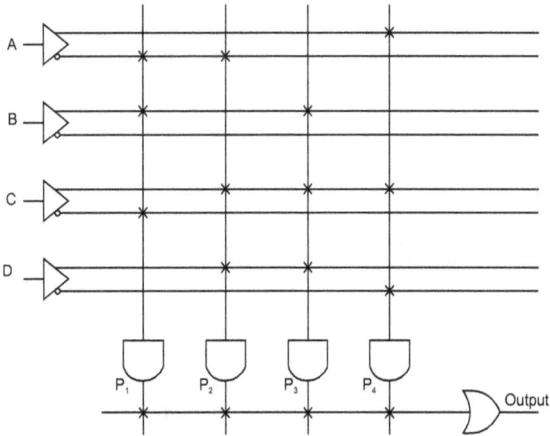

Fig. 5.14 : Programmed PLA for example 5. 1

Example 5.3 :

Implement Full Adder Circuit Using PLA.

Solution : Now, we will first draw the Truth Table of Full Adder

Table 5.2 : Truth table of Full Adder

Inputs			Outputs	
A	**B**	**C**	**Sum**	**Carry**
0	0	0	0	0
0	0	1	1	0
0	1	0	1	0
0	1	1	0	1
1	0	0	1	0
1	0	1	0	1
1	1	0	0	1
1	1	1	1	1

From the above truth table, we can write the equations for sum and carry as.

$$\text{Sum} = \Sigma m \ (1, 2, 4, 7) \qquad \qquad \qquad \text{...(5. 1)}$$

$$\text{Carry} = \Sigma m \ (3, 5, 6, 7) \qquad \qquad \qquad \text{...(5. 2)}$$

The K-maps are used to simplify the above equations.

K - map for sum

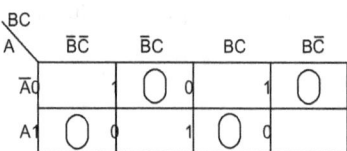

Fig. 5.15

We can write the SOP as

$$\text{Sum} = \bar{A} \bar{B} C + \bar{A} B \bar{C} + A \bar{B} \bar{C} + ABC$$

Similarly, the K-map for carry is

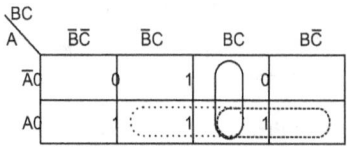

Fig. 5.16

SOP for carry is $\text{Carry} = AC + AB + BC$

Thus, PLA realization of a full adder is as shown in Fig. 5.17.

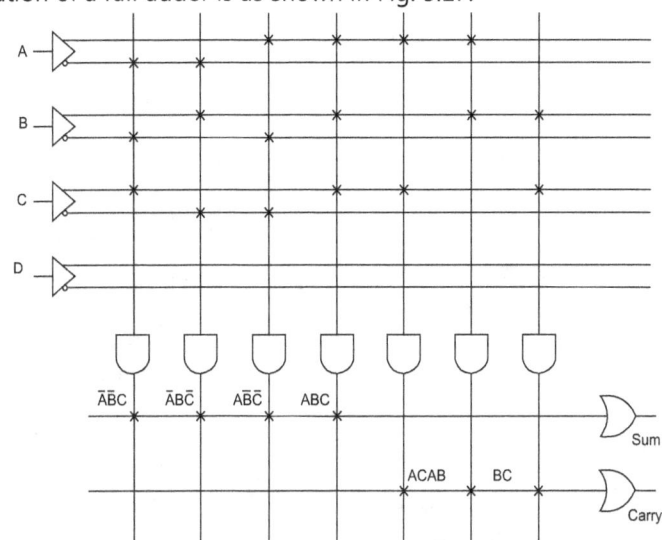

Fig. 5.17 : Programmed PLA for a full adder

Example 5.4

Design a BCD to Excess-3 code converter and implement it using a suitable PLA

[Dec. 06, 07, 8M]

Solution :

The first step to the solution is to draw a truth table. For different combinations of BCD inputs, the Excess-3 output is as shown in the truth table.

Table 5.3 : Truth table for BCD to Excess -3 conversion

Decimal	BCD inputs				Excess – 3 outputs			
	D_3	D_2	D_1	D_0	E_3	E_2	E_1	E_0
0	0	0	0	0	0	0	1	1
1	0	0	0	1	0	1	0	0
2	0	0	1	0	0	1	0	1
3	0	0	1	1	0	1	1	0
4	0	1	0	0	0	1	1	1
5	0	1	0	1	1	0	0	0
6	0	1	1	0	1	0	0	1
7	0	1	1	1	1	0	1	0
8	1	0	0	0	1	0	1	1
9	1	0	0	1	1	1	0	0

The K-maps for the Excess-3 output E_0, E_1, E_2, E_3 are as shown:

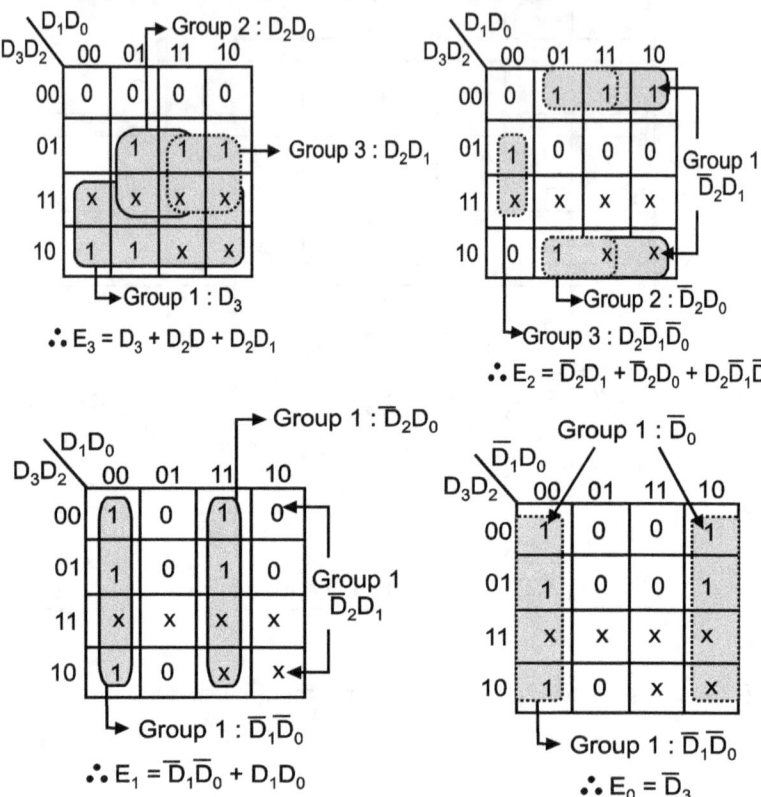

$$\therefore E_3 = D_3 + D_2 D + D_2 D_1$$

$$\therefore E_2 = \overline{D}_2 D_1 + \overline{D}_2 D_0 + D_2 \overline{D}_1 \overline{D}_0$$

$$\therefore E_1 = \overline{D}_1 \overline{D}_0 + D_1 D_0$$

$$\therefore E_0 = \overline{D}_3$$

Fig. 5.18 : K-maps

- From SOP obtained different bits, the PLA can be realized as shown in Fig. 5.19.

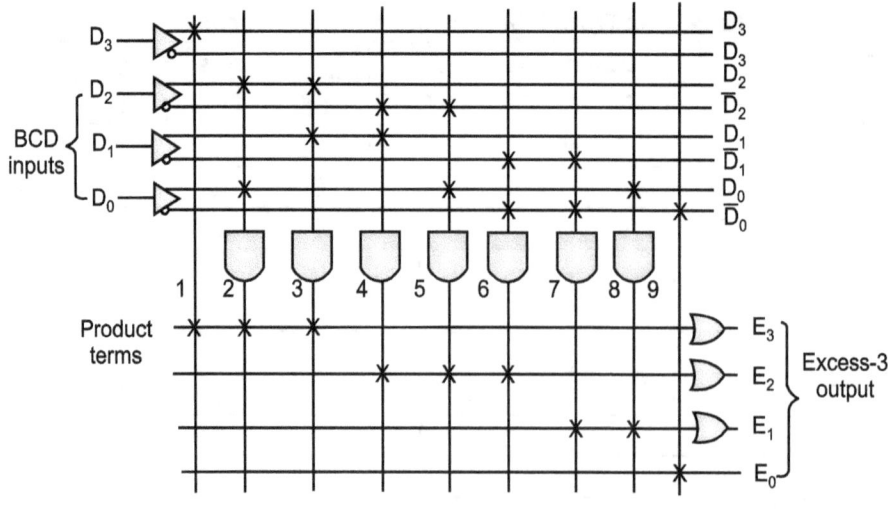

Fig. 5.19 : PLA realization for BCD-to-Excess-3 conversion

Example 5.5 : Design a 3-bit Gray to Binary converter and implement it using a PLA.

Solution :

Draw a truth table from Gray to Binary conversion.

Table 5.4 : Truth table for Gray to Binary conversion

Decimal	Gray input			Binary output		
	G_2	G_1	G_0	B_2	B_1	B_0
0	0	0	0	0	0	0
1	0	0	1	0	0	1
3	0	1	1	0	1	0
2	0	1	0	0	1	1
6	1	1	0	1	0	0
7	1	1	1	1	0	1
5	1	0	1	1	1	0
4	1	0	0	1	1	1

The K-maps for the binary outputs is as shown in the figure below.

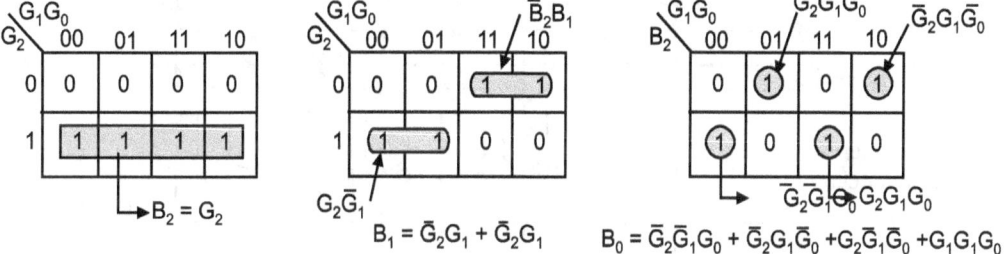

$$B_2 = G_2$$
$$B_1 = \bar{G}_2 G_1 + \bar{G}_2 G_1$$
$$B_0 = \bar{G}_2 \bar{G}_1 G_0 + \bar{G}_2 G_1 \bar{G}_0 + G_2 \bar{G}_1 \bar{G}_0 + G_1 G_1 G_0$$

Fig. 5.20 : K-maps for the binary outputs B_0, B_1, B_2

The PLA realization for the above K-maps can be drawn as given in Fig. 5.21.

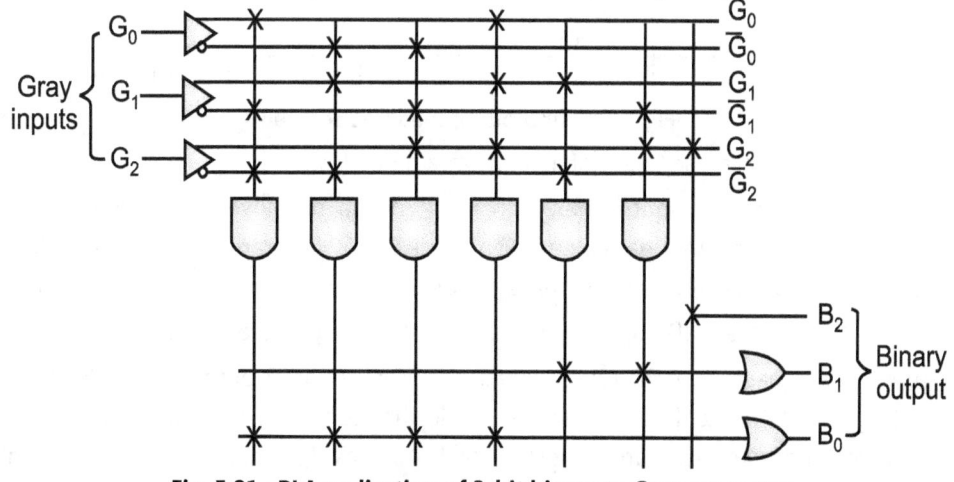

Fig. 5.21 : PLA realization of 3-bit binary to Gray converter

5.4 PROGRAMMABLE ARRAY LOGIC (PAL)

Q. Explain PAL with the help of neat diagram.   **[Dec. 09, 2 M]**

- In programmable array logic, the AND array is programmable and the OR array is fixed. The basic structure of the PAL is the same as PLA. PAL is less expensive than PLA because only the AND array is programmable.

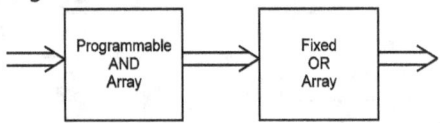

Fig. 5.22 : Structure of PAL

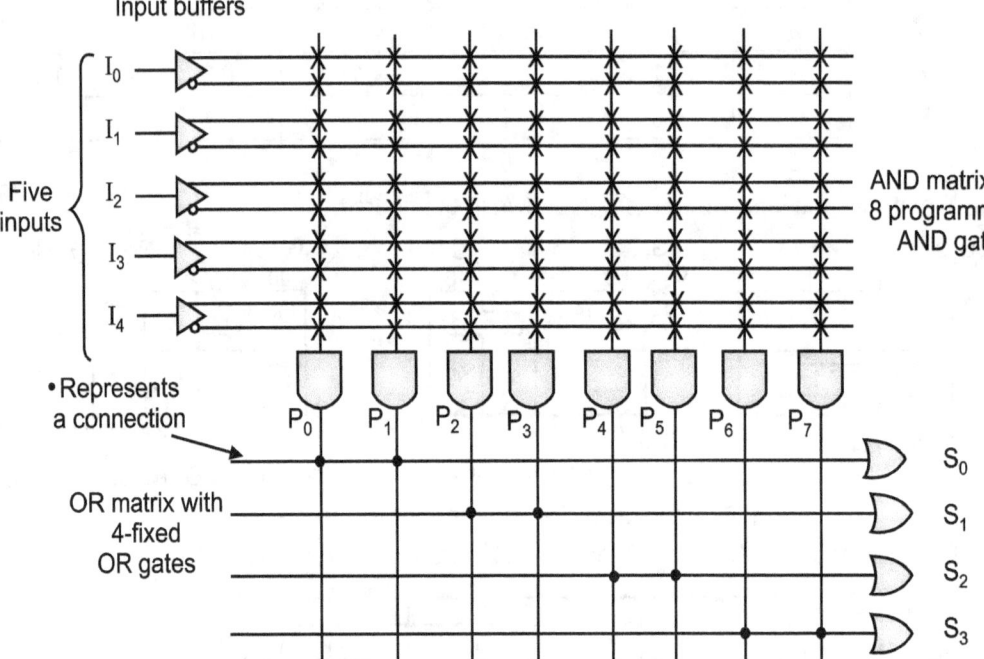

Fig. 5.23 : Unprogrammed PAL segment

- Fig. 5.23 represents a segment of an unprogrammed PAL.

- The figure shows an input buffer, with inverted and non-inverted outputs. A buffer is used to drive many AND gate inputs. When the PAL is programmed, the fusible links (F1, F2 - - F8) are selectively blown to leave the desired connections to the AND gate inputs.

- Connections to the AND gate inputs in a PAL are represented by 'X', as shown.

- Typical PALs have from 10 to 20 inputs and from 2 to 10 outputs, 2 to 6 AND gates driving each OR gate. PALs are also available that contain D flip-flop with inputs driven from the programmable array logic. Such PALs provide a convenient way of realizing sequential networks.

Example 5.6 :

Implement the following output function using PAL.

$$f_1(x, y, z) = \sum m \ (0, 1, 3, 6, 7)$$
$$f_2 (x, y, z) = \sum m \ (1, 2, 4, 6)$$

Solution : In PAL, the OR array is fixed and AND array is programmable. Since the OR array is fixed the number of product terms per OR gate cannot be changed. In PALs, unlike the PLAs, a product term cannot be shared among two or more OR gates. First, we need to simplify the functions f_1 and f_2 using k - map.

k-map for f_1

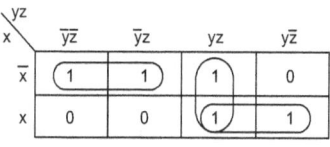

Fig. 5.24(a)

$\therefore$ $\qquad\qquad\qquad f_1 = x\bar{y} \ + \ yz \ + \ xy$

k -map for f_2

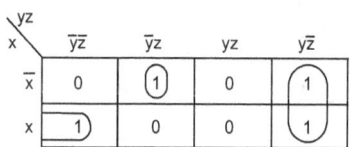

Fig. 5.24(b)

$$f_2 = x\bar{z} \ + \ \bar{y}z \ + \ \bar{x}\bar{y} z$$

From above equations, we require 3 inputs, 2 outputs and maximum 3 product terms per OR gate.

Now, we will prepare a PAL program table.

Table 5.5 : PAL Program Table

Product Terms		AND Inputs			Outputs
		x	y	z	
$\bar{x}\bar{y}$	1	0	0	–	
yz	2	–	1	1	$f_1 = x\bar{y} \ + \ yz \ +$
xy	3	1	1	–	xy
$x\bar{z}$	4	1	–	0	
$\bar{y}z$	5	–	1	0	$f_2 = x\bar{z} \ + \ \bar{y}z \ +$
	6	0	0	1	$\bar{x}\bar{y} z$
$\bar{x}\bar{y} z$					

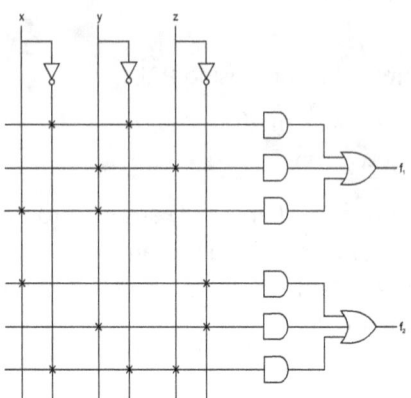

Fig. 5.25 PAL realization of the given function

Example 5.7 :

Design a BCD to Excess-3 converter and implement it using PAL.   **[Dec 12, 8 M]**

Solution : The truth table for BCD to Excess- 3 converter can be made as shown

Table 5.6 : Truth table for BCD to Excess-3 conversion

Decimal	BCD inputs				Excess – 3 outputs			
	D_3	D_2	D_1	D_0	E_3	E_2	E_1	E_0
0	0	0	0	0	0	0	1	1
1	0	0	0	1	0	1	0	0
2	0	0	1	0	0	1	0	1
3	0	0	1	1	0	1	1	0
4	0	1	0	0	0	1	1	1
5	0	1	0	1	1	0	0	0
6	0	1	1	0	1	0	0	1
7	0	1	1	1	1	0	1	0
8	1	0	0	0	1	0	1	1
9	1	0	0	1	1	1	0	0

Based on the truth table the k-map for the outputs E_0, E_1, E_2, E_3 are drawn.

Output E_3

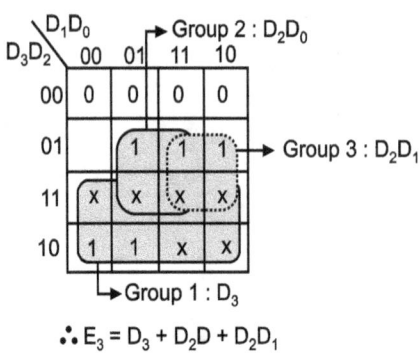

$\therefore E_3 = D_3 + D_2D + D_2D_1$

Output E_2

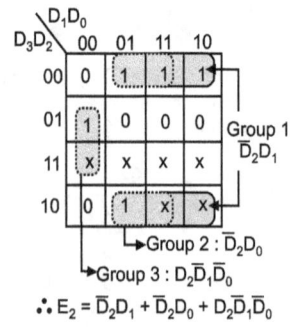

$\therefore E_2 = \overline{D}_2D_1 + \overline{D}_2D_0 + D_2\overline{D}_1\overline{D}_0$

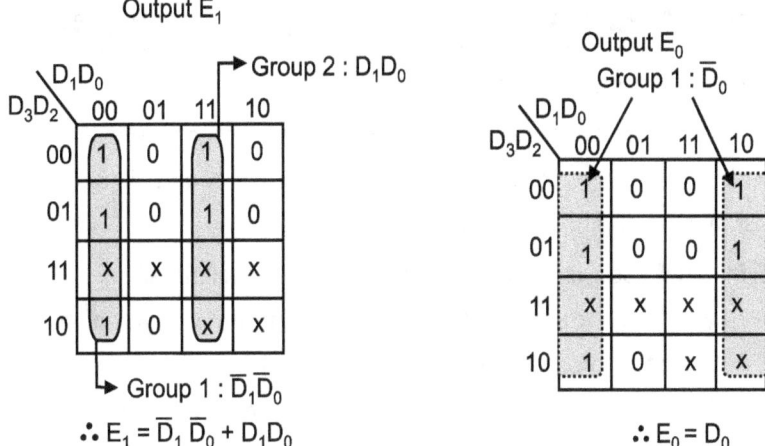

$$\therefore E_1 = \overline{D}_1\,\overline{D}_0 + D_1 D_0$$

$$\therefore E_0 = D_0$$

Fig. 5.26 : K-maps for Excess-3 outputs

The PAL realization based on the k-map minterms are implemented as shown below.

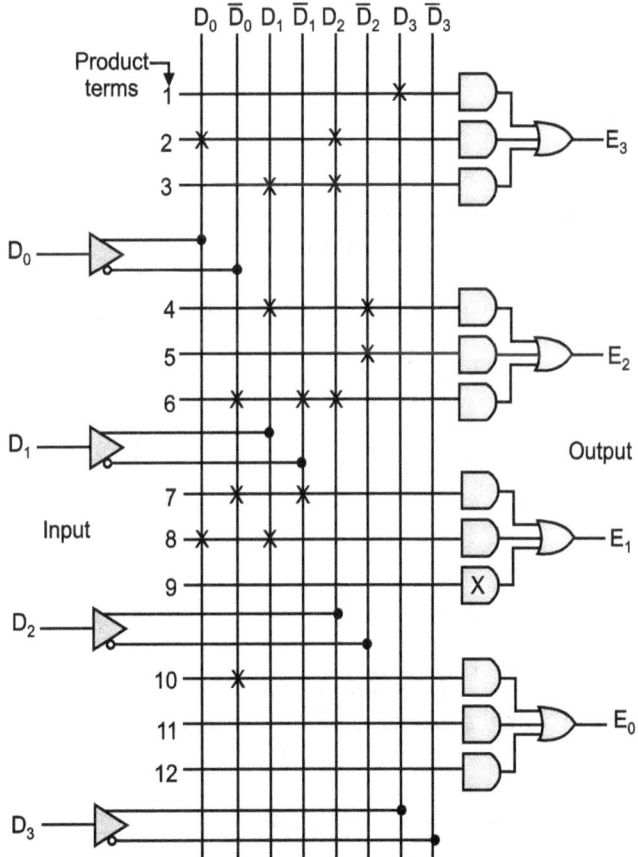

Fig. 5.27 : Implementation of BCD to Excess-3 code converter using PAL.

5.5 PROGRAMMABLE READ ONLY MEMORY (PROM)

- ROM means "Read Only Memory".

- Initially the diodes are connected between every rows and columns through the possible links, therefore initial information stored in all the locations and all the bits are zero; i.e. at the time of fabrication, the information in memory is zero.

- The fuse material used is either nichrome or polycrystalline silicon, these fuse can be blown OFF by passing large current through it. During the programming, the fuse will be blown OFF, where the information is to be stored as '1'.

- If nichrome is used as the fuse material, then 20 to 50 mA current is required to blow OFF the fuse. The fusing time varies between 5 µs and 200 µs and programming rate is 5 ms per bit.

- The PROM is one time programmable, once programmed the information stored cannot be changed. It can be read only.

Example 5.8 :

Design a 3-bit gray to binary code converter. Implement it using suitable PROM. Draw the PROM table and logic diagram.   **[May 07, 6 M]**

Solution :

1. Truth table for gray to binary converter.

Table 5.7

G_2	G_1	G_0	B_2	B_1	B_0
0	0	0	0	0	0
0	0	1	0	0	1
0	1	1	0	1	0
0	1	0	0	1	1
1	1	0	1	0	0
1	1	1	1	0	1
1	0	1	1	1	0
1	0	0	1	1	1

So after this we will calculate the expression for the truth table.

$$B_2 = G_2$$

$$B_1 = \overline{G_2}G_1 + G_2\overline{G_1}$$

$$B_0 = \overline{G_2}\,\overline{G_1}G_0 + \overline{G_2}G_1\overline{G_0} + G_2G_1G_0 + G_2\overline{G_1}\,\overline{G_0}$$

PROM is required 3 input variable G_2, G_1, G_0.

So, there will be $2^3 = 8$, memory locations so each location can store 4-bit word.

Table 5.8 : Truth table for gray to binary code conversion

Memory Location Number	Inputs			Output			
	G_2	G_1	G_0	B_3	B_2	B_1	B_0
0	0	0	0	0	0	0	0
1	0	0	1	0	0	0	1
2	0	1	0	0	0	1	1
3	0	1	1	0	0	1	0
4	1	0	0	0	1	1	1
5	1	0	1	0	1	1	0
6	1	1	0	0	1	0	0
7	1	1	1	0	1	0	1

Logic diagram for this truth table.

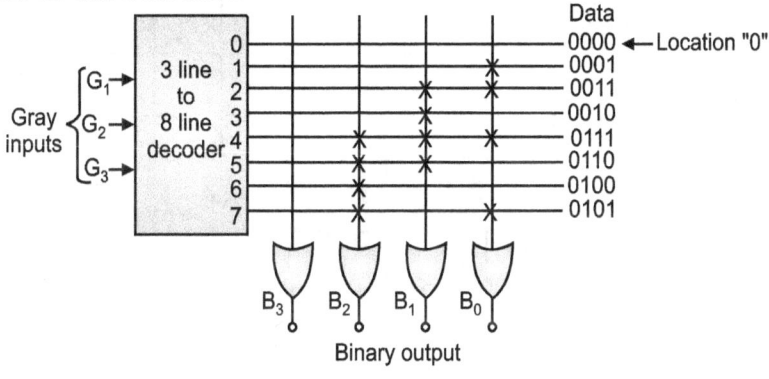

Fig. 5.28

5.6 SEMICONDUCTOR MEMORIES

Q. Explain the ROM memory in detail.

The semiconductor memories are classified as shown below.

Table 5.9

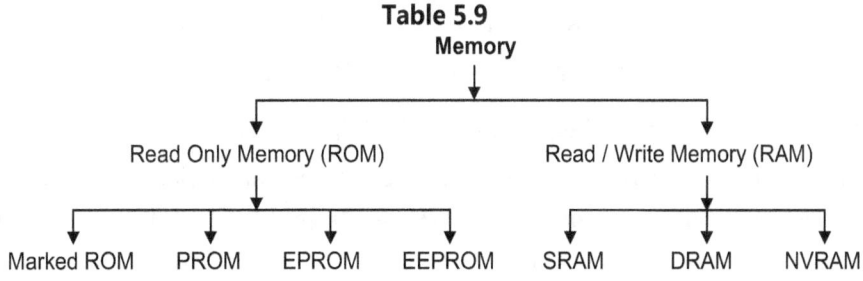

5.7   ROM (Read Only Memory)

Q. What do you mean by ROM ?

Q. Define ROM.

- As the name indicates, it is a Read Only Memory. It means, the user cannot write data in this memory. It is non - volatile memory. Non - Volatile means, it can hold data even if the power is turned off. ROM is generally used to store instructions and look up tables.

- There are four types of ROM memories; Masked ROM, PROM, EPROM and EEPROM.

Organization of ROM Memory :

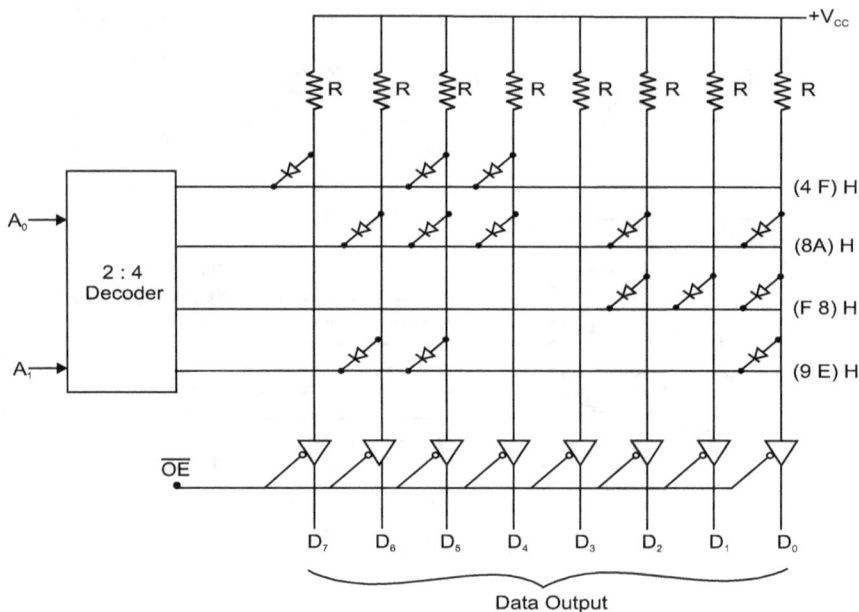

Fig. 5.29 : Four byte diode ROM

- Fig. 5.29 shows a simple 4 byte diode ROM. Diode ROM consists of only diodes and a decoder. As shown, address lines A_0 and A_1 are decoded by 2 : 4 decoder and used to select one of the four rows. As the decoder output is active low, it places a logic '0' on the selected row.

- When the output of the decoder goes low, the diode conducts and logic 'o' is available at that data line. It means that the presence of diode indicates logic 'o'. Data is available on the output data line only when output enable ($\overline{OE}$) signal is low.

- As shown in Fig 5.29 when the first row is selected, the data available at the output is (4F) H. Similarly second, third and fourth row generates (8A) H, (F8) H and (9E) H as the output.

Table 5.10 : Shows the contents of ROM at four locations.

Address	Binary Data								Data in
	D_7	D_6	D_5	D_4	D_3	D_2	D_1	D_0	Memory
00	0	1	0	0	1	1	1	1	4 F
01	1	0	0	0	1	0	1	0	8A
10	1	1	1	1	1	0	0	0	F8
11	1	0	0	1	1	1	1	0	9E

- Now-a-days ROMs use MOS technology instead of diode. In this the diodes and pull up resistors are replaced by MOS transistors.
- These ROMs are called as Mask - programmed ROMs. Masked ROMs are used in microprocessor based systems such as TV games, toys etc.

5.7.1 PROM : (Programmable Read only Memory)

> **Q.** Explain the PROM in detail. **[2 M]**

Four byte PROM is shown in Fig. 5.30.

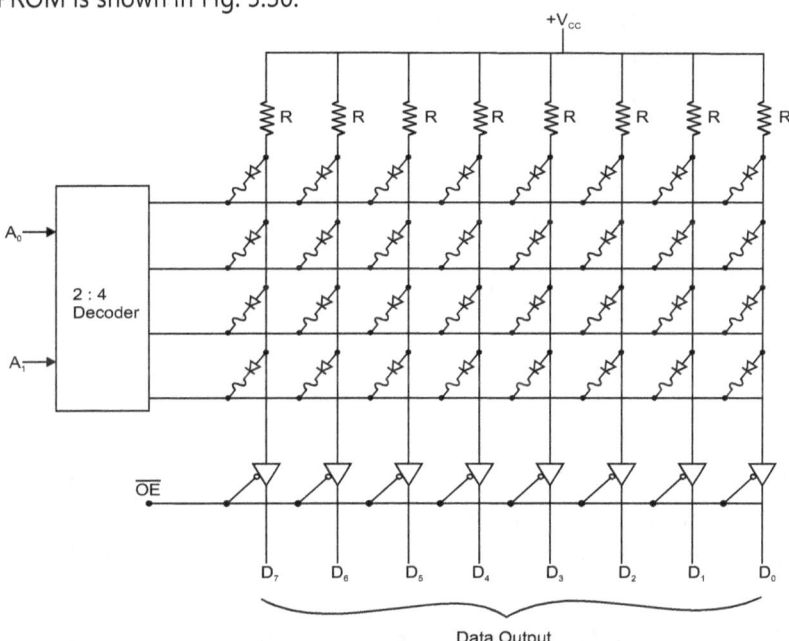

Fig. 5.30 : Four byte PROM

- It has diodes in every bit position. Therefore, the output is initially all 0s. Each diode has fusible link in series with it. By applying proper current pulse at the corresponding output, we can blow out the fuse, storing logic '1' at that bit position. The fuse uses material like Nichrome and Polycrystalline. To blow out the fuse, it is necessary to pass a current around 20 to 50 mA for the period of 5 to 20 μs. The blowing of fuses according to the Truth Table is called Programming of ROM.

- There is a special device available called as PROM Programmer to program the PROM. The PROM programmer is used to selectively burn the fuses according to the bit pattern to be stored. This process is known as burning of PROM. PROM's are called as OTP. i.e. One Time Programmable. Once programmed, the information stored is permanent.

5.7.2 EPROM (Erasable Programmable Read Only Memory)

Q. Explain basic description of EPROM.

- As the name indicates, we can erase the stored data in the EPROM. To erase and program the EPROM, a special device is used called as EPROM Programmer. To erase the data stored in EPROM, it is exposed to the ultraviolet light through its Quartz window for 15 to 20 minutes as shown in Fig. 5.31.

- The chip can be reprogrammed. EPROM memory is ideally suitable for the product development experiment projects. These chips are used in college laboratories, since this chip can be reused many times.

- When EPROM is erased each cell in the EPROM contains '1'. Data is introduced by selectively programming '0's into the desired bit locations.

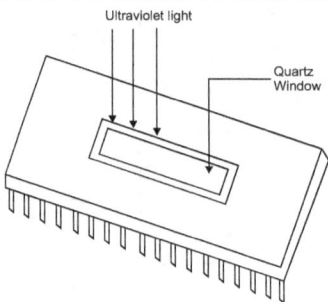

Fig. 5.31 : EPROM IC

- During programming of the EPROM, address and data are applied to the address and data pins of the EPROM. When the address and data are stable then program pulse is applied to the program input of the EPROM. The program pulse duration is about 50 ms and its amplitude depends on the EPROM IC. The amplitude of EPROM pulse is typically 5.5 V to 25V.

5.7.3 EEPROM (E^2PROM) (Electrically Erasable Programmable Read Only Memory)

Q. Explain in brief EEPROM.	**[Dec. 04, 3 M]**
Q. Discuss in detail characteristics of EEPROM.	**[May 27, 2 M]**

- EEPROM are similar to the EPROM but in EEPROM the data is erased by using electrical signal, instead of ultraviolet light. E^2 PROM uses, MOS circuitry very similar to that of EPROM.

- Data is stored as charge or no charge on an insulated layer or an insulated floating gate in the device. In this the insulating layer is made very thin (< 200° A). Therefore a voltage as low as 20 to 25 V can be used to move charge across the thin barrier in either direction for programming or erasing.

- E^{2}PROM allows selective erasing at the register level rather than erasing all the information since the information can be changed by using electrical signals.

- The E^{2}PROM IC also has a special chip erase mode, by this chip entire chip can be erased in 10 ms. The advantage of using EEPROM is that the time required to erase the data is very less as compared to EPROM. Also, EEPROM can be erased and reprogrammed with device right in the circuit. But the disadvantage of EEPROMs is that they are most expensive and the least dense ROMs.

5.8   RANDOM ACCESS MEMORY AND ITS ORGANIZATION (RAM)

- In RAM, we can perform both the read and write operations, so it is also called as read/write memory.

- RAM is a volatile memory, means that it cannot hold data when power is turned OFF.

- There are different types of RAM's such as SRAM, DRAM and NVRAM.

5.8.1 Static Random Access Memory (SRAM)

Q. Discuss in detail characteristics of SRAM.	**[May 07, 2 M]**
Q. Write short note on SRAM.	**[Dec. 12, 4 M]**
Q. What is mean by SRAM ? Explain in detail.	**[Dec. 10, 3 M]**
Q. Draw circuits of SRAM cell of each and explain its working.	

Static RAM's are of two types based on manufacturing technology.

(i) SRAM built by using bipolar technology.

(ii) SRAM built by using MOS technology.

5.8.8.1 TTL RAM Cell

- Fig. 5.32 shows, the simplified schematic of a bipolar memory cell. The memory cell is implemented by using TTL (Transistor-Transistor Logic) Multiple emitter technology. It stores 1 bit of information. It is also called as Flip Flop. It can store either logic '0' or logic '1' as long as power is applied.

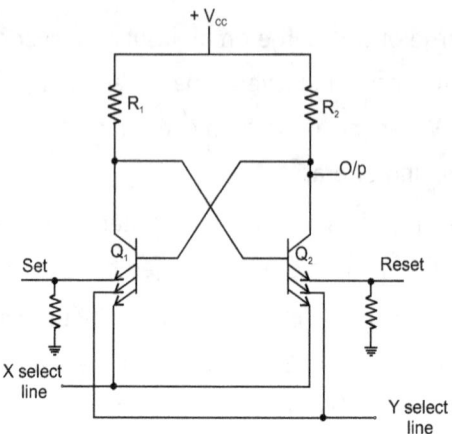

Fig. 5.32 : TTL RAM cell

- Select lines are used to select a cell from the matrix. The Q_1 and Q_2 are cross coupled inverters, hence one is always OFF and the other is always ON.

- Logic '1' is stored in the cell, if Q_1 transistor is conducting and Q_2 is OFF. Similarly, logic '0' is stored in the cell, if Q_2 is conducting and Q_1 is OFF.

- The state of the cell is changed by pulsing a HIGH on the Q_1 (SET) emitter. This turns Q_1 OFF. When Q_1 is turned OFF, Q_2 is turned ON. As long as Q_2 is ON, its collector is LOW and Q_1 is held OFF.

- Large number of these memory cells are organised in a row and column basis to form a memory chip. Fig. 5.33 shows the row and column orgnisation of a memory chip.

- As shown in Fig. 5.33 there is row decoder to select one row and column decoder to select one column. When the decoded row and column cross, they select the desired individual memory cell.

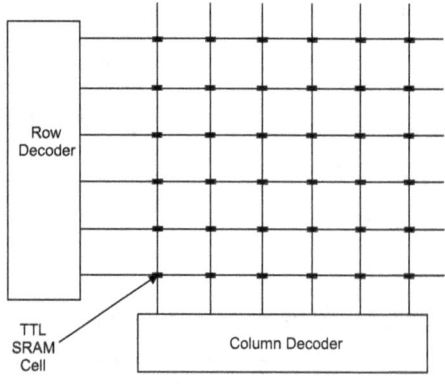

Fig. 5.33 : Row and Column organisation for static RAM

5.8.8.2 MOS Static RAM Cell

Q. Draw basic cells of static RAM and mention two differences.	**[Dec. 07, 6 M]**

- It is very similar to the TTL RAM cell but instead of using transistor, enhancement mode MOSFET is used for MOS static RAM cell.
- T_1 and T_2 transistors form the basic cross coupled inverters. T_3 and T_4 act as load resistors for T_1 and T_2 transistors. X Row select line and Y column select lines are used to address the cell. When X and Y both are high, cell is selected.

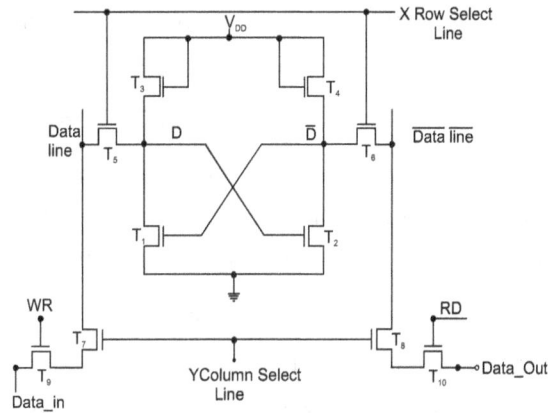

Fig. 5.34 : A MOS Static RAM cell.

- When X = 1, T_5 and T_6 becomes ON and the cell is connected to the data and data line. When Y = 1, T_7 and T_8 becomes ON. Due to this either read or write operation is possible

Write Operation of MOS SRAM :

- Write operation can be enabled by making WR signal High.
  Suppose Data_in signal is at logic '1' then D signal is at logic '1'. This turns ON T_2, at that time T_1 is OFF.
- Similarly, when Data_in signal is at logic '0', then D signal is at logic '0'. This will turn OFF T_2. At the same time T_1 is ON.

Read Operation in MOS SRAM :

- It is enabled by making RD signal high. With read operation enabled, T_{10} becomes ON. When T_{10} is ON, the Data line is connected to the Data_out line.
- Thus the complement of the bit stored in the cell is available at the output.

5.8.2 Dynamic RAM

Q. What is meant by DRAM ? Explain in detail.	**[Dec. 10, 3 M]**
Q. Draw basic cells of dynamic RAM and mention two differences.	**[Dec. 07, 3 M]**
Q. Discuss in detail, characteristics of DRAM.	**[Dec. 08, 2 M]**

- In dynamic RAM capacitor is used to store the charge. Fig. 5.35 shows the dynamic RAM cell.

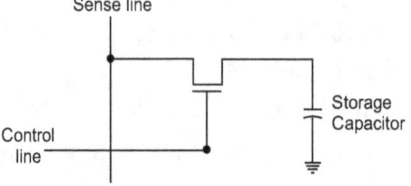

Fig. 5.35 : Dynamic RAM

- A dynamic RAM contains thousands of such memory cells. When the column line and sense line goes high, the MOSFET conducts and charges the capacitor. When the column line and sense line goes low, the MOSFET opens and the capacitor retains its charge. In this way, it stores 1 bit.

- Dynamic RAM contains more memory cells, as only a single MOSFET and capacitor is needed. This is the advantage of DRAM as compared to SRAM.

- The main disadvantage of Dynamic RAM is that it needs refreshing of charge on the capacitor after every few milliseconds. Therefore, it complicates the system design, since it needs the extra hardware control refreshing of dynamic RAMS.

- In Dynamic RAM, the transistor acts as a switch.

5.8.3 Comparison between SRAM and DRAM

Q. Give the comparison between SRAM and DRAM.

	Dynamic RAM	**Static RAM**
1	DRAM contains more memory cells as compared to SRAM per unit area.	SRAM contains less memory cells per unit area.
2	The Access time is greater in DRAM. i.e. speed is less than SRAM.	The Access time is less, i.e. speed is more in SRAM than DRAM.
3	It stores the data as a charge on the capacitor. It consists of MOSFET and the capacitor for each cell.	SRAM consists of number of Flip Flops. Each flip flop stores one bit.
4	Refreshing circuitry is required to maintain the charge on the capacitor.	Refreshing circuitry is not required.
5	Cost is less.	Cost is more.

5.8.4 NVRAM – Non Volatile RAM

Q. Explain the characteristics of NVRAM.   **[Dec. 08, 2 M]**

- These types of memories are Non-volatile types of memories. i.e. it retains data even though the power supply is switched OFF. NVRAM is manufactured by using a combination of a SRAM and an EEPROM.

- SRAM and EERPOM are available on the same IC chip. SRAM is a volatile memory. When the power is ON, it functions as a normal SRAM. But, when the power supply is switched OFF, the data in SRAM is stored in EEPROM.

- The transfer of data from SRAM memory to EEPROM memory occurs in less than 4 ms. When the power supply is switched ON, all the contents of EEPROM are again loaded in SRAM. Therefore the combination of SRAM and EEPROM works as a Non-Volatile memory. Hence, it is called as the NVRAM.

- Two most commonly used signals in NVRAM are STORE and RE CALL. STORE signal is used to store data in EEPROM. RECALL signal is used to transfer the data back into SRAM from EEPROM. RECALL signal is used to transfer the data back into SRAM from EEPROM. NVRAM is most commonly used in computers to store important information such as time, date, computer configurations and settings of the monitor.

Advantage : Battery Backup is not required to save the data, in case of power failure.

5.9 MEMORY IC

- The external pins of memory chip are shown below.

- As shown in Fig. 5.36, there are different pins for memory IC's such as Address lines, Data lines, read $\left(\overline{RD}\right)$, write $\left(\overline{WR}\right)$ and chip select $\left(\overline{CS}\right)$. The functions of these pins are given below.

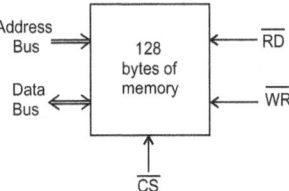

Fig. 5.36 : Memory IC

Address Bus : Address line are unidirectional lines. These lines are used to select one of the memory locations out of the 128 memory locations. The address lines required for the selection of memory location is given by

No. of memory location = 2^n (n=No. of address lines)

Therefore for 128 bytes of memory locations, we require, seven address lines, as

$$2^7 = 128$$

Similarly, if 1024 memory locations are required 10 address lines as

$$2^{10} = 1024$$

Data Bus : Data Bus is used to read or Write the data into the selected memory location. Suppose the size of memory is 128 bytes. It means that one byte corresponds to 8 bit in one memory location. Therefore, we need 8 data lines to store 8 bits of information into one memory location.

Data lines are **bi-directional** lines.

Read signal $\left(\overline{RD}\right)$: When this pin goes low $\left(\text{active low } \overline{RD}\right)$, then read operation is performed.

Write Signal $\left(\overline{WR}\right)$: When this pin goes low $\left(\text{active low } \overline{WR}\right)$, then write operation is performed.

Chip select signal $\left(\overline{CS}\right)$: This pin is used to enable or select the IC for performing different operations.

5.10   Memory Operations

> **Q.** With the help of timing diagram, explain the write operation of memory.

Basic two memory related operations performed are

(i)   Memory Write operation

(ii) Memory Read operation.

5.10.1 Memory Write Operation

The following sequence of events, takes place during memory write operation.

(i)   Address of the desired memory location is loaded on the address bus.

(ii) Select the IC, using $\overline{CS}$ signal $\left(\text{i.e. send } \overline{CS} = \text{'0'}\right)$.

(iii) The data to be stored is loaded on data input lines.

(iv) Write signal goes low $\left(\overline{WR} = \text{'0'}\right)$. At the same time $\overline{RD} = \text{'1'}$

As shown in Fig. 5.37, first the address of memory location is sent on the address lines. After that, chip select signal $\overline{CS}$ and write signal $\overline{WR}$ goes low. Then the data is transferred on Data lines. $\overline{RD}$ signal remains high during write operation.

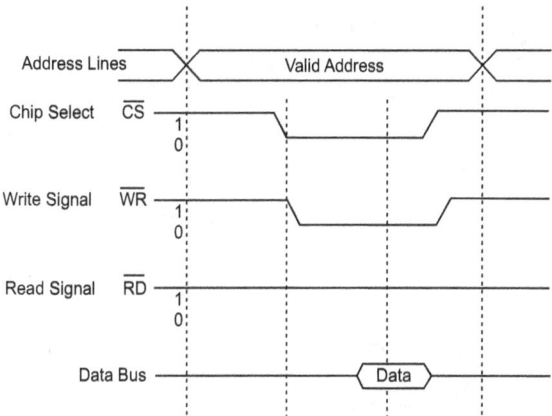

Fig. 5.37 : Memory write operation

5.10.2 Memory Read Operation

Q. With the help of timing diagram, explain the read operation of memory.

[Dec. 04, 3 M]

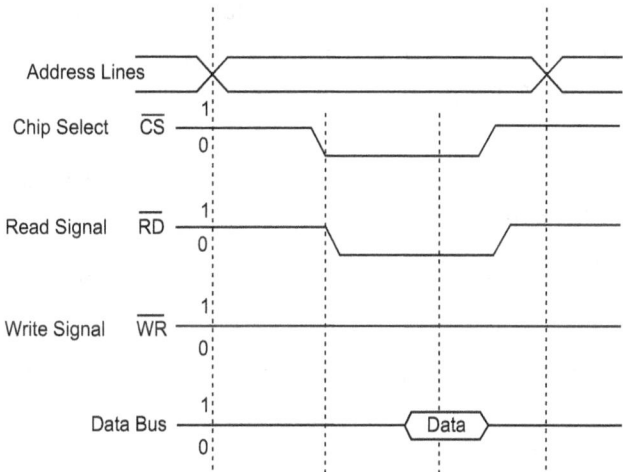

Fig. 5.38 : Memory Read Operation

- The following sequence of event s takes place during memory Read operation.
- Address of the desired memory location is loaded on the address bus.
- Select the IC using $\overline{CS}$ signal $\left(\text{i.e. send } \overline{CS} = \text{'0'}\right)$
- Read signal goes low, $\left(\overline{RD} = \text{'0'}\right)$
- The data to be read is available on the data bus from the selected memory location.
- In memory Read operation the Read signal goes low and write signal remain High.

5.11 EXPANDING SIZE OF MEMORY

- In most of the General purpose or commercial applications, the single IC of memory does not satisfy the required memory capacity. Therefore, we need to connect several memory IC's in series or in parallel to increase the size of the memory.
- There are various methods to expand the size of the memory, such as.
- Expanding word size.
- Expanding word Capacity
- Expanding word size and word capacity.

5.11.1 Expanding Word Size

Q. How to expand memory size memory locations ?	**[May 07, 2 M]**
Q. Explain how will you expand memory capacity location wise ?	**[Dec. 06, 3 M]**

- Suppose we have memory IC of 8 Data lines (D_0 – D_7), But the requirement is of Data lines is 16 bit (i.e. D_0 – D_{15}).

- In such case , we need two memory IC's of 8 Data lines. Now, to get 16 bit data bus, there is some interfacing required between two memory chips. The interfacing required to get the expanded word size is as follows.

(i) The address lines of each IC are connected together.

(ii) The data lines of each memory IC are connected separately with data bus to get desired expanded size of data bus.

(iii) The control signals $\overline{RD}$, $\overline{WR}$ and $\overline{CS}$ are also connected together.

Example 5.7 :

We have Memory IC of size 1K × 8 bits. But in the system, we require memory of size 1K × 16 bits. Draw the interfacing diagram to get the required memory size of 1K × 16 bits by using two memory IC's of size 1K × 8 bits.

Solution :

The required number of IC's to get the memory size of 1K × 16 bits is 2.

- As shown in Fig. 5.39 two memory IC's, each of size 1K × 8 bits are connected to get memory of size 1 K × 16 bits. Address lines A_0 – 9 are connected directly to both the IC's.

  Similarly $\overline{RD}$, $\overline{WR}$ and $\overline{CS}$ pins are common to both the IC's.

- There is a difference , while connecting data lines. For IC1, the data lines D_0 – D_7 of system bus are connected to D_0 – D_7 data lines, but for IC2 data lines D_8 – D_{15} of system bus are connected to D_0 – D_7 data lines of IC2.

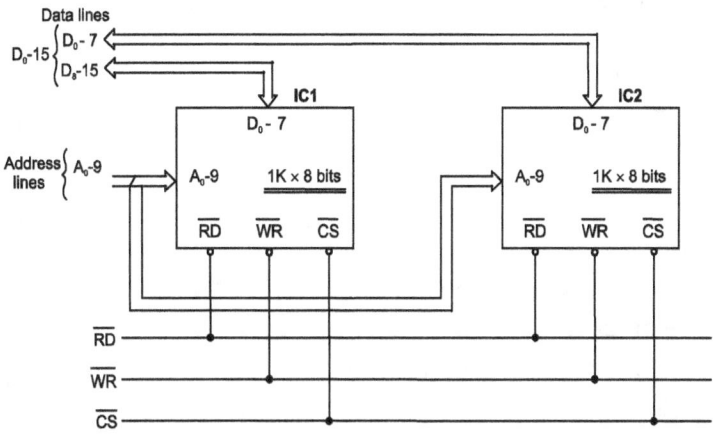

Fig. 5.39 : Memory of size 1K × 16 bits, using two 1K × 8 bits

5.11.2 Expanding Word Capacity

Q. Explain how will you expand memory capacity location.　　　　**[Dec. 04, 3 M]**

- Word capacity of memory means the number of memory locations available. Suppose, we have 1K × 8 bits of memory IC. But the system requirement is of 2K × 8 bits of memory. In such case, we need to use two memory IC's of 1K × 8 bits to get 2K × 8 bits of memory.

- 1K × 8 bits means, 1K memory locations, and each memory location has 8 bits of data lines.

Example 5.8 :

Requirement of the system is of 2K × 8 bits of memory. Draw the interfacing diagram of generating 2K × 8 bits of memory, using two memory IC's of 1K × 8 bits.

Solution :

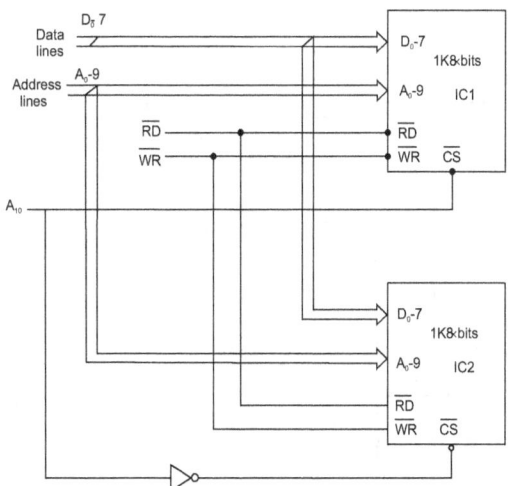

Fig. 5.40 : 2K × 8 bits Memory, using 1K × 8 bits of Memory

Fig. 5.40, shows the interfacing diagram of 2K × 8bits of memory, using 1K × 8 bits of memory IC's.

The different connections of signals are given below,

- The eight data lines D_0– 7 of IC1 and D_0 – 7 of IC2 are connected to get common data lines D_0 – 7.

- Control signals, $\overline{RD}$ and $\overline{WR}$ of IC1 and IC2 are connected to get common $\overline{RD}$ and $\overline{WR}$. control signals.

- For 1K × 8 bits, total 10 address lines required. Therefore, the address lines A_0 – 9 of IC1 and A_0– 9 of IC2 are connected together to get A_0– 9.

- Address line A_{10} is directly connected to IC1. The same address line, A_{10} is connected to IC_2 **using Inverter**.

For 2K × 8 bits, total Eleven address lines are required from A_0 to A_{10} as $\boxed{2^{10} = 2\,K}$.

5.11.3 Expanding Word Size and Word Capacity of Memory

To increase both word size and word capacity of memory we need to connect memories in series and parallel as given in the following example.

Example 5.9 :

Desired memory size is 4K × 8 bits and available memory chip is 2K × 4 bits. Draw the interfacing diagram of interfacing, 4 IC's, each of size 2K × 4 bits to get desired memory size of 4K × 8 bits.

Solution :

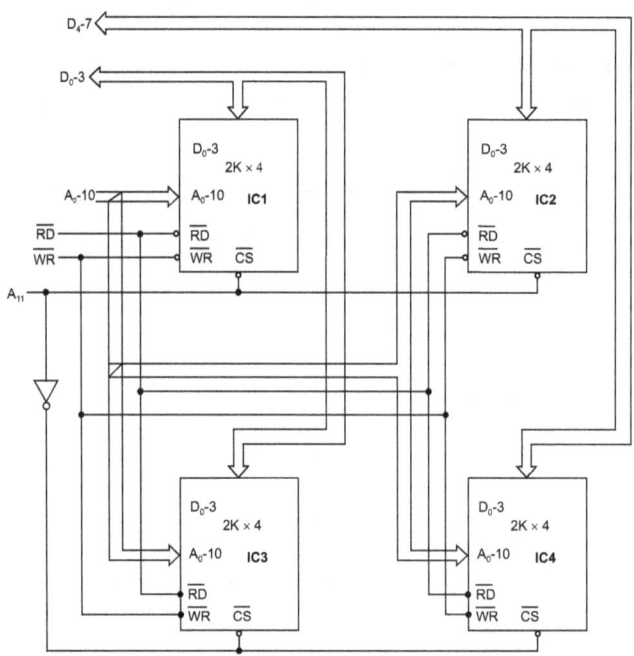

Fig. 5.41 : Interfacing of 4K × 8 bits of memory using 2K × 4 bits of memory

- As shown, in Fig. 5.41 IC1 and IC3 has common Data lines D_0- 3. Similarly, IC2 and IC4 has common data lines $D_4 - D_7$.
- For IC1 and IC2 the address line A_{11} is connected directly. For IC3 and IC4 the address line A_{11} is connected through Inverter.

Example 5.10 :

Draw the interfacing diagram to interface 64 K $\times 8$ bit of memory using 32 K $\times 8$ bits of memory IC's.

Solution :

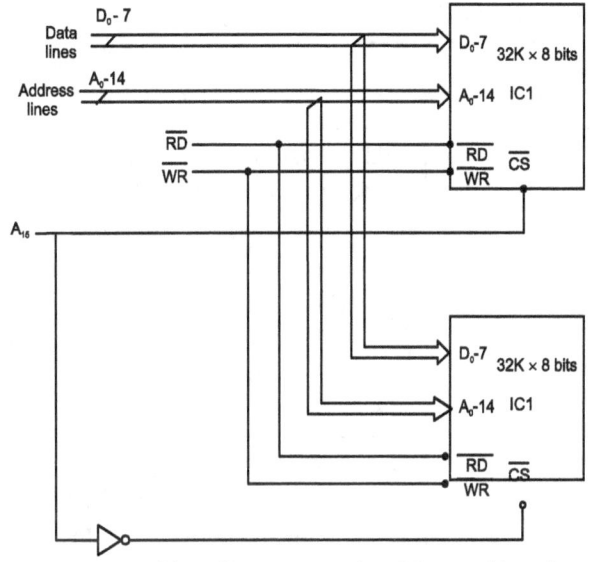

Fig. 5.42 : 64 K $\times 8$ 8 bits of memory, using 32 K $\times 8$ bits of memory.

As shown in Fig. 5.42, Data lines $D_0 - 7$ of system bus are directly connected to the Data lines $D_0 - 7$ of IC_1 and IC_2. For 64 K $\times 8$ bits of memory, total 16 address lines are required, as, 2^{16} = 64 K. But IC is of capacity 32 K $\times 8$ bits. Therefore 15 address lines $A_0 - 14$ are connected to IC1 and IC2 as, 2^{15} = 32 K.

5.12 COMPARISONS

5.12.1 Comparison between PROM, PLA, PAL

Parameters	PROM	PLA	PAL
Circuit	There are fixed AND arrays and programmable OR arrays.	AND and OR arrays are programmable.	Only the AND array is programmable OR array is fixed.
Implementation	SOP functions in the standard form only can be implemented.	Any SOP function can be implemented.	Any SOP function can be implemented.

Solution	It is possible to decode any minterm.	Desired minterm can be obtained by programming the AND matrix.	Desired minterm can be obtained by programming the AND matrix.
Cost	Cheap	Expensive than PAL and PROM	Moderately expensive
Use	Easy to use	Complicated	Moderately complicated

5.12.2 Comparison between CPLD and FPGA

Sr. No	Parameters	CPLD	FPGA
1.	Structure	CPLD constitutes PAL like blocks which contain 16 microcells each. Each microcell consists of AND–OR combinations followed by EXOR gate, FF, MUX and tristate buffers.	FPGA constitutes of configurable logic blocks (CLBs) and I/O blocks (IOBs) which can be configured as per requirement of application.
2.	Circuit structure	CPLD contains PAL like blocks, I/O blocks and interconnection wires.	FPGA does not contain the AND / OR matrices. Instead, logic blocks (configurable) are provided for implementing the logic circuits.
3.	Programming Technique used	In system programming (ISP)	In system programming (ISP)
4.	Available packages	Available in packages such as PLCC, QFP, PGA and BGA.	Available in packages such as PLCC, QFP, PGA and BGA.
5.	Available IC package	XC 9500 family.	Xilinx 4000 family.

INTRODUCTION TO HDL

6.1 INTRODUCTION

- In this unit we discuss Library, Entity, Architecture, Modelling styles, Data objects, concurrent and Sequential statements, Design examples, using VHDL for basic combinational and sequential circuits, Attributes.

- We know that, any digital circuit consists of only a few basic circuits; AND, OR, and NOT gates, a memory element flip-flop, irrespective of the size and complexity of the circuit. The digital circuits can be designed using manual methods, such as simplification of Boolean expressions using Boolean algebraic theorems, graphical methods, tabular methods, using available SSI and MSI devices (mux/demux, registers, counters etc). These design (synthesis) methods or tools are well for design of systems which are small in size and are not complex enough in today's context.

- However, the increasing size and the complexity of digital systems require design methods with the use of computers. These methods are known as Computer Aided Design (CAD) methods. The number of CAD tools have been developed for this purpose.

- CAD tools made it possible to design modern complex logic circuits, and also made the design work much easier. Many tasks in the design process are performed automatically by the CAD tools resulting in faster and efficient design.

- A number of Hardware Description Languages (HDLs) have been developed for describing the structure and behavior of complex digital circuits and number of HDL based CAD tools have been developed for the design of digital systems.

6.2 VLSI DESIGN

Q. What is the VLSI technology ? Give classification of IC technology.   **[4 M]**

- VLSI stands for Very Large Scale Integration. It is the process of integrating milion of transistors on tiny silicon chips. VLSI circuit technology is one of the basic components of today's high technology. VLSI device are found in all varieties of applications from simple home appliances to complex space crafts. The main benefits are complex functionality in very small package.

Classification of IC technology :

Type	Device	Year	Function
SSI	1-100	1960	Gates, op-amps
MSI	100-1k	1965	Filters
LSI	1k-10k	1970	Microprocessor, ALU
VLSI	> 10k	1975	Memory, DSP

6.3 INTRODUCTION OF VHDL

Q. Give comparison between VHDL and Verilog.

Q. What is VHDL ?   **[Dec. 10, 12, 2 M]**

VHDL	Verilog
1. It is somewhat difficult and complex than verilog.	1. Relatively simple especially for 'c' language users.
2. It result in slower simulation.	2. Results in fast simulation.
3. It is superior in higher system level designs.	3. It has a very good acceptance in ASIC.
4. Procedures and functions may be placed in a package. So that they, can be used for any design.	4. There is no concept of package in VERILOG.
5. A library is a store for complied VHDL code.	5. No concept of a liabrary.
6. VHDL allows concurrent procedure calls.	6. VERILOG does not allow concurrent task calls.

6.4 LEVELS OF ABSTRACTION

Q. Explain levels of abstraction in detail.

- Different styles are adopted for writing VHDL code. Abstraction defines how much detail about the design is specified in a particular description. There are four main levels of abstraction.

(i) Layout level :

- It is lowest level of abstraction. It specifies actual layout of design on silicon. Detailed timing information, analog effects are specified.

(ii) Logic level :

- A model is described by the logic gates and the connection between logic gates. This design has information about function, architecture, technology, detailed timing. Layout information and analog effects are ignored.

(iii) Register transfer level :

- This model describes the flow of data between registers and how a design processes the data. The design is specified using register and the logic in between.

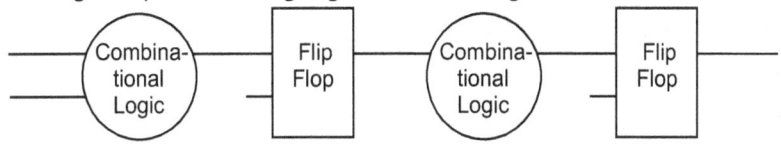

Fig. 6.1

- Design contains architecture information, no details of technology, no specification of absolute timing delays.
- Entire code is partitioned between clocked and combinational processes.

(iv) Behavioral level :

- The model is specified by describing functionality of the design using HDL's without specifying the architecture of registers.
- It contains timing information required to represent a function.

e.g. Behavioral model of an AND gate with A and B inputs, and C as output.

```
process (A, B)
  begin
    if   (A = '1' and B = '1') then
          C <= '1' ;
    else
          C <= '0' ;
          end if ;
          end process ;
```

6.5 DATA OBJECTS

Q.	With the help of suitable example explain data objects	
	(i) constant (ii) variable (iii) signal (iv) file	**[May 09, 12, 8 M]**
Q.	Explain data objects in detail.	**[May 10, 8 M]**
Q.	Give different types of data object.	
Q.	Write a note on data types of VHDL.	

A VHDL object consist of one of the following :

- Constant
- Variable
- Signal
- **Constant :**

Constant objects are names assigned to specific values of a type. Constant is an object whose value can not be changed once defined for the design. By use of constant, model becomes more readable and easy to update.

The syntax is

constant constant_name : type_name := value ;

The value specification is optional

e.g. constant PI : real := 3.1414 ;

constant WIDTH : integer := 8 ;

constant delay : time := 10 ns ;

- **Variable**

A Variable is an object with single current value. The value of variable may change. Variables are used for local storage in process statements and subprograms. All value assignments to variable occur immediately.

The variable declaration syntax is

variable variable_name : type_name := initial value ;

e.g. variable P, Q : bit ;

variable DELAY : time ;

Variable WIDTH : std_logic_vector (7 downto 0) ;

- **Signal**

Signal objects are used to connect entities together to form models. Signals are communication media between entities. Signals are nothing but the wires (which connect two or more components) lying inside an IC.

Signals can be declared in entity declaration section, architecture declaration section, and package declarations. Signals declared in packages can be shared among entities and called global signals.

The syntax is

signal signal_name: signal _type := initial value ;

The value specification is optional.

e.g. signal VCC : bit := '1' ;

signal GROUND : std_logic := '0' ;

signal INT_BUS : bit_vector(7 downto 0) ;

signal CONTROL : std_logic_vector(15 downto 0) ;

Signals declared in entity declaration section are global to any architecture for that entity. Signals declared in architecture can only be referenced in that architecture only.

- **Variable Vs Signal**

Variable	Signal
1. The value of variable is updated immediately, after the execution of variable assignment statement.	1. The value of signal is updated after an amount of time or after a delta delay, after the execution of signal assignment statement.
2. Variables are declared in the process.	2. Signals are declared in architecture before begin statement.
3. A variable has only two properties attached to it : Type and Value.	3. A signal has three properties attached to it : Type, Value, and Time.
4. During simulation, variables occupy less storage than signal.	4. During simulation, signals occupy more storage than variables.
5. Variable assignment is ': =' i.e. Y : = A OR B	5. Signal Assignment is '< =' i.e. Y < = A OR B

6.6 VHDL COMPONENT

Q. Write short note on VHDL component.   **[2 M]**

1. Entity

2. Architecture

Q. Write short note on Entity.   **[Dec. 11, 2 M]**

Q. Describe the main component of a VHDL description.   **[Dec. 11, 2 M]**

A component is a very important concept in VHDL. A component can be a complete design or a small part of a system.

VHDL component has two parts :

1. Entity

2. Architecture

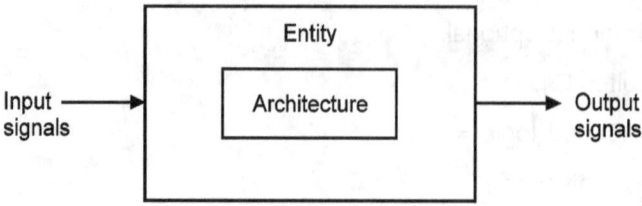

Fig. 6.2 : A VHDL component

Entity : It is actually used for port declaration for inputs and outputs. An entity is the most basic building block in VHDL. So, entity acts as a black box, which gives the external view of the design. Entity does not know about the internal behaviour of the component.

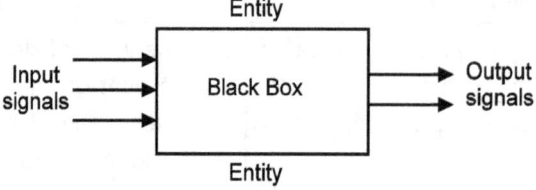

Fig. 6.3 : Entity

Entity name is the same as the component name.

For example, the entity of full adder looks like as shown in Fig. 6.4.]

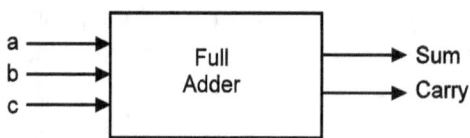

Fig. 6.4 : Entity for Full Adder

6.6.1 Entity

Q. Explain entity in detail with one example.	**[6 M]**
Q. Explain entity in detail.	**[4 M]**

- The entity describes the design's interface to the external circuit. It is equivalent to pin configuration of an IC. Entity declaration defines the input and output ports of the design. Each port in the port list must be given a name, data flow direction and a type. Entity can be used as a component in other entities after being compiled into a library.

- The syntax for entity declaration is :

  entity ENTITY_NAME is

  port (Port list) ;

  end ENTITY_NAME ;

e.g entity OR_ GATE is

    port   (A1, A2, A3, A4: in bit ;

           B1, B2, B3, B4: in bit ;

           Y1, Y2, Y3, Y4: out bit) ;

           end OR_GATE ;

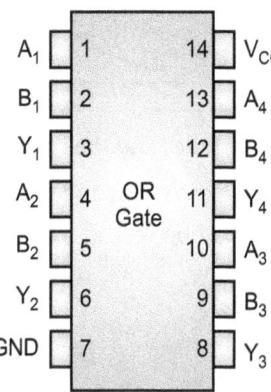

Fig. 6.5

- Entity declaration starts from keyword entity and ends with keyword end. Between this ports are defined with keyword port. Ports are declared with their name, mode and type.

- Mode specifies the direction of ports. Four types of modes are defined in VHDL as follows.

Mode   in – value can be read but not assigned. i.e. input port.

Mode   out – value can be assigned but not read. i.e. output port.

Mode   inout – value can be read and assigned. i.e. input/output port. (bidirectional signals)

Mode   buffer – output port with internal read capability.

- In above example, entity OR_GATE is declared for an IC of OR gate as shown. Ports A1, A2, A3, A4, B1, B2, B3, B4 are defined as an input port of bit type.

Y1, Y2, Y3, Y4 are declared as output ports. There is no semicolon after last line in port list.

- Every VHDL code must start with entity. VHDL design description must include only one entity and at least one corresponding architecture.

Buffer :

- Once a port is declared as mode buffer, it is similar to a port which is declared as mode out, but out mode does not allow for internal feedback.

- Mode buffer is used for ports, which are readable within the entity, such as for counter outputs. In counter, present state used to determine the next state, so the value of counter must be in the feedback loop, therefore counter outputs are declared as buffer.

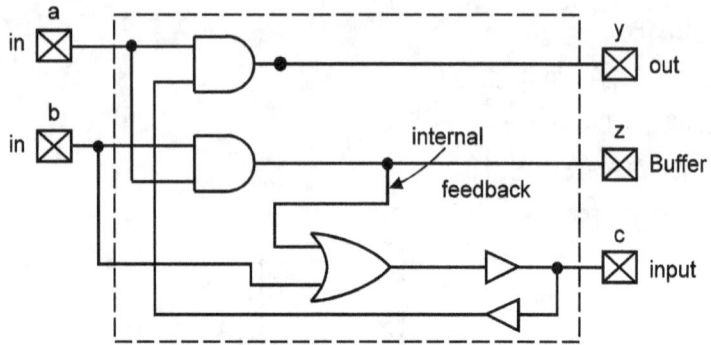

Fig. 6.6 : Modes and their signal sources

As shown in Fig. 6.6, signals a and b act only as the input, signal y acts only as output. Signal z is declared as buffer, therefore, it can be reread internally. Signal c acts as the bidirectional signal; i.e. input or output.

Examples of entity :

Q. Write entity for an IC, ALU. **[4 M]**

Example 6.1 : Write entity for an IC shown in Fig. 6.7.

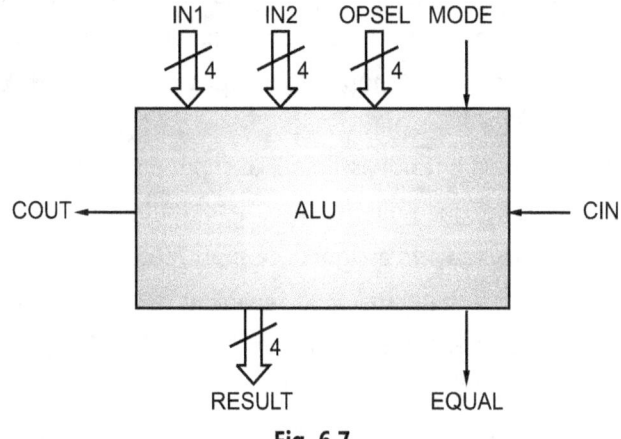

Fig. 6.7

Solution :

entity ALU is

    port (IN1, IN2, OPSEL : in bit_ vector (3 downto 0) ;

        MODE, CIN : in bit ;

        COUT, EQUAL : out bit ;

        RESULT : out *bit _vector* (3 *downto* 0)) ;

    end ALU ;

Example 6.2 :

Write the entity construct for the R-S flip flop circuit as shown below.

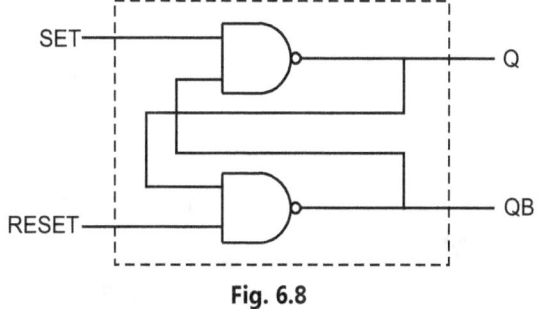

Fig. 6.8

Solution :

Let the name of the entity be RSFF. It has two input ports SET and RESET and two bidirectional ports Q and QB. Then entity construct will be

    entity RSFF is

    port   (SET, RESET: in bit ;

            Q, QB: buffer bit) ;

    end   RSFF;

6.6.2 Architecture

> **Q.** Explain architecture component of VHDL in detail.   **[4 M]**

- Architecture describes a design's behavior and functionality (internal behaviour of entity). Architecture specifies behavior, function, interconnections, relationship between inputs and output of an entity.

- Architecture can contain only concurrent statement. An entity can have more than one architecture. There can be no architecture without an entity.

- The syntax of architecture body is

    architecture ARCHITECTURE_NAME of ENTITY_NAME is

        [declarative part]

    begin

    [Statement part]

    end ARCHITECTURE_NAME ;

    The words architecture, of, is, begin and end are keywords in VHDL.

Architecture_Name

- Architecture must be given a name consisting of a text string which should be assigned by a designer in a way meaningful to the design.

ENTITY_NAME

Must write the name of entity for which the architecture is to be written.

Declarative part

It appears before the keyword begin. It can be used to declare signals, user_defined types, constants, components, subprogram etc.

Statement part

It is contained between the keywords begin and end. All the statements are executed concurrently (simultaneously).

The functionality of the design can be expressed in terms of following styles which are called styles of modeling.

1. Data flow

2. Behavioral

3. Structural

Example 6.3 :

Write the VHDL code for the circuit shown in Fig. 6.9.

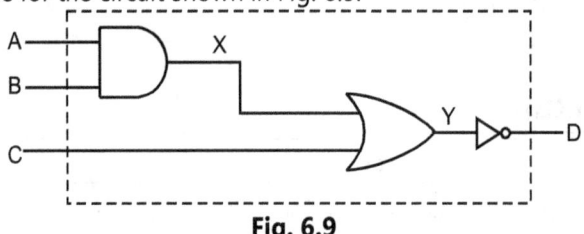

Fig. 6.9

Solution :

This circuit is having three inputs A, B, C and one output D. To express D in terms of A, B, C, we have to consider intermediate wires X and Y. Inputs A, B, C and output D must be defined in entity declaration.

The intermediate wires (wires running inside an IC) X, Y should be declared as signal in declarative part of architecture body.

        entity ANDORNOT is
          port (A, B, C: in bit ;
                D: out bit) ;
          end ANDORNOT ;
     architecture ANDORNOT_ARCH of ANDORNOT is
            signal X,Y: bit ;
              begin
                X <= A and B ;

Y <= X or C ;

D <= not Y ;

end ANDORNOT_ARCH ;

The sequence of statement is not important.

> **Q.** Consider a simple example of half adder. How will you write a VHDL entity declaration for half adder ? Also write an architecture of half adder ? Also write an architecture of half adder in structural style of modeling and data flow style of modeling.   **[Dec. 10, 8 M]**

Example 6.4 :

Write the VHDL code to design half adder.

Solution :

The truth table and circuit of half adder is as shown.

Input		Output	
IN1	IN2	Sum	Carry
0	0	0	0
0	1	1	0
1	0	1	0
1	1	0	1

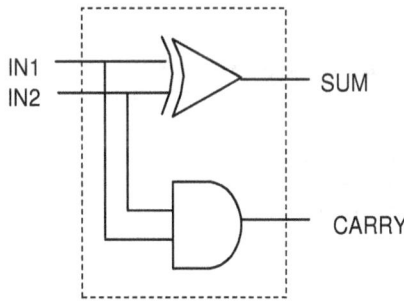

Fig. 6.10 : Half adder

Half adder is having two inputs IN1, IN2 and two outputs SUM, CARRY.

No need of signal declaration.

entity HALFADDR is

      port (IN1, IN2: in bit ;

         SUM, CARRY: out bit) ;

   end HALFADDR ;

architecture HALFADDR_ARCH of HALFADDR is

begin

    SUM < = IN1 xor IN2 ;

    CARRY < = IN1 and IN2 ;

end HALFADDR_ARCH ;

6.7 CONCURRENT STATEMENTS

Q. Give classification of different types of concurrent statement   **[2 M]**

A VHDL architecture body consists of a set of interconnected concurrent statements. Concurrent statement in a design executes simultaneously. All concurrent statements describe the functionality of multiplexer structure. It is not possible to design storage elements like flip-flop using concurrent statements only.

The concurrent statements defined in VHDL are :

- Concurrent signal assignment
- Block statement
- Component Instantiation statement
- Generate statement
- Process statement

6.7.1 Concurrent Signal Assignment

Q. Explain concurrent signal assignment with example.   **[4 M]**
Q. Describe the types of concurrent signal Assignment.   **[6 M]**

(i) Simple Concurrent Signal Assignment

The syntax is

    Target <= expressions ;

i.e. Target signal receives the value of an expression. A signal assignment is defined by '<='

    e.g.   Z <= A and B ;

The logical AND of A and B is assigned to Z. This statement is executed whenever either A or B has an event occurred on it. An event on a signal is a change in the value of that signal. [Whenever value of A or B changes, statement will execute].

A signal assignment statement is said to be sensitive to changes on any signal that are to the right of the <= symbol. The above statement is sensitive to A and B.

Signal assignment statement creates the driver. Z <= A and B statement will create one AND gate with A and B inputs and Z as output.

i.e. It has created driver for Z.

Let, X <= Y; It will connect nodes X and Y. Driver for X will be created like.

In concurrent statements, there are no implied registers.

(ii) Conditional Concurrent Signal Assignment

The syntax is

    target <=   Boolean expression1 when condition

          else

          expression2 ;

   when statement can also be nested.

While executing when statement,

Each condition is tested in the order in which it is written.

The value of that expression whose associated condition is true will be assigned to the target.

If none of the conditions are true, the value of expression associated with last else is assigned to the target.

e.g.   Z < = A when ASSIGN_A = '1'

                         else

                         B when ASSIGN_B = '1'

                         else

                         C;

ASSIGN_A is tested; if it is '1', then the value of A will be assigned to Z.

If ASSIGN_A is not equal to '1', then condition ASSIGN_B is tested, if it is '1' then Z will be equal to B.

If ASSIGN_B is not equal to '1' then the value of C will be assigned to Z.

(iii) Selected Concurrent Signal Assignment

The syntax is

   with choice_ expression select

                 target < = expression1 when choice1,

                         expression2 when choice2,

                         expressionN when choiceN,

                         expression when others ;

'with_select' statement evaluates choice_expression and compares that value to each choice value in the order in which they are written. The value of that expression where match is found is assigned to the target. If no match is found, expression associated with others will be assigned to target.

- No two choices can overlap.
- All possible choices must be enumerated.
- Each choice can be either a static expression (such as 3) or a static range (such as 1 to 3).
- Each value in the range of the choice expression type must be covered by one choice.
- "others" clause is optional.
- All choices for the expression must be included, otherwise "others" clause must be the last choice.

Example 6.5 :

Write VHDL code for 2 bit comparator.

Solution :

For 2 bit comparator, there are two, 2 bit inputs A, B and three outputs Y0, Y1, Y2.

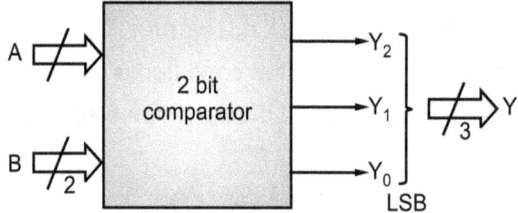

Fig. 6.11 : 2 bit comparator

Truth table :

If A = B then Y2 = 0, Y1 = 0, Y0 = 1   i.e. Y = 001

If A > B then Y2 = 0, Y1 = 1, Y0 = 0   i.e. Y = 010

If A < B then Y2 = 1, Y1 = 0, Y0 = 0   i.e. Y = 100

From truth table itself, we can describe the relationship between input and output and hence no need of gate circuitry for this design.

```
entity COMP1 is
     port (A, B,: in bit_vector (1 downto 0) ;
   Y: out bit_vector (2 downto 0) ;
end COMP1 ;
   architecture COMP1_ARCH of COMP1 is
               begin
Y <= "001" when A = B
         else
         "010" when A > B
```

else

"100" when A < B ;

end COMP1_ARCH ;

- Single bit value must be specified in single quotes i.e. '1', '0'.

  Multi bit value must be specified in double quotes i.e. "100", "1010".

- Let Y = Y2 Y1 Y0

If declared as Y: out bit_vector (2 downto 0) ; then Y0 is considered as LSB and Y2 as MSB.

If declared as Y: out bit_vector (0 to 2) ; then Y2 is considered as LSB and Y0 as MSB.

6.7.2 Block Statement

Q. Explain the Block statement with syntax.   [4 M]

Main purpose of block statement is organizational only. It constructs only separate part of the code without adding any functionality. It allows the designer to logically group areas of the model.

Each block represents a self-contained area of the model. Signals, types, constants etc. declared in the block are local to that block and can not be referenced outside of that block.

The syntax is

label: block

[block declarative item]

begin

concurrent statements   optional

end block [label] ;

label → is required to name the block.

e.g. ALU: block

signal QBUS: bit_vector (31 downto 0) ;

begin

C <= A add B ;

C <= A sub B ;

end block ;

Block can also be nested.

e.g. BLK1: block

signal QBUS: bit_ vector (31 downto 0) ;

begin

BLK2: block

signal QBUS: bit_ vector (31 downto 0) ;

```
    begin
        -- BLK2 statements
    end block BLK2 ;
        -- BLK1 statements
    end block BLK1 ;
```

In this example, signal QBUS is declared in two blocks. One block is contained in the other. BLK1 is the parent block of BLK2. The QBUS signal from BLK1 has been overridden by a declaration of the same name in BLK2.

Example 6.6 :

Write VHDL code to design D-latch using Block statement.

Solution :

The pin configuration of D-latch is as shown in Fig. 6.12.

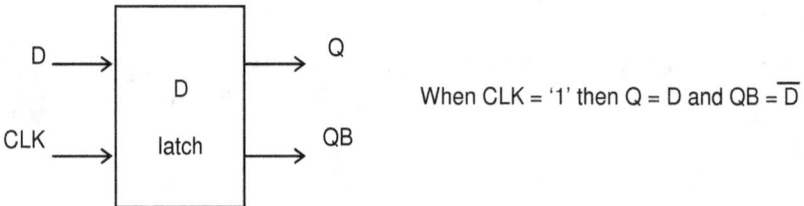

When CLK = '1' then Q = D and QB = $\overline{D}$

Fig. 6.12

```
entity DLATCH is
    port (D, CLK: in bit ;
            Q, QB: out bit) ;
end DLATCH ;
architecture DLATCH_ARCH of  DLATCH is
begin
    B1: block (CLK = '1')              -- guard expression
        begin
        Q <= guarded  D ;             -- statement 1
    QB <= guarded  not ( D ) ;        -- statement 2
        end block B1 ;
end  DLATCH_ARCH ;
```

• When CLK is equal to '1' then value of D and its complement will be assigned to Q and QB respectively.

When CLK is not equal to '1' then statement 1 and statement 2 (guarded statement) will disable or turned off (does not execute).

6.7.3 Component Instantiation Statement

Q. Explain component instantiation statement.   **[4 M]**

Component is predesigned, preanalyzed, precompiled entity_architecture pair (VHDL model). Components are normally placed in design library. Component specifies a subsystem, which can be instantiated in another architecture leading to a hierarchical specification.

The component can be defined in package, design entity, architecture, or block declarations. Components must be declared before *begin* statement of architecture, if it is declared in architecture. A component must be declared before it is instantiated. e.g. Suppose VHDL code for half adder is written, compiled and verified, and placed either in design library or in working directory, then for full adder design, we can use half adder as component because full adder can be designed using two half adders and one OR gate.

The syntax for component declaration is :

    component   component_name

        port (port_list) ;

    end component;

e.g.   component HALFADDR

        port (IN1, IN2: in bit ;

            SUM, CARRY: out bit) ;

        end component ;

Component_name should be same as entity name of VHDL code which is using as component. In port list copy the port list of entity (entity of VHDL code which is using as component).

Component Instantiation :

It is selecting a compiled specification of component in the library and linking it with the architecture where it will be used.

Component Instantiation statement is used to build a net list in VHDL by referencing a previously defined hardware component in current design.

It introduces a subsystem declared elsewhere as a component in current design.

The syntax for component instantiation is :

    Instance_name: component_name

        port map ([port_name =>] expression

            [port_name =>] expression.);

Instance_name is name of the instance of the component.

Component_name is name of the component to be instantiated.

Port map connects each port of this instance of component_name to a signal valued expression in the current entity.

Ports can be mapped to signals by 'named' or 'positional' notation.

Ports of the component are called formal ports. Ports of top_level entity (entity of main design) are called actual ports. Named association is port maps by names are preferred because it makes the code more readable and pins can be specified in any order.

All positional port mapping should be placed before any named port mapping.

Example 6.7 :

Write VHDL code for NAND gate and write VHDL code for the logic circuit shown in Fig. 6.13 by using NAND gate design as component.

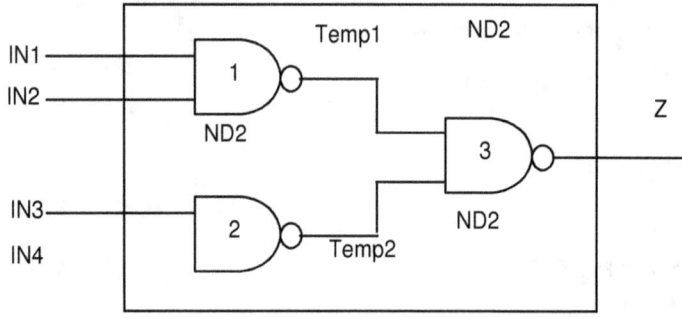

Fig. 6.13 (a)

Solution :

(a) Design of NAND gate

Let

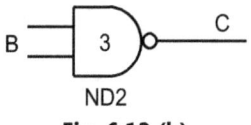

Fig. 6.13 (b)

```
    entity ND2 is
        port (A, B: in bit ;
            C: out bit) ;
            end ND2 ;
    architecture  ND2_ARCH  of ND2  is
    begin
      C <= A  nand  B ;
      end  ND2_ARCH ;
```

If we save the VHDL file, it will save with its entity name.

i.e. This file will save as ND2.VHDL. Now if this file is compiled, verified and placed either in design library or in working directory, then this VHDL code can be used as component in design of any other circuit.

(b) Design of given circuit (Structural Model)

    entity COMPND2 is

        port (IN1, IN2, IN3, IN4 : in bit ;

        Z: out bit) ;

    end COMPND2 ;

    architecture COMPND2_ARCH of COMPND2 is

    component ND2

        port   (A, B : in bit ;

        C: out bit) ;

        end component ;

        signal TEMP1, TEMP2 : bit ;

    begin

    I1: ND2 port map (IN1, IN2, TEMP1) ;   -- Positioned port mapping

    I2: ND2 port map (A => IN3, B => IN4, C => TEMP2) ;   -- Named port mapping

    I3: ND2 port map (TEMP1, TAMP2, C=> Z) ;   -- Mixed port mapping

    end COMPND2_ARCH ;

ND2 design is declared as component in architecture before begin statement. Signals TEMP1 and TEMP2 are declared. Three component instantiation statements I1, I2, and I3 are written.

I1 instance creates one copy of ND2 design i.e. NAND gate1 with two inputs mapped IN1, IN2 and one output named TEMP1.

Similarly, I2 instance creates NAND gate2 with input named IN3, IN4 and an output TEMP2.

I3 instance creates NAND gate3 with input TEMP1 which gets connected to the output of NAND gate1 and TEMP2 connected to the output of NAND gate2 and output Z

6.7.4 Generate Statement

Q. Explain the generate statement in detail with example.	**[6 M]**
Q. Explain the forms of generate statement.	

Generate statement is used to select concurrent statements conditionally or to replicate concurrent statements. It is used to create multiple copies of components, processes, or blocks i.e. it provides a compact description.

Generate statement has two forms :

    (i) for...generate   (ii) if...generate

(i) for...generate

It creates multiple copies of components, processes, or block i.e. it executes concurrent statements number of times.

The syntax is :

    label: for identifier in range generate

        {concurrent statements}

    end generate [label] ;

Number of copies is determined by a discrete range. Range must be computable integer, in either of following forms :

integer_expression to integer_expression

integer_expression downto integer_expression

Each integer_expression evaluates to an integer

for_generate statement declares a new local integer variable with the name identifier. Identifier is assigned the first value of range, and each concurrent statement is executed once. Identifier is then assigned next value in range, and each concurrent statement is executed once more. This is repeated until identifier is assigned the last value in range. Each concurrent statement is then executed for the last time and execution continues with the statement following *end generate* statement. The loop identifier is then deleted.

(ii) if...generate

It made zero or one copy, conditionally.

The syntax is

    label : if expression generate

        {concurrent statement}

        end generate [label] ;

If expression is true, then concurrent statements are executed once, otherwise no execution of concurrent statements.

e.g.   CKO : if K=0 generate

    DFF : D_FLIP port map (COUNT, CLOCK, QCK) ;

    end generate CKO;

Example 6.8 :

Design 4 bit full adder with 1 bit full adder as a component using generate statement.

Solution :

Refer Example 6.7.

Where four copies of one bit full adder are created by instantiating component full adder four times. For this four instances, (FA0, FA1, FA2, FA3) are written.

Same can be done by writing one instance and using for-generate statement as follows :

```
entity ADDRGEN is
    port ( A, B : in  bit_ vector ( 3 downto 0 ) ;
                CIN : in  bit ;
                  S : out  bit_vector (3  downto  0 ) ;
            COUNT : out bit) ;
end  ADDRGEN ;

architecture ADDRGEN_ARCH of ADDRGEN is
    component  FULLADDR
        port ( A, B, CIN : in  bit  ;
                    S, C : out  bit ) ;
    end component ;
    signal  TEMP :  bit_vector (4  downto  0 ) ;
begin
        TEMP(0) <= CIN ;
        GK: for K in 0 to 3 generate
            FA : FULLADDR  port map (A(K), B(K), TEMP(K), S(K), C(K+1) ) ;
            end generate GK ;
        COUT <= TEMP(4) ;
end ADDRGEN_ARCH ;
```

6.7.5 Process Statement

Q. Explain the process statement in detail.	[6 M]

In VHDL, process statement contains only sequential statement.

Process is the primary concurrent VHDL statement used to describe sequential behavior (i.e. sequential statements). All the statements in the process, are executed sequentially, hence order of statements is important. All process in an architecture executes concurrently.

Signals to which some value is assigned within a process are not updated with their new values until the process suspends.

The syntax for process declaration is :

```
process (sensitivity list)
            Declaration part
begin
            Sequential statements
end process;
```

In declaration part, types, variables, constants, subprograms can be declared. Statement part contains only sequential statement.

Process never stops, it repeats forever, unless suspended.

To suspend the process, either sensitivity list or wait statements are used.

- **Sensitivity list**

Sensitivity list is a list of signals to which process is sensitive. Sensitivity list defines the signals that cause the statements inside the process statement to execute whenever one or more elements of the list changes its value.

Process executes when any one of the signals in the sensitivity list changes. A process with a sensitivity clause must not contain an explicit wait statement. Process should either have a sensitivity list or wait statement at the end. Only static signal names are allowed in the sensitivity list.

Wait Statement

Wait statement is only used in the process statement. This statement provides an alternate way to suspend the execution of a process.

A process can be suspended by means of a sensitivity list, i.e. when a process has a sensitivity list it always suspends after executing the last sequential statement in the process. For example, given in listing. This process executes, when there is an event on a or c and suspends after executing the last statement.

e.g. process statement with sensitivity list.

```
process (a, c)
begin
    if a > c then
        y <= '1';
    else
        y <= '0';
    end if;
end process;
```

The alternate way to suspend the process is by using a wait statement.

listing ----- process statement with wait statement.

```
process
begin
    if a > c then
        y <= '1';
    else
        y <= '0';
    end if;
    wait on a, c;
end process;
```

The wait statement is placed at the end of a process. If wait statement was the last statement in the process, the process resumes execution from the first statement in the process.

There are basically **three types** of wait statements.

1. wait on sensitivity_list;
2. wait until Boolean_expression;
3. wait for time_expression;

We can also combine these statements into a single statement as,

wait on sensitivity_list until boolean_expression for time_expression;

Examples of wait statements are

1. Wait until Clk = '1'

It means that for the wait condition to be satisfied and execution of the code to continue, there must be an event on signal Clk, i.e. change in value and that value of Clk must be equal to '1' i.e. a rising edge for Clk.

2. Wait on x, y, z

In this the execution of wait statement causes the enclosing process to suspend and then wait for an event to occur on signals x, y or z. When there is an event on x, y or z, the process resumes execution from the next statement onwards after the wait statement. If the wait statement is the last statement in the process, the process resumes execution from the first statement.

3. Wait for 12 ns

This wait statement causes the enclosing process to suspend for 12 ns, and when the simulation time advances to T + 12 ns, the enclosing process resumes execution from the statement following the wait statement. We can also use the command as

 constant period : time := 12 ns;

 wait for 3 period;

4. Wait on clock for 15 ns

The execution of wait causes the enclosing process to suspend and then wait for an event to occur on clock for a time_out interval of 15 ns. If there is no event on clock within 15 ns, the process resumes execution with the statement following the wait.

5. Wait until answer > 80 for 10 ms

When wait statement executes, it suspends the process. The boolean condition (answer > 80) is evaluated every time there is an event on answer. If the answer > 80, (after the event on answer) then it will resume the execution of the next statement.

If there is no event on answer or if the boolean condition is false, then it will wait for maximum 10ns 10 ms and resumes the execution of the next statement.

6. Wait on clock until answer > 80

When this wait statement executes, it suspends the execution of process. It checks the boolean condition only after there is an event on clock, if the boolean condition is true, then only go to the next statement, otherwise continue to wait.

7. Wait for 0 ns

It means to wait for one delta time. This statement is useful when we want the process to be delayed so that delta-delayed signal assignments within a process can take effect. For example,

    process
    begin
        wait on a;
        y <= a;
        wait for 0 ns;
        z < = y;
    end process;

Process takes very less time to execute (less than delta delay). If signal a changes at 20 ns, y is scheduled to get the new value of a at 20 ns + 1 delta. The wait statement (wait for 0 ns) causes the process to suspend for one delta. Signal y gets updated with it's new value. Process resumes at 20 ns + 1Δ, z gets the new value of y at 20 ns + 2Δ.

If the "wait for 0 ns" statement was not present, then both the statements (y <= a and z <= y) get executed sequentially at time 20 ns and in that case, y gets the new value of a, but z gets the old value of y i.e. logic '0'.

It is an error if both a sensitivity list and a wait statement are present within a process.

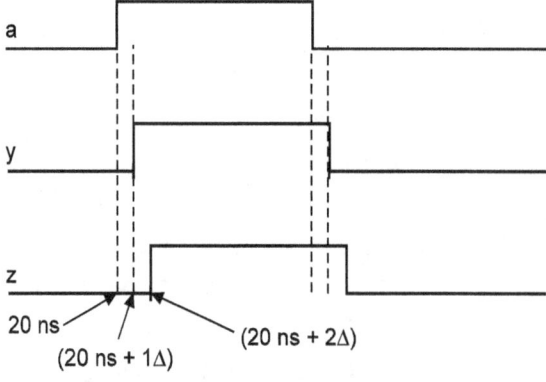

Fig. 6.14 : Effect of 'wait for 0 ns'

It is permissible to have several wait statements, inside the same process.

Example 6.9 :

    process
    begin

        – –

        wait until clock = '0';

        – –

        wait until clock = '0';

        – –

        wait until clock = '0';

    end process;

The wait is actually a sequential command. The wait command can not be used in functions, but wait can be used in procedures and processes.

6.8 SEQUENTIAL STATEMENTS

Q. Explain the following statements used in VHDL with suitable example.

   (i) Process (ii) case (iii) if then else (iv) signal assignment   **[May 13, 8 M]**

Q. What is the difference between concurrent and sequential statement of VHDL ?

                      [May 10, Dec. 09, 12, 6 M]

Q. Compare if and case statement ?

Q. Explain the types of sequential statements.   **[6 M]**

Sequential statements are executed one after the another, in the order in which they are written. Sequential statements can appear only in process or subprograms. Only sequential statements can use variables.

6.8.1 If Statement

The syntax is :

    if condition then

sequential statements end if ;

   If condition is true then statements will execute.

     if _else statement

The syntax is

    if condition then

            statement1 ;

    else

```
                statement2 ;
      end if ;
```

If condition is true then statement 1 will execute, otherwise statements compact 2 will execute.

Nested if_else

The syntax is

```
      if  condition1 then
                    statement1  ;
      elseif  condition2  then
                statement2 ;
      else
                statements3 ;
      end if ;
```

If condition 1 is true then statement 1 will execute. Then it checks condition 2, if it is true, statements 2 will execute. Otherwise statement 3 will execute.

if statement evaluates each condition in order. It generates a priority structure. It is same as concurrent statement when_else.

Use of if statement is suitable or easy upto three or four levels (conditions).

e.g.

```
      process ( A,B,C,X )
      begin
      if ( X = "0000") then
              Z <= A ;
      elsif ( X <= "0101") then
              Z <= B ;
      else
         Z <= C ;
         end if ;
      end process ;
```

6.8.2 Case Statement

Q. Explain the case statements in detail.

The syntax is :

```
      case expression is
          when choice1 => statement1 ;
          when choice2 => statement2 ;
```

```
        when choiceN=>  statementN;
        when others  => statements;
    end case ;
e.g.
        process ( A,B,C,X )
        begin
        case X is
                when   0 to 4 => Z <= B ;
                when     5    => Z <= C ;
                when   6 to 9 => Z <= A ;
                when   others => Z <= '0' ;
        end case ;
    end process ;
```

"case" statement selects for execution, one of the number of alternative sequence of statements. Statements following each "when" clause is executed, only if the choice value matches the expression value. Each choice can be either a static expression   (such as 4) or a static range (such as 1 to 5).

Every possible value of the case expression must be covered in one and only one when clause i.e. no choices can overlap.

It corresponds to "with_select " in concurrent statement.

"case" statement produces parallel logic whereas "if " statement produces priority encoded logic.

Example 6.10 :

Design 8:1 multiplexer using case statement

Solution :

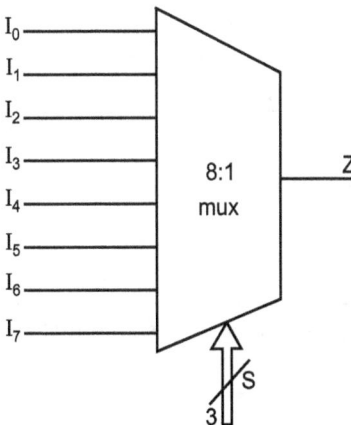

Fig. 6.15 : 8 : 1 Multiplexer

```
entity  MUX81  is
    port ( I0, I1, I2, I3, I4, I5, I6, I7 : :  in bit ;
                S : in  bit_vector (2  downto 0) ;
                Z : out  bit ) ;
    end MUX81 ;
architecture  MUX81_ARCH  of  MUX81  is
begin
    process ( I0, I1, I2, I3, I4, I5, I6, I7, S )
    begin
    case S is
        when "000"  =>  Z<= I0 ;
        when "001"  =>  Z<= I1 ;
        when "010"  =>  Z<= I2 ;
        when "011"  =>  Z<= I3 ;
        when "100"  =>  Z<= I4 ;
        when "101"  =>  Z<= I5 ;
        when "110"  =>  Z<= I6 ;
        when "111"  =>  Z<= I7 ;
        when  others => Z<= '0';
        end case ;
    end process ;
    end MUX81_ARCH ;
```

6.8.3 Null Statement

null statement does not perform any action. It can be used to indicate that when some condition is met, no action is to be performed.

```
e.g.     case S is
            when "00"    => Z<= '1' ;
            when "01"    => Z<= '0' ;
            when  others => Z<= null
        end case ;
```

6.8.4 Loop Statement

loop statement is used to execute sequence of sequential statements repetitively.

while loop statement

The syntax is :

```
    loop_label : while condition loop
```

Sequence_of_statements

end loop loop_label ;

Sequence of statement will execute till condition is true.

e.g.   process (A)

begin

L1 : while P <= 4 loop

Z (I) <= A(I+4) ;

I = I +1 ;

end loop L1 ;

end process ;

It has a Boolean iteration scheme. Condition is evaluated before execution.

for loop statement

The syntax is :

loop_label: for loop_parameter in range loop

sequence_of _statements

end loop loop_label ;

The loop is executed once for each value in the range. Range determines number of execution of loops. The range is tested at the beginning of loop execution.

The loop parameter is a constant, which may be used but not altered. Loop counter only exists within the loop.

e.g. FACTORIAL := 1 ;

L1: for NUMBER in 2 to10 loop

FACTORIAL := FACTORIAL * NUMBER ;

end loop L1 ;

6.8.5 Next Statement

The syntax are :

(i) next ;

(ii) next loop_label when condition ;

"next" statement is used only inside a loop. "next" statement skips the remaining statement in the current iteration of the loop and execution starts from the first statement of the next iteration of the loop.

e.g.   for X in 1 to 10 loop

SUM := SUM +5 ;

if (SUM =100) then

next ;

```
        else
                null ;
        end if ;
        Y := Y + 1 ;
    end loop ;
```

The next statement also cause an inner loop to be existed.

```
    L1: for X  in 10  downto 1  loop
            Statement group 1 ;

    L2 : loop
        Statement group 2 ;
         next  loop L1  when flag = '1' ;
        Statement group 3 ;
        end  loop L2 ;
        Statement group 4 ;
        end loop L1 ;
```

When flag = '1', statement group 3 and 4 are skipped and execution starts from the first statement of loop L1 and L2 was terminated.

6.8.6 Exit Statement

"exit" statement entirely terminates the execution of the loop in which it is located.

The syntax are :

(i)   exit ;

(ii) exit loop_ label when condition ;

e.g. 1

```
    exit  L1_LOOP when (I < 5) ;
```

This statement completes the execution of the loop labelled L1_LOOP when the expression (I < 5) is true.

The exit statement provides a quick and easy method of exiting a loop statement when all processing is finished or an error or warning condition occurs.

e.g. 2

```
    SUM :=1 ;   J := 0 ;
    L3: loop
        J := J + 21 ;
```

SUM := SUM * 10 ;

If (SUM > 100) then

exit L3 ;

end if ;

end loop L3 ;

Loop L3 will execute till condition SUM > 100 is false. When SUM > 100 becomes true, execution of loop L3 will completely terminate.

6.8.7 Report Statement

The syntax is :

report string-expression ;

[severity expression] ;

"report" statement is used to print or display the specified string and the severity level to be reported to the simulator for appropriate action.

The severity is specified in the STANDARD package and contains following values.

note,   warning,   error,   failure

Default value is note.

Normally, report statement is used with assertion statement.

Assert Statement :

It is basically used for Error Management in VHDL. With Assert statement, it is possible to test function and time constraints on a model inside a VHDL component.

If the condition for an **assert** is not met (false) during simulation of a VHDL code, a **message** of a certain **severity** is sent to the user (to the simulator).

Syntax :

Assert <condition>

Report <message>

Severity <error_level>

If the condition is not met (condition is false), the report statement is executed and gives the message to the simulator. Also there are four different severity levels for the message (error_levels). These are

- Note is the Default severity level.
- Warning
- Error
- Failure

The message and severity level are displayed in the VHDL simulator's command window.

An Assert is both a sequential and a concurrent command.

We will see an example of a concurrent assertion statement used in SR flip-flop model. The code is written to ensure that the input signals R and S are never simultaneously zero. The VHDL code is given below. As shown, in the assert command, when both, S and R are '0', at that time, Assert command becomes false. As "not   (S='0' and R='0')", is false when both S and R are '0' simultaneously, then the message is given as "R and S are both low, not valid inputs".

```
library ieee;
use ieee.std_logic_1164.all;
entity SRFlip_Flop is
    for (S, R : in std_logic; Q, Qbar : out std_logic);
end SRFlip_Flop;
architecture SR_arch of SRFlip_Flop is
begin
    assert not (S = '0' and R = '0')
Report "S and R are both low, not valid input"
severity ERROR;
end SR_arch;
```

Similarly, the equivalent process statement for above example is given below :

```
process
begin
    assert not (S = '0' and R = '0')
    report "S and R are both low, not valid inputs";
    severity ERROR;
    wait on S, R;
end process.
```

Next, we will see a program, to check that the simulator time does not exceed, 1000 ns. The code is given below.

Now is a predefined function that returns the current simulation time.

```
process (clk)
begin
    assert now < 1000 ns
    report "simulator time exceeds 1000 ns"
    severity Failure;
end process;
```

Next, we will see a program of Rising edge triggered D-flip-flop. It uses assertion statement to check for setup and hold times.

```
library ieee;
use ieee.std_logic_1164.all;

entity D-Flipflop is
    port (D, clk : in Bit ; Q, Qbar : out Bit);
end D-Flipflop;

architecture DFF_arch of D-Flipflop is
constant Hold_Time : TIME := 4 ns;
constant Setup_Time : TIME := 3 ns;
begin
process (D, clk)
    variable LastEventonD, LastEventonclk : TIME;
begin
    -- check for hold time
    if D'Event then
        assert Now = 0 ns or (Now – LastEventonD) > = Hold_Time;
        report "Hold Time is too short";
        severity ERROR;
        LastEventonD : = Now;
        end if;
        -- check for setup time
        if clk = '1' and clk'Event then
        assert Now = 0 ns or (Now – Last EventonD) >= Setup_Time;
        report "Setup time is too short"
            severity Error;
        LastEventonclk := Now;
        end if;
                        -- Behavior of FF
        if clk = '1' and clk event then
                        Q <= D;
                        Qbar <= not D;
                    end if;
        end process;
    end DFF_arch;
```
The hold time is the minimum time the data must remain stable **after** the clock changes.

The setup time is the minimum time the data input must be stable **before** the clock changes as shown in Fig. 6.16.

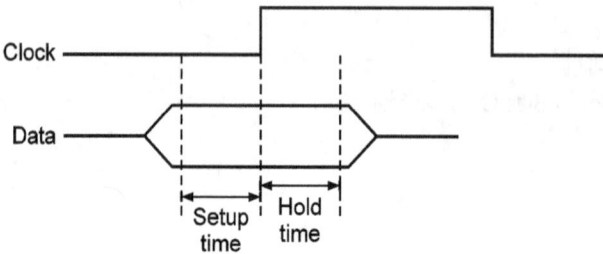

Fig. 6.16 (a) : Set up and Hold time

As already discussed, Now is a function which returns the current simulation time. All processes are executed until they suspend during the initialisation phase. To prevent misleading message appearing during initialisation phase of simulation, the expression "Now = 0 ns" is used in the assertion statement. In the DFF example, as shown already when there is an event on signal D or clk, the process executes. The first if statement is executed when there is an event on D. The assertion statement

    (Now = LastEventonclk) >= Hold_time

checks for the Hold_time. The difference between the current simulation time and the last time an event occurred on signal clk is greater than a constant Hold_time. If this statement is false, it means the Hold_time is short and it prints the message.

Similarly, the setup time is checked. The last if statement describes the latch behavior of the D type flip-flop.

We will see one more example to check spikes at the input of a buffer.

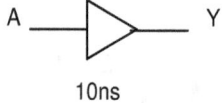

10ns

Fig. 6.16 (b)

The buffer has 10 ns propagation delay. If the spike has width of 5 ns or less, then print the message as "spike is detected".

    library ieee;
    use ieee.std_logic_1164.all;
    package PACK is --- package to store propagation delay and min-pulse
        constant min_pulse : TIME := 5 ns;
        constant propagation_delay : TIME : = 10 ns;
    end PACK;
    library ieee;

```
use ieee.std_logic_1164.all;
use work.PACK.all;
entity buffer is
    port (A : in bit;
            Y : out bit);
    end buffer;
    architecture buffer_arch of buffer is
begin
    process (A)
        variable LastEventonA : TIME := 0 ns;
    begin
        assert Now = 0 ns or (Now–LastEventonA) > = min_pulse;
        report "spike detected on input of buffer";
        severity WARNING;
        LastEventonA := Now;
        Y <= A after propagation_delay;
    end process;
end buffer_arch;
```

6.9 STYLES OF MODELING

Q. Explain the types of sequential statements.	**[6 M]**
Q. Write short note on architecture with modeling styles.	**[Dec. 11, 4 M]**
Q. Describe different modeling styles of VHDL with suitable examples.	**[May 10, 12, 8 M]**

The styles or ways in which functionality of design is described are called styles of modeling.

Three modeling styles are

- Data flow
- Behavior
- Structural

6.9.1 Data Flow Modeling

Q. Explain the concept of data flow modeling.	**[May 10, 12, 8 M]**

In this modeling, the flow of data through the entity is expressed using concurrent signal assignment statements, i.e. it has a set of concurrent assignment statements. Each statement is executed when any of its input signal changes its value. This modeling needs Boolean equations as design specification.

e.g.   Design of AND gate
       entity AND1D is
          port (A, B : in bit ;
                C : out bit) ;
       end AND1D ;
       architecture AND1D_ARCH of AND1D is
       begin
          C <= A and B ;
       end AND1D_ARCH;

Example 6.11 :

Write down VHDL code for the given AND_OR network using structural modeling.

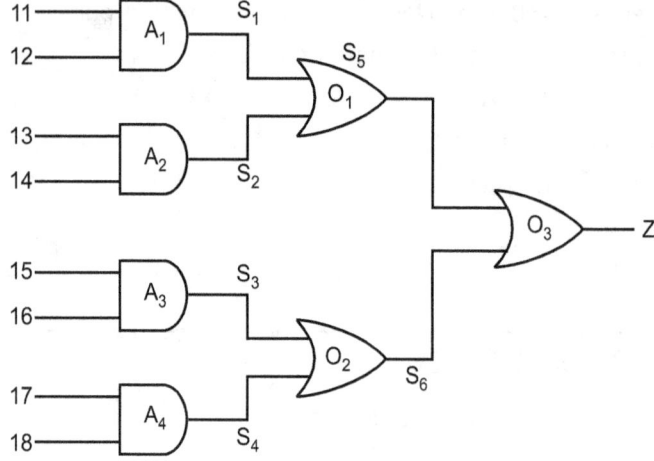

Fig. 6.17

Solution :

Assume AND1 and OR1 entity_architecture pair are precompiled, verified and are available in working directory.

    entity STRUCT is
        port (I1, I2, I3, I4, I5, I6, I7, I8 : in bit ;
             Z : out bit) ;
    end STRUCT ;
    architecture STRUCT_ARCH of STRUCT is
        component AND1
        port (A, B : in bit ;
              C : out bit) ;
      end component ;
        component OR1

        port (P, Q : in bit ;

               R : out bit) ;

end component ;

    signal S1, S2, S3, S4, S5, S6 : bit ;

begin

A1   :   AND1 port map (I1, I2, S1) ;

A2   :   AND1 port map (I3, I4, S2) ;

A3   :   AND1 port map (I5, I6, S3) ;

A4   :   AND1 port map (I7, I8, S4) ;

O1   :   OR1   port map (S1, S2, S5) ;

O2   :   OR1   port map (S3, S4, S6) ;

O3   :   OR1   port map (S5, S6, Z) ;

end STRUCT_ARCH ;

6.10 PACKAGE AND LIBRARY

6.10.1 Package

Package is a collection of commonly used subprograms, data types, constants etc. A package is common storage area. Packages are used to hold the data to be shared among a number of entities. The data declared inside a package can be referenced by other entities.

A package consists of two parts :

(i) Package declaration   (ii) Package body

(i) Package declaration

It defines the interface for the package (similar to entity).

The package declaration section can contain the following declarations.

- Subprogram declaration
- Type subtype declaration
- Constant, deferred constant declaration
- Signal declaration creates a global signal
- File declaration
- Alias declaration
- Component, attribute declaration
- Use clause.

All the items declared in the package declaration section are visible to any design unit that uses the package with a use clause.

The constants whose name and types are declared in the package declaration section, but actual values specified in the package body section are called as deferred constant.

The syntax for package declaration is

> package package_name is
>
> > declarations ;
>
> end [package] package_name ;

e.g.   package P1 is

> constant RISE, FALL : time ;
>
> > end P1;

RISE and FALL are deferred constants.

(ii) Package body

Package body is used to define the values for deferred constants, to specify the subprograms bodies for subprogram declared in package declaration.

Package body also contains

- Subprogram declaration
- Subprogram body
- Type, subtype declaration
- Constant, file, alias declaration
- Use clause.

It specifies the actual behavior of the package (similar to architecture).

A package declaration can have only one package body, both having the same name.(contrast to entity_architecture).

Writing of package body is optioned.

It contains the hidden details of a package (i.e. package body is not visible).

The syntax for package body is

> package body Package_name is
>
> > Declarations ;
> >
> > subprograms body ;
>
> end Package_name ;

e.g. package body P1 is

> > RISE := 5 ns ;
> >
> > FALL :=10 ns ;
>
> end P1 ;

Packages are stored in libraries for convenience purposes. User-created packages by default stored in work library.

"use" statement is used to access a package from a library and "library" keyword is used to access particular library.

The syntax is

    library   Library_name;

    use Library_name. package_name. particular_name;

    e.g.

    library BLIB ;   -- allows your design to access library BLIB

    use BLIB.P1.all ;   -- allows your design to use entire P1 package from library BLIB.

    use BLIB.P1.NAND2 ;   -- allows your design to use only component NAND2 from package P1 which is kept in library BLIB.

6.10.2 Design Libraries

A design library is an area of storage in the file system of the host environment. The management of the design libraries is not defined by the language and is tool - implementation - specific.

Generally, there are three types of libraries in VHDL :

1. Library IEEE

2. Library WORK

3. Library STD

When a VHDL component is compiled, it is saved in the work library as default. The work library is not the name of a directory on the PC, on which the compilation is being done, but a logical name.

VHDL tools usually define the work library automatically when the tool is started up. This means that different work libraries will be obtained depending on where the VHDL compiler is started. All compiled components are stored in a library. Packages too are usually stored in a library. The VHDL standard is defined in such a way that the Work and STD libraries are always visible. These two libraries do not, have to be specified in the VHDL code. The following invisible lines are always included in every VHDL code.

Library work;

Library std;

use std.standard.all;

The std library has the package named standard. In standard package itself, data types such as bit, bit_vector, character, time and integer are defined.

STD library has two packages predefined, these are standard and TextIO.

Package standard is a predefined package that contains the definitions for the predefined types and functions of the language. This package contains the following types – Boolean, Bit, character, severity_level, integer, real, time, string, file_open_kind and file_open_status.

Standard package also contains the following subtypes such as : Delay_length (from type time), natural (from type Integer), positive (from type Integer). Standard package also contains the function Now.

Package TEXTIO

It contains declarations of types and subprograms that support formatted I/o operations on text files.

TEXTIO package contains types such as LINE, TEXT, SIDE, WIDTH. It has standard text files such as Input and output. It has input procedures such as Readline and Read, and output procedure write.

Library IEEE

It contains the package STD_Logic_1164, which defines a nine value logic type and its associated overloaded functions and other utilities.

Package STD_LOGIC_1164 :

This package shall be compiled into a design library. It contains the following :

type STD_ULOGIC is ('U' – Uninitialized

'X' – Forcing unknown

'0' – Forcing '0'

'1' – Forcing '1'

'Z' – High impedance

'W' – Weak unknown

'L' – Weak 0

'H' – Weak 1

'–' – don't care

);

It also contains STD_ULOGIC_VECTOR as type,

function RESOLVED, subtype STD_LOGIC.

subtype STD_LOGIC is Resolved STD_ULOGIC,

    -- STD_LOGIC is Resolved from STD_ULOGIC

type STD_LOGIC_VECTOR is array (Natural range < >)

    of STD_LOGIC;

This package also contains subtypes such as, X01, X01Z, UX01, UX01Z etc.

There are also functions available. These functions are and, nand, or, nor, xor, xnor, not.

The conversion functions are To_BIT, To_BITVECTOR, To_STDULOGIC, To_STDLOGICVECTOR, To_STDULOGICVECTOR.

Edge detection functions such as RISING_EDGE, FALLING_EDGE etc.

Library Clause :

The library clause makes visible the logical names of design libraries. The format is library TTL, CMOS;

Above statement makes the logical names TTL and CMOS visible in the design unit.

The library clause

   library STD, work;

is implicitly declared for every design unit.

Use Clause :

Two forms of use clause

       use library_name . primary_unit_name;

       use library_name . primary_unit_name.item;

If all items within a primary unit are to be made visible, the keyword all can be used. For example,

       use IEEE.STD_LOGIC_1164.all;

If we need to use TEXTIO package, then it must be declared in the VHDL code,

       use STD.TEXTIO.all;

6.11 VHDL CODES

6.11.1 Mux Code

1. Mux using with statement

```
library ieee;
    use ieee.std_logic_1164.all;
entity mux_using_with is
    port (
        din_0   :in  std_logic;-- Mux first input
        din_1   :in  std_logic;-- Mux Second input
        sel     :in  std_logic;-- Select input
        mux_out :out std_logic -- Mux output
    );
    end entity;
architecture behavior of mux_using_with is
begin
    with (sel) select
    mux_out din_0 when '0',
                din_1 when others;
end architecture;
```

2. Mux : using when statement

```
entity mux_using_when is
    port (
        din_0  :in  std_logic;-- Mux first input
        din_1  :in  std_logic;-- Mux Second input
        sel    :in  std_logic;-- Select input
        mux_out :out std_logic -- Mux output
        );
end entity;
architecture behavior of mux_using_when is
begin
mux_out <= din_0 when      (sel = '0') else
            din_1
end architecture;
```

3. Mux : using if statement

```
library ieee;
    use ieee.std_logic_1164.all;
entity mux_using_if is
    port (
        din_0  :in  std_logic;-- Mux first input
        din_1  :in  std_logic;-- Mux Second input
        sel    :in  std_logic;-- Select input
        mux_out :out std_logic -- Mux output
    );
end entity;
architecture behavior of mux_using_if is
begin
    MUX:
    process (sel, din_0, din_1) begin
        if (sel = '0') then
            mux_out <= din_0;
        else
            mux_out <= din_1;
        end if;
end process;
end architecture;
```

4. Mux : Using case statement

```vhdl
library ieee;
use ieee.std_logic_1164.all;
entity mux_using_case is
    port (
        din_0  :in  std_logic;-- Mux first input
        din_1  :in  std_logic;-- Mux Second input
        sel    :in  std_logic;-- Select input
        mux_out :out std_logic -- Mux output
    );
end entity;
architecture behavior of mux_using_case is
begin
    MUX:
    process (sel, din_0, din_1) begin
        case sel is
            when '0'   => mux_out <= din_0;
            when others => mux_out <= din_1;
        end case;
    end process;
end architecture;
```

6.11.2 Binary Adder VHDL Code

1. Program for 4-bit binary adder

```vhdl
library IEEE;
use IEEE.STD_LOGIC_1164.all;
entity adder_4bit is
    port(
    a : in STD_LOGIC_VECTOR(3 downto 0);
    b : in STD_LOGIC_VECTOR(3 downto 0);
    carry : out STD_LOGIC;
    sum : out STD_LOGIC_VECTOR(3 downto 0)
    );
end adder_4bit;
architecture adder_4bit_arc of adder_4bit is
```

```
Component fa is
    port (a : in STD_LOGIC;
        b : in STD_LOGIC;
        c : in STD_LOGIC;
        sum : out STD_LOGIC;
        carry : out STD_LOGIC
        );
end component;
signal s : std_logic_vector (2 downto 0);
begin
    u0 : fa port map (a(0),b(0),'0',sum(0),s(0))
    u1 : fa port map (a(1),b(1),s(0),sum(1),s(1));
    u2 : fa port map (a(2),b(2),s(1),sum(2),s(2));
    ue : fa port map (a(3),b(3),s(2),sum(3),carry);
end adder_4bit_arc;
```

2. Program for N bit binary adder

```
entity BitAdder2 is
generic (N: natural :=2);
    Port ( X : in std_logic_vector(N-1 downto 0);
        Y : in std_logic_vector(N-1 downto 0);
        SUM : out std_logic_vector(N-1 downto 0);
        CARRY : out std_logic);
end BitAdder2;
architecture Behavioral of BitAdder2 is
signal result: std_logic_vector(N downto 0);
begin
        result <= ('0' & X)+('0' & Y);
        SUM <= result(N-1 downto 0);
        CARRY <= result(N);
end Behavioral
```

6.11.3 Counter VHDL Code

1. 4-bit unsigned up counter with Asynchronous clear

```
library ieee;
    use ieee.std_logic_1164.all;
    use ieee.std_logic_unsigned.all;
```

```
entity counter is
    port(C, CLR : in  std_logic;
        Q : out std_logic_vector(3 downto 0));
end counter;
architecture archi of counter is
    signal tmp: std_logic_vector(3 downto 0);
    begin
        process (C, CLR)
            begin
        if (CLR='1') then
            tmp <= "0000";
        elsif (C'event and C='1') then
            tmp <= tmp + 1;
        end if;
    end process;
    Q <= tmp;
end archi;
```

2. 4-bit unsigned down counter with synchronous set

```
library ieee;
use ieee.std_logic_1164.all;
use ieee.std_logic_unsigned.all;

entity counter is
    port(C, S : in  std_logic;
    Q : out std_logic_vector(3 downto 0));
end counter;
architecture archi of counter is
  signal tmp: std_logic_vector(3 downto 0);
  begin
   process (C)
    begin
    if (C'event and C='1') then
        if (S='1') then
        tmp <= "1111";
      else
        tmp <= tmp - 1;
```

```
      end if;
      end if;
   end process;
   Q <= tmp;
end archi;
```

3. 4-bit unsigned up counter with asynchronous load from primary input

```
library ieee;
use ieee.std_logic_1164.all;
use ieee.std_logic_unsigned.all;


entity counter is
  port(C, ALOAD : in  std_logic;
     D : in std_logic_vector(3 downto 0);
     Q : out std_logic_vector(3 downto 0));
end counter;
architecture archi of counter is
  signal tmp: std_logic_vector(3 downto 0);
  begin
    process (C, ALOAD, D)
     begin
      if (ALOAD='1') then
        tmp <= D;
      elsif (C'event and C='1') then
         tmp <= tmp + 1;
      end if;

  end process;
  Q <= tmp;
end archi;
```

4. 4-bit unsigned up counter with synchronous load with a constant

```
library ieee;
use ieee.std_logic_1164.all;
use ieee.std_logic_unsigned.all;
entity counter is
  port(C, SLOAD : in  std_logic;
     Q : out std_logic_vector(3 downto 0));
```

```
end counter;
architecture archi of counter is
  signal tmp: std_logic_vector(3 downto 0);
  begin
   process (C)
    begin
     if (C'event and C='1') then
      if (SLOAD='1') then
       tmp <= "1010";
      else
       tmp <= tmp + 1;
      end if;
     end if;
   end process;
   Q <= tmp;
end archi;
```

5. 4-bit unsigned up counter with asynchronous clear and clock enable

```
library ieee;
use ieee.std_logic_1164.all;
use ieee.std_logic_unsigned.all;

entity counter is
  port(C, CLR, CE : in std_logic;
      Q : out std_logic_vector(3 downto 0));
end counter;
architecture archi of counter is
  signal tmp: std_logic_vector(3 downto 0);
  begin
    process (C, CLR)
     begin
      if (CLR='1') then
       tmp <= "0000";
      elsif (C'event and C='1') then
       if (CE='1') then
        tmp <= tmp + 1;
       end if;
```

```
      end if;
   end process;
   Q <= tmp;
end archi;
```

6. 4-bit unsigned up/down counter with asynchronous clear

```
library ieee;
use ieee.std_logic_1164.all;
use ieee.std_logic_unsigned.all;
entity counter is
  port(C, CLR, UP_DOWN : in std_logic;
      Q : out std_logic_vector(3 downto 0));
end counter;
architecture archi of counter is
  signal tmp: std_logic_vector(3 downto 0);
  begin
    process (C, CLR)
      begin
        if (CLR='1') then
          tmp <= "0000";
        elsif (C'event and C='1') then
          if (UP_DOWN='1') then
            tmp <= tmp + 1;
          else
            tmp <= tmp - 1;
          end if;
        end if;
    end process;
   Q <= tmp;
end archi;
```

7. 4-bit signed up counter with asynchronous reset

```
library ieee;
use ieee.std_logic_1164.all;
use ieee.std_logic_signed.all;

entity counter is
  port(C, CLR : in  std_logic;
```

```
      Q : out std_logic_vector(3 downto 0));
end counter;
architecture archi of counter is
  signal tmp: std_logic_vector(3 downto 0);
  begin
    process (C, CLR)
      begin
        if (CLR='1') then
          tmp <= "0000";
        elsif (C'event and C='1')   then
          tmp <= tmp + 1;
        end if;
    end process;
    Q <= tmp;
end archi;
```

6.11.4   Shift Register VHDL Code

1. Design of 4 Bit serial in - Serial out shift register using behavior modeling style.

```
library ieee;
use ieee.STD_LOGIC_1164.all;
entity siso_behavior is
    port(
        din : in STD_LOGIC;
        clk : in STD_LOGIC;
        reset : in STD_LOGIC;
        dout : out STD_LOGIC
        );
end siso_behavior;
architecture siso_behavior_arc of siso_behavior is
begin
    siso : process (clk,din,reset) is
    variable s : std_logic_vector(3 downto 0) := "0000" ;
    begin
      if (reset='1') then
        s := "0000";
      elsif (rising_edge (clk)) then
        s := (din & s(3 downto 1));
```

```
    dout <= s(0);
      end if;
    end process siso;
end siso_behavior_arc;
```

2. 8-bit shift-left register with positive-edge clock, serial in, and serial out

```
library ieee;
use ieee.std_logic_1164.all;
entity shift is
 port(C, SI : in  std_logic;
     SO : out std_logic);
end shift;
architecture archi of shift is
 signal tmp: std_logic_vector(7 downto 0);
 begin
  process (C)
   begin
    if (C'event and C='1') then
     for i in 0 to 6 loop
       tmp(i+1) <= tmp(i);
     end loop;
     tmp(0) <= SI;
    end if;
  end process;
  SO <= tmp(7);
end archi;
```

3. 8-bit shift-left register with negative-edge clock, clock enable, serial in, and serial out

```
library ieee;
use ieee.std_logic_1164.all;
entity shift is
 port(C, SI, CE : in  std_logic;
     SO : out std_logic);
end shift;
architecture archi of shift is
 signal tmp: std_logic_vector(7 downto 0);
 begin
  process (C)
   begin
```

```
    if (C'event and C='0') then
      if (CE='1') then
        for i in 0 to 6 loop
          tmp(i+1) <= tmp(i);
        end loop;
          tmp(0) <= SI;
        end if;
      end if;
    end process;
    SO <= tmp(7);
end archi;
```

4. 8-bit shift-left register with positive-edge clock, asynchronous clear, serial in, and serial out

```
library ieee;
use ieee.std_logic_1164.all;
entity shift is
  port(C, SI, CLR : in std_logic;
      SO : out std_logic);
end shift;
architecture archi of shift is
  signal tmp: std_logic_vector(7 downto 0);
  begin
    process (C, CLR)
      begin
        if (CLR='1') then
          tmp <= (others => '0');
        elsif (C'event and C='1') then
          tmp <= tmp(6 downto 0) & SI;
        end if;
    end process;
    SO <= tmp(7);
end archi;
```

5. 8-bit shift-left register with positive-edge clock, synchronous set, serial in, and serial out

```
library ieee;
use ieee.std_logic_1164.all;
entity shift is
  port(C, SI, S : in  std_logic;
```

```vhdl
        SO : out std_logic);
end shift;
architecture archi of shift is
  signal tmp: std_logic_vector(7 downto 0);
  begin
    process (C, S)
      begin
        if (C'event and C='1') then
          if (S='1') then
            tmp <= (others => '1');
          else
            tmp <= tmp(6 downto 0) & SI;
          end if;
        end if;
      end process;
    SO <= tmp(7);
end archi;
```

6. 8-bit shift-left register with positive-edge clock, serial in, and parallel out

```vhdl
library ieee;
use ieee.std_logic_1164.all;
entity shift is
  port(C, SI : in  std_logic;
       PO : out std_logic_vector(7 downto 0));
end shift;
architecture archi of shift is
  signal tmp: std_logic_vector(7 downto 0);
  begin
    process (C)
      begin
        if (C'event and C='1') then
          tmp <= tmp(6 downto 0)& SI;
        end if;
      end process;
    PO <= tmp;
end archi;
```

7. 8-bit shift-left register with positive-edge clock, asynchronous parallel load, serial in, and serial out

```vhdl
library ieee;
use ieee.std_logic_1164.all;
entity shift is
```

```
port(C, SI, ALOAD : in std_logic;
    D  : in std_logic_vector(7 downto 0);
    SO : out std_logic);
end shift;
architecture archi of shift is
 signal tmp: std_logic_vector(7 downto 0);
 begin
  process (C, ALOAD, D)
   begin
    if (ALOAD='1') then
     tmp <= D;
    elsif (C'event and C='1') then
     tmp <= tmp(6 downto 0) & SI;
    end if;
  end process;
  SO <= tmp(7);
end archi;
```

8. 8-bit shift-left register with positive-edge clock, synchronous parallel load, serial in, and serial out

```
library ieee;
use ieee.std_logic_1164.all;
entity shift is
 port(C, SI, SLOAD : in std_logic;
    D : in std_logic_vector(7 downto 0);
    SO : out std_logic);
end shift;
architecture archi of shift is
 signal tmp: std_logic_vector(7 downto 0);
 begin
  process (C)
   begin
    if (C'event and C='1') then
     if (SLOAD='1') then
      tmp <= D;
     else
      tmp <= tmp(6 downto 0) & SI;
     end if;
    end if;
```

```
  end process;
   SO <= tmp(7);
end archi;
```

9. 8-bit shift-left/shift-right register with positive-edge clock, serial in, and parallel out

```
library ieee;
use ieee.std_logic_1164.all;

entity shift is
port(C, SI, LEFT_RIGHT : in std_logic;
    PO : out std_logic_vector(7 downto 0));
end shift;
architecture archi of shift is
  signal tmp: std_logic_vector(7 downto 0);
  begin
    process (C)
     begin
      if (C'event and C='1') then
       if (LEFT_RIGHT='0') then
         tmp <= tmp(6 downto 0) & SI;
       else
         tmp <= SI & tmp(7 downto 1);
       end if;
      end if;
     end process;
    PO <= tmp;
end archi;
```

www.ingramcontent.com/pod-product-compliance
Lightning Source LLC
Chambersburg PA
CBHW081144020726
47504CB00009B/1993